EXCITED ACCLAIM
FOR JOSHUA FERRIS'S

Then We Came to the End

One of the Best Books of the Year

—*Boston Globe*
—*Christian Science Monitor*
—*New York* magazine
—*New York Times Book Review*
—*St. Louis Post-Dispatch*
—*Time* magazine
—*Salon*

"Hilarious in a *Catch-22* way, but with an undercurrent of sadness that works counterpoint to all the absurdity."

—Stephen King, *New York Times Book Review*

"Not too many authors have written the Great American Office Novel. Joseph Heller did it in *Something Happened* (the one book of his to rival *Catch-22*). And Nicholson Baker pulled it off in zanily fastidious fashion in *The Mezzanine*. To their ranks should be added Joshua Ferris, whose *Then We Came to the End* feels like a ready-made classic of the genre.... A truly affecting novel about work, trust, love, and loneliness."

—Michael Upchurch, *Seattle Times*

"Ah, the doldrums of office life: so pervasive, yet so easily alleviated by doses of modest, company-sponsored delight. This mood—or rhythm, really—is adroitly captured in Joshua Ferris's funny debut novel. Perhaps in the era of the professionalization of writing itself, many novelists have avoided chronicling the subtleties of office life because it's not perceived as 'literary'—or because they have no experience of it. But as *Then We Came to the End* begins to suggest, it is one of the richest settings of our time."

—Meghan O'Rourke, *Slate*

"Fabulous.... The emotional oscillation as employees strive to stay alive (read: employed) is played out by Ferris with the sort of exuberance and energy that marked Jay McInerney's *Bright Lights, Big City,* to which *Then We Came to the End* might seem a Midwestern cousin.... Ferris's writing displays a strong descriptive flair, but the greatest asset of *Then We Came to the End* is the nuance of its narrative voice, which has the gossipy warmth and seeming closeness of a conspiratorial coworker leaning over a partition to impart the latest rumor."
—Art Winslow, *Chicago Tribune*

"What looks at first glance like a sweet-tempered satire of workplace culture is revealed upon closer inspection to be a very serious novel about, well, America. It may even be, in its own modest way, a great American novel."
—Darcy Cosper, *Los Angeles Times*

"Ferris brilliantly captures the fishbowl quality of contemporary office life, where nothing much happens and the smallest events take on huge significance.... The narration (done in the technically challenging first-person collective) never falters, making this a masterwork of pitch and tone, in which individual characters are less important than the general mood of boredom leavened with camaraderie."
— *The New Yorker*

"It should be said upfront that this is a very funny book; reading it is like tagging along on a corporate tour led by Joseph Heller and Mike Judge, with occasional color commentary by Sam Kinison.... Like all successful comedy, *Then We Came to the End* isn't just schtick and gags. It's propelled by—and gets its heart from—an effort to contextualize the anger, remorse, loneliness, and isolation felt or, perhaps more accurately, vaguely sensed, by the characters.... The jokes, disaffection, apathy, the elaborate and ingenious ways of wasting time—it's a pleasure to be around (and, with the use of 'we,' actually part of) this group."
—Ethan Rutherford, *Minneapolis Star Tribune*

"We in office world know these people. We work with them. But Joshua Ferris, in his virtuoso first novel, makes us see them. He writes in a conspiratorial tone of such delicious knowingness that I read *Then We Came to the End* with a great grin on my face. By turns hip, wicked, and incisive, the novel plumbs the nuances of office humiliation, soaring entitlement, goofy pranks, busy-making maneuvers, low-grade venality, and ever-present schadenfreude.... *Then We Came to the End* is a beautiful beginning for Joshua Ferris. You won't want to miss it."

—Karen Long, *Cleveland Plain Dealer*

"This is a *novel*, by God! News that stays news, oldest subject there is—what part of a human being might outstay his visit on earth? I read this novel remembering why I ever wanted to read fiction, why I want to write it....It is also one of the funniest novels I have ever read."

—Geoffrey Wolff, author of *The Duke of Deception* and *The Age of Consent*

"A perceptive and darkly entertaining novel...expansive, great-hearted, and acidly funny."

—James Poniewozik, *New York Times Book Review*

"Office workers nationwide, from Madison Avenue to Market Street, will be spending their lunch hours reading Ferris's hilarious account of a group of Chicago advertising employees scrabbling to survive the dot-com bust....The office is a breeding ground for collective consciousness, and it's in the interstices between the collective and the personal where things get interesting. And, in Ferris's world, very, very funny."

—Amy Woods Butler, *St. Louis Post-Dispatch*

"A terrific first novel...awfully funny."

—Nick Hornby, *The Believer*

"Emotionally resonant and quite funny."

—Amy Virshup, *New York Times*

"A wildly original, totally off-the-wall, all-round wonderful first novel. *Then We Came to the End* moves only briefly beyond the confines of the workplace but encompasses a whole world of feeling. Laugh? It almost made me wish I had a job."

—Geoff Dyer, author of *Out of Sheer Rage* and *But Beautiful*

"Wonderfully comic. . . . Ferris masters all this with a subtle technical skill in which inane office patter becomes a kind of joyous celebration of the possibilities of prose. He knows, like other masters of the form, that great comedy has a hard bite." —*O, The Oprah Magazine*

"An impressive first novel . . . Altmanesque." —*Details*

"A keen humorist. . . . We're happy to read about this pathetic and noble workforce from the 'inside,' all the way to the end."

—Stephen Barbara, *Wall Street Journal*

"Funny yet piercing. . . . If Ferris had written only about the petty, childish nature of office life, he might have turned out a funny but forgettable book. But he also writes about the dark places to which our work and personal lives sometimes take us, and the relief our colleagues can bring in those moments."

—Soyia Ellison, *Atlanta Journal-Constitution*

"*Then We Came to the End* is the *Catch-22* of the business world: it's a hilarious and heartbreaking and surreal portrait of the modern American corporation as a carnival—preschool?—of infantile misbehavior and breathtakingly futile and petty and despairing competition. The real revelation here is how *moving* it all becomes: how much humanity and genuine emotional weight finally, against all odds, shine through."

—Jim Shepard, author of *Love and Hydrogen* and *Like You'd Understand, Anyway*

"*Then We Came to the End* exposes the delusions people in groups are susceptible to, the surprising little cruelties they're capable of. But it is not the sort of 'small, angry book about work' one of Ferris's characters is endlessly writing. Instead, it is an insightful, expansive, and often hilarious story, a novel so complex it may well deserve Jim Shepard's assessment: 'the *Catch-22* of the business world.'"

—Maud Newton, *Newsday*

"Mr. Ferris has our number. He smells our fear, our vulnerability.... His observations are often ticklish, making the book feel like the one we have rattling in our heads."

—Emily Bobrow, *New York Observer*

"Wickedly funny and painfully real." —*Redbook*

"An assured debut and an entertaining read.... *Then We Came to the End* is very good at capturing the interactions between coworkers, depicting a company as a family of sorts, with all a family's love and annoyance, the kind that make you defend a coworker vigorously one day and want to stick a knife in him the next."

—Reagan Upshaw, *San Francisco Chronicle*

"A charming and sometimes very funny story of worker bees pushed past the brink of boredom.... Ferris maintains a wonderfully wry tone and has a fine observational eye for all the absurdities of the modern workplace." —David Daley, *USA Today*

"A haunting and funny first novel. The brilliance of the book is that it somehow seems totally true—you'll read each successive act of petty office politics and think, 'I work with people like that'—while at the same time it's a completely artful piece of storytelling. Ignore the *Office Space*–reminiscent cover; the only thing this book shares with that film (or TV's *The Office*) is that it's ridiculously good. Seriously, even if you don't like books, get this and read it: You will laugh your ass off." —Erik Pedersen, *E! Online*

"Several pages into Joshua Ferris's very funny and impressively observed first novel, we start comparing it with other memorable novels about the world of advertising. But after a few chapters we broaden the parameters and consider it in terms of the corporate novel, the office novel, the cube farm novel...we conclude that categorizing *Then We Came to the End* as anything other than an original and inspired work of fiction would be doing it a great disservice.... Ferris skillfully balances the comic with the authentic, the insightful with the absurd, and we can't help but be transfixed by their stories."

—James P. Othmer, *Washington Post*

"*Then We Came to the End* is a vicious send-up of cubicle culture that somehow manages not to lose sight of its characters' humanity.... Ferris allows enough sunlight to filter in through the fluorescents that a reader is left wishing his characters well as they polish up their résumés, dry-clean their interview suits, and head off to the next chapter in their lives." —Yvonne Zipp, *Christian Science Monitor*

"Ferris is a warmhearted satirist, leveling a gently mocking eye at the absurdities of corporate America, in particular the arm dedicated to raising consumerism to a pseudo-art form....This entertaining and accomplished novel lives up to its *Catch-22* pedigree. After reading Ferris brilliantly render the world of advertising, one wonders to which subculture he will turn his talents next. Wherever he goes, we would do well to follow, in order to learn about ourselves."

—Sean Kinch, *Tennessean*

"As funny as *The Office*, as sad as an abandoned stapler, *Then We Came to the End* is that rare novel that feels absolutely contemporary, and that rare comedy that feels blisteringly urgent." —*Time*

Then We Came to the End

Then We Came to the End

A Novel

Joshua Ferris

BACK BAY BOOKS

Little, Brown and Company

New York Boston London

Back Bay Books / Little, Brown and Company
Hachette Book Group USA
237 Park Avenue, New York, NY 10017
Visit our Web sites www.ThenWeCametotheEnd.com and
www.HachetteBookGroupUSA.com

Originally published in hardcover by Little, Brown and Company, March 2007
First Back Bay paperback edition, February 2008

Library of Congress Cataloging-in-Publication Data
Ferris, Joshua.
Then we came to the end : a novel / Joshua Ferris—1st ed.
p. cm.
ISBN 978-0-316-01638-4 (hc) / 978-0-316-01639-1 (pb) /
978-0-316-03387-9 (special edition)
1. Office workers—Illinois—Chicago—Fiction. 2. Chicago (Ill.)—
Fiction. I. Title.
PS3606.E774T47 2007
813'.6—dc22 2005036677

10 9 8 7 6 5 4

RRD-C

Design by Nancy Singer Olaguera/ISPN Publishing Services

Printed in the United States of America

To Elizabeth

Is it not the chief disgrace in the world,
not to be a unit; — not to be reckoned one
character; — not to yield that peculiar fruit
which each man was created to bear, but
to be reckoned in the gross, in the hundred,
or the thousand, of the party, the section,
to which we belong . . .

— *Ralph Waldo Emerson*

Then We Came to the End

You Don't Know What's in My Heart

WE WERE FRACTIOUS AND overpaid. Our mornings lacked promise. At least those of us who smoked had something to look forward to at ten-fifteen. Most of us liked most everyone, a few of us hated specific individuals, one or two people loved everyone and everything. Those who loved everyone were unanimously reviled. We loved free bagels in the morning. They happened all too infrequently. Our benefits were astonishing in comprehensiveness and quality of care. Sometimes we questioned whether they were worth it. We thought moving to India might be better, or going back to nursing school. Doing something with the handicapped or working with our hands. No one ever acted on these impulses, despite their daily, sometimes hourly contractions. Instead we met in conference rooms to discuss the issues of the day.

Ordinarily jobs came in and we completed them in a timely and professional manner. Sometimes fuckups did occur. Printing errors, transposed numbers. Our business was advertising and details were important. If the third number after the second hyphen in a client's toll-free number was a six instead of an eight, and if it went to print like that, and showed up in *Time* magazine, no one reading the ad could call now and order today. No matter they could go to the website, we still had to eat the price of the ad. Is this boring you yet? It bored us every day. Our boredom was ongoing, a collective boredom, and it would never die because we would never die.

Lynn Mason was dying. She was a partner in the agency. Dying? It was uncertain. She was in her early forties. Breast cancer. No one could identify exactly how everyone had come to know this fact. Was it a fact? Some people called it rumor. But in fact there was no such thing as rumor. There was fact, and there was what did not come up in conversation. Breast cancer was controllable if caught in the early stages but Lynn may have waited too long. The news of Lynn brought Frank Brizzolera to mind. We recalled looking at Frank and thinking he had six months, tops. Old Brizz, we called him. He smoked like a fiend. He stood outside the building in the most inclement weather, absorbing Old Golds in nothing but a sweater vest. Then and only then, he looked indomitable. When he returned inside, nicotine stink preceded him as he walked down the hall, where it lingered long after he entered his office. He began to cough, and from our own offices we heard the working-up of solidified lung sediment. Some people put him on their Celebrity Death Watch every year because of the coughing, even though he wasn't an official celebrity. He knew it, too, he knew he was on death watch, and that certain wagering individuals would profit from his death. He knew it because he was one of us, and we knew everything.

We didn't know who was stealing things from other people's workstations. Always small items — postcards, framed photographs. We had our suspicions but no proof. We believed it was probably not for the loot so much as the excitement — the shoplifter's addictive kick, or maybe it was a pathological cry for help. Hank Neary, one of the agency's only black writers, asked, "Come on, now — who would want my travel toothbrush?"

We didn't know who was responsible for putting the sushi roll behind Joe Pope's bookshelf. The first couple of days Joe had no clue about the sushi. Then he started taking furtive sniffs at his pits, and holding the wall of his palm to his mouth to get blowback from his breath. By the end of the week, he was certain it wasn't him. We smelled it, too. Persistent, high in the nostrils, it became worse than a dying animal. Joe's gorge rose every time he entered his office. The following week the smell was so atrocious the building people got involved, hunting the office for what turned out to be a sunshine roll — tuna, whitefish, salmon, and sprouts. Mike Boroshansky, the chief of security, kept bringing his tie up to his nose, as if he were a real cop at the scene of a murder.

We thanked each other. It was customary after every exchange. Our thanks were never disingenuous or ironic. We said thanks for getting this done so quickly, thanks for putting in so much effort. We had a meeting and when a meeting was over, we said thank you to the meeting makers for having made the meeting. Very rarely did we say anything negative or derogatory about meetings. We all knew there was a good deal of pointlessness to nearly all the meetings and in fact one meeting out of every three or four was nearly perfectly without gain or purpose but many meetings revealed the one thing that was necessary and so we attended them and afterward we thanked each other.

Karen Woo always had something new to tell us and we hated her guts for it. She would start talking and our eyes would glaze over. Might it be true, as we sometimes feared on the commute home, that we were callous, unfeeling individuals, incapable of sympathy, and full of spite toward people for no reason other than their proximity and familiarity? We had these sudden revelations that employment, the daily nine-to-five, was driving us far from our better selves. Should we quit? Would that solve it? Or were those qualities innate, dooming us to nastiness and paucity of spirit? We hoped not.

Marcia Dwyer became famous for sending an e-mail to Genevieve Latko-Devine. Marcia often wrote to Genevieve after meetings. "It is really irritating to work with irritating people," she once wrote. There she ended it and waited for Genevieve's response. Usually when she got Genevieve's e-mail, instead of writing back, which would take too long — Marcia was an art director, not a writer — she would head down to Genevieve's office, close the door, and the two women would talk. The only thing bearable about the irritating event involving the irritating person was the thought of telling it all to Genevieve, who would understand better than anyone else. Marcia could have called her mother, her mother would have listened. She could have called one of her four brothers, any one of those South Side pipe-ends would have been more than happy to beat up the irritating person. But they would not have understood. They would have sympathized, but that was not the same thing. Genevieve would hardly need to nod for Marcia to know she was getting through. Did we not all understand the essential need for someone to understand? But the e-mail Marcia got back was not from Genevieve. It was from Jim Jackers. "Are you talking about me?" he wrote. Amber Ludwig wrote, "I'm not Genevieve." Benny Shassburger wrote, "I think you goofed." Tom Mota wrote, "Ha!" Marcia was mortified. She got sixty-five e-mails in two minutes. One from HR cautioned her against sending personal e-mails. Jim wrote a second time. "Can you please tell me — is it me, Marcia? Am I the irritating person you're talking about?"

Marcia wanted to eat Jim's heart because some mornings he shuffled up to the elevators and greeted us by saying, "What up, my niggas?" He meant it ironically in an effort to be funny, but he was just not the man to pull it off. It made us cringe, especially Marcia, especially if Hank was present.

In those days it wasn't rare for someone to push someone else down the hall really fast in a swivel chair. Games aside, we spent most of our time inside long silent pauses as we bent over our individual desks, working on some task at hand, lost to it — until Benny, bored, came and stood in the doorway. "What are you up to?" he'd ask.

It could have been any of us. "Working" was the usual reply.

Then Benny would tap his topaz class ring on the doorway and drift away.

How we hated our coffee mugs! our mouse pads, our desk clocks, our daily calendars, the contents of our desk drawers. Even the photos of our loved ones taped to our computer monitors for uplift and support turned into cloying reminders of time served. But when we got a new office, a bigger office, and we brought everything with us into the new office, how we loved everything all over again, and thought hard about where to place things, and looked with satisfaction at the end of the day at how well our old things looked in this new, improved, important space. There was no doubt in our minds just then that we had made all the right decisions, whereas most days we were men and women of two minds. Everywhere you looked, in the hallways and bathrooms, the coffee bar and cafeteria, the lobbies and the print stations, there we were with our two minds.

There seemed to be only the one electric pencil sharpener in the whole damn place.

We didn't have much patience for cynics. Everyone was a cynic at one point or another but it did us little good to bemoan our unbelievable fortunes. At the national level things had worked out pretty well in our favor and entrepreneurial cash was easy to come by. Cars available for domestic purchase, cars that could barely fit in our driveways, had a martial appeal, a promise that, once inside them, no harm would come to our children. It was IPO this and IPO that. Everyone knew a banker, too. And how lovely it was, a bike ride around the forest preserve on a Sunday in May with our mountain bikes, water bottles, and safety helmets. Crime was at an all-time low and we heard accounts of former welfare recipients holding steady jobs. New hair products were being introduced into the marketplace every day and the glass shelves of our stylists were stocked with tidy rows of them, which we eyed in the mirror as we made small talk, each of us certain, *there's one up there just for me.* Still, some of us had a hard time finding boyfriends. Some of us had a hard time fucking our wives.

Some days we met in the kitchen on sixty to eat lunch. There was only room for eight at the table. If all the seats were full, Jim Jackers would have to eat his sandwich from the sink and try to engage from over in that direction. It was fortunate for us in that he could pass us a spoon or a packet of salt if we needed it.

"It is really irritating," Tom Mota said to the table, "to work with irritating people."

"Screw you, Tom," Marcia replied.

Headhunters hounded us. They plied us with promises of better titles and increases in pay. Some of us went but most of us stayed. We liked our prospects where we were and didn't care for the hassle of meeting new people. It had taken us a while to familiarize ourselves and to feel comfortable. First day on the job, names went in one ear and out the other. One minute you were being introduced to a guy with a head of fiery red hair and fair skin crawling with freckles, and before you knew it you had moved on to someone new and then someone after that. A few weeks would go by, gradually you'd start to put the name to the face, and one day it just clicked, to be wedged there forever: the eager redhead's name was Jim Jackers. There was no more confusing him with "Benny Shassburger" whose name you tended to see on e-mails and handouts but hadn't come to recognize yet as the slightly heavyset, dough-faced Jewish guy with the corkscrew curls and quick laugh. So many people! So many body types, hair colors, fashion statements.

Marcia Dwyer's hair was stuck in the eighties. She listened to terrible music, bands we had outgrown in the eleventh grade. Some of us had never even heard of the music she listened to, and it was inconceivable that she could enjoy such noise. Others of us didn't like music at all, some preferred talk radio, and there was a large contingent that kept their radios tuned to the oldies station. After everyone went home for the night, after we all fell asleep and the city dimmed, oldies continued to play inside the abandoned office. Picture it — only a parallelogram of light in the doorway. A happy tune by the Drifters issuing in the dark at two, three o'clock in the morning, when elsewhere murders were taking place, drug deals, unspeakable assaults. Crime was down, but it had yet to be rendered obsolete. In the mornings, our favorite DJs were back on, playing our favorite oldies. Most of us ate the crumb toppings first and then the rest of the muffin. They were the same songs that would play throughout a nuclear winter.

We had visceral, rich memories of dull, interminable hours. Then a day would pass in perfect harmony with our projects, our family members, and our coworkers, and we couldn't believe we were getting paid for this. We decided to celebrate with wine at dinner. Some of us liked one restaurant in particular while others spread out across the city, sampling and reviewing. We were foxes and hedgehogs that way. It was vitally important to Karen Woo that she be the first to know of a new restaurant. If someone mentioned a new restaurant Karen didn't know about, you could bet your bottom dollar that Karen would be there that very night, sampling and reviewing, and when she came in the next morning, she told us (those of us who didn't know about the other person's knowing about the new restaurant) about the new restaurant she'd just been to, how great it was, and how we all had to go there. Those of us who followed Karen's suggestion gave the same advice to those of us who hadn't heard Karen's suggestion, and soon we were all running into one another at the new restaurant. By then Karen wouldn't be caught dead there.

Early in the time of balanced budgets and the remarkable rise of the NASDAQ we were given polo shirts of quality cotton with the agency's logo stitched on the left breast. The shirt was for some team event and everyone wore it out of company pride. After the event was over, it was uncommon to see anyone wearing that polo again — not because we had lost our company pride, but because it was vaguely embarrassing to be seen wearing something everyone knew had been given to you for free. After all, our portfolios were stuffed with NASDAQ offerings and if our parents had only been able to buy us outfits from Sears, we could now afford Brooks Brothers and had no need for free shirts. We gave them to the Goodwill or they languished in our drawers or we put them on to mow the lawn. A few years later, Tom Mota exhumed his company-pride polo from some box of clothes under his bed. Likely he found it when the Mota chattels were being divided up by order of a judge. He wore it to work. He had worn the polo along with the rest of us on that polo-wearing day, but his life had changed dramatically since then and we thought it was an indication of where his head was at that he didn't mind being seen in a shirt most of us used to wash our cars. It really was a very handy cotton. Then Tom wore the same shirt the next day. We wondered where he was sleeping. On the third day, we were concerned about his showering. When Tom passed an entire week in the same polo, we expected it to give off an odor. But he must have been washing it, and we pictured him bare-chested at the Laundromat watching his one polo turn in the dryer, because his wife wouldn't let him return to his Naperville home.

By the end of the month, we figured out finally it had nothing to do with Tom's divorce. Thirty straight days in the same corporate polo — it was the beginning of Tom's campaign of agitation.

"You ever going to change out of it?" asked Benny.

"I love this shirt. I want to be buried in it."

"Would you take mine, at least, so you can switch off?"

"I would love that," said Tom.

So Benny gave Tom his polo, but Tom didn't use it to switch off. Instead he wore Benny's on top of his own. Two polos, one under the other. He approached the rest of us and solicited our polos as well. Jim Jackers grasped at any opportunity to ingratiate himself, and soon Tom was walking around in three polos.

"Lynn Mason's starting to ask questions," said Benny.

"Company pride," said Tom.

"But three at a time?"

"You don't know what's in my heart," said Tom, pounding his fist against the corporate logo three times. "Company pride."

Some days green was on top, some days red, some days blue. Later we found out he was the one responsible for taping the sunshine roll to the back of Joe's bookshelf. He was responsible for many things, including changing everyone's radio stations, making pornographic screensavers, and leaving his seed on the floor of the men's rooms on sixty and sixty-one. We knew he was responsible because once he was laid off, the radios went unmolested and the custodians no longer complained to management.

It was the era of take-ones and tchotchkes. The world was flush with Internet cash and we got our fair share of it. It was our position that logo design was every bit as important as product performance and distribution systems. "Wicked cool" were the words we used to describe our logo designs. "Bush league" were the words we used to describe the logo designs of other agencies — unless it was a really well-designed logo, in which case we bowed down before it, much like the ancient Mayans did their pagan gods.

We, too, thought it would never end.

Enter a New Century

1

LAYOFFS — TOM'S FINAL HOUR — JANINE GORJANC'S TRAGEDY — THE DOWNTURN — DRASTIC MEASURES — THE DEBATE OVER TOM — CREEPY PICTURES — THE STORY OF TOM MOTA'S CHAIR — WALKING SPANISH DOWN THE HALL — SANDERSON — TWO E-MAILS — THE STORY OF TOM MOTA'S CHAIR, PART II — THE PRO BONO FUND-RAISER ADS — LASTIVE ACID — LYNN MASON

LAYOFFS WERE UPON US. They had been rumored for months, but now it was official. If you were lucky, you could sue. If you were black, aged, female, Catholic, Jewish, gay, obese, or physically handicapped, at least you had grounds. At one point or another we have all been deposed. We plan on being deposed for Tom's suit — we have no doubt there will be one. Though he has no grounds unless asshole has been added to the list. And that's not just us talking. His ex-wife *hates* the guy. Restraining order. He can't see his two young kids without supervision. She moved to Phoenix just to get away from him. We wouldn't call him an asshole without having reached a very high consensus. Amber Ludwig objects to the specific designation because she has objected to profanity since becoming pregnant, but really there is no other word, and her objection is really just an abstention.

When Tom found out he was being let go, he wanted to throw his computer against his office window. Benny Shassburger was in there with him. Benny wasn't like a great friend of Tom's or anything but he was the guy who on occasion would have lunch with Tom and then report back to the rest of us. Word spread fast that Tom had been laid off and naturally Benny was the guy to go down there. He said Tom was pacing in his office like a man recently jailed. He said he could picture what Tom had looked like the night he went to the Naperville house with the aluminum bat and the authorities were called to restrain him. We had never heard that story before. Right there and then we had to stop Benny from telling us the story of Tom's final hour so he could first tell us the story of the aluminum bat. Benny was shocked we had never heard that story; he was sure we had. No, we never had. "Get out of here," he said. "You've heard that story." No, we hadn't. This was always how these conversations went. So Benny told us the story of Tom and the bat and then he told us the story of Tom's final hour. Both were good stories and together they killed a good hour. Some of us loved killing an hour of the company's time and others felt guilty for it afterward. But whatever your personal feelings on the matter, you still had to account for the hour, so you billed it to a client. By the end of the fiscal year, our clients had paid us a substantial amount of money to sit around and bullshit, expenses they then passed on to you, the consumer. It was the cost of doing business, but some of us feared it was an indication that the end was near, like the profligacy that preceded the downfall of the Roman Empire. There was so much money involved, and some of it even trickled down to us, a small amount that allowed us to live among the top one-percent of the wealthiest in the world. It was lasting fun, until layoffs came.

Tom wanted to throw his computer against the window, but only if he could guarantee it would break the glass and land on the street below. He was under his desk removing cords. "That's sixty-two stories, Tom," Benny said. And Tom agreed it was a bad idea if he couldn't break the glass. If glass didn't break they would say Tom Mota couldn't even fuck up right — he didn't want to give them the satisfaction of *that,* the bastards. We were the bastards he was referring to, in part. "But I don't think it'll break the glass," said Benny. Tom stopped tooling around with his computer. "But I gotta do *some*thing," he said, sitting back on his heels.

We lacked that kind of urgency. Our building was on the Magnificent Mile, in downtown Chicago, on a corner a few blocks from Lake Michigan. It had tones of art deco and two gilded revolving doors. We shuffled up the stairs toward the revolving doors slowly, afraid of what awaited us inside. In the beginning, we were let go in large numbers. Then, as the practice was refined, one by one, as they saw fit. We feared ending up on Lower Wacker Drive. Unemployed, we would be unpaid; unpaid, we'd be evicted from our homes; evicted, we would end up on Lower Wacker, sharing space with shopping carts and developing our own winterized and blackened feet. Instead of scrabbling for the addition of "Senior" to our current titles, we would search the alleyways for smokable butts. It was fun, imagining our eventual despair. It was also despairing. We didn't really believe we would be honked at from the Lexuses of our former colleagues as they drove down Lower Wacker on their way home to the suburbs. We didn't think we would be forced to wave at them from our lit oil drums. But that we might have to fill out an unemployment form over the Internet was not out of the question. That we might struggle to make rent or a mortgage payment was a real and frightening prospect.

Yet we were still alive, we had to remember that. The sun still shone in as we sat at our desks. Certain days it was enough just to look out at the clouds and at the tops of buildings. We were buoyed by it, momentarily. It made us "happy." We could even turn uncommonly kind. Take, for instance, the time we smuggled Old Golds into Frank Brizzolera's hospital room. Or when we attended the funeral of Janine Gorjanc's little girl, found strangled in an empty lot. It was hard for us to believe something like that could happen to someone we knew. You have never seen someone weep until you have witnessed a mother at the funeral of her murdered child. The girl was nine years old. She was removed at night from an open window. It was all over the papers. First she was missing. Then her body was found. To watch Janine at the funeral, surrounded by pictures of Jessica, her family trying to hold her up — even Tom Mota's heart broke. We were outside the funeral home afterward, in the parking lot speaking somberly to one another, when Tom began to beat on his '94 Miata. It didn't take long before everyone noticed him. He hit the windows with his fists and let out terrible cries of "Fuck!" He kicked the doors and the tires. Finally he collapsed near the trunk, wracked with sobs. It was not unreasonable behavior given the circumstances, but we were a little surprised that Tom appeared the most affected. He was sprawled out on the funeral home parking lot in his suit and tie, sobbing like a child. A few people went over to comfort him. We assumed in part his behavior had something to do with his ex-wife taking his kids to Phoenix. One thing we knew for certain — despite all our certainties, it was very difficult to guess what one individual was thinking at any given moment.

We believed that downturns had been rendered obsolete by the ingenious technology of the new economy. We thought ourselves immune from things like plant closings in Iowa and Nebraska, where remote Americans struggled against falling-in roofs and credit card debt. We watched these blue-collar workers being interviewed on TV. For the length of the segment, it was impossible not to feel the sadness and anxiety they must have felt for themselves and their families. But soon we moved on to weather and sports and by the time we thought about them again, it was a different plant in a different city, and the state was offering dislocated worker programs, readjustment and retraining services, and skills workshops. They'd be fine. Thank god we didn't have to worry about a misfortune like that. We were corporate citizens, buttressed by advanced degrees and padded by corporate fat. We were above the fickle market forces of overproduction and mismanaged inventory.

What we didn't consider was that in a downturn, *we* were the mismanaged inventory, and we were about to be dumped like a glut of imported circuit boards. On the drive home we puzzled over who was next. Scott McMichaels was next. His wife had just had a baby. Sharon Turner was next. She and her husband had just purchased a house. Names — just names to anyone else, but to us they were the individuals who generated our greatest sympathy. The ones who put their things in a box, shook a few hands, and left without complaint. They had no choice in the matter, and they possessed a quiet resignation to their ill-timed fates. As they departed, it almost felt to us like self-sacrifice. They left, so that we might stay. And stay we did, though our hearts went out to them. Then there was Tom Mota, who wanted to throw his computer against the window.

He wore a goatee and was built like a bulldog, stocky, with foreshortened limbs and a rippling succession of necks. He didn't belong where we were. That's not condescension so much as an attempt at a charitable truth. He would have been happier elsewhere — felling trees in a forest, or throwing nets for an Alaskan fishery. Instead, he was dressed in khakis, drinking a latte on a sectional sofa, discussing the best way to make our diaper client's brand synonymous with "more absorbent." That is, when we still had our diaper client. After deciding not to throw his computer against the window, Tom fixated on his magazines. He said to Benny, "Benny, man, you gotta get my magazines from Jim. That fuck's had them two months. I'm not leaving here without them — but I can't go out there. I don't want to have to see anybody." When Benny told us that, we felt pity for Tom. Of course Tom would not have wanted that. He would have spit our pity back in our faces. Nobody wants pity. They just want to get the hell out of there, out of sight, to alleviate the sting of ridicule, and then they want to forget about the entire miserable experience. They can't do that walking the halls to retrieve magazines. Benny returned to Tom's office ten minutes later with back copies of *Car and Driver, Rolling Stone, Guns and Ammo.* Tom was sitting on the floor of his office, winding his watch. Benny said, "Tom." Tom didn't answer. "Tom?" said Benny. Tom continued to wind his watch. Then he stood, opened a desk drawer, and pulled out one of the corporate polos he used to wear many days in a row. The blue one (Benny's) and the green one (Jim's) were also in the desk drawer. Tom took off his button-down and put the red polo on. "They think I'm a clown," he said to Benny. Benny replied, "No. Nobody thinks you're a clown, Tom. They got you by the balls, man — everybody knows that." "Hand me those scissors," said Tom. Benny said he looked behind him and saw a pair of scissors on Tom's bookshelf. Benny told us he didn't want to hand scissors to Tom. "They think I'm a clown," Tom repeated as he walked over to his bookshelf and grabbed the scissors himself and began to cut into his nice pleated slacks at the knee. "What are you doing, Tom?" asked Benny, with an uneasy chuckle. He was still holding Tom's old magazines. He watched as Tom cut all the way around with the scissors until the trouser leg fell to his ankle. Then he started working on one sleeve of the polo, on the opposite side to the cut-off trouser leg. "Tom," said Benny. Tom's tan-lined arm was soon visible all the way to the shoulder. A tattoo of barbed wire snaked around his biceps. "Tom, seriously — what are you doing?"

"Will you do me a favor," asked Tom, "and cut a hole from the backside of my shirt?"

"Tom, why are you doing this?"

Sometimes drastic measures were called for. There were occasions when someone needed to get into a car with a package and drive all the way out to Palatine to the FedEx station that had the latest drop-off time *in the state* just to guarantee the arrival of an overnight delivery. A new client pitch due Monday meant a full week of one o'clock nights and a few hours of sleep on random sofas on Sunday. It was called a fire alarm, and when one came along you had to drop everything. There was no going to the gym. Theater tickets were canceled. You saw no one, not your five-year-old, not your marriage counselor, not your sponsor, not even your dog. We feared the fire alarm. At the same time, we were all in it together, and we could be taken by surprise, after five days of grind, by the transformation of the team. Eating takeout, laughing around a cubicle, putting our minds together to solve something hard — five or six days of that and there was no immunization against the camaraderie. The people we worked with, with all their tics and pieties and limitations — we had to admit it to ourselves, they weren't all that bad. Where did *that* come from? Whence this *friendliness?* "'The love flooding you for your brother,'" said Hank Neary, quoting something or other. He was always quoting something or other and we hated him for it, unless we were in the middle of a fire alarm, in which case we loved him like a brother. That love would dissipate in a week. But while it lasted, work was a wellspring, a real source of light, the nurture of a beloved community.

Then the downturn came and there were no more fire alarms. No speeding out to Palatine, no one o'clock nights, no love flooding us for our brother.

Benny went down the elevator with Tom. With his clothes cut to shreds, Tom looked like someone washed up on shore after a shipwreck, tattered and clinging to a single plank. His shoes and socks were off, left inside the office with the abandoned magazines, the Kmart portraits of his kids, and the discarded swatches from his trousers and polo.

"What are you going to do?" asked Benny.

"What do you think I'm gonna do?" Tom asked rhetorically, just as they had reached the lobby. "I'm gonna find a new job."

"No," said Benny. "I mean right now. What are you doing right now?"

They exited the elevator. Tom had emptied out the pens and pencils from a mug he kept on his desk and that empty mug was now his only possession. Tom stopped in the marble elevator bank and watched for the descent of the other elevators. "You ever read Ralph Waldo Emerson?" Tom asked Benny. Benny didn't know where to stand. He told us he didn't know why they had just stopped in the elevator bank. "What are you planning to do, Tom?" "Listen to what Emerson said," said Tom. Tom began to quote. " 'For all our penny-wisdom,' " he said, " 'for all our soul-destroying slavery to habit, it is not to be doubted that all men have sublime thoughts.' Did you hear that, Benny? Did you hear it, or you need me to repeat it to you?" "I heard it," Benny replied. "They never knew me," Tom said, shaking his head and pointing up at those bastards. "They never did."

The first elevator arrived, and lunchgoers from the law firm emerged. Tom held his empty mug before them. "Help out the unemployed?" he asked them, shaking the cup. "Hey, help out the jobless?"

"Tom," said Benny.

"Benny, get the fuck off me! — Help me out, guy, please? I just lost my job today."

And that was Tom's final hour.

We heard it from Benny just after he told us the story of how Tom arrived at the Naperville house with an aluminum bat when he knew the children were at the grandmother's and everything deemed legally "Tom's" in the divorce settlement, everything that was "Tom's" and could be smashed or shattered with an aluminum bat, suffered Tom's swing until the authorities arrived to subdue him.

Amber Ludwig, who had the compact, athletic body of a seal, with very small hands and dark, closely set eyes, said she feared Tom was going to return like you hear on the news and open fire. "No, seriously," she said. "I think he's come undone. I don't think he was ever *done* to begin with."

Amber wasn't showing yet but everyone already knew. She was debating an abortion but, to Larry Novotny's great disappointment, looked to be leaning against it. Larry would have to decide what to do about his wife, who had just had a child herself not that long ago. We felt sorry for Larry, who worried the curved, finger-smudged bill of his Cubs cap endlessly that spring, but we also thought it was pretty obvious that he should have kept his pecker in his pants. We felt sorry for Amber, too, but as everyone knows, it takes two to tango. We just hoped they weren't doing it on our desks.

We asked Amber if she really, honestly thought Tom capable of a bloodbath.

"Yes," she said. "I wouldn't put anything past him. He's a madman."

We tried to convince her that that sort of thing happened only in factories and warehouses, and then only on the South Side. A debate ensued. Was Tom certifiable? Or was he just a clown? What was that at Janine's little girl's funeral, when he wept and continued weeping even after we got to the bar? Wasn't that proof the guy had a heart?

"Okay," said Amber, "okay, but what do you call standing on the heating vent and mooning the swimmers from his office window? What was that?" she asked.

She was referring to the Holiday Inn rooftop pool Tom's office looked down on, and Tom's tendency to get right up to the glass with his butt cheeks. Hijinks! we cried. Fun! That's not insanity. Amber was outvoted. We knew Tom. We knew Alan Glew, Linda Blanton, Paul Saunier. We knew Neil Hotchkiss and Cora Lee Brower and Harold Oak. They weren't any of them coming back here with a nightmare in a backpack. They had been let go. They packed their things. They left us for good, never to return.

— — —

IT WAS A SURPRISE to everyone when Janine came back. Of course it was understood she could come back whenever she wanted. We just didn't think, given all she had gone through, that coming back here, resuming the old routine — how could that ease her suffering? But maybe it was exactly what she needed, something to take her mind off it. She looked older, especially in the eyes. Her blouses were all wrinkled. Her brown hair was flat and dry where before she had styled it every day, and some days she smelled bad. Her first day back, she thanked us for the flyers. Lynn Mason had had the idea of printing up flyers when we heard that the girl had gone missing. Genevieve Latko-Devine, arguably the kindest and sweetest among us, drove out to North Aurora, where the Gorjancs lived, to get a photograph of Jessica. She returned to the office by noon with a fourth-grade school portrait. We scanned it, loaded it onto the server, and began to build the ad.

Genevieve was at the computer doing the work. Jessica was a plain girl with fair hair and pale skin and an unfortunately crooked smile. We told Genevieve that Jessica was getting washed out.

"What do you want me to do about that?" she asked.

"Let's work on her," said Joe Pope. "Drop her into Photoshop."

We worked on Macs. Some of us had new Macs, some had high-powered notebooks, and some unfortunate souls had to pedal furiously under their desks to keep a spark running through their extinct models. We made layouts in QuarkXPress; all our image manipulation we did in Photoshop. Genevieve dropped the image of the girl into Photoshop and started playing up the girl's hair and freckles. We took a look and everyone agreed she was still getting washed out.

"Try making this area here darker," said Joe, circumscribing the girl's face with a finger. "God, your screen is filthy," he added. He removed a tissue from her box and dusted it. He took a new look. "Now she's more washed out than ever."

Genevieve tried a few things. We looked at the girl. Joe shook his head. "Now she looks sunburned," he said. "Bring it back some."

"I think we're losing sight of what our ultimate goal is here," said Genevieve.

But we feared that if she was washed out, people would look right past the flyer.

Genevieve didn't lack for more suggestions. "Pump 'MISSING' up a little," said Jim Jackers.

"And play up the $10,000 reward," suggested Tom. "I don't know how, just . . . use a different font or something."

"And you have some kerning issues," Benny reminded her from the sidelines.

We all wanted to help. Genevieve worked on it another hour, tweaking this and that, until someone recommended that she fix the little girl's smile to be less crooked. Jessica would look prettier that way.

"All right," she concluded, "we're officially through here."

That afternoon we ripped color print after color print and scored them in the mount room. Several of us drove out to North Aurora and spent the evening posting them — in the public library, the YMCA, the entrance aisles of the grocery stores, in the Starbucks and movie theaters and in the Toys "R" Us, and on all the neighborhood telephone poles. Three days later she was found in an empty lot wrapped in plastic sheeting.

We put up bunting and had cake for Janine's return. Next day Joe Pope found her crying in front of the mirror in the men's room. She had gotten confused and gone through the wrong door. It was rare to get news by way of Joe Pope, since he didn't talk to many people, so we probably shouldn't have known that he found Janine in the men's room. But he did talk to Genevieve Latko-Devine, and Genevieve talked to Marcia Dwyer, and Marcia talked to Benny Shassburger, and Shassburger talked to Jim and Amber, who talked to Larry and Dan Wisdom and Karen Woo, and Karen never met anybody she didn't talk to. Sooner or later everyone found out everything, which is how we came to know that Janine was not over her grief, not by a long shot, because she had gotten confused and wandered into the men's room. We pictured her at the sinks, holding on to the marble ledge for support, her head downcast and her tired eyes shedding momentous tears, oblivious to the urinals in the mirror. After her return, she almost never spoke at lunch.

We talked about Janine wandering into the men's room. No one thought it should be kept a secret, but we were careful not to ridicule the event or turn it into a joke. A few of us did, but not many. It was obviously a tragic thing. We knew about it, but how could we possibly know the first thing about it? Some of us discussed the matter to break up the routine, but most of us used the information to explain why she was quiet at lunch. Then we filed the incident away. That is, until Janine started bringing pictures of Jessica into the office and placing them on the credenza and the bookshelves and hanging them from the walls. The pictures crowded in, elbowing each other for room. A hundred pictures of her dead daughter in the seventy-five square feet of her office. The three on the wall facing her were the most mournful things we'd ever seen. It was also downright creepy. It got to the point where we tried to avoid entering her office. When we were forced to, for some pressing item of business, we never knew where to rest our eyes.

— — —

ON A TUESDAY IN MAY at twelve-fifteen in the afternoon, Lynn Mason scheduled an input meeting. We gathered in her office to be a part of it. Input meetings made us happy because they meant we had work to do. We worked in the creative department developing ads and we considered our ad work creative, but it wasn't half as creative as the work we'd put in to pad our time sheets every Monday morning since layoffs began. An input meeting meant we'd have actual work that would make our time sheets less intimidating the following week. But some of us didn't like input meetings when they were scheduled for twelve-fifteen. "That's when most of us — hello? — go to lunch," said Karen Woo. Lunch for Karen was a sacrament. "Why not schedule it for eleven-fifteen?" she asked. "Or even one o'clock?" Most of the rest of us just thought, no big deal, so lunch comes an hour late. "But I'm hungry," said

Karen. She didn't seem to have much sympathy for the fact that Lynn Mason had just found out she had cancer and might have other things on her mind. Besides, Lynn could schedule an input whenever she wanted — she was a partner. "Of course she *can* schedule an input whenever she wants," said Karen. "But *ought* she? That's the question. *Ought* she." Many of us thought Karen should consider herself lucky to still have a job.

While waiting for Lynn to arrive, we killed time listening to Chris Yop tell us the story of Tom Mota's chair. We loved killing time and had perfected several ways of doing so. We wandered the hallways carrying papers that indicated some mission of business when in reality we were in search of free candy. We refilled our coffee mugs on floors we didn't belong on. Hank Neary was an avid reader. He arrived early in his brown corduroy coat with a book taken from the library, copied all its pages on the Xerox machine, and sat at his desk reading what looked to passersby like the honest pages of business. He'd make it through a three-hundred-page novel every two or three days. Billy Reiser, who worked on another team and walked with a limp, was a huge Cubs fan. He had a friend who installed satellites. They gained illegal access to the roof, secured a remote satellite in an out-of-the-way place, and situated it so that the signal beamed off the next-door building into Billy's office. Then Billy's friend set up a television under his desk, mounted at an angle so if Billy was sitting just a foot back in his chair, he could look down and see the picture. When it was all through, he had two hundred stations and could watch the Cubs even on away games. We gathered down there in limited numbers when Sammy Sosa was going for the home run record. The problem was Billy was worried someone would find out about the satellite, so every time Sammy hit a homer and we cheered like mad, we got kicked out.

Tom Mota had been laid off the week before Chris Yop told us the story of his chair. Yop said he had been cleaning off his desk when he looked up and found the office coordinator standing in his doorway. Our office coordinator smelled of witch hazel and carpet fiber, had a considerable mole on her left cheek, and never said hello to anyone. It was rumored that, like an ant, her back could bear the burden of something several times her body weight. She stood in Yop's doorway with her arms crossed, leaning against the doorjamb and peering in at Yop's bookshelves. She asked if they were Tom Mota's. "So I say to her," Yop said to us, " 'Tom Mota's? What, those?' 'The bookshelves,' she says. 'Are those Tom's?' 'The bookshelves? No,' I say, 'those aren't Tom's. Those are mine.' 'Well, someone took Tom's bookshelves out of his office,' she says to me, 'and I have to get them back.' At this point, Tom's been shitcanned, what? a day? This was last Tuesday — I mean, the body's not even cold yet, and she's standing in my doorway accusing me of stealing? So I repeat to her, I say, 'Those aren't his bookshelves, those are my bookshelves.' But then she walks into my office, right, get this. She walks into my office and she says, 'Is that his chair? Is that Tom's chair you're sitting on?' She's pointing at it, right. She thinks it's his chair. It's my chair. Those are his bookshelves, sure. I took them out of his office when he got shitcanned and brought them down to mine. But it's for damn sure not his chair. It's my chair! So I say, 'This? This is my chair. This chair is mine.' And she says, she walks into my office and stands very close to me, she says, she's about a foot, maybe two feet from me, she says, pointing at my chair, 'Do you mind if I look at the serial numbers?' Now, who knew about this?" he asked us. "Who knew about these serial numbers?" None of us had ever heard anything about serial numbers. "Yeah, serial numbers," Yop continued. "They keep serial numbers on the back of everything. That way they can track everything, who has what and what office it's in. Did you know about this?"

We let him go on about the serial numbers because his outrage was typical of the time. Chris was a nervous man, and as he spoke, his whole face seemed to quiver. His animating hands shook a little, as if battling a caffeine dip. He had encouraged us to call him Yop because it made him feel younger, cooler, and more accepted. He kept his graying hair long, so it curled up near the ears, but age had thinned it on top. He was married to a woman named Terry and on weekends he played bad rock songs for a seventies cover band. He was always asking everyone what they were listening to these days. We considered it half-noble, half-pathetic when passing his office to hear some new rap album issuing from his CD player, when everyone knew what he really wanted to be listening to was *Blood on the Tracks.* We listened to his story about Tom Mota's chair from various locations in Lynn's cluttered office. She had a glass-top table and a white leather sofa and we hung in the doorway and leaned against the walls, killing time while waiting for her. Karen Woo kept looking at her watch and sighing because Lynn was running late to her own meeting.

"I was like, 'Serial numbers?'" Yop continued. "And she says, she's standing behind me, right, she says, 'Have a look.' So I get off my chair, I take a look — serial numbers! On the back of my chair! 'Where'd these come from?' I ask her. She doesn't answer me. Instead she says, 'Can I borrow a pen?' She wants to borrow a pen so she can take down the serial numbers! I'm thinking, what sort of fascist organization — 'Hello?' I say. 'This is my chair.' But she's not paying any attention to me — she's taking down the serial numbers! Then she goes over to the buckshelves, she starts taking down the serial numbers on them and she says, 'And what about these buckshelves?' Now I'm in a fix, because I lied about the buckshelves, sure, but I'm telling the truth about the chair. I could give a *shit* about the buckshelves. Take the buckshelves. Just leave me my chair."

We told Yop he meant to say *bookshelves.*

"What'd I say?" he asked us.

We told him he was saying *buck*shelves.

"Buckshelves?"

Right — at first it was *book*shelves, but then he started saying *buck*shelves.

"Listen, don't pay any attention to me," he said. "That's just me getting my words wrong. The point is, take the bookshelves. Just leave me my chair. It's my chair. 'But are they *yours?*' she asks me. It's a moral question for this woman, whose they are. So I say, 'Yeah, they're mine, but you take them, okay. I don't want them anymore.' I don't want them anymore? Who wouldn't want those bookshelves? But I don't want to lose my chair — my *legitimate* chair, so I say, 'Go ahead, take 'em.' "

We didn't want to interrupt him again, but we felt the need to remind him that it was her job, as the office coordinator, to keep track of office furniture and the like.

Yop ignored us. "What is that she has on her wrist?" he asked.

Yop was asking about the office coordinator's tattoo. It was of a scorpion whose tail wrapped around her left wrist.

"Now why would a woman do that to herself?" he asked. "And why would we hire a woman who would do that to herself?"

It was a good question. We assumed he knew the joke.

"What's the joke?" he asked.

The scorpion was there to protect her ring finger.

"Let me tell you something," he said. "That's funny, but that ring finger doesn't need any protecting. But okay, whatever—she's just doing her job. How we *ever* hired a person with a scorpion on her wrist is *far* beyond me, but okay, she's doing her job. But that's my legitimate chair. It's *my* chair. She takes my chair, that's not her mandate. So she says to me, she says, 'Why would you offer me your buckshelves if, as you say, they're really your buckshelves? I don't want them if they're yours,' she says, 'I only want them if they're Tom's. All of Tom's stuff has disappeared and it's my job to get it back.' So I say, trying to act all innocent and unknowing, I say, 'What all did they take?' And she says, 'Well, let's see. His desk,' she says. 'His chair, his buckshelves, his —' "

We apologized for interrupting, but he was doing it again.

"What's that?" he asked.

Saying *buck*shelves.

Yop raised his arms in the air. He was wearing a ratty Hawaiian shirt — the hair on his arms was going gray. "Will you *listen* to me, please?" he cried. "Will you all just please hear what I'm trying to say? I'm trying to tell you something really important here. *They know everything!* They knew everything we'd taken! So what choice did I have? 'You can have the buckshelves, okay?' I say to her. *Just don't take my chair.* 'But are they *Tom's?*' she asks me. *That's* what's important to her. She wants to know, 'Did you take these buckshelves from Tom's office?' And that's when it hits me. I'm going to get shitcanned just because I took Tom's buckshelves."

*Book*shelves! we cried out.

"Right!" he cried back. "And for something as simple as that I'm going to get shitcanned! Hey, I have a mortgage. I have a wife. I'm a fucking professional. I get shitcanned this late in my career, that's it for me. It's a young man's game. I'm too old. Who's going to hire me if I get shitcanned? I see no alternative but to come clean, so I say to her, 'Okay, listen. These buckshelves, right? I'll get them back down to Tom's office. I promise. I'm sorry.' And she says, 'But you're not answering my question. *Are* they his? *Did* you take them?' So you *know* what I'm thinking at this point. I've tried to be somewhat honest with her. I've tried to tap into something human and feeling in her. But it's not working. She ain't nothin' but a bureaucrat. So what I say is, I say, 'All I know is, they were here when I came back from lunch.' And she says, she looks at her watch, she says, 'It's ten-fifteen.' And I say, 'Yeah?' 'Ten-fifteen in the morning,' she says. 'You took lunch at, what? Nine-thirty?' Then she points at the buckshelves and she says, 'And I guess all these bucks just appeared when you came back from lunch, too, huh? Your nine-thirty lunch?' And I don't say anything, and she says, 'And what about the nice chair you're sitting on? That suddenly appear out of nowhere, too?' And I don't say anything, and she says, 'I'll be back after I've had a chance to crosscheck your serial numbers. I would suggest that if those are Tom's buckshelves you have them back in his office pronto. And the same goes for anything else that belongs to Tom.' And that's when I say to her, 'Hey, hold the fuck up, missy. What do you mean, *belongs* to Tom? Nothing belongs to Tom. Tom just worked here. Nothing *ever* belonged to Tom. Nothing belongs to *anyone* here, because they can take it away from you like *that.*'" Yop snapped his fingers. "Listen to how she responds," he said. "'Uh, sorry, no,' she says. 'I'm afraid all of this belongs to me.'"

Yop threw out his hands in supplication and his eyes bulged out. He expected us to be outraged that the office coordinator would say a thing like that, but the truth was, it didn't surprise us at all. In a way, it did belong to her. She wasn't going to be laid off. Everyone needs an office coordinator.

"Oh, I was so fucking irate," he said. "*Nothing* gets me more than the petty-minded people around here who have just *this* much power, and then they wield it and they wield it until they have TOTAL control over you. And now she's going to check her serial numbers and find out that I have Ernie Kessler's old chair."

Wait a minute. It wasn't his chair?

"From when he retired," Yop said, in a calmer voice. "Last year."

We couldn't believe it wasn't his chair.

"It is now. It *was* Ernie's chair. From when he retired."

We felt deceived. He had given us the impression that at the very least it was his chair.

"It *is* my chair," he said. "He rolled it down to me. Ernie did. I asked him for it and he rolled it down to me and he rolled my chair away and put it in his office. When he retired. We just swapped chairs. We didn't know about the serial numbers. Now that I know about the serial numbers, I'm thinking, That's it for me. This office coordinator, she's going to tell Lynn I took Tom's buckshelves — and that I took Ernie Kessler's chair, too, even though he gave it to me. So what choice do I have? If I want to keep my job I have to pretend it *is* Tom's chair and roll it down to his office! It's not his chair — somebody else has Tom's chair — but last week, that's exactly what I did. I rolled Ernie Kessler's chair down to Tom Mota's office after everyone had gone home. I had to pretend it was Tom's chair, and for a week now I've gone on pretending, while I've had to sit on this other chair, this little piece-of-crap chair, just so I can avoid getting shitcanned. That was my *legitimate* chair," he said, his fists quivering in anguish before him.

We didn't blame him for being upset. His chair was a wonderful chair — adjustable, with webbed seating, giving just a little when you first sat down.

— — —

THE AUSTERITY MEASURES BEGAN in the lobby, with the flowers and bowls of candy. Benny liked to smell the flowers. "I miss the nice flowers," he said. Then we got an officewide memo taking away our summer days. "I miss my summer days even more than the flowers," he remarked. At an all-agency meeting the following month, they announced a hiring freeze. Next thing we knew, no one was receiving a bonus. "I couldn't give a damn about summer days," he said, "but my bonus now, too?" Finally, layoffs began. "Flowers, summer days, bonuses — fine by me," said Benny. "Just leave me my job."

At first we called it what you would expect — getting laid off, being let go. Then we got creative. We said he'd gotten the ax, she'd been sacked, they'd all been shitcanned. Lately, a new phrase had appeared and really taken off. "Walking Spanish down the hall." Somebody had picked it up from a Tom Waits song, but it was an old, old expression, as we learned from our *Morris Dictionary of Word and Phrase Origins.* "In the days of piracy on the Spanish Main," Morris writes, "a favorite trick of pirates was to lift their captives by the scruff of the neck and make them walk with their toes barely touching the deck." That sounded about right to us. In the song, Tom Waits sings about walking toward an execution, and that sounded right, too. We'd watch the singled-out walk the long carpeted hallway with the office coordinator leading the way, and then he or she would disappear behind Lynn Mason's door, and a few minutes later we'd see the lights dim from the voltage drop and we'd hear the electricity sizzle and the smell of cooked flesh would waft out into the insulated spaces.

We would turn at our desks and watch the planes descend into O'Hare. We would put our headphones on. We would lean our heads back and close our eyes. We all had the same thought: *thank god it wasn't me.*

Jim knocked at Benny's doorway. "You seen Sanderson around lately, Benny?"

"Who?"

"Sanderson. Will Sanderson."

Benny still didn't know who Jim was talking about.

"Come on, Benny. Sanderson. With the mustache."

"Oh, right," said Benny. "Bill Sanderson? I thought his name was Bill."

"His name is Will," said Jim.

"I haven't seen that guy around for . . . weeks."

"Weeks? You don't think . . ."

They were quiet.

"Sanderson," said Benny. "Man oh man," he said. "They got Will Sanderson."

A FUN THING TO DO to let off steam after layoffs began was to go into someone's office and send an e-mail from their computer addressed to the entire agency. It might say something simple like "My name is Shaw-NEE! You are captured, Ha! I poopie I poopie I poopie." People came in in the morning and read that and the reactions were so varied.

Jim Jackers read it and immediately sent out an e-mail that read, "Obviously someone came into my office last night and composed an e-mail in my name and sent it out to everyone. I apologize for any inconvenience or offense, although it wasn't my fault, and I would appreciate from whoever did this a public apology. I have read that e-mail five times now and I still don't even understand it."

We knew who did it. There was never an apology. Jim knew who did it because he was one of us, and Jim confronted Tom

Mota about it. This was some months before Tom walked Spanish. What do you think Tom did? Tom told Benny about the encounter at lunch, about how Jim's fury was off the charts, and how Tom egged Smalls on to hit him. "Smalls" was Tom's nickname for Jim, though both men were about the same height. "Come on, Smalls, you little fucker, *please* hit me," Tom told Benny he told Jim, and how funny it all was. We were only into our third month of layoffs then. Jim never left the office again without closing out of his e-mail program.

Tom's e-mails were not always antic provocations — sometimes they were earnest and came from his own computer. We were amused by his sincere tone and his talk of man's infinite worthiness. These heartfelt, long-winded missives, of sentiment wildly clashing with Tom's real-life behavior, were laughably inappropriate, schizophrenic in tone and content, and always welcome respites in an otherwise ordinary day. He was written up for their profanities and for composing them on company time, because he had the balls to send them not only to all of us, including Lynn Mason, but to the other partners as well — always organizing the send-to list according to seniority, an unspoken rule. He also cc'd the accounts people, the media buyers, project services, human resources, the support staff, and the barista manning the coffee bar. "I passed a bad night last night," his final e-mail in this vein began. The subject line read, "I Consign You and Your Golf Shoes to Lower Wacker Drive." "The tomatoes in my garden are not coming out," he continued. "Maybe because I only have the weekend to work the garden, or maybe because the garden keeps getting mowed over by the goddamn Hispanics who tend to the grounds of the apartment complex I've been living in since the state forced me to sell my house in Naperville and Barbara took the kids to Phoenix to live with Pilot Bob. Do I have an actual garden? The answer to that is a big fat no, because the goddamn woman in the property office won't listen to reason. She keeps insisting that this is a *rental* property, *not* your backyard. Flower borders, that's all we want, she says. So the goddamn Hispanics go out and tend the marigolds along the borders. But do you understand, I'm talking about fat, ripe, juicy, delicious red tomatoes that I want to grow with my own two hands through the bountiful mystery and generosity of nature! That dream ended when Barb started sleeping with Pilot Bob and we gave up Naperville. Anyway, would I like a garden? YES. Matter of fact I would like a farm. But at the present moment I'm afraid all I have is apartment 4H at Bell Harbor Manor, which is neither a harbor nor a manor and contains NOT ONE SINGLE BELL. Which one of you wit-wizards came up with the name 'Bell Harbor Manor'? May your clever tongues be ripped from their cushy red linings and left to dry on pikes under the native sun of a cannibal land. Ha! I will be called into the office for that one but I'm leaving it, because what I'm trying to get at here is that I'M NOT SURE ANY OF US KNOWS just how far we have removed ourselves not only from nature but from the natural conditions of life that have prevailed for centuries and have forced men to the extreme limits of their physical capacity in order simply to feed, clothe and otherwise provide for their families, sending them every night to a sweet, exhausted, restorative, unstirred, deserved sleep such as we will never know again. Now there's Phoenix, and airplanes to get you there, and Pilot Bob who can take care of EVERYTHING, though he probably doesn't even know how to mow his own lawn. But don't forget, Bob, and all you Bobs out there, that 'Manual labor is the study of the external world.' I believe that to be true. Now, the question you're all probably asking yourselves is, what is he doing then, Tom Mota? Why is Tom wasting his days in a carpeted office trying to hide the coffee stain on his khakis? How is he any better than Pilot Bob? Unfortunately, I don't think I am any better. I'm not studying the external world. What I'm doing is trying to generate a buck for a client so as to generate a quarter for us so that I can generate a nickel for me and have a penny left over after Barbara gets what the court demands. For that reason I love my job and never want to lose it, so I hope no one reading this finds me smug or ungrateful. I'm only trying to suggest that as we find ourselves in this particularly unfortunate, misconstrued, ungodly juncture of civilization, let's not lose sight of the nobler manifestations of man and of the greater half of his character, which consists not of taglines and bottom lines but of love, heroism, reciprocity, ecstasy, kindness and truth. What a bloated bunch of horseshit, you will say. And good for you. I welcome you to shoot me up close in the head. Peace, Tom."

Not long after hitting send, Tom was let go, and if not for the paltry severance, we might have been inclined to think that his was not another in a series of layoffs, but an outright firing. But the truth was, Tom was probably in the pipeline already. His e-mail just hastened things along, the way pneumonia can spell doom for a cancer patient.

LYNN MASON WAS STILL running late to the twelve-fifteen meeting on that Tuesday in May, so Chris Yop continued telling us the story of Tom Mota's chair. That very morning he had looked up from cleaning his desk to find the office coordinator standing in his doorway once again, arms folded. "So she says to me," he said to us, "'I see you put Tom's buckshelves back.' So I act totally ignorant, I say, 'I'm sorry, I don't know what it is you're talking about,' and I go back to cleaning my desk, but she's not leaving, so I look up again and she says, 'And I see you no longer have his chair, either.' So I say, 'I would appreciate you not harassing me anymore. There are rules against that sort of thing in the employee handbook.' And she says, 'You think I'm harassing you?' And I say, 'Yes. And I don't appreciate it.' And she says, 'Well, maybe we should take it up with Lynn.' And I say, 'I would welcome that,' and she says, 'What are you doing right now?' and I say, 'Well, unlike some people, I'm trying to get some work done. Some people actually generate revenue around here, you handjob.' I shouldn't have said that — I was just, you know, pointing out the difference between an office coordinator and a copywriter like me who generates revenue. So she says back to me, 'Oh, sure, I understand how *incredibly* important you are, how everything would just *crumble* all around us without you, but if you wouldn't mind, will you follow me, please?' And I say, 'Follow you? Follow you where?' And she says, 'Lynn would like a word.' 'What, now?' I say. And she says, 'If you can pull yourself away.' And I say, 'She wants to see me *right now?*' She doesn't say another word — just motions for me to follow. So I get off my chair, that piece of crap — I mean, my ass is like on Novocain on that thing — and together we head down to Lynn's office. I mean, what choice do I have? If she's telling me Lynn wants to see me, what choice do I have?"

We asked Yop how long ago this was.

"Maybe an hour ago," he said. "So we go down there. I'm not going to lie to you. My heart's going. I'm forty-eight. This is a young man's game. Who's going to hire me if I get shitcanned? I don't know Photoshop. Some days, I don't even understand Outlook, okay. You know me and the e-mail. I get shitcanned, who's going to pay me what I deserve? I'm an old man. I get paid too much. But I gotta go down there. The office coordinator goes in first. I follow her in and close the door. 'Okay,' says Lynn. And you know how she can lean forward at her desk and look at you like she's about to carve your skull out with her laser eyes? She says, 'Now what's going on?' The office coordinator comes right out of the gate — first, I stole Tom's buckshelves. 'Where's the proof?' I cry out. I mean she's not letting me talk. 'Huh? Where's the proof?' I ask. She doesn't answer. Then she tells Lynn I've been harassing her. Me harassing her! I can't believe my ears. But what she doesn't say a thing about, not one word about — she says *not one word* about the chair. The whole point is the chair! That's the reason we're here! I was trying to protect my chair. So I say, 'What about the chair?' And she says, you want to know what she says? She says, 'What chair?' What do you mean, what chair, right? So I say, 'Come on, what chair. *The* chair. My chair.' And she says, 'I don't know what he's talking about, this chair.' To Lynn she says this! She denies there was ever a chair! So I say, I'm so pissed off, I say, 'COME ON, WHAT CHAIR! You know what chair, goddamn it!' And there's silence, and then she says, 'I'm sorry, Lynn. I don't know what he's talking about.' And I say, 'YOU GODDAMN WELL KNOW WHAT CHAIR! She knows what chair, Lynn! She tried to take my chair away from me. My *legitimate* chair.' So there's silence, and then Lynn says, 'Kathy —' Kathy — did any of you know her name was Kathy? She says, 'Kathy, can you give Chris and me a minute please?' So 'Kathy' says of course and Lynn says, 'Can you shut the door, please, Kathy?' and 'Kathy' says, 'Sure,' and we hear the door close, and my heart's going, you know, and Lynn says, 'Chris, I'm sorry, but we're going to have to let you go.'"

Yop stopped speaking. He shook his lowered head slowly. There was silence. "I was speechless," he continued after a while. His voice had dropped. "I asked her if it had something to do with Ernie Kessler's chair. She says no. She says it has nothing to do with Ernie's chair. 'Because I don't need Ernie's chair,' I tell her. 'Honest — I've been sitting on one of the cheap plastic ones for the past week and it's fine. It's a fine chair.' And she says, 'This has nothing to do with Ernie's chair.' I can't believe it. I can't believe what she's telling me. So I say, 'Is it the mistakes? Because I'm getting better,' I tell her. 'It's how my brain works sometimes,' I tell her, 'but I'm getting better. Most of them get caught when we run spell-check anyway. I know it's not ideal in a copywriter, I appreciate your patience,' I say to her. 'But I am getting better.' And she says, 'It's not the mistakes, Chris.' 'So what is it then?' I ask. 'It's nothing personal,' she says to me. 'It's just business.' 'Is it because I make too much money? Is that it?' And she says, 'No, not exactly.' 'Can I maybe take a cut in pay?' I ask. I'm asking her, 'Can I take a pay cut and stay on?' 'It's not exactly the money, Chris,' she says. So what the hell is it then, right? 'Now, listen,' she says. 'We're going to give you a month's severance, and COBRA will cover your health benefits through the year. It's really nothing personal,' she says. She keeps saying that — it's nothing personal, Chris — so I figure it must be something personal. 'So what is it then, Lynn?' I ask her. And maybe my voice cracks a little. 'If it's not personal, what is it?' 'Chris, please,' she says. Because by now I'm breaking down . . ."

We asked him what he meant by that.

"I started crying," he said. "It wasn't just the job," he added. "It was the whole feeling of being me. Being old. Thinking about Terry. Not having a kid. And now, not having a job." He and his wife had tried to conceive for years, and by the time they gave up, they were considered too old to adopt by the agencies. "I was thinking about having to go home to Terry and telling her I'd been shitcanned. I didn't want to cry," he said, "god knows, I just got overcome. I put my head down, and I lost it for a minute. I just wasn't in control. So, you know, I had to leave. I never cried in front of someone like that before. I couldn't stick around. 'Come on, Chris,' she says to me. 'Come back. You're going to be fine,' she says. 'You're a fine copywriter.' This is what she's saying to me while I'm being shitcanned. I haven't talked to her since."

We couldn't blame him for being upset, but it would be just like Yop, tough-acting Yop, to give up the chair he fought so hard for just like *that* if it would save his ass, and if that didn't work, it would be just like Yop to beg for a cut in pay, and if that still didn't save his job, Chris Yop would be the one among us to break down. Tom Mota wanted to throw a computer through the window; Chris Yop threw himself at Lynn's feet.

Just before Lynn showed up, fifteen minutes late for her own input, we asked Yop what he was still doing here.

"I don't know," he said. "I can't go home, not yet. It doesn't feel right."

But should you really be *here?* we asked him. In Lynn's office?

"Well, Lynn and me," he said, "we didn't get a chance to finish our conversation. I broke down. I left. You guys don't think I should have to *leave* leave, do you, when we didn't get a chance to finish our conversation?"

No one replied — meaning, well, yeah, Yop. You should probably leave.

"I don't know," he said, looking around. "This meeting's been on my calendar for a long time."

— — —

ALL TALK TAPERED OFF when Lynn finally arrived. When the time came to get down to business, we got down to business. We didn't fuck around in input meetings. We fucked around before them and sometimes we fucked around after them, but during them, there might be the occasional wisecrack, but otherwise we were solemn as churchgoers. Any one of us could be let go at any time, and that fact was continually on our minds.

Lynn Mason was intimidating, mercurial, unapproachable, fashionable, and consummately professional. She was not a big woman — in fact, she was rather petite — but when we thought of her from home at night, she loomed large. When she was in a mood, she didn't make small talk. She dressed like a Bloomingdale's model and ate like a Buddhist monk. On the day of the twelve-fifteen she was dressed in an olive-hued skirt suit and a simple ivory blouse. What you really admired about her, though, were her shoes. As aficionados of design, we — the women among us especially — sat in awe of their sleek singularity, exquisite color, and contoured elegance, marveling at them as others might the armrest of a chair by Charles Eames, or the black wing of a Pentagon jetfighter. Each pair — and she must have had fifty of them — deserved their own Plexiglas display case at the Museum of Contemporary Art, next to that polyethylene thing and those neon signs. We had never seen anything so beautiful as those shoes. When someone finally got up the nerve to ask her what brand they were, no one recognized the name, leaving us to conclude that they were made by boutique Italian designers who refused to export their product, but which Lynn's friends picked up for her on their international travels, because everyone knew Lynn never took vacation.

When she entered, disrupting Chris Yop at his story, she was carrying input documents fresh from the copy machine; a scent of toner trailed behind her. Without a word she set the copies on her desk and began to collate them, moistening her finger and thumb and stapling the sheets together and passing the packet to Joe, who sat immediately to her right. "Stapler on the machine's broken," she explained. Joe passed the document to his right, and it wound its way to Karen Woo, who was seated farthest from him. Lynn stapled a few minutes more, then stopped to remove her leather heels. "Why does it feel like I just walked in on a funeral?" she asked, finally looking around at us. No one said a word. "I hope it's nobody I know," she added. She went back to collating and stapling.

Our information had come from reliable sources but it was only the barest details. Her surgery was scheduled for the following day. The tumor had invaded her chest wall. She was going in for a full mastectomy. We had questions for her — was she scared? did she like her doctors? what were her chances of complete recovery? But she had not yet said a word about it to any of us and we knew nothing of her state of mind. We might have wondered why she was at work the day before. She needed to get her priorities straight, we thought. But then none of us ever had our priorities straight. Each and every one of us harbored the illusion that the whole enterprise would go straight to hell without our individual daily contributions. So what was this fantasy about straight priorities, this dream that would never be realized? Besides, what else should she do but carry on? We had to think that by coming into work the day before surgery, she was refusing to let the specter of death distract her from the ordinariness of life that could very well be both a comfort and an armament to someone diagnosed with breast cancer. She was exactly right to come into work the day before. Unless she should have stayed at home and ordered in and played with her cats on the sofa. It was really not for us to say.

Without so much as a word about Chris Yop's presence among us, the input documents got handed around. Everyone took a copy; Chris Yop took a copy, too. Did he really plan to sit through the entire input meeting though he was no longer an employee?

Lynn took her jacket off and flung it over her chair, sat down, and said, "Okay. Let's get this funeral started." She began to read from the input document. When we turned the page, Yop turned the page. It was hard to concentrate on anything else. There was Lynn, reading from the input document, and then there was Yop reading from the input document, and the one had just fired the other, but there they both were, carrying on as if nothing at all had happened. Maybe she hadn't noticed him? Maybe she had other things on her mind?

Our project turned out to be pro bono. The agency had donated our services to a popular breast cancer fund-raising event sponsored by the Alliance Against Breast Cancer. Our job, Lynn explained, reading from the input document, was to raise awareness of the event and to boost donations across the country. We would be doing so by advertising in nationally distributed magazines and on the backs of cereal boxes.

We had to wonder, was this just a bizarre coincidence? We thought she might finally say something to us about her diagnosis. We watched her, but she never wavered from her steady reading of the input document. She gave no indication that this project was different in any way from any other project. We looked around at one another. Then we looked back down at the input document. When she was through, she explained a few extraneous matters, and then she asked us if we had any questions. We told her it sounded like a great project, and we inquired how we happened to get involved. "Oh, I know the committee chair," she replied. "I've been saying no for two years and I just didn't have the energy to say no anymore." She shrugged. Noticing something in the corner of her eye, she turned and picked lint off the shoulder of her blouse. "Any other questions?" No one said a word. "Okay," she said.

"Funeral's over." And with that, we all got up and left her office. Yop almost made it out into the hall when she called him back in. "Chris," she said, "can I have a word with you, please? Joe," she added, "get the door on your way out, will you?" Yop turned back, downcast and hesitant. Lynn got up to draw her blinds. Yop walked back in, the door closed, and that was the last we saw of them.

We set off for our offices and cubicles, immediately leaving them again to gather in small clusters, in doorways and print stations, to discuss the almost surreal pro bono project we had on our hands. During the input she had asked us to envision a loved one being diagnosed with the disease — a wife, a mother — so that we could really sympathize with cancer sufferers and design a more effective communication. Well, *she* had the disease. If someone could give us insight to sympathize with the sick for a more effective communication, who better than she? And yet not a word. Everyone knew she was a private person. And we had a reputation for gossip. We didn't expect that she would just come out and announce that she had cancer. But she was also a very dedicated marketer, and in that respect, it was perhaps odd, despite her sense of privacy, that she did not extend herself to help us better understand the horror of a diagnosis, for example, or the misery of treatments, if understanding those things were necessary for coming up with a better ad. We didn't know if we should believe that she just happened to know some committee chair who had pestered her and pestered her until she agreed to donate our time.

She had a command of business politics like no one we had ever known. In 1997 she quarreled with Roger Highnote. He departed, and our lives improved dramatically. She was an enemy of the lowest common denominator. The cardinal rule of advertising has always been, make your communication dumb enough for an eighth grader to understand. Lynn Mason's mentor, the fabled Mary Wells, had the fabled Bernbach as mentor, and Bernbach once said, famously, "It's true that there's a twelve-year-old mentality in America. Every six-year-old has it." Like Wells and Bernbach, Lynn respected American intelligence, and a lot of good had come from it: the talking llama campaign, the Cold Sore Guy spots. Sure, she was the one walking everyone Spanish down the hall, but she hadn't walked any of *us* Spanish down the hall yet — that was an important distinction.

Lynn Mason was also scrupulous as hell. Once Karen Woo and Jim Jackers were redesigning the packaging for a box of cookies made by a big conglomerate who later broke our hearts when they left us for another agency. The box was standard stuff, overanimated with recognizable cookie characters and catchy little phrases like "Chocolicious!" and "Dunkable!" in colorful arching fonts. These mandatories had to stay; they had become scripture in the client's thick red binder of branding guidelines. So Karen and Jim's job was pretty simple — they were just being asked to find some way to play up the cookie's nutritional value. In an increasingly health-conscious and weight-wary world, every cookie box was doing it. So Karen wrote some copy for one of the panels that spoke to the importance of niacin and folic acid. Then she went down to Jim's cube and stood over his computer while instructing him to write, in a smallish font near the bottom of the front of the box, "0 g of Lastive Acid." Jim did as he was instructed.

"What's lastive acid?" he asked.

"Not something you want in your body," replied Karen.

They took the box down to Lynn, who looked over the changes. Practically everything was the same except for the copy box on the side panel discussing the good effects of niacin and folic acid, and Lynn was happy with that until she came to the part that read — and here she stopped reading silently and began to recite out loud — "'And our chocolicious cookies contain zero grams of lastive acid, making them the health-conscious choice for totally dunkable snacking.' What is lastive acid?" she inquired.

"I thought it was like a, you know," said Karen, "something unhealthy."

"But what is it?"

"Sounds terrible, whatever it is," said Jim.

"It's probably not something you want in your body," said Karen, "from the sound of it. Lastive acid. Sounds like it would stay with you longer than the formaldehyde."

Meanwhile Lynn had gone searching through the input document provided by the accounts people. "I don't see anything about 'lastive acid' in here," she said, gazing at Karen.

"No, I came up with it," said Karen.

Lynn's face, which had aged into the early years of her forties with little modification of her cool detached beauty, was architecturally designed for such outrageous confessions. Her high cheekbones kept her eyes buttressed from the collapse of a disbelieving brow, her nearly crow's-feet-free eyes never gave way to an off-putting squint, and her mouth, flanked on both sides by a single parenthesis of a gently etched laugh line, remained in perfect equipoise when presented with revelations that would have provoked in lesser professionals fallen jaws of slackened disgust or a steady stream of rebuke. She simply gazed across the desk at Karen and asked soberly, "You just made it up?"

"Well, not the part about there being zero grams."

"Karen," she said — and Jim told us later that the only show of irritation she allowed herself was to pull her chair closer to her desk and to place two fingers at her left temple.

"I was trying to think out of the box," explained Karen.

"I . . . myself, Lynn, I didn't know . . ." Jim stammered.

Lynn shifted her focus briefly to address him. "Jim, will you excuse us for a minute, please?"

It was this sort of thing that showed us how Lynn had developed over the years a moral principle that guided her in the practice of advertising, which she abided by with strict authority. We respected her for it and wanted to live up to those high standards. Whenever we did something thoughtless or dull, or when we didn't perform at the level we had hoped to on one project or another, we would, in our own individual ways, try to hint to her that we were just as disappointed in ourselves as she was while implying that we were making every effort to improve. Failing, perhaps, to pick up on these subtle apologies — not wanting to advertise our shortcomings, we rarely came right out and admitted them — she usually didn't respond, but when she did, her communiqués were brief, inconclusive, and often bewildering. She might leave us a voice mail that said, "Forget about it," or drop an e-mail that said only, "Don't worry so much — Lynn." We spent hours trying to decode these simple messages. We went into other people's offices, demanded they stop what they were doing, and conscripted them into the ceaseless political labors of puzzling out her woefully inadequate responses to our pleas for reassurance. "Don't worry *so much?*" we asked each other. "Why not *at all?*" We wanted to ask her directly but no one dared, except Jim Jackers, whose insatiable demand for confirmation that he wasn't a hopelessly unreformed boob sent him into Lynn's office with the regularity of therapist appointments. Where she found the time, and why she had a soft spot for Jim, were mysteries on the order of her gnomic e-mails, and someone's absurd suggestion that she might be just as receptive to any of the rest of us if we only had the nerve to knock at her door was dismissed as sadly out of touch.

So she wasn't going to say anything to us about her diagnosis. We were disturbed and upset and at a bit of a loss. We wanted her to open up, if only for ten minutes. What were we here for if not, on occasion, that? Just work? We hoped not. Yet we got nothing. Not even for the sake of a better ad. We still had no official word that she would be out of the office while recuperating from surgery. Officially, she'd be in all week, and when the time came, we'd be expected to show her ad concepts for what she had sold to us as a pain-in-the-ass fund-raiser she had been pestered into doing against her will.

2

MORNINGS — BENNY'S CHALLENGE — WHO IS JOE POPE? — CARL GARBEDIAN — THE FIRST INTERRUPTION — KAREN WOO WEIGHS IN — TAKE ME HOME — THE SECOND INTERRUPTION — THE JOE POPE DOLL — A BETTER STORY THAN THIS ONE — BENNY UPLOADS — BRIZZ'S BEQUEST TO BENNY — WALKING BLITHELY PAST BRIZZ — TOM'S GIFT TO CARL — CARL'S CONFESSION — TOM'S "ANGER" — GOD IN THE WORKPLACE — COLD SORE GUY — THE WRITING ON THE WALL

THE BEST TIME WAS always early in the morning. Mornings had going for them the quiet in the hallways, the lights not yet at full capacity, and a forestalled sense of urgency. It was the worst time, too, because of the anticipation of the end of those things.

We liked to gather in Benny's office. He came back with a full mug and said, "So yesterday —"

We could hardly look at him. "What?" he said. We told him he had something — "Where?" It was on his lip. He went searching. It was on the other side. We hoped to god he would find it soon. Finally he thumbed it off and looked at it. "Cream cheese," he said. There were bagels? "In the kitchen," he replied. Benny's story would have to wait for those of us wanting bagels. Those of us more interested in his story stuck around. "All right, so yesterday," he resumed, "I wanted to see if I could go the entire day without touching my mouse or my keyboard." He settled himself with constrained gusto into his chair, careful not to spill. "The whole day without touching my mouse or my keyboard — impossible, right? I mean, how many times a day do we use those two things? If you're like me and you're putting an ad together, you're clicking or keying maybe ten thousand times a day. Twenty thousand. I don't even know, I never counted. The point is, a lot of times. You start to think your whole life is slowly clicking away. So I decided yesterday, what if I could go the whole day? What do I have to do? I have to click and open, click and drag, click and color, click and align, click and resize, click and drop-shadow —"

He went on and on, using his chubby fingers to count off.

"Then there's keyboard functions, right? Control-x, control-c, control-v, control-f —"

We told him to get on with it. We liked wasting time, but almost nothing was more annoying than having our wasted time wasted on something not worth wasting it on.

"So listen to how I did it," said Benny, his dough face smiling wryly.

"You did no work all day long," said Marcia.

"Not true," Benny objected, suddenly uncharacteristically solemn. "I had things to give Joe, I had deadlines. I *had* to use my mouse and my keyboard yesterday. So listen to how I did it."

So Benny told us the story of how he went the entire day without clicking by teaching Roland how to use Photoshop. Roland said he didn't think he could learn Photoshop, he had never even been to college. But Benny told him that was crazy talk. What with the right instructor, it wouldn't take more than a couple hours. Roland worked for security. He stood watch at the front desk in the downstairs lobby, or else he trolled the perimeter of the building in his security guard's generic navy suit coat. All day long he sat at his lonely lobby post or he went back and forth around the building on his aching feet. To sit in an office with Benny would be a pleasure. The only stipulation he gave Benny was that if he got chirped on the Motorola by Mike Boroshansky, chief of security, he'd probably have to go. We expected so little from security in those days.

"So what I want to know," Benny had said to him, "is which one of these photos do you think works best for this ad?" Roland looked at Benny's screen and said, "I don't know. That one?" and Benny said, "Come on, Roland, man — you have over a thousand photos to choose from up there, and you've looked at a total of six. Scroll down, man! Click through." So Roland ended up clicking through about an hour's worth of stock photos while Benny sat off to the side mouse-free. It was a pleasure for Roland — good company and a cushioned seat. "No, not that one," Benny kept saying. "You don't have much of an artistic intuition, Roland, no offense." "Hey, Benny," Roland said defensively, "I didn't go to school for this or anything, if you don't mind." But still he clicked to the next page, and scrolled down, and clicked to the next page and scrolled down. Whenever Roland came across a photo Benny liked, Benny wrote down its reference number on a Post-it. When he had enough reference numbers, he kicked Roland out of his office and called the rep from the stock house and they messengered over the thumbnails for him to choose from. That's when he went to lunch. Then, when he got back from the Potbelly and it was time to start putting the ad together, he picked up the phone and called down to security and asked for Roland.

When Roland returned to Benny's office, he was only more than happy to be back there giving his feet a rest. "You know how many miles a day I walk around in this building?" he asked Benny. "How many?" said Benny. "I don't know," he said. "I never counted." "You should get one of those pedometers," said Benny. Two hours later they had finished the rough layout of an ad Joe Pope needed first thing in the morning. Benny's moratorium on clicking would be over by the morning, and he could put the finishing touches on the ad then. So that's how he did it. The whole day and not one click for Benny. Except he ruined it at a quarter to five when he allowed himself to check numbers on fantasy baseball.

"You know," said Amber Ludwig, "I don't find this story very amusing. What if Tom Mota comes back here and one of our security guys is inside your office putting an ad together?" she asked. "I'm *so* sure that makes me feel real safe, Benny."

"Oh, Amber," said Benny. "Tom Mota's not coming back here."

Suddenly Joe Pope appeared in Benny's doorway. "Morning," he said.

"Oh!" Amber shrieked instinctively, gripping her pregnant belly. She wasn't showing, we shouldn't have known the first thing about it, but we did because we knew everything. "Oh, Joe," she cried. "You scared me!"

"Sorry," said Joe. He stood in the doorway with his right pant leg still cuffed against the threat of grease. Joe Pope rode his bicycle into work on all but the most inclement days. Most mornings he came up the elevator like a courier with his sleek fluorescent helmet and his cuffed leg and his daypack. He walked the bike down to his office and parked it against the wall. Then he locked the front tire to the frame. Inside the office he did that, locked his bicycle, like he was beset on all sides by thieves and barbarians. That bicycle was the only personal item in Joe Pope's office. He had no posters, postcards, doodads, snow globes, souvenirs, framed pictures, art reproductions, mementos, no humor books on the shelves and nothing to clutter his desk. He had been in that office three years, and it still looked temporary. Every day we had to wonder — who the hell was this Joe Pope, anyway? It wasn't that we had anything against him. It was just that he was maybe an inch shorter than he should have been. He listened to weird music. We didn't know what he did on the weekends. What sort of person showed up on Monday and had no interest in sharing what transpired during the two days of the week when one's real life took place? His weekends were long dark shadows of mystery. In all likelihood, he spent his days off in the office, cultivating his master plan. Mondays we'd come in refreshed and unsuspecting and he would already be there, ready to spring something on us. *Maybe he never left.* Certainly he never came around with a coffee mug to palaver with us on a Monday morning. We didn't judge him for that, so long as he didn't judge us for our custom of easing into a new workweek.

When he did come around, it was only to say things like "Sorry to interrupt, Benny, but did you happen to put that ad together for me yesterday?"

"Got it right here, Joe," trumpeted Benny, with a sly wink in our direction as he handed over Roland's handiwork.

Joe's sudden presence was the dissolving agent, and we picked our individual bodies up and returned to our desks, heavy and yawning. Morning was officially upon us.

Why was it so terrifying, almost like death, one morning of a hundred, to walk back to your own office and pass alone through its doorway? Why was the dread so suffocating? Most days, no problem. Work to be done. A pastry. Storm clouds out the window that looked, in their menace, sublime. But one out of a hundred mornings it was impossible to breathe. Our coffee tasted poisonous. The sight of our familiar chairs oppressed us. The invariable light was deadening.

We fought with depression. One thing or another in our lives hadn't worked out, and for a long period of time we struggled to overcome it. We took showers sitting down and couldn't get out of bed on weekends. Finally we consulted HR about the details of seeing a specialist, and the specialist prescribed medication. Marcia Dwyer was on Prozac. Jim Jackers was on Zoloft and something else. Dozens of others took pills all day long, which we struggled to identify, there were so many of them, in so many different colors and sizes. Janine Gorjanc was on a cocktail of several meds, including lithium. After Jessica's death, Janine and her husband, Frank, divorced. We understood divorce to be a common repercussion of the death of a child. There was no bitterness between them, just a parting of ways. Now they each lived alone with their memories. Pictures of Frank with Jessica also hung in Janine's office, and, to be honest, it was almost as moving to see pictures of him as it was to see all the ones of the lost girl. Frank with Jessica on his knee, Frank caught in an apron with hot mitts on his hands during some holiday — that man was as gone from the world as Jessica was. The woolly sideburns were gone and the thick black glasses were gone and he no longer had a wife or child. Spend two minutes in Janine's office looking over those pictures and contemplating the destinies of the happy people involved, and you too would reach for one of the prescription containers scattered about the place.

Yet for all the depression no one ever quit. When someone quit, we couldn't believe it. "I'm becoming a rafting instructor on the Colorado River," they said. "I'm touring college towns with my garage band." We were dumbfounded. It was like they lived on a different planet. Where had they found the derring-do? What would they do about car payments? We got together for going-away drinks on their final day and tried to hide our envy while reminding ourselves that we still had the freedom and luxury to shop indiscriminately. Invariably Tom would get drunk and berate the departing with inappropriate toasts. Invariably Marcia would find hair bands on the jukebox and subject us to their saccharine ballads while recalling the halcyon days of George Washington High. Invariably Janine would silently sip her cranberry juice, looking mournful and motherly, and Jim Jackers would crack dull, tasteless jokes, and Joe would still be at the office, working. "'Every ship is a romantic object,'" Tom would blather, "'except that we sail in.'" Concluding, he would stand and lift his glass. "So good luck to you," he toasted, finishing off his martini, "and fuck you for leaving, you prick."

WE HAD WIDE HALLWAYS. Some contained offices running along both sides, while others had offices on one side and cubicles on the other. Jim Jackers' cubicle was unique in that it was set off in a corner. He had a wonderful view because of that location and we questioned whether he deserved it. To get there you had to walk past the toner stain in the carpet on sixty. He shared that prime space with one other person, a woman named Tanya something who worked on a different partner's team. A retractable wall separated them, made of thick privacy glass, the kind used in shower windows. Behind it, one moved about, it seemed to the other, as if scrubbing and deodorizing, when really they were just filing or inputting.

We were into the first few weeks of layoffs when Benny told us the story of Carl Garbedian saying good-bye to his wife. We were gathered at Jim's cube for some arbitrary reason — it was a mystery how and why some of us found ourselves gathering at the same place at the same time. Benny's stories were more frequent in the days before the downturn, when we felt flush and secure. We were less mindful of being caught gathering. Then the downturn hit, our workload disappeared, and, though we had more time than ever to listen to Benny's stories, we were more conscious of being caught gathering, which was one indication that our workload had disappeared and that layoffs were necessary. We were in a bind — what to do about Benny's stories? We compromised by continuing to listen, but without enjoying them because we were too worried someone would come by and see us. We would listen with only one ear, and with one eye always over our shoulders, in case we needed to bolt back to our desks and commence the charade that our workload was as strong as ever, because only then would we not be laid off.

Carl Garbedian was in his midthirties. He had a gut like the male equivalent of a second trimester. He wore off-brand, too-tight jeans and generic tennis shoes, which, to us, conveyed the extent to which he'd given up. His wife dropped him at the curb one morning and he refused to get out of the car. Benny had seen much of this himself, but what he couldn't get firsthand, he got later from Carl, when he prodded it out of him during the lunch hour. Practically everyone shared their thoughts with Benny because everyone loved Benny, which was why some of us hated his guts.

Just before stepping out of the car, right as she should have been kissing Carl good-bye, Marilynn's cell phone rang. She was an oncologist and always felt obligated to answer the phone in case of emergency. "Hello?" she said. "Go ahead, Susan, I can hear you just fine."

Carl was immediately annoyed. Benny told us that Carl hated the way his wife always reassured people that she could hear them just fine. He hated how she plugged her finger in her opposite ear, effectively shutting out all other noise. And he hated that her other obligations always preempted him. They were just about to say good-bye, for chrissake. Didn't it matter, wasn't it important, their kiss good-bye? The thing he really hated, which he would never admit to her, was how he felt the lesser of the two of them for having no obligation that could compare with hers, which he might use to preempt *her.* She had people calling about patients who were dying. Let's face it, there was zero chance one of us would call Carl with a question of mortal urgency. Whatever question we might have for Carl, it could wait until we ran into him in the hall the next day. That made Carl feel that his wife's job was more meaningful than his own; and, because of his particular way of thinking at the time, that *she* was therefore more meaningful. Carl's thoughts were *dark,* man. It didn't make for an easy marriage. If only you heard the fragments of phone conversations we sometimes overheard when passing Carl's office.

Benny told us that when Marilynn answered her cell, Carl considered stepping out of the car and storming off, but instead chose to stay and gaze out the window. He caught sight of the man who panhandled outside our building. He was always there, this man, sitting near one of the revolving doors, lifting and shaking a Dunkin' Donuts cup as we entered, while his legs remained outstretched and crossed at the ankles. The sight of him, just the sight of him alone — which five years ago might have inspired Carl to empty his pockets of change — was a mnemonic torture device that now dropped with thundering anguish the whole memory load of innumerable days back upon Carl's shoulders. They had lifted the night before, for an hour or two. But now, even before entering the building — by god, even before he had the chance to run screaming from another bit of Karen Woo gossip, or see the shine clinging to Chris Yop's brow — they had reappeared, all the compounded days of Carl's tenure, with the additional crushing weight of yet another day.

Do something! he had wanted to scream at the bum. He was close to rolling down the window and doing just that. He was offended that the man just sat there for his money. Other bums had *positioned* themselves. They had brands. "Vietnam Vet with AIDS." "Unemployed Mother of Three." "Trying to Get Back to Cleveland." This guy had *nothing* — no words on a piece of cardboard, not even a dog or some bongos. For some reason it infuriated Carl. Yeah, there was a time he'd have given whatever was in his pockets; now he'd give the guy half his life savings, if he'd just *choose a different building!*

Benny had seen the Garbedians idling at the curb and had snuck up from behind and pounded on Carl's window. Carl irritably waved him off. Benny assumed they were fighting so he left them alone. But Benny being Benny, he loitered around the front entrance where he wasn't easy to spot, over by the post-office drop box. He had a good view of the car from there.

Inside Marilynn was still on the phone. She was discussing a matter of medical importance in a language Carl envied. He decided to make a call of his own. He took his cell phone out of his jeans pocket, hit speed-dial, and put the phone to his ear. His wife said into her phone, "Can you hold on a minute, Susan? I'm getting another call." She looked down at the screen and then she looked over at Carl, who was looking straight out the window.

"What are you doing?" she asked him.

He turned to her. "Making a call," he replied.

"Why are you calling me, Carl?" Marilynn asked with a firm, cautious bemusement.

Mornings had turned tetchy of late between the two Garbedians, sometimes downright traitorous. "Hold on one second," Carl said to Marilynn, putting a finger up in the air. "I'm just leaving a voice mail. Hi, Marilynn, it's me, Carl. I'm calling at about" — he lifted his arm and looked at his watch, a formal gesture — "it's about half-past eight," he said. "And I know you're real busy, Sweetie, but if you could do me a favor and call, I'd love to just . . . catch up. Chat. You have my number, but in case you don't, let me give it to you now, it's —"

Marilynn put her phone back to her ear and said, "Susan, I'm going to have to call you back."

"Okay, bye-bye, Sweetie," said Carl.

They both hit end on their cell phones at the same time. At some point, the new-message light on Marilynn's phone began to blink.

— — —

JOE POPE STUCK his head over Jim Jackers' cubicle just as Benny was coming to the good part in his story. Some of our cube walls were made of particleboard wrapped in a cheap orange or beige fiber and were so flimsy they wobbled from nothing more than the in-house draft. Other cube walls, like Jim's, had been purchased just before the downturn and could withstand hurricane winds. Benny's story came to an abrupt halt. Some of us departed Jim's cube immediately, while the rest of us peered up at Joe nervously. Joe asked Jim if the mock-ups he was working on would be ready for the five o'clock pickup.

Joe had a tendency to interrupt. Sometimes it was a good thing. We could lose ourselves in one of Benny's stories and the time would fly and then someone more important than Joe might come around and see us and that would be worse. We liked him at first, very early on. Then one day Karen Woo says, "I don't like Joe Pope," and she gives us her reasons. She goes on and on about it, for close to a half hour, a very spirited rant, until finally we had to excuse ourselves so we could get back to work. After that there was no doubt in anyone's mind how Karen Woo felt about Joe Pope, and more than a few people agreed that she had a legitimate gripe — that if in fact the situation was as Karen reported it, Joe was not a likable person at all. It's tough to say now what that gripe actually was. Let's see, here . . . trying to remember . . . nope, not coming. Half the time we couldn't remember three hours ago. Our memory in that place was not unlike that of goldfish. Goldfish who took a trip every night in a small clear bag of water and then returned in the morning to their bowl. What we recalled was that Karen didn't let up on the story, day after day for an entire week, and when that week was over, we all had a better idea of Joe than we had gotten in his first three or four months.

Jim Jackers looked up from his computer. "Yeah, Joe, they'll be ready," he replied. "I'm putting the final touches on them now."

Jim's remark was Joe's cue to depart, but instead he lingered over the cube wall. This was between the time of his first promotion and his second. "Thanks, Jim," he said. He looked at us. We held our ground. We didn't want to be bullied back to our desks by Joe Pope when Benny was in the middle of a good story. "How is everybody?" asked Joe. We looked around. We shrugged. Pretty good, we told him. "Good," he said. He finally left and we raised our brows at one another.

"That was a disgusting display of power," said Karen Woo.

We told Jim he had to leave if he was the one attracting Joe Pope's attention. If he was the reason Joe was on the move in our direction, Jim had to go.

"But this is my cubicle," said Jim.

"Maybe he was just trying to be friendly," Genevieve Latko-Devine suggested. Genevieve had blond hair, cobalt eyes, and a tall, gelid grace. Even the women admitted her superior beauty. For Christmas one year, she was given as a gag gift a set of twisted redneck teeth, which she was instructed to wear year-round in an effort to even us all out. But when she put them on, we discovered — the men among us, that is — a desire for rotted teeth we never knew we had. We told Benny to go on with his story.

He picked up where he'd left off. Carl and his wife sat in silence a long time after hanging up their respective cell phones. Finally Marilynn, with tender, firm insistence, turned to him and said, "You need help, Carl."

Shaking his head resolutely, Carl replied, "I don't need help."

"You need medical attention," said his wife, "and you won't admit it, and you're hurting our marriage because of it."

"I'm not depressed," said Carl.

"You are a *textbook* case of depression," Marilynn persisted, "and you need medication *so* badly —"

"How would you know?" he asked, cutting her short. He had turned at last to stare at her with an outraged and lonely expression. "You aren't a psychiatrist, Marilynn, are you? You can't know *every* angle of medicine — can you, can you possibly?"

"Cancer patients, Carl," she said, exasperation rising in her tone, "are not the happiest people, believe it or not. I recommend antidepressants for many, many of my patients. I know a depressed person when I see one, I know the symptoms, I know the damage it can do to families, to . . ."

He let Marilynn fade out. Just then, crossing the street on her way to work, was Janine Gorjanc.

Janine looked to Carl perfectly motherlike. Unpretty but not ugly. Hippy but not fat. Puffy about the face but with a youthful cuteness buried somewhere in there that might have caused someone to be crazy about taking her to the high school prom. A child, thought Carl, is not the only result of childbirth. A mother, too, is born. You see them every day — nondescript women with a bulge just above the groin, slightly double-chinned. Perpetually forty. Someone's mother, you think. There is a child somewhere who has made this woman into a mother, and for the sake of the child she has altered her appearance to better play the part. Insulated from her as he was by the car, he could look without the urge to turn and flee, and it was the first time he had seen her in months, maybe years. "Carl?" Marilynn was saying. "Carl??"

"Marilynn," he said. "Do you see that woman? That woman there, in the wrinkled blouse. She looks like a mother, doesn't she?" Marilynn followed his gaze. "That's Janine Gorjanc," he said. "That's the woman, I've told you about her," he said. "Her daughter was killed. You remember? She was abducted. I told you about her. I went to the funeral?"

"I remember," she said.

"She stinks," he said.

"She stinks?"

"She emits some kind of smell, I don't know what it is. It's not every day. But some days, I think she just lets herself go. She doesn't shower or something." He watched her enter the building. Marilynn was looking at her husband, not at Janine. She was listening, trying to understand. "Marilynn," he said, "I hate the woman for how she smells."

"Have you ever tried talking to her about it?" she asked.

"But I hate myself even more," he continued, unbuttoning his oxford, "for hating her. Can you even imagine what she's been through?"

"Carl," Marilynn said, "what are you doing?"

"The abduction," he continued obliviously, "then the waiting, the terrible waiting."

"*What* are you doing?" she cried.

"Then finding the body. Imagine finding the body, Marilynn."

He was naked to his waist by then. He had removed the oxford and flung his undershirt over his head. "I don't want to go into work today," he announced, turning to his wife. He was breathing up and down with his paunch exposed, a hair-brushed hillock of pale, glowing belly. When Benny recounted all this to us, he said Carl had told him later he hoped Lynn Mason would walk by right then and see that unattractive feature and walk him Spanish for the sake of aesthetics. "Put your clothes on!" cried Marilynn.

"I don't want to be the person that hates Janine Gorjanc," he said. "If I go inside I will be that person because I will smell her. I don't want to have to smell her. If I smell her I will hate her and I don't want to be that person. You have to take me home."

"Have you gone *completely* out of your mind?" she asked as she watched him yank off his tennis shoes, unzip his jeans and pull them down to his ankles.

He sat up in the front seat in nothing but his underwear. "I'm wearied," he said, turning to her. "That's what it is, Marilynn. I'm really very wearied. If you make me go inside, I'm going inside like this."

"That," she bellowed, "no —" She shook her head and laughed. "That is no threat *to me,* Carl."

"I'm so wearied," he repeated.

"Carl, put your clothes on," she said, "and go inside, and by this afternoon, I will have made you an appointment to see a very good psychiatrist."

"I'm not putting my clothes on until you take me home," he said.

"Carl," she cried, "I have to be in surgery in ten minutes! I can't take you home!"

"Don't make me get out," he said. "Please don't make me get out, Marilynn."

"Oh, Jim, just one more thing —"

We looked up and saw Joe Pope just as he was peeking his

head over Jim Jackers' cube wall a second time. Benny shut up and Jim swirled around and Amber Ludwig started in fright and Marcia Dwyer took the opportunity to grab her Diet Coke and leave, while the few of us who stuck around listened to Joe inform Jim that he had just come back from Lynn Mason's office. They had been discussing the mock-ups due out later that day, and they had thrown around some ideas about making changes to this and making changes to that, and when we heard *that,* one by one we got up and left because we knew what Joe Pope's changes were all about — more work. It was always more work with that guy. The last of us overheard Joe saying, "I'm sorry to interrupt, Jim — is it an okay time?" and Jim replied, "Sure, sure, Joe, it's a fine time. Come in and have a seat."

Later that day it spread like wildfire. Joe Pope had received his second promotion.

He was our new Roger Highnote. He had a unique fashion sense that didn't exactly fall in line with seasonal approbation and we wondered where he'd picked it up. What magazines was *he* reading? The following year we were all wearing similarly pre-stressed denims but by that point it hardly mattered. For an entire year he looked like an idiot. "Good-looking?" we said to Genevieve. "Joe Pope?" No, he was seriously one inch too short. He made our lives a living hell. And he was very awkward. But how to explain it? For it wasn't the same awkwardness we felt with Jim Jackers. In the hallways Jim greeted everyone by saying, "What up, dawg?" a question he had the temerity to ask even Lynn Mason when passing her by. That was confused behavior. We all went to a party once, and Jim carried around his own box of wine. He also referred openly to his bowels as "Mr. B." "Excuse me," he would say, before departing for the restroom. "But Mr. B's making it happen."

Jim made us wince with awkwardness, but we winced for *his*

sake. Joe Pope's awkwardness caused an entirely different brand of wincing and it was hard to put a finger on. "'He was not only awkwardness in himself,'" declared our own poetaster Hank Neary, "'but the cause that was awkwardness in other men.'" And like always, we had no earthly clue what Hank was talking about. Unless he meant to say that Joe Pope's presence made *us* feel awkward. That was very true. Joe felt no obligation to speak. He would greet and be greeted like a normal human being, but beyond that he remained brazenly, stoically silent. Even in a meeting or a conference call, the man could let long episodes of silence fill the room while he was thinking of what he wanted to say, without hemming and hawing nervously in order to fill the oppressive silence bearing down upon us all. Perhaps that could be called composure, but it made the rest of us uneasy, so much so that Hank, determined to get it right, returned with a second quote pulled from his infinite lode of worthless erudition — "'He inspired uneasiness. That was it! Uneasiness! Not a definite mistrust — just uneasiness — nothing more.'" — and when that quote went from one of us to the other via e-mail, we congratulated Hank on finally saying something comprehensible. Uneasiness. That was it precisely.

He had a way of coming upon you suddenly. This happened a lot at print stations. One time, Tom Mota was standing at a print station when Joe sidled up next to him and said, "Morning." Just at that moment, Tom had something awkward coming out of the color printer. Let's just say it wasn't exactly work-related. This was before the copy-code policy was implemented as part of the austerity measures, which also prevented Hank Neary from photocopying library books in the morning and reading the Xeroxed pages all day at his desk. Joe's job no doubt *was* something official, and it was queued up behind Tom's. Bad luck for Tom. So Tom said to him, "Are you just going to wait? You're just going to wait there for your job to come out?" Joe's response was to remain imperturbably silent. So Tom just came clean. "I have something coming out," he said, "and be honest with you, Joe, I'd rather you not see it. It's got some titties in it, and I know who you talk to," he said. "And why do you always feel the need to rush over to the printer when your job is queued up behind all these other jobs, anyway?" he continued. "Why are you so eager? You do know it takes a while for these jobs to come out if they're all queued up, don't you?"

Who knows how Joe reacted to that. He was levels above Tom in the hierarchy but he probably suffered the man with more silence, patiently waiting for his job to come out. Maybe he tried to get a glimpse of whatever Tom was printing out, as Tom claimed, or maybe he kept his eyes straight ahead and thought, "Like I could give a good goddamn what this guy's got printing out." Either way he was probably inscrutable.

That was the word for him — inscrutable. His inscrutability created a pervasive uneasiness. Why did he have to be such a dull mystery? Nothing on his walls, nothing in his office but a bicycle. Which he *locked*. We heard it click every morning and tried not to take offense. Our opinion of Joe, he was too young to be inscrutable. If you're thirty years old, you have *interests*. You make engagements with the world. Why was this guy always at his desk, surrounded by bare walls? "We have to show you this, this is our Joe Pope doll." That's probably how we'd explain Joe Pope to a new person. Not that we'll ever hire someone new again. But if we did, we'd probably say, "We keep it in Karen Woo's office. She hates Joe Pope. Come check it out. Now watch, it's going to do a perfect imitation. Watch. Did you catch it?" "But it just sat there," the new hire would say. *"Exactly!"* we'd cry. "Joe's *always* at his desk. Now watch as he bends at the knees and pulls his chair in! Watch Joe

Pope interrupt us over the cube wall! Pull the string and listen to Joe Pope say nothing! It's the new Inscrutable-Action Joe Pope doll by Hasbro!"

WE HAD HAD A TOY client, a car client, a long-distance carrier, and a pet store chain. We did TV, print, direct mail, and Internet. We had a business-to-business division. We drank too much on the weekends. We had the great good fortune and shortcomings of character that marked every generation that had never seen war. If we had been recovering from the aftereffects of a significant campaign, we might have been grateful to be where we were. Eager, even. As it was, it was just us and our struggles to move up a notch chairwise. It was counting ceiling tiles in everyone's office to determine who had the higher tile count. Sean Smith was in the first Gulf War but that hardly impressed us because all he did was drive a tank around a bunch of sand woefully devoid of enemy craft and when pressed, that was the extent of his recall. Frank Brizzolera might have seen World War II, but he died before we could ask him. We had one Vietnam vet but he never spoke of his experiences and quit within a year. Maybe he knew firsthand the blind jungle warfare we had learned about in school, had the sound of pitched battles in his head, and when he looked out his window at that proud parade of flags flying over the bridge across the Chicago River, he thought about particular sacrifices, men with names who had died, and said those names aloud to himself, and felt with palpable gratitude the simple luxury of returning to a chair in a building that was safe. Imagine the stories he might have told! Set in burning villages during darkest night — flares over riverbeds — choppers landing in rice paddies. We were always looking for better stories of more interesting lives unfolding anywhere but within the pages of an Office Depot catalog. But he never spoke of his experiences, and two months after he quit, no one could remember his name.

A better story than ours might be the one of two interoffice competitors, one male, one female, finding true love through rivalry in the workplace, written by our very own Don Blattner. Blattner was all Hollywood by way of Schaumburg, Illinois. He had another screenplay about a disaffected and cynical copywriter suffering ennui in the office setting while dreaming of becoming a famous screenwriter, which he claimed was not autobiographical. He was always talking about potential investors and wouldn't let us read any of his screenplays unless we signed confidentiality agreements, as if we had positioned ourselves surreptitiously in these cornered lives so as to steal Blattner's screenplays and whisk them off to Hollywood. Like Jim, he made us wince, especially on those occasions he called Robert De Niro "Bobby." He studied the weekend box-office grosses very seriously. If a movie failed to perform as the industry expected, Blattner would come into your office on Monday morning carrying his *Variety* and say, "The boys at Miramax are going to be *awfully* disappointed by this." It was such horseshit, yet we felt something had been lost the day he announced he was giving it up. "I gotta face it," he declared in a resigned and unsentimental voice. "The workshops aren't helping, the how-to books aren't helping, and nobody's optioning any of my shit." We took back all our ridicule and practically begged the man to continue, but he remained firmly and pathetically committed to his sober-eyed conclusion that he would never be anything but a copywriter. Months passed before one of us experienced the relief of startling him at his desk again as he secretly tried to close out of his screenplay software. Hope had risen like a perennial once again.

There *had* to be a better story than this one, which was why so many of us spent so much time lost in our own little worlds. Don Blattner was not the only one. Hank Neary, our black writer who wore the same brown corduroy suit coat day after day, so that either he never cleaned the one, or had an entire closet full of the same, was working on a failed novel. He described it as "small and angry." We all wondered who the hell would buy small and angry? We asked him what it was about. "Work," he replied. A small, angry book about work. Now there was a guaranteed best seller. There was a fun read on the beach. We suggested alternative topics on subjects that mattered to us. "But those don't interest me," he said. "The fact that we spend most of our lives at work, that interests me." Truly noble, we said to him. Give us a Don Blattner screenplay any day of the week.

Dan Wisdom had gotten encouragement in college from Miles Buford, the painter, who said in his twenty-year teaching career he had never seen a talent like Dan's. Then Dan graduated and went to work, where he sat behind a Mac manipulating pixels for a sugar-substitute client and wondered if Professor Buford's flattery was just an attempt to get laid. Dan continued to paint, though, at night and on the weekends, and if his portraits were a little grotesque, we could nevertheless discern a unique vision and a steady line. Maybe it would happen for him. He said no. He said figurative painting was dead. But we liked what he could do with fish.

Deliver us! You could practically hear that plea crying out from the depths of our souls, because none of us wanted to end up like Old Brizz.

Among the very first to be let go, Brizz walked Spanish down the hall like no one before or since. The season of layoffs was interminable, and to give a sense of that, Old Brizz's termination took place a full year before Tom Mota got the ax. Old Brizz handled it much better than Tom did. He came by all our offices to say farewell. Usually people raced out to escape our gaze. Brizz said he didn't want to leave without saying good-bye. That was grace under fire, and he carried himself with dignity and pride. He didn't mind knowing that we knew that they didn't value him as much as they valued us. Because that's basically what they said when they walked you Spanish down the hall. He didn't mind talking to us even after they said that to him in so many words. Or maybe he didn't even think of it that way. Maybe he wouldn't have understood our talk of value. "This has nothing to do," he might have said, "with who's worth more. Is that what you think? You guys, take it from an old man who's been in this business a long time. This process has nothing to do with weeding out the worst of us so that the only ones left are the talented and the productive. Come on, don't fool yourselves. Ha, don't be foolish. Ha ha, don't be naive!" We could hear his rattling lungs laughing at us. His coming around to fare us well, so calm, so self-controlled — it was a little unnerving. What did it mean that minutes after walking Spanish down the hall he had the poise to encourage us not to worry about him? He came by each one of our individual offices, he visited the cubicles and the receptionists. We even saw him talking to one of the building guys. They hardly said anything to anyone, the building guys. Just stood on their ladders handing things up and down to one another, speaking in hushed tones. There was never much of an opportunity to get to know them. But Old Brizz was standing at the elevator talking to one building guy in particular for half an hour while holding his box of personal items. One would speak, the other would nod. Then they'd laugh. Who knows what you laugh about with a building guy. But Brizz found it — the funny thing to be shared, even on the day he had been shitcanned. He filed for unemployment right away. A few months later, he still hadn't found work. He took on a few freelance jobs. Then we didn't hear from him. Next we knew he was in the hospital. No insurance. He went quick. It was unfortunate, how prescient we were when we said the guy had six months, tops. We visited him — ours seemed his only flowers. We wanted to ask him, Hey, Brizz, man, where's your family? Instead we snuck him cigarettes, strictly forbidden when one is laid out in the cancer ward. We put one of those smoke-be-gone ashtrays right on his chest, and it caught the exhaust good, so Brizz got in three smokes before the old guy next slot over complained and we were reprimanded by the nurse. When he died, it was hard to believe he was gone. Not just walked Spanish down the hall. Gone gone.

Benny came around to collect. We couldn't believe it. Benny wasn't really going to profit from this, was he?

"He was on my list," he said innocently.

We all shouted, Benny! Come on!

"Come on what?" he cried. "He was at the top of my list! Those are the rules."

He wasn't wrong. Those were the rules of Celebrity Death Watch. We all paid him his ten bucks.

At Brizz's funeral we discovered he had some family after all, a brother with a health-club glow. We called him Bizarro Brizz because he had good skin with a good color. Probably never smoked a cigarette in his life. It was as if jowly, ruddy Brizz had taken off a terrible mask. We offered him our condolences. After preparing ourselves in the pews for a while, some of us braved the front. Brizz in the box looked much healthier than Brizz at his desk. Afterward, at the wake, we tried to recall memories of him. We remembered one thing, the time we stood with him at the parking garage waiting for the bow-tied Hispanics to pull up with our cars. We had our single-dollar tips folded in the palms of our hands. God was it freezing. We were out of the way of the wind under the bright light of the garage, but Chicago in February, if you'll allow an homage to Brizz, was colder than a witch's tit in an icebox. He still called a refrigerator an icebox. He sat at his desk once and told us of being a kid and having the ice delivered. "That's how old I am," he confided to us in a rare moment. "I remember the ice being delivered." "Did you used to call Australia 'Tasmania Land'?" asked Benny. "Not that old," said Brizz. Just then, Joe Pope arrived at Brizz's doorway and asked him if he had those headlines ready. That's what we were talking about with Old Brizz as we waited for our cars in the final freezing February of his tenure as one of us, certain aspects of Joe Pope's character. We couldn't pin Old Brizz down, though, try as we might. His car was the first to come out. It was a gray Peugeot, a one-time looker, but rusted around the trim now and dented in places high and low. The real story was the interior. Stuff — crap — accumulated junk — how else to put it? — filled the backseat windows *to the roof.* Paper mostly, but smashed against the glass we also made out a winter hat, a beer cozy, an unopened package of nude hose — things like that. Along the ledge of the doorframe we noticed scattered coins and green plastic houses from the game of Monopoly. "Brizz," said Benny. "All these extras come from the dealership?" "Have you guys never seen my car before?" Brizz asked with pride. "Is that what this is?" asked Larry Novotny. "A car?" He bent at his knees and resettled his Cubs cap on his thinning hair while peering through the windows at the trash heap inside. The front passenger seat was hardly any better than the back, but there was a nice niche carved out for the driver behind the wheel. We had to wonder — who keeps a car like that? Was he really one of *those* people? The car-park man got out and turned the car over to Brizz, but Brizz never tipped. That was another thing about Brizz: he usually stayed in and ate his baloney sandwiches, but when he came out to lunch with us, we had to supplement his share of the tip so as not to screw the waitress, which made us hate him momentarily. "I got a *tip* for you," he replied, when someone asked him once why he was so cheap. "Never take no wooden nickels."

We heard that time and again — "Never take no wooden nickels" — until we wanted to clobber him over the head with a mallet. Except for the surprise of his homeless-man's car, and his half-hour conversation with the building guy on the day he was terminated, Old Brizz was fatiguing in his predictability. He came in, he proofread in a pair of nineteen-fifties eye frames, he left at ten-fifteen for the day's first smoke break. Good god, we could still see him standing in the winter freeze outside the building in nothing but a ratty sweater vest, jowls like a hound dog's, pulling on his pointy cigarette. He came back in smelling like fifty butts in an ashtray. He brought out his baloney sandwiches at quarter past noon and chased them down with a Thermos of black coffee that he made at home because he claimed the stuff down the hall was too gourmet for his taste.

One day not long after Brizz's death, Benny started calling us into his office. Benny's office had all the cool stuff in it. A gumball machine, remote-controlled cars. He put an anatomical skeleton against the wall just inside the doorway, so it stared back at him at his desk. Everyone asked where he got the skeleton. His answer was always "Some dead guy." He duct-taped a Buck Rogers gun to the skeleton's hand and crowned the smooth skull with a cowboy hat.

Benny was uploading a finished ad to the server when Jim walked by. "Jim, get in here. I got news for you."

Jim came into Benny's office and sat down.

"I'm uploading," said Benny.

"That's your news?"

"Brizz named me a beneficiary in his will. Blattner! Get in here, I got news for you."

Blattner came in and sat down next to Jim across the desk from Benny.

"Listen to this," said Benny. "Brizz named me a beneficiary in his will."

"Get out," said Blattner. "That's funny because —"

"Marcia!"

Marcia walked past and then reappeared. She stepped inside the doorway and stood next to Buck, the space cowboy skeleton. "Brizz named Benny a beneficiary in his will," said Jim, craning his neck so he could see Marcia. She came in and sat down on the barstool.

"That's funny because it sounds just like this screenplay I'm working on," said Blattner.

"Genevieve!" said Benny.

Genevieve stopped in the doorway.

"Genevieve," said Blattner, "remember that screenplay I was telling you about? It happened to Benny in real life."

"What screenplay?" asked Genevieve.

"Just listen," said Benny. While his computer uploaded, he told us of receiving a letter from a lawyer on the South Side.

Genevieve had second thoughts. "I'm sorry, Benny, I can't listen right now," she said, rattling some revisions in her hand. "I have to get these down to Joe." She abandoned the doorway.

Hank showed up. "What's going on?" he asked, adjusting his big black eyeglasses.

"Brizz made Benny a beneficiary in his will," said Marcia.

"And Blattner stole the idea for a screenplay," said Jim.

"No," said Blattner. "No, that's not —"

"Wait until I tell you what he left me," said Benny.

"Why should he leave *you* anything?" asked Karen Woo, who had walked in with Hank. "You benefited financially from his death."

"Karen," said Benny, for the thousandth time. "Those are the rules of Celebrity Death Watch. What was I supposed to do?"

Benny arrived at a storefront law office on Cicero Avenue for the reading of the will. Brizz's brother was the only other person in attendance. Benny and Bizarro Brizz recognized each other from the funeral. After handshakes and offers of coffee, the lawyer took a seat behind his big cherrywood desk. "Frank's will," said the lawyer, lifting an envelope. He removed the letter and looked down through his bifocals. Then he looked up and explained that the benefactor had written a few preliminary words.

Life had been very good to him, the letter explained. He had been blessed with loving parents, and growing up he had had a wonderful companion in his younger brother, whom he had loved, even if they had drifted a little once they reached adulthood. He had loved his wife, who had given him a delightful seventeen years. The thing he loved about life the most, Brizz had written, was the day-to-day living of it — the *Chicago Sun-Times* arriving on his front porch in the morning, a hot cup of black coffee and a good cigarette, and being alone in his warm house in winter.

"Brizz was married?" said Marcia.

"Is that the meaning of life?" asked Hank. "Coffee, a newspaper, and a cigarette?"

"And a warm house in winter," said Blattner. "A Warm House in Winter — god, that's a good title. Benny, toss me that pen."

"Just listen," said Benny. "It gets even better."

The lawyer began. " 'I, Francis Brizzolera, a resident of Chicago,

Illinois, being of sound mind and memory . . .'" The lawyer skipped down silently. "'To my brother, Philip Brizzolera, I will and bequeath the following property: all my financial holdings present upon my death — including any stocks, bonds, mutual funds, savings and checking accounts, and all contents of my safety deposit box. I also leave to my brother Phil my car —'"

"Let me tell you," Benny said to us, "how relieved I was to hear that Brizz hadn't left me his car with all that crap in it."

"'— and my house,'" continued the lawyer, "'along with all of its contents, except that which I bequeath to Benjamin Shassburger.'"

Benny's computer made a noise indicating his uploading was complete. It was probably time for us to get back to work. We were six months into layoffs at that point, with no end in sight.

"'To Benny Shassburger,'" said the lawyer, "'I will and bequeath my totem pole.'"

Benny said he shifted forward in his chair. He leaned an ear into the lawyer. "I'm sorry," he said. "His what?"

The lawyer looked down again through his bifocals at the will. "It says here totem pole," he said.

In the backyard of Brizz's house, a single-family dwelling on the South Side to which Phil had to get both keys and directions from the lawyer, stood an enormous totem pole, roughly twenty-five feet tall. The two men walked around it in silence. All manner of heads had been carved into it — eagles' heads, scary heads, heads of hybrid creatures. Some heads had pointy ears, some had long snouts. It was intricately carved and painted myriad bright colors. It had been driven into the ground so firmly that when Benny gave it a push — it was his now, after all — he felt no give whatsoever. Benny told us that as a kid, he and his father had participated in the YMCA's Indian Guides, which he described as the Jew's alternative to the Boy Scouts. His name was Shooting Star;

his father's name was Shining Star. He was a very dedicated collector of all things Indian back then, including cheap, poorly carved totem poles, which, over time, lost their attraction. But the one he had just inherited, with its rich scarlet luster and deep browns, contained an authentic and magical power that left him in awe. Because of its size and complicated carvings, but also because it was standing in a backyard in an old Irish neighborhood among the telephone wires, the lawn chairs and bird feeders, even a trampoline in the yard across the way. Some little girl had bounced up and down, up and down as Brizz's totem pole stood impervious and resolute. Men in white tank tops had gone back and forth, back and forth with their lawn mowers, while that mute and primitive object refused to vacate the corners of their eyes. It could be glimpsed between houses driving down the street. Boys probably stopped to stare at it from their bicycles. Neighbors had to pull their barking dogs away. And all the while, the man inside, warm at his kitchen table reading the newspaper with a cigarette burning in a nearby ashtray, was content to know that in the backyard he had staked into the ground the relic, the symbol, the manifestation of his — what?

"What was Brizz doing with a totem pole?" asked Marcia.

"This is nothing like my screenplay, by the way," Don Blattner announced to the room.

"Come on, Benny," said Jim. He had his geisha-sized feet up on Benny's desk in a shiny new pair of Nikes. "A totem pole?"

"There it was before me," said Benny, standing suddenly and gesturing as if before some wild spectacle, a full moon or an alien. "And there was no denying it. So I asked Phil, I said, 'Do you know, was your brother an Indian enthusiast?' 'Not that I ever knew of,' Phil said. 'Then did your family maybe have some Indian blood in it?' I asked him. He had his arms akimbo, like this," said

Benny, demonstrating, "and he was staring up at the totem pole like this, just staring up at it, and without turning to me he just shook his head slowly, like this, and said, 'Brizzolera. We're one hundred percent Italian.' "

Benny followed Bizarro Brizz inside. The kitchen counters were cluttered with various plates and bowls and serving containers, as if on display at a secondhand shop. More cutlery than a single man could use in six months sat in a clean pile on top of a dish towel. Brizz had two toasters lined up back to back, next to a toaster oven. The kitchen walls had been yellowed by cigarette smoke and the linoleum curled up at the edges of the floor. Curiously, in the surfeit of garage-sale-like clutter that defined not just the room they were in but all the rooms, Brizz had only one chair at the kitchen table.

Benny watched Phil open drawers full of utensils, hot mitts, pan lids. "We did more than just drift apart a little," explained Phil, "or however it was he phrased it. I'd call him every couple of months, you know, but if not for that, I'm pretty sure we wouldn't have spoken at all. Not out of malice, just . . . him. Who he was."

"That's so strange," said Benny, "because he was really one of the most pleasant guys to work with."

"Oh, he was a sweet guy, my brother, you get no argument from me. But he sure was aloof. Hey, tell me about that," said Phil. "What was it like working with Frank?"

Benny gave the question some thought: what was it like to work with Brizz? "Like I said, he was always just really pleasant," said Benny. "He wasn't one of those people you work with and they're always creating friction, you know?"

That, he thought, was one lame answer to Phil's question. He wanted to come up with a good story about Brizz that would give him a real sense of his departed brother at work, something he'd done that made us say, That's good old Brizz for you, which would sink in and become part of Phil's memory. But Benny couldn't think of anything.

"What should I have told the man?" Benny asked us, long after his uploading was complete, and all we could agree on was the sight of Brizz smoking outside the building in winter in nothing to keep him warm but his sweater vest. That was a story Brizz *owned,* but was it a story? Or we might have told him about the talk with the building guy, but that wasn't much of a story either. To be honest, what we remembered most about Brizz was his participation, along with the rest of us, in the mundane protocols of making a deadline — Brizz's nicotine stink in a conference call listening to a client's change in directions, Brizz sitting behind his desk with his reading glasses, carefully and methodically proofreading copy before an ad went to print. Hard to build an anecdote out of that. Good god, why had nobody stopped him? Why had we never, not one of us, stopped, turned around, and said, Knock knock. Sorry to interrupt you when you're proofreading, Brizz. Why had we not gone in, sat down? Yeah, you smoke Old Golds, you keep a messy car — but what else, Brizz, what else? Would closing the door help? What fucked you up as a kid and what woman changed your life and what is the thing you will never forgive yourself for? What, man, *what?* Please! We walked past. Brizz never looked up. How many times did we end up down at our own offices, doing pretty much the same thing, preparing for some deadline now come and gone, while Brizz lived and breathed with all the answers a hundred feet down the hall?

"He ate two baloney sandwiches for lunch almost every day," Benny said to Phil. "That's what I remember about your brother the most."

Genevieve reappeared in the doorway after having handed off her revisions to Joe.

"What'd I miss?" she asked.

— — —

SOME OF US WENT out for lunch to a new place every day and made lunch an event. Others, like Old Brizz, stayed in and had the same thing, day after day. Sometimes it was to save money. Other times it was to avoid the company of people who, from nine to noon and from one to six, we had to give ourselves over to unconditionally. For an hour in between, time reverted back to us, and sometimes we took advantage of that hour by closing our doors and eating alone.

Carl Garbedian shut his door every day and ate a Styrofoam clamshell of *penne alla vodka* from the Italian joint a block away and never went out to lunch with us unless it was a free team event. The free team event was a thing of the past, and so it had been months since we'd last seen Carl sliding into a booth, opening a menu, and considering his options.

Six months before being sacked, Tom Mota knocked on Carl's door. This was only a few days or so after Benny told us the story of Carl undressing in his car. Tom apologized to Carl for interrupting his lunch and asked if he had a minute. Carl invited him in and Tom took a seat. "So I heard from Benny some things about how you were feeling lately," Tom began, "that when I heard them, I found I could relate, so I bought you something." Tom handed Carl a book across the desk. "Don't be mad at Benny, you know how he likes to talk. And that," he added, indicating the book, "that's nothing. That's just something everybody should have on their shelves. Do you know this guy at all?" he asked.

Gazing down upon the book — the complete essays and poems of Ralph Waldo Emerson — Carl shook his head.

"Nobody does anymore," said Tom. "But everybody should. And I know that sounds like a bunch of pretentious bullshit, but it's bullshit I believe in."

Carl inspected the book and then looked up at Tom as if he needed an explanation of how to use the thing.

"And I know it's maybe a little funny, me buying you a book," Tom continued. "We don't buy each other books around here. But I was listening to Benny and he said you weren't feeling yourself lately, and when I asked him why and he tried to explain, I thought that what might help you was a little guidance from this guy here."

"Thanks, Tom," said Carl.

Tom shook his head dismissively. "Please don't thank me, it's a six-dollar book. Odds are you won't even read it. It'll sit on your bookshelf and every once in a while you'll come across it and think, now why'd that fuck ever buy me this book for? I know what it's like to get a random book," he said, "trust me, but listen — let me read you a few things so you see better where I'm coming from maybe. Can I do that?"

"If you'd like," said Carl. He handed the book back to him.

Tom paused. "Unless maybe you'd rather me just leave you to your lunch," he said.

Carl removed the napkin from his lap and wiped his hands. "It's fine if you want to read some of it, Tom," he said.

So Tom opened the book. "It might help, I don't know," he said. He thumbed nervously through the pages for the passage he wanted. It was probably a fraught moment for both men, a self-conscious and brittle silence as Tom prepared to read. When he finally located the passage he wanted, he began quoting but immediately cut himself off again. "And listen," he qualified himself, thrusting forward in his chair with abrupt eagerness, "I know it's maybe a little funny, here's me talking to you about how you can improve your life with this book and look at me, I'm a total fuckup. This last year has been . . . let's just say I see the error of my ways. But what it is with me, it's funny. I see the error of my ways, but I can't seem to get my head out of my ass, basically, is the basic fact of my life since my wife left me. So, please, forgive the hypocrisy of the unconverted sitting here preaching to you, but I do find that when I read Emerson, at the very least it calms me down."

"Tom," said Carl, "I appreciate the gesture."

Tom waved him off. " 'Let a man then know his worth,' " he read, " 'and keep things under his feet.' " Tom reading out loud to Carl — the self-consciousness in that room must have been *palpable.* " 'Let him not peep or steal, or skulk up or down with the air of a charity-boy, a bastard, or an interloper, in the world which exists for him. But the man in the street, finding no worth in himself . . .' I'm just going to skip down a little ways here," said Tom. "Okay, this is the part. 'That popular fable of the sot,' " he continued, " 'who was picked up dead drunk in the street, carried to the duke's house, washed and dressed and laid in the duke's bed, and, on his waking, treated with all obsequious ceremony like the duke, and assured that he had been insane, owes its popularity to the fact, that it symbolizes so well the state of man, who is in the world a sort of sot, but now and then wakes up, exercises his reason, and finds himself a true prince.' " Tom ended his quotation there and shut the book.

"Well," he said. "Anyway. I think he has a lot of good things to say. 'Finds himself a true prince.' That's hard to keep in mind here, you know? But he tries to remind us, Carl, you and me both — everybody, really — that underneath it all, if we exercise our reason, we're princes. I know I lose sight of that myself half the time when all I want to do is open fire on these bastards. You see, the problem with reading this guy," he continued, "is the same problem you have reading Walt Whitman. You read him at all? Those two fucks wouldn't have lasted two minutes in this place. Somehow they were exempt from office life. It was a different time, back then. And they were geniuses. But when I read them I start to wonder why *I* have to be here. It almost makes it harder to come in, be honest with you." Tom handed the book back across the desk. He added with a huffy, defeated chuckle, "That's a ringing endorsement, huh? Anyway, I'll let you get back to your lunch."

When Tom had nearly reached the door, Carl called out to him. "Can I tell you something in confidence, Tom?" he asked. Carl gestured for Tom to return to the chair.

Tom sat, and Carl looked at him for a long time before speaking. Earlier in the week, he confided, he had slipped quietly into Janine Gorjanc's office after everyone else had gone home for the night and taken a bottle of antidepressants from her desk drawer. Since that time, he told Tom, he had been taking a pill a day.

"Is that wise?" Tom asked.

"Probably not," said Carl. "But the last thing I want is for her to know that I'm depressed."

"You don't want Janine to know that you're depressed?"

"No, not Janine. My wife. Marilynn. I don't want Marilynn to know I'm depressed."

"Oh," said Tom. "Why's that?"

"Because she thinks I'm depressed."

"Oh," said Tom. "You aren't depressed?"

"No, I am depressed. It's just that I don't want her knowing that I'm depressed. She knows I'm depressed. I just don't want her knowing that she's right that I'm depressed. She's right too much of the time as it is, you see."

"So this is a matter of pride," said Tom.

Carl shrugged. "I guess so. If that's how you care to phrase it."

Tom shifted in his chair. "Well, you know, Carl, I understand that, man. I can understand that perfectly well, being married for a number of years to a woman who was always goddamn right about everything herself. But man, if you're taking a drug that hasn't been prescribed for you specifically —"

"Yeah, I know," said Carl, cutting him short. "I know all about that, trust me. I'm married to a doctor."

"Right," said Tom. "So what I guess I'm asking is, why steal it? Why not have somebody prescribe something that's right for you?"

"Because I don't want to have to see a doctor," said Carl. "I hate doctors."

"Your wife's a doctor," said Tom.

"It's a problem," said Carl. "Plus if I did that, it might get back to her somehow, and then she would know that she was right about me being depressed. It's just easier to go into Janine's and take it from her. She has a million of these things in there," he said.

He reached into his desk drawer and pulled out a prescription bottle and handed it to Tom.

"Do you know anything about what's in here?" asked Tom, shaking the bottle gently and reading the label. It was a three-month supply. "Three hundred milligrams," he said. "That sounds like a lot."

"I just follow the instructions on the label," said Carl.

Tom asked him if he had noticed any change in his mood.

"It's only been a week," Carl replied. "It's probably too early yet."

There was a knock at the door. In silence Tom handed Janine's drugs back to Carl and Carl returned the bottle to his desk. When Carl called out, Joe Pope appeared.

"Sorry to interrupt you at your lunch, Carl," he said.

"That's okay."

"I'm actually here for Tom," said Joe.

Tom turned in his chair and gave Joe a sidewinder gaze.

"I wondered if you wouldn't mind joining us for an input meeting later this afternoon," Joe inquired of him.

"Sure," Tom said. "What time?"

"Three-thirty, Lynn's office?"

"You bet."

When *that* got around — *Sure, what time? You bet.* — we didn't know *what* to make of it. All Tom would say was, "What was I supposed to say — no? Go shove it up your ass, Joe, no input meeting for me? I got child support to pay, man. Believe it or not, I need this job."

We didn't doubt that. It was just that we could recall a time in the Michigan Room when Tom Mota was less agreeably disposed toward Joe Pope. All of our conference rooms were named after streets running along the Magnificent Mile, and the view from Michigan was stupendous. The whole city was spread out before our eyes, layer after layer of buildings tall and squat, wide and thin, a giant matrix of architectural variation cut up by taxi-glinting thoroughfares and back alleyways and the snaking Chicago River, and every surface from burnished window to ancient brick was brightening under the August sun. The irony of the view from the Michigan Room was that it drove us mad with desire to be out there, walking the city sidewalks, looking up at the buildings, joining the swell of other people and enjoying the sun, but the only time we ever felt that urgency was when we were stuck at the window in the Michigan Room. Otherwise we left for the night and all we could think about was getting around the goddamn tourists and heading the fuck home.

On the day Tom and Joe really had it out, a month or so before

Tom's gift to Carl, it had evidently gotten back to Joe what was said here and there — at a lunch, before a meeting. Idle speculation, you know. Sometimes material for an honest debate where everyone took sides, but more often just as a joke. It's what we did, we *talked.* We weren't doing anything the Greeks weren't doing around their shadowy, promiscuous campfires. And neither, apparently, was Joe Pope, because just as we were capping our pens, all our notes taken and questions answered, and now only a half minute's distance from the restroom or telephone or coffee bar — whatever beckoned loudest — Joe, who was running his own input meetings by then, said to us, "Oh, one last thing." He paused. "Sorry, just give me one more minute here." We settled back down. "I feel the need to bring this to our attention," he said. "Look, I understand the need to talk. Most of the time, that's a good thing. We talk, we laugh. It makes time go faster. But I'm not sure we're always aware of some of the things we're saying. We might not mean anything by them, this or that or the other thing might just be a joke, but it gets around, and sometimes, one person or another hears about it and they get upset. Not everybody. Some people just laugh it off. Look, as an example, I know I'm talked about. No big deal to me. I take no offense. But other people, they hear things, it hits them in a certain way. You can't blame them. They get bothered, or hurt, or it embarrasses them. I'd prefer those type of things we try to keep to a minimum. I'm not saying don't talk. I'm just saying, reduce the volume a little, make sure that what you're saying doesn't hurt anybody. Okay?"

There was a long, unendurable pause as he looked around at all of us in case we had questions. "Okay, that's my little speech," he concluded. "Thanks for indulging me." At last we were released. We started to get up again. We had no idea Joe carried with him the reformer's spirit. We had mixed feelings about reformers. Some of us thought they were noble, and likely to change nothing. Others were outright hostile. *Who the fuck is he* — that sort of response.

"You know, Joe," Tom Mota said, just as we had started to file out. "There's really nothing wrong with being gay."

Joe cocked an ear at him, but managed still to look him firmly in the eye. "With what?" he asked.

"Hank Neary's gay," Tom continued, avoiding the direct question. Hank was just then pushing his chair in. He looked startled to be the sudden subject of conversation. "Aren't you, Hank? And he has no problem with it."

"Tom," said Joe. "You must not have heard anything I just said."

"No, I heard you, Joe. I heard you loud and clear."

People halfway out the door halted in their tracks.

"Then maybe you didn't understand," Joe tried to clarify. "The point was there's right talk, Tom, and there's wrong talk, and who's gay or who isn't gay, that's the wrong talk, understand? That kind of talk could be construed as slander."

"Slander?" said Tom. "Whoa, slander — Joe, that's an expensive word, slander. Do we need to involve lawyers? I have lawyers, Joe. I have so many fucking lawyers it would be no problem putting them to work on this one."

"Tom," said Joe. "Your anger."

"Excuse me?" said Tom.

"Your anger," Joe repeated.

"What the fuck does that mean," said Tom, "'Your anger'? Is that what you just said, 'Your anger'?" Joe didn't reply. "What the fuck does it mean, 'Your anger'?" Joe left the room. "Does anybody know what the fuck he means by 'Your anger'?" asked Tom.

We knew what "Your anger" meant because we suffered from the same anger from time to time. We suffered all sorts of ailments —

heart conditions, nervous tics, thrown-out backs. We had the mother of all headaches. We were affected by changes in weather conditions, by mood swings and by lingering high school insecurities. We were deeply concerned about who was next, and what criteria for dismissal the partners were operating under. Billy Reiser came in with a broken leg. At first everyone was excited. How did it happen? We gathered down at his office as soon as word spread, as if guided by a voice or a high-pitched frequency. Talk was like the flu: if it started with one, soon it infected all. But unlike the flu, we couldn't afford to be left out if something was going around. We wanted Billy to tell us how it happened. "Softball," he explained. That was it? "Bad slide," he elaborated. We couldn't help feeling disappointed. We told Billy we hoped he felt better soon and left again for our desks. A reason like that was hardly worth getting up for. Then over the next ten or twelve months, Billy proceeded to hobble around on his crutches, and swear to god you could hear the guy coming from six miles away. Jesus, we said eventually, aren't you off those things yet? "Complications," he said. He went through a series of surgeries. There were metal pins involved. Doctors said he might walk forever with a limp, so he was considering a lawsuit. We felt sorry for him, but at the same time, Billy heaving himself across a hallway, the joints of his crutches creaking like a nineteenth-century whaler — it might not sound like much, but day-in day-out, it started to grate. We understood "Your anger" whenever Billy passed by, irrational and unforgiving anger which caused some of us to call him, at one point or another, every derogatory name for a handicapped person in the book — mean and insensitive names like "crip," "gimp," and "wobbler" — while others we made up on our own. "The guy's name is Reiser," said Larry Novotny, "but he can't even stand up on his own two legs." Amber clucked at him for shame and the rest of us for the poverty of the pun but from then on we never called Billy by his first name again. It was always Reiser. Of course we took pains not to let Reiser get wind of our frustrations with him, most days. Most days we let human foibles run right off of us, as Jesus commanded. "Let he that is without sin cast the first stone," for we had among us our fair share of believers. We had a Bible study group. They met for lunch every Thursday in the cafeteria. A motley crew of condo-board executives, South Siders, recovering anorexics, building people, receptionists. It was an ebb-and-flow crowd, mimicking faith itself. The Word was the source that brought us all together. We drifted in and out of it, trying to make sense of the Word as it applied to us in our personal lives as well as in the corporate setting, but most of us just stayed away. More power to them, we liked to say. What were we missing? we wondered at night. How boring to listen to them go on and on about God, we thought every Thursday around noon. We had to ask, was this *really* the place for God? The sight of a dozen Bibles open on a cafeteria table and the familiar heads now bowed in a wild transformation of our long-established expectations of who they were shook us a little, as if forcing us to confront the possibility that we knew nothing, absolutely nothing about the inner lives of anyone here. But that soon passed. Our scope was infinite, our reach almighty, our knowledge was complete. Goddamn it, sometimes it felt like we *were* God. Was it such a blasphemy? We knew everything, we had terrible powers, we would never die. Was it a surprise that most of us did not join in at Bible study?

"I don't really give a shit if the guy's a homo or not," said Tom Mota, a week or so after his encounter with Joe Pope in the Michigan Room. "I just want to know what the fuck he means by 'Your anger.'" There was an opening between two clusters of cubicles that allowed enough room for a couple of round tables and several chairs where we found ourselves congregating some mornings around a box of Krispy Kremes or a bag of bagels that someone, inspired by the possibility of a brightened day, purchased and brought in and shared with the rest of us. The human spirit shining through against all adversity. We were enjoying our breakfast, drinking our first cups of coffee of the morning, when Joe Pope comes by carrying some ad freshly ripped from the printer and asks who brought in the bagels. "May I have one?" he asked. Genevieve Latko-Devine said of course he could and he thanked her and we expected him to be on his way after that but he lingered to spread some cream cheese and then he sat down among us, thanking Genevieve again. It was all very casual, as if routine, nothing out of the ordinary. We felt it, though, right *here* — Joe Pope's unexpected presence. Bonhomie took a holiday.

Things got very quiet, until Joe himself finally broke the ice. "By the way," he said. "How are you all doing with the cold sore spots?"

We were in the process of coming up with a series of TV spots for one of our clients who manufactured an analgesic to reduce cold sore pain and swelling. We took in Joe's question kind of slowly, without any immediate response. We might have even exchanged a look or two. This wasn't long after his second promotion. Doing okay, more or less, we said, in effect. And then we probably nodded, you know, noncommittal half nods. The thing was, his question — "How are you all doing with the cold sore spots?" — didn't seem a simple question in search of a simple answer. So soon after his promotion, it seemed more like a shrewd, highly evolved assertion of his new entitlement. We didn't think it was actual concern or curiosity for how we were progressing on the cold sore spots so much as a pretense to prod our asses.

"You do know, Joe," Karen Woo finally said, "that it's only

nine-thirty in the morning, right? Believe it or not, we *are* going to get to the cold sore spots today."

Joe looked genuinely misunderstood. "That's not why I was asking, Karen," he said. "I have every confidence you'll get to it. I was asking because I've been having trouble coming up with something myself."

We remained suspicious. He rarely had a hard time coming up with anything.

"The difficulty I'm having," he explained, "is that they want us to be funny and irreverent and all that, but at the same time, they don't want us to offend anybody who suffers from cold sores. It seems to me those two things are mutually exclusive. At least it makes it hard for me to come up with an ad that's worth a damn."

By noon, we knew that the son of a bitch was *right.* It was extremely tough to strike a balance between being funny about the unsightly effects of a cold sore while protecting against offending anyone watching who might suffer the unsightly effects of cold sores. It was one of those impossible, harebrained paradoxes that only a roundtable of corporate marketers smelling of competing aftershaves could have dreamed up — in a different land, in a different era, those tools would have come up with the dynasty's favorite koans. We had to admit maybe Joe Pope had no other intention in asking his question that morning but to inquire if we were having as hard a time with the cold sore spots as he was, and that our hasty assumptions were the result of a miscommunication. Some of us continued to suspect him, however, and as the fine points faded, on balance the episode probably didn't go in his favor.

It didn't improve matters when we gathered down at Lynn Mason's cluttered office two days later to present to her our concepts for cold sore spots and Joe and Genevieve unveiled Cold Sore Guy. We knew right away that not only would Cold Sore

Guy be one of the three concepts we'd send to the client, but that it would be the spot they ran, and ran, and ran, until you and everybody else in America grew intimate with Cold Sore Guy. The fucker *nailed* it, he and Genevieve, who was the art director of the pair, just fucking nailed the great koan of the cold sore marketers. Door opens on the background of suburbia, and standing in the bright doorway is a pair of attractive young lovebirds. "Hi, Mom!" says the girl. "I'd like you to meet my special someone." Cold Sore Guy offers Mom his hand. He indeed has an unsightly, somewhat exaggerated cold sore on the right corner of his upper lip. "Hi, I'm Cold Sore Guy." "Of course you are!" says Mom, taking Cold Sore Guy's hand. "Come on in!" Cut to Kitchen. Stern-looking Father. "Daddy," says the girl. "I'd like you to meet Cold Sore Guy." "Cold Sore Guy," says Daddy sternly. "It's nice to finally meet you, sir," says Cold Sore Guy, giving Daddy's hand a firm shake and smiling wide as a bell with his egregious cold sore. Cut to Living Room. Alzheimer's-looking Grandmother. "Grandma?" says the girl, shaking the frail woman vigorously. "Grandma?" Grandma comes to, sits up, looks at Cold Sore Guy and says, "Well, you must be Cold Sore Guy!" "Hi, Grandma," says Cold Sore Guy. Voice-over explains features and benefits of the product. Tagline: "Don't let a cold sore interfere with *your* life." Final cut to Dining Room. Stern-looking Father: "More mashed potatoes, Cold Sore Guy?" "Oh, love some, sir!" Fade.

We had all this for the first time only on storyboards, but the immediacy was undeniable, and we just knew he'd nailed it, him and Genevieve. The entire family was welcoming. They liked the guy. They shook hands with him. It was funny, but the subject of the fun was *embraced.* Cold Sore Guy was the hero. Plus, he could eat mashed potatoes. No one eats mashed potatoes with a cold sore like his, but superhero Cold Sore Guy did. And what's more, *it never said we could cure a cold sore.* That was always the toughest maneuver we had to make with that particular client. We could say we could treat a cold sore, but we were forbidden from saying that we could cure one. Joe's spot said nothing about treating or curing — he just managed to make the cold sore sufferer a sympathetic person. The client loved it. And when they cast it with the right actor, the guy looked even more sympathetic and performed it hilariously, and the ad was replayed on the Internet and took home awards and all the rest.

The day following the unveiling of Cold Sore Guy, Joe came into his office with his bicycle as he did every morning and found the word *FAG* written on the wall with a black Sharpie. It slanted up, in the hand of a child or a man in haste, not unlike what you might see on the back of a stall door in a bar. *Now* something was on his wall — nothing big, but definitely noticeable. We thought, sure, we're a dysfunctional office sometimes, but nobody we know could do a thing like that. Maybe it was somebody harboring animosity against Joe in some other realm of his life, who snuck past security one night, found Joe's office, and Sharpied away his soul. But in the end, that didn't sound very likely, and we had no choice but to conclude that Joe, in search of some local attention, had put it up there himself before leaving late the night before.

3

MORE LAYOFFS — WHY MEDIA BUYERS SUCK — THE BILLBOARD — YOP AT THE PRINT STATION — THE DOUBLE MEETING — LYNN IN SURGERY — WE KNOW WHAT JOE KNOWS — THE TWO-MARTINI LUNCH — AMBER'S REAL CONCERN — HONEST WORK — SOME GUY TALKS TO BENNY — GENEVIEVE'S ACCUSATION — JANINE GORJANC IN THE POOL OF PLASTIC BALLS — THE SETUP — WE APOLOGIZE — PAINTBALLS

IN THE EARLY WEEKS of 2001, they let go of Kelly Corma, Sandra Hochstadt, and Toby Wise. Toby had a custom-made desk in his office, which he'd commissioned out of a favorite surfboard — he was a great surfing fanatic. The desk took a while to dismantle, extending his period of stay beyond the usual protocol. Then he asked for help carrying the pieces down to the parking garage. We loaded the desk in the back of his new Trailblazer and prepared to say good-bye. This was always the most awkward time. Everyone had to decide — handshake, or hug? We heard Toby shut the tailgate on the Trailblazer and expected him to come around to where we had congregated. Instead he hopped into the driver's seat and powered down the tinted window. "So I guess I'll be seeing ya," he said, with a jolly lack of ceremony. Then he powered up the window again and took off. We felt a little slighted. Was a handshake too much to ask? If he was just bluffing his way out of a bad hand, if that was just his poker face, it sure was an exuberant and bouncy one. He stopped at the curb to look for cars and then pulled out with a little squeal. It was the last we ever saw of him.

In the weeks leading up to Tom Mota's termination, in the

spring of that year, Tom was found departing Janine Gorjanc's office with great frequency. Hard to say what they were talking about. We loved nothing more than to lay waste to a half hour speculating about office romance, but we could not conceive of a stranger pair. The petulant, high-strung Napoleon exiled to an Elba of his own mind, and the acrid mother in mourning. Love worked in funny ways. We forgot they had things in common — lost children. They consoled each other, perhaps. They shared the long indefatigable nightmare of not knowing what to do with the burden of a materialized love that refused their private requests to wane, to break, to please just go away, and so they found themselves directing that love toward each other. But that was only how we killed time. In fact, there was no love affair. Tom just wanted the billboard to come down.

Our media buyers, like Jane Trimble and Tory Friedman, tended to be small, chipper, well-dressed women who wore strong perfume and had an easy knack for conversation. They kept bags of sweets in their desk drawers and never gained any weight. They spent most of their time on the phone talking with vendors, the deadening prospect of which made us gag, and for their services, they received random gifts and tickets to sporting events, the blatant unfairness of which angered us with a blind and murderous envy. Because they put the orders in and talked with friendly inflections in their voices, they were bribed with largesse, like dirty checkpoint guards, and we thought they deserved a special ring of hell, the ring devoted to corrupt mayors, lobbyists, and media buyers. That was how we felt, anyway, during our time in the system. When one of us walked Spanish and got out of the system, we thought back on those loquacious and smiling media buyers as just some of the nicest people.

Tom's gripe was with Jane. "He's got to take that goddamn

billboard down," he said to her after walking into her office without a knock or a greeting. Unfortunately Jane knew just what he was referring to: the vendor with whom she had placed the order. Flyers of the missing girl were not the only effort we had made to help Janine and Frank Gorjanc during the days of their short-lived search for their daughter. Using some of their money, supplemented by hastily raised funds, we had the same image of Jessica from the fourth grade with the word MISSING and a number to call placed on a billboard on I-88 facing westbound traffic. Long after the girl had been found, that billboard was still up there. Jane tried to explain that nobody wanted to see that billboard come down as much as she did, but that these things took time when there was no immediate turnover. "No immediate turnover?" cried Tom. "It's been six months!" "He promises me he's working on it," Jane replied with the courtesy and patience expected of media buyers. "Well that's not good enough," Tom barked at her. "At least have him strip it." "Stripping," explained Jane sheepishly, knowing how crass she must have sounded, "unfortunately costs money, Tom."

It was an unpopular space, that was the problem. Far out on I-88, west of the Fox River, metropolitan Chicago effectively came to an end, yielding its industrial parks and suburban tract housing to fields of alfalfa and small towns with single gas stations. Billboards in North Aurora were good for casino boat and cigarette ads, and maybe the occasional AIDS awareness campaign, but little else. The vendor might have taken a hit on the rental fee but to rent it at all was likely a great boon to him, and he probably never had a client complain about continued exposure after the lease expired. Free advertising — who could complain about that?

If there was an opportunity to complain, we complained. The creative team complained about the account team. The account team complained about the client. Everybody complained at one time or another about human resources, and human resources complained among themselves about each and every one of us. About the only people not complaining were the media buyers, because they were showered with bribes of tickets and gifts, but when Janine complained to Tom about the billboard, Tom Mota took that complaint to them. The billboard, he said, advertised Jessica as missing, when Jessica had not been missing for months. Jessica had been found. Jessica had been buried. He complained that Janine had to see that billboard on the side of I-88 every day on her way home from work, had to be reminded of the week she spent waiting in numb and desperate hope that that billboard might help in some way to bring her little girl back, and of her devastation when she learned that it would not. Now that billboard was nothing but a vicious reminder, broadcasting from a great height the girl's cruel fate. Tom wouldn't stand for it. He complained about the son-of-a-bitch vendor who moved unconscionably slowly, and about the bright, uncomplaining dispositions of media buyers like Jane Trimble — complained so much that Jane had to get on the phone with the vendor and complain. When she got off the phone with the vendor, Jane called Lynn Mason to complain about Tom Mota — just one more complaint that must have contributed to his eventual termination.

On the morning in May Lynn Mason was scheduled to be in surgery, the day after she let go of Chris Yop, Yop was back in the building, standing at a print station. Marcia Dwyer was startled to find him there. It was early morning. Marcia had come to photocopy the inspiring tale of a cancer survivor featured in an outdated issue of *People* magazine. When Yop turned and saw her, he gave a start like a cornered animal. "Christ Almighty," he said. "I thought you were Lynn."

"Lynn's in surgery today," she said, "remember?"

Marcia spoke with a hardcore South Side accent and wore the accompanying tall hair with bangs. Her black curls in back were held in place by some miraculous fixative. If we knew her at all, as she spoke with Yop she probably had one hand on her hip with her wrist turned inward.

"What are you doing back here, Chris?" she asked.

"Working on my resume," Yop said defensively.

Marcia told us about this encounter a half hour later, when the day officially began. We had congregated by the couches for a double meeting. The day after a meeting with Lynn we usually had a postmeeting meeting conducted by Joe, where the finer points of the project were hammered out without wasting any more of Lynn's time. Of late, Lynn spent her days in meetings with her fellow partners in an effort to keep us solvent. Not wasting her time had become an imperative.

It was just like us to have two meetings for one project. No one ever wondered if the existence of double meetings might have some bearing on Lynn's need to have solvency meetings — or if they did, they kept their mouths shut. After all, we liked double meetings. Only in a double meeting could you ask the questions you were reluctant to ask in the first meeting for fear of looking stupid in front of Lynn. We wanted to die looking stupid in front of Lynn, but we didn't mind it in front of Joe.

One agency we knew about, out in San Francisco, had architects come in to design a floor plan that included live trees, dartboards, flagstones, sun panels, coffee kiosks, and a half-court big enough for a game of three-on-three. Those lucky bastards knew no such thing as a conference room or a frosted-glass door. We had to suffer such insults, but in recompense, we were given mismatching recreational furniture intended to inspire the creative impulse and upon which we were encouraged to lounge. Located in open spaces where the windows lengthened and allowed sunlight to pour in, these little hot spots were a nice break from corridors and cubicles, and where we always went to double meet. Marcia was perched on the edge of one of the recliners, and her hair was particularly tall and sculptural that morning.

She told us Yop seemed offended when she asked him what he was doing at the print station. "It was like he expected me to be a major bitch about it and start hollering for security," she said, "but I was just asking what he was doing. I mean, just yesterday the guy was laid off, right — and this morning he's back in the building? What's that about?"

We couldn't believe Yop was back in the building.

"I asked him, I says, 'You shouldn't be here, right?' And he says to me, 'No, I shouldn't be here.' So I says, 'So what happens if somebody catches you?' and he says, 'Well, then I'm fucked.' 'What's that mean, you're fucked?' I says, and he says, 'Trespassing!' "

We couldn't believe that. Trespassing? Would he be arrested?

"Yeah, can you believe that?" Yop asked Marcia. "That's what I was told right after the input yesterday when Lynn called me back into her office, remember? My presence in the building will be construed as *criminal action.* I was like, 'Lynn, you have to be kidding me, right? After all I've done for this place, you're going to have me arrested for trespassing?' She stops drawing the blinds — she wasn't even looking at me when she said it! But anyway, she sits down, and you know that look she can give you, where it's almost like she's burning your brain out with her laser eyes? She pulls her chair in and she gives me that look and she says, 'I'm sorry, but you can't still be here, Chris. You've been terminated.' So I say to her, 'Yeah, I know that, Lynn, but when we were having our conversation earlier and I couldn't keep it together, remember?

and I had to leave your office? I didn't think I would have to *leave* leave until we had a chance to finish our conversation, like how we're doing now. Because I still have one important thing to say before I go.' So she says to me, 'Chris, tell me whatever it is you have to tell me, but then you need to leave. Understand? I can't take any chances with you in the building.' What the fuck, right? She can't take any chances with me in the building? What am I going to do, steal Ernie's chair? Maybe I could get down the hall with it into the freight elevator. I'd still have to walk it past security. How am I going to get out of the building with Ernie's chair? 'So go ahead,' Lynn says to me. 'What do you have to say?' 'Okay, I just want to know one thing,' I tell her. 'Do you know or have you ever known anything about serial numbers?' This is what I ask her. 'Does the phrase *serial numbers* mean anything to you personally?' How does she respond? She says, 'Serial numbers?' Yeah, she looks at me like I'm crazy. 'I don't know what you're talking about, Chris,' she says to me, 'serial numbers.' You see — I KNEW IT!" Yop howled in a frantic whisper, flinging a furtive glance in the direction of the print-station doorway. And in a softer voice, "*I fucking knew it!* That office coordinator made the whole thing up! *It's her own personal system.* There's nothing official whatsoever about the serial numbers! She has a punch gun. You know what I'm talking about, with the wheel? That's where they come from! The serial numbers! *Lynn didn't even know about them!* She was like, 'Serial numbers?' So I tell her everything about the serial numbers, about how the office coordinator made them up, keeping tabs on everything like Big Brother or something. But so anyway, she listens, very politely, but then she says, 'Is that it?' And I'm like, 'Well, yeah, but —' I thought at the very least she would call the office coordinator back in and we'd start over and this time I'd get a fair shake. But it was obvious there was no chance she was going to give me my job back. So that's when she tells me that if she finds me in the building again, she's going to have to report me to security, who will call the police, who will arrest me for trespassing. Can you believe that?" Yop's tumid, rheumy eyes bulged out at Marcia. He really wasn't in the best of health. "After all my time here," he continued. "So that's when I thought, 'Oh, yeah? Well, watch me come back here tomorrow and print out my resume using your machines. You know what they charge at Kinko's for printing like this? No way I'm spending my last paycheck at Kinko's. I've given a lot to this place, and I think I should be allowed to save a few bucks on printing. By the way," he said. "Would you proofread it for me?"

"So I says to him, 'Proofread what?'" Marcia said to us just before the double meeting began. "He wanted me to proofread his resume! I couldn't believe it. I was like, 'Chris, I'm an art director. You're the copywriter. You do the proofing, remember?' I mean, honestly, I spell like a person in an institution. But still he says, 'Yeah, I know, but I really need another pair of eyes on it.' And then he stands there holding out a pen. A red pen! He wants me to do it right there in the print station!"

So Marcia stood at the copier proofreading Yop's resume, stealing glances at the door now and again because she didn't want to be seen with somebody who could be arrested for trespassing. As she worked, he engaged her in conversation. He asked if she wanted to know the twisted thing about being terminated. "The really sick and twisted thing," he said. "You wanna know what it is?"

"I was trying to concentrate on his resume," she said to us, "and I was also watching the door because I didn't want anyone to walk in and see me with the guy. I already knew the sick and twisted thing: that sorry drip was back in the building. But I didn't say that, because I was trying to be nice."

"The sick and twisted thing," Yop confessed, "is that I *want* to work. Can you believe that? I *want* to work. Isn't that sick? You understand what I'm saying here, Karen? I've just been terminated, and inside my head I'm still working!"

"Oh my god," said Marcia, looking up from his resume. "My name is Marcia."

"At that point," Marcia said to us, "I was *through.* He doesn't even know my *name?*"

"What did I say?" said Yop.

"You just called me Karen," replied Marcia.

"Karen?" Yop looked away and shook his head. "Did I? I said Karen? I'm sorry," he said. "I know you're not Karen, you're Marcia, I know that. You and me worked together a long time, I know who you are. You're Marcia, you're from Berwyn."

"Bridgeport."

"I know who you are," said Yop. "Karen's someone else. Karen's the Chinese girl."

"Korean."

"My mind is just totally fried this morning, that's all," he said. "I hope you forgive me. Anyway, the point I was trying to make . . ."

"WHAT?" Marcia cried at us from her perch on the recliner. "WHAT is the point you're trying to make, you stuttering jackass? *Berwyn?* I could not *believe* that the guy got my name wrong."

"The point I was trying to make," Yop continued, "is that I find myself thinking about the fund-raiser. Can you believe that?"

"What fund-raiser?" asked Marcia.

"The fund-raiser," Yop replied. "The fund-raiser we have to come up with ads for."

"Oh, for breast cancer," said Marcia, nodding. "The pro bono project." She was reminded that in a few minutes she had a double meeting to attend.

"But then I thought, *he* doesn't!" cried Marcia. "I just wanted to say to him, 'Oh my god, Chris — you don't *work* here anymore. Give the fund-raiser ads up. Leave the building. Proofread your own frickin' resume! But my god," she said, "he wouldn't stop talking. He says to me, 'Can you believe I can't stop working in my head? I keep working and working and working — isn't that sick and twisted?' Well, *yeah.* Yeah it's sick and twisted. *You don't work here anymore!* But I didn't say that. I was trying to be nice. I do try to be nice sometimes. So even though he didn't know my name I went on proofreading his stupid resume, which had *so* many mistakes. How did we ever hire that guy to be a copywriter? I'm pointing them out to him, all these misspellings and typos and things, when he says, totally out of the blue — I mean, I have *no* idea where this comes from. I know something's wrong, though, because he's not talking talking talking, he's just looking at me, so I look up from his resume and I says, 'What?' and he says, 'It'll happen to you, too, you know. Don't think it won't.' And I says, 'What will happen to me?' 'Getting fired,' he says. 'It'll happen to you just like it's happened to everyone else, and then you won't be above everybody like how you act now.' I could not believe what I was hearing," she said to us. "I was proofreading the fucking guy's resume — *me!* — making *improvements* on the thing, and he tells me that I'm going to get laid off? And not just that, but also that I hold myself above everybody else? Just because I hold myself above that sorry drip doesn't mean I hold myself above everybody. I was trying to help him get a new job, for god's sake! Wasn't that nice of me? I mean, what an ass crack! Isn't he a total ass crack," she asked us, "to say to me, 'Oh, and by the way, this bad thing that just happened to me? It's going to happen to you, too.' What if Brizz had done that? What if Brizz had said, 'Thanks for visiting me in the hospital, guys, but just so you know, one day you'll all be dying, too, and when that day comes, you won't be able to breathe, either, you'll be in such pain and misery, and then you'll die. So good luck, you jerks.' So I ripped his resume up into little pieces and threw them in his face, and one little piece stuck on his forehead, he was sweating so much. And I said something really mean to him. I couldn't help it, I says, 'You sweat so gross it makes me sick.' I shouldn't have said that. But I loved saying it, because it *is* gross when he sweats. What a fucking jerk! Telling me I'm going to get laid off. You guys have to remember," she said. "You have to understand. I've been on *eggshells* since the input yesterday."

We asked Marcia why she should be on eggshells. She looked around conspiratorially, unusual for her, because she typically didn't give a damn who heard her say what. Marcia was never on eggshells. She was born and raised in Bridgeport, she changed her own oil, she listened to Mötley Crüe.

"Because *I'm* the one who took Tom Mota's chair," she confessed. "You understand? Tom's chair is in *my* office. It's always been the rule that when someone leaves, if you get in there first you can take their chair. I got in there first, I took Tom's chair. I didn't know anything about serial numbers. Not until that tool started jabber-assing about them yesterday at the input. Since then I've been on eggshells. It's made me crazy. I want to get rid of it, but because he took Ernie's chair down to Tom's office, trying to pretend it was really Tom's and not Ernie's, I can't take Tom's real chair down there because then Tom would have *two* chairs. Isn't that going to look suspicious? But if they look and see I have the chair with Tom's serial numbers on it — don't you see, I have the chair with the serial numbers! What should I do? Who knew about these serial numbers? I didn't. Did you?"

She was as breathless and worked up as Yop himself. We told her to get ahold of herself. Chris Yop was not let go just because he was caught with Tom Mota's buckshelves. He was let go because he can't even draw up his own resume without filling it with typos. Lynn Mason and the other partners couldn't trust million-dollar ad campaigns to sloppy copywriters — that is, if we ever had million-dollar ad campaigns again. That's why Chris Yop was let go.

All the same, we thought it would be prudent of her to go into Tom's office and swap Ernie's chair with Tom's. It was a delicate time, and in delicate times it made sense to take every precaution. Better to be caught with Ernie's chair than with Tom's. And just as we said that, we caught ourselves talking about such things as which chair Marcia would be better off being caught with, and we realized then how far we had fallen.

JOE SHOWED UP TO the double meeting carrying his day planner, which was predictable and annoying. We were irked by the steadfast familiarity of that goddamn day planner. Sometimes we almost thought we could like Joe if just one time out of ten he left that leather-bound diary behind at his desk. But no. The couch and the two loveseats and the leather recliners were all taken so Joe had to sit on the floor.

At a double meeting a couple things always happened. Joe split us up into teams, one art director for every copywriter. Ideally, after the double meeting, each team would get together and brainstorm ideas. How it worked in practice was always a little different, however. The copywriter went off on his own and the art director did the same, generating ideas independently of one another. Then they got together to battle it out. Who was wittier, who had more savvy, who had sailed it out of the park. We all had the same prayer: *please let it be me.* Regardless of who that me was, he or she tried to be very discreet about it, but there was no denying it, they reigned victorious for a day while the rest of us returned to our desks to chew silently on our own spines. We had lost, and our dimwittedness made us vulnerable to low opinion, whispered denigrations, and the dread prospect of being next.

So imagine our surprise, and our chagrin, when we sat down at the couches with our coffees to double meet — during which time we only refined details, we only requested clarifications — and Karen Woo announced that she already had ad concepts. She had an entire *campaign.* "You know what, I'm sick of seeing attractive sixtyish-type women smiling into the camera and saying, 'Look at me, I'm a survivor. I defeated breast cancer.' That's bullshit," she said. "This industry needs to cut through the happy-smiley clutter and get nasty with some truth."

We looked at her with our chins floating in our coffee cups. Hold up! we wanted to shout. You can't have concepts. We haven't even double met yet!

"What's your idea?" asked Joe.

Her idea? We'll tell you her idea, Joe. To slaughter. Nobody talks about it, nobody says a word, but the real engine running the place is the primal desire to kill. To be the best ad person in the building, to inspire jealousy, to defeat all the rest. The threat of layoffs just made it a more efficient machine.

"It surprises me that you have concepts already, Karen," said Larry Novotny. Karen and Larry didn't get on so well. "It really surprises me."

"Initiative," Karen said smugly.

"I don't want to speak for anybody else," Larry added, "but to be honest, it really surprises the hell out of all of us."

Karen leaned forward on the sofa and turned to Larry in his recliner, his eyes hard to see under the arced canopy of his Cubs cap. He was wearing one of his boring flannel shirts. They had a stare-down. Karen and Larry didn't get on because Larry was an Art Director and Karen a Senior Art Director and titles meant everything. Every AD wanted to be a SAD. If you were a SAD you had your eyes on becoming an Acker. Acker was our phonetic translation of Associate Creative Director. Ackers wanted to be Creetors (Creative Directors), and every Creetor envied the Eveeps. You could either be a Creveep (Creative Executive Vice President) or an Ackveep (Account Services Executive Vice President), but both species hoped equally to be invited one day into partnership. What the partners dreamed of was the stuff of Magellan, da Gama, Columbus, et al.

The point was we took this shit very seriously. They had taken away our flowers, our summer days, and our bonuses, we were on a wage freeze and a hiring freeze, and people were flying out the door like so many dismantled dummies. We had one thing still going for us: the prospect of a promotion. A new title: true, it came with no money, the power was almost always illusory, the bestowal a cheap shrewd device concocted by management to keep us from mutiny, but when word circulated that one of us had jumped up an acronym, that person was just a little quieter that day, took a longer lunch than usual, came back with shopping bags, spent the afternoon speaking softly into the telephone, and left whenever they wanted that night, while the rest of us sent e-mails flying back and forth on the lofty topics of Injustice and Uncertainty.

"Karen," said Joe. "What's your idea?"

Karen broke off from Larry and turned to Joe.

"Take a look," said Karen. She unveiled three polished concepts she called the "Loved Ones" campaign. From the stock houses she had secured close-ups of individual faces, all male. The first was a black boy, the second an Asian man, the last an older white gentleman. They looked directly at the camera without expression. We all thought, she's been on Photonica's website for the past eighteen hours looking for these gems. The headlines were an exercise in simplicity and the art of the tease. Each was a quote. With some work in Photoshop, Karen had the black boy holding a white placard that read, "My Aunt." The Asian man's placard said, "My Mother." The old white guy's said, "My Wife." That was it, the images and the headlines. They were arresting enough, Karen believed, that anyone coming across them would be prompted to read the body copy, where a first-person testimonial explained the anguish of losing a loved one to breast cancer and the dire need for a cure.

"Bit of a downer," suggested Larry, "don't you think?"

"No, Larry. I don't think. It's gripping and honest and motivating, is what it is."

"Not very palatable."

"It is too palatable, Larry!"

"It's like seeing African kids starve on the TV, Karen. Maybe we can get Sally Struthers involved."

"Joe," said Karen.

"Larry," said Joe.

"I'm just saying, Joe," said Larry.

We hated Karen Woo. We *hated* hating Karen Woo because we feared we might be racists. The white guys especially. But it wasn't just the white guys. Benny, who was Jewish, and Hank, who was black, hated Karen too. Maybe we hated Karen not because she was Korean but because she was a woman with strong opinions in a male-dominated world. But it wasn't just the men; Marcia couldn't stand her and she was a woman. And Marcia loved Donald Sato, so she couldn't be a racist. Donald wasn't Korean but he was Asian of some kind, and everybody liked him as much as Marcia did even though he didn't say a whole lot. One time,

Donald did say, as he turned away from his computer for a brief moment, toward a group of four or five of us, "My grandpa has this weird collection of Chinese ears." We had been discussing something, it wasn't like it just came out of nowhere. But at the same time, it wasn't unusual for an entire day to go by where Donald said only, "Uh, maybe," like four or five times, half of them without even directing his attention away from his computer, and then five o'clock hit and no more Donald. Now he's telling us about his grandpa's — "What do you mean, a collection of ears?" asked Benny. "Are you talking real ears, like real ears?" "Ears from the heads of Chinese people, yes," Donald assented, having turned back to his computer screen. "A whole sack of them." The mystery deepened. "A sack? What kind of a sack?" Sam Ludd, who smoked a lot of pot and frequently smelled like Funyuns, turned to Benny to communicate something to him in the secret language of laughter. "But seriously," Benny persisted, pivoting on the window ledge to look at Donald straight on, "what the fuck are you talking about, Don?" "And what would constitute a nonweird collection of Chinese ears?" asked Sam, who lasted about two and a half seconds after layoffs began. "They're from the war," Don told the screen. "He doesn't like to talk about it." "But you've seen it?" said Benny. "There's more than just one," said Don. "No, the sack, the sack," said Benny. Don looked at him and nodded. "Yeah." "Well did he, like, cut them off himself? did he buy them? were they given to him as a gift? Don, talk to me." "I don't really know much more. I know he was in the war. Maybe he cut them off, I don't know. That's not something you can really ask your grandpa." "Okay, but . . ." Benny was flustered, "you shouldn't bring it up then, man, if you don't have more information." "I think you're wrong, Don," said Sam. "I think you can ask a grandpa if he cut the ears off Chinese people." "What did they look like?" asked Benny. "Can you tell me that?" Don told the screen he didn't really know what they looked like. They looked like ears. Dead old shriveled ears. And the sack was just a felt thing with a drawstring. Benny nodded and bit his cheek.

Anyway, Karen Woo. Did we dislike her because we were racists, because we were misogynists, because her "initiative" rankled and her ambition was so bald, because she wore her senior title like a flamboyant ring, or because she was who she was and we were forced by fate to be around her all the time? Our diversity pretty much guaranteed it was a combination of all of the above.

"I think the problem I'm having with this project, Joe," said Benny, astraddle a sofa arm, "is knowing the fundamental approach we should be taking here. Is this just a benign reminder that breast cancer research needs money, or do we want to kick some ass à la Karen's dead relatives there and get people to send checks overnight?"

"Maybe somewhere in between," Joe answered, after a moment's thought. "That's not to rule these out, Karen. I like them. Let's just have some of us go in one direction and the rest of us go in the other."

We discussed print dates, who the project services people would be, and then we broke into teams. Joe was the first to stand. Just before leaving he announced that we would not be showing finished concepts to Lynn; we would be showing them to him.

We all wanted to know how come. Joe replied that it was because Lynn would be out of the office for the rest of the week.

"The rest of the week?" said Benny. "Is she on vacation?"

"I don't know," said Joe.

But he did know. He knew just as we knew that she was in surgery that day and would be in recovery when the concepts were due — the difference being that he probably got his information straight from Lynn, whereas we had to get ours from other sources. We never disliked Joe more than when he had information that we had, too, which he then refused to tell us.

"CAN WE PLEASE STOP talking about Joe Pope for two minutes?" asked Amber Ludwig when Joe had left the couches after the double meeting. We had stuck around to discuss the fact that we knew what he didn't think we knew and how annoying that was.

"What should we be talking about, Amber?" asked Larry. "Karen's dead people?"

"They're called Loved Ones, Larry."

Amber was, we all knew, preoccupied by something that had come to light just last week, when Lynn Mason received a call from Tom Mota's ex-wife informing her that Tom had apparently dropped out of sight.

Barbara, the ex-wife, had received some curious communications — voice mails, e-mails, handwritten letters — full of quotations from various sources: the Bible, Emerson, Karl Marx, *The Art of Loving* by Erich Fromm, but also, disconcertingly, *The Anarchist's Philosophy,* a McLenox publication. Amber looked on the McLenox website and discovered they brought out such titles as *Hiding Places Both Underwater and Underground* and *How to Make a Fake Birth Certificate on Your Home Computer.*

Tom's messages to his wife were oddly lucid arguments for correcting the awful predicament of an individual who found himself stuck in a rut, with many allusions to love, compassion, tenderness, humility, and honesty, along with some not-so-lucid references to doing something that would "shock the world," as he put it, that would make his name go down in history. "'All history resolves itself very easily into the biography of a few stout and earnest persons,'" quoted Tom in an e-mail that had, by three o'clock the previous Friday afternoon, been forwarded to everyone in the office. "Barbara," it concluded, "you laugh, but I intend to be one of those persons."

Barbara called Lynn to find out if anyone else had heard from Tom. "And I guess to sort of warn you," Barbara added. "I hate to put it that way, because I never used to think of him like that. But then he shows up at the house with a baseball bat and destroys everything in sight, which causes you to think, maybe I never really knew this person. I didn't know him then and I don't know what he's capable of now, and I don't really want to stick around to find out."

"I can't say I blame you," Lynn replied.

"So I'm calling just to say that I've been trying to get in touch with him, just to make sure . . . you know. But . . . and I don't want you to think he's going to do anything . . . unexpected. I just thought I should let you know I can't find him."

"I appreciate the call," said Lynn.

She got off the phone and called Mike Boroshansky, the South Side Pole in charge of building security. Mike let everyone on security detail know about the possible situation. They taped a picture of Tom to the security desk in the lobby, and during the day, Benny's friend Roland compared it with visitors coming in through the revolving doors, and at night, the other security guard did the same.

We alone had perspective. Tom Mota was not going to do anything crazy. He was crazy, but he wasn't *crazy*. We couldn't believe how worried they were. Posting a picture of Tom? Everyone knew that was nuts.

Everyone except Amber Ludwig, who could remember with characteristic anxiety Tom Mota after he'd had two martinis at lunch. How rare it was for anyone to have a martini at lunch anymore. To watch Tom have two, it was a pure delight. "What has happened to America," he would ask, and then stop himself. "Hey, I'm talking here." We had to halt our conversations and pay attention to him. "What has happened to America," he continued, "that the two-martini lunch has been replaced by this, this . . ." He gazed at us with disdainful shakes of his bulldog's head. ". . . this boothful of pansies, all dressed up in your khakis and sipping the same iced tea? Huh?" he said. "What has happened?" He genuinely wanted to know. "Didn't General Motors," he continued, lifting the new martini in the air delicately, so as not to spill, "IBM, and Madison Avenue establish postwar American might upon the two-martini lunch?"

It was only the beginning of the vodka talking in him. "Cheers," he said. "Here's to your Dockers and your Windbreakers." He reached out for the glass with his full, flushed lips while trying to hold the stem steady in his hand.

After returning to the office on those days, in the dull hours from two to five, we never knew what to expect from him. Sometimes he would nap in a stall in the men's room. Sometimes he would stand on his desk in his socks and remove the panels of fluorescent lighting from his ceiling. Passing by, we'd inquire just what he was doing up there. "Why don't you go fuck your own asshole?" he'd suggest. That was always lovely. But it wasn't the behavior of a madman, in our opinion. He was someone inconsolably trapped and going stir-crazy, aggressive and in need of release, which was, after all, the reason for the two-martini lunch. We spent a lot of time talking about how the job and the divorce were turning Tom Mota into an alcoholic.

Who was an alcoholic, whether early onset, functional, or fall-down drunk — that was always a topic of conversation. Who was fucking who, that was another. It was no secret that Amber Ludwig was fucking Larry Novotny. Amber would like us to stop talking about that now. But was it not true? If not true, not another word on the subject. Well? Amber? Unresponsive. Okay — what, then? If not the subject of fucking Larry, and if you've just asked that we stop talking about Joe Pope, what should we talk about? After all, the democratic principle underpins this madness. The floor is yours. Argue, once again, that you don't feel safe here anymore, that Tom Mota always gave you the creeps, and that what we call antics and low comedy you call homicidal insanity. Amber?

"Last night I tried to sleep," she said, "but I couldn't stop worrying."

We tried telling her for the fiftieth time that he was not coming back. She gazed around as if she were Marcia, as if she had Marcia's power to reduce us with a single withering glance to small and ridiculous beings. But when Amber did it, the gaze turned inward and revealed something about her, that she felt misunderstood and therefore hurt.

"What are you talking about?" she asked. "Are you guys talking about Tom Mota again? How can you be talking about Tom Mota at a time like this?"

Who was *she* talking about?

"Who else?" she said. "Who could I *possibly* be talking about right now?"

By then it was certainly time for us to get up, return to our desks, and try to catch Karen in the pursuit of the best fund-raiser concept, but for some reason nobody moved. "Can you believe she might be in surgery right now?" Amber asked us. "I mean this very minute. Does anybody know what time it was scheduled for?"

"I don't think anybody knows that," said Genevieve.

"Last night," continued Amber, "I don't know why, but I was wondering if she had a boyfriend."

"Oh, I actually know something about this," Genevieve announced.

Amber was startled. "What, what do you know?"

"That she was dating a lawyer."

"How do you know that? She told you?"

"Oh, no. I saw them at a restaurant with my husband. He knew the guy. They were opposing counsel on a case."

"You saw them at a restaurant?" said Amber. "What did he look like?"

"Kind of heavyset, if I remember. But not fat. Sexy, I thought. I thought they made a good-looking couple."

"So what happened? Are they still together?"

"Oh, I don't know that," said Genevieve. "I only saw them once at a restaurant."

There was silence. It seemed pretty clear we were all wondering what Lynn Mason did at night when she went home. Did she watch TV, or did she think TV was a waste of time? What hobbies did she have? Or had she sacrificed hobby-having to professional ambition? Did she exercise? Was her diet particularly bad? Did she have a history of cancer in the family? Who was her family? Who were her friends? What had happened between her and the lawyer? And how did she feel, being in her forties, never having married?

"I wanted to call her last night and offer to drive her to the hospital," said Amber. "Can you imagine that? She'd have been like, 'Amber, please don't call me at home at eleven o'clock at night.' Click."

"Oh, I don't know," said Genevieve. "She might have been touched. Remember her birthday?" We had made an infomercial for her on her birthday, editing together testimonials from everyone about how great she was. "She was very touched," said Genevieve. "I don't think we give her enough credit for being human."

"It's hard," said Benny. "She's scary."

"I can't picture her on a date," said Larry.

There was more silence, until Genevieve asked, "Do you really think she needed a ride to the hospital?"

— — —

WE BROKE APART, climbing down to fifty-nine and up to sixty-three and to the floors in between. If something was on the radio we kept it low. The weather outside, telling from our windows, was overcast but not cold. Spring had finally arrived. We settled down to the fund-raiser ads. We opened a new Quark document, or took out our pencils. Every once in a while a nicely sharpened pencil would crack on the page upon impact and we'd have to go in search of the one electric pencil sharpener. That was annoying. Back in our chairs we drummed the eraser between our teeth. If a stray paper clip happened to be lying around we were likely to bend it out of shape. Some of us knew how to turn a misshapen paper clip into a projectile that could hit the ceiling. If our attention was drawn to the ceiling, we usually recounted our tiles. When we returned to our computer screens, we erased whatever false starts we found there, suddenly embarrassed by them. We had the feeling that our bad ideas were probably worse than the bad ideas of others. Those of us who worked on sketch pads were engaged by that point in the great unsung pastime of American corporate life, the wadded paper toss. This, more than anything, was what "billable hour" implied. It was always annoying when an eyelid started to twitch. We did some drag-and-drop. What was missing was an interesting color palette, so we leaned back in our chairs and gave it some thought. What Pantone would be perfect for a fund-raising event? No one ever admitted to it publicly, but there were days of extreme sexual frustration. The phone would ring. It was nothing. We checked our e-mail. We clicked back into Quark and established new snap-to guides. Sometimes our computers froze and we would have to call down to IT. Or we needed something from the supply room. Lately inventory in the supply room seemed half of what it used to be, and the woefully bereft shelves recalled to mind TV programs that documented seasons of drought and low crop production in the history of a foregone people. But usually we needed nothing from the supply room. We took out our bags of snacks from our desk drawers, or we chewed our fingernails. Suddenly a blinding flash of the obvious would strike, and a flurry of keyboard noise filtered out into the hall. We thought, "This is not a half-bad idea." That was all we needed, one little insight. Soon the roughest look, the crudest message, started to shape itself into coherence. Inevitably when we reached that point, we stopped to use the restroom.

What was the likelihood, if we were being honest, that this one fund-raiser, one of a thousand, no matter how many donations it might receive, would really get us any closer to a cure for breast cancer? Who knows, maybe it would. None of us understood how advances in medical science worked. Maybe they needed only one more dollar and our solicitations would put them over the top.

We also saw our work that day as doing a personal favor for Lynn, even if we couldn't help feeling that, by choosing not to tell us that she had cancer, she had cheated us of one of our most dearly held illusions — namely, that we were not present strictly for the money, but could also be concerned about the well-being of those around us.

MAYBE THIS WAS why she didn't tell us:

Not long after layoffs began, things started going missing from our workstations. Marcia Dwyer's handcuffs, Jim Jackers' Mardi Gras beads. At first we thought we must have misplaced these things. We had loaned them out, or maybe they'd fallen behind a bookshelf. Don Blattner ran framed movie stills around his walls, with a particular emphasis on scenes from *The Lost Boys* and *From Here to Eternity.* Larry Novotny had a collection of World Series pennants dating back to 1984. Who could say why we felt the need to display such things in our offices? For some it helped to say, Hello, this is me. Others just liked having their useless shit around in the place where they spent most of their time. When that useless shit began to disappear, we got angry.

We never suspected the cleaning crew. Those quiet souls weren't likely to risk their legal status for a paperweight and a few plastic wind-up toys. It was a marvel — never a CD Walkman, never a wallet left by accident on a desk overnight. Instead, Karen's snow globe of Hawaii. Chris Yop's gold-plated nameplate. Pictures in cheap frames of our fat parents on vacation. Things of sentimental or practical value to no one but us.

Benny's friend Roland from security worked an occasional night shift. One Friday morning during this time, Benny asked him, "So what'd you find in there?"

"Well, I looked," said Roland. "The filing cabinets first off. Nothing in them. I even looked through the file folders themselves. I looked through the bookshelves next, but there aren't a whole many books there on his bookshelf."

He was talking about Joe Pope's bookshelf. Some people had convinced Benny to have a talk with Roland, if just to see what would come of it, and Roland had taken Benny seriously.

"And I looked through his desk drawers, too," Roland continued. "There wasn't nothing there, either, except this lucky rabbit's foot."

"A rabbit's foot?" said Benny. "Let me see it."

Roland handed over a keychain attached to a rabbit's foot. Before the day was through Benny had shown it to everyone and we all said no, none of our useless shit had ever included a rabbit's foot keychain.

"Must belong to the prior occupant," Roland concluded when Benny handed it back to him.

After that, somebody who shall remain anonymous went into Benny's office; he said he had something he wanted to float by Benny. Benny got a chuckle out of it. Then the guy said, "But hold on, Benny — we're not joking. We're serious." And Benny, still chuckling, said, "Yeah, it's funny, it's clever." The guy cut him off. Benny wasn't *listening,* Benny wasn't *hearing* him. "We're dead serious," the guy said. Now Benny could see the guy wasn't kidding. "Are you serious?" said Benny. "Are you listening to me or not, Benny?" the guy asked. "We are dead, dead, *dead* serious." "Oh," said Benny. "I thought you were just joking." "No, we're not joking," he said. "We are not joking." "Who's 'we'?" asked Benny. "Benny," said the guy, "don't be so fucking dense. What do you say, are you in or not?" "You're talking about deliberately setting him up," Benny said. "As a joke!" the guy cried. "Just as a stupid practical joke!" "That doesn't sound right to me," said Benny. "Why not?" "I don't know," he said. "It's just not something I think I want to do." The guy could only clap his hands on his knees and stand up. "Okay," he said. "Suit yourself."

After the guy left, Benny called down to security. "What can I do you for, Benjamin?" asked Roland. "Look," said Benny. "I think you should stop making inspections of Joe's office. How many times have you been in there now?" Roland told him that he stopped by there every time he worked a night shift, so every Thursday night. "And have you ever found anything?" "Nothing," said Roland, "except that lucky rabbit's foot." "Listen," Benny said, "we were just kidding around one day, saying he could be the one because he's really the only guy who stays here until nine or ten at night. He makes us feel like we're not working hard enough because we don't stay here half as long as he does. But it was just a joke, Roland. He's not your guy. He doesn't want our knickknacks." "So if it's not him," said Roland, "who is it?" "Hey, Roland, you're the security man here. You should be telling me that." "But I thought you said you knew who it was." "It was a joke!" cried Benny. "A joke! It's not him!" "Well, I won't go in there anymore, then, if you're telling me I should be looking elsewheres." "I'm telling you," said Benny. "You're not going to find anything if you go in there."

A day or two after this conversation, Joe Pope went in search of a woman named Paulette Singletary. Paulette was a sweet black woman of forty or so with hair parted in the middle almost exactly like a thatched roof. She had a greeting for everyone. It might not sound like much to have a greeting for everyone, but in an office as big as ours, we saw people every day whose faces we knew better than our own mothers', yet we'd never been introduced to them. Maybe we'd sat together in a meeting or seen them at an all-agency function, but because we'd never been introduced, we averted our eyes as we passed them down the hall. Paulette Singletary was the only one among us who would stop someone and say, "You and I haven't met yet, I don't think. My name's Paulette." It might have been a southern thing. Paulette came from Georgia and retained an accent you could hear ever so faintly. With a greeting for everyone, a warm smile, and an easy laugh, Paulette was everyone's favorite. It was a challenge finding someone so universally approved, unless it was Benny Shassburger, and even Benny had his detractors.

Joe went in search of Paulette, but not finding her at her workstation he took the liberty of replacing the small piece of stained glass in his hand — an angel of blue and russet — which he knew belonged on Paulette's cube wall, because he had seen it there over a succession of weeks and months. From the minute he saw the glass glinting unexpectedly from the corner of his office, Joe knew where it belonged.

The following day, one of the new high-powered laptops went missing.

"You all are up to something," Genevieve Latko-Devine said, sweeping her finger across a good number of us, "and I think you should knock it off."

This was maybe a day or two after the stolen computer. Tough to recall if her remark — an accusation, really, a broad and mostly unfair one — came before an input, at lunch, or at the coffee bar, or maybe in an off-moment when several of us were gathered around some workstation before returning to our desks. Joe had told her how puzzled he'd been to find Paulette Singletary's stained glass in his office. He wouldn't have noticed if the door had remained open at that hour of the afternoon, but he had closed it to get some work done and there it was, catching sunlight in the corner.

Most of us honestly had no idea what Genevieve was talking about. "Oh? Was that also the case," she asked us, "when someone Sharpied *FAG* on his wall?"

"That was Joe who did that," said Karen Woo.

"Oh, give me a break, Karen. That's ridiculous and you know it."

"I don't think it's so ridiculous," said Tom.

"You guys are sick in the head," said Genevieve.

"Prove it," replied Tom.

"Okay," said Genevieve. "What about the time you decorated his office in biohazard tape?"

A few people earlier that year had gotten their hands on a roll of yellow plastic biohazard tape and given Joe's office a good dressing. Whether he ever figured out the insinuations being made by that particular tape — that as a "fag," he was a carrier of unpleasant disease — was unknown. In fact he never discussed the event. He just removed the tape from his doorway and his chair and, after parking and locking his bicycle, carried on as though nothing had happened. He didn't seek names or run to Lynn Mason. He just placed the tape in his wastebasket.

"Or," continued Genevieve, "what about the time — and this is one of my personal favorites — you locked him out of the server?"

Because all of our jobs were located on one central server, if one person had a job open on his or her computer, nobody else could open that job. It was a matter of protocol — only one person working on any one job at any given time. That way we eliminated redundancies and things of that nature. Word spread that Joe was on deadline on a project and needed access to a specific document. All it took to lock him out of that document was one person pulling it up on-screen. When Joe discovered he was locked out, he sent one e-mail, and then another, and then a third asking whoever had the document open to please close it, he was on deadline. Nobody replied. He was forced to walk around looking at everyone's computer. When he found it at last the computer's owner apologized to him, closed out of the job, then called someone else on a different floor on a faraway computer who would then open the job before Joe even got back to his desk, locking him out again. He'd return to the first guy, who would plead innocent, a half hour later he'd find the second guy, who would apologize, close out, and call someone new, starting the cycle over again. According to them, the idea was, if Joe Pope likes a late night, let's give him a late night.

"Sick in the head," said Genevieve.

First of all, we told her, we had nothing to do with Paulette Singletary's stained glass ending up in Joe Pope's office. And the whole *FAG* incident? Mike Boroshansky investigated and personally cleared every one of us of responsibility, and that included Tom Mota. Was it really so crazy, we asked Genevieve, to suggest that Joe had done it himself? Maybe he was seeking attention, or had a persecution complex. Besides, we continued in our defense, we weren't trying to excuse anyone's behavior, but Joe Pope wasn't the most social guy in the world. After-work drinks for Joe Pope? No chance. Joe, you want to grab some lunch? Forget about it.

"When was the last time," Genevieve asked us, before shaking her head and walking away, "that any of you asked Joe to lunch?"

GENEVIEVE MADE HER ACCUSATION around the same time that Karen Woo stopped by Jim Jackers' cubicle one afternoon and made her infamous announcement.

"I've just come back," she said, "from McDonald's."

It was like some kind of revelation, the way she said it. Jim looked up from whatever preoccupied Jim when he was at his desk. "Oh my god," said Karen, moving closer, taking a seat in the plastic chair beside his desk, "I have just come back —" she paused for effect "— from McDonald's."

"What's at McDonald's?" asked Jim.

In Jim's defense, it was impossible not to engage Karen when she stopped by your workstation. Her voice was a force of nature, her conversation a fast-moving rapid full of deadly churning eddies. She was like Hitler without the anti-Semitism, MLK without the compassion or noble cause. At the same time, Jim was an easy mark. He'd stop whatever he was doing and listen to just about anyone.

"Okay, I *never* go to McDonald's," said Karen. "I haven't been to a McDonald's probably since college. I wake up this morning, I have the biggest jones for a Filet-O-Fish." "That's weird," said Jim. "Isn't it?" said Karen. "*So* random. It's seven in the morning, and I have the biggest jones. So, okay, I have to wait till lunch. I make it to eleven-thirty. But it's still only eleven-thirty! I can't go over to McDonald's at eleven-thirty and order a Filet-O-Fish. That's gross." "Is it really called Filet-O-Fish?" asked Jim. "What, you think it's Fish-O-Filet?" "No, I thought it was McFilet," said Jim. "No it's not *Mc*Filet, Jim," said Karen. "That's dumb. That's seriously dumb. It's not *Mc*Filet. Will you just listen to my story? So I wait an extra half hour, it *kills* me, but I wait. I go over there. They're fucking *out* of Filet-O-Fishes. I'm standing at the counter, I'm like, *uh* . . . *uh* . . . and then I basically just fall over and die." "So what'd you order?" "No, Jim, that's not my point. I ordered nothing. I *hate* McDonald's. I'm not ordering any cow product from McDonald's, that's disgusting. I *wanted* a Filet-O-Fish." "So where'd you end up going?" Karen rolled her eyes and threw her head back in a display of monumental exasperation. "Jim," she said, "you're just not getting it. That's not my point. Will you please just listen to my story? I had to pee real bad," she continued, "so I went through the dining area to the back, and you've been to that McDonald's, right? You know that to the left is the bathrooms, and to the right is the play area. You know what I mean by the play area, right? With the McFry guys, and the cheeseburger merry-go-round and all that?" "The PlayStation," said Jim.

"PlayStation, whatever," said Karen. "No, PlayStation is the videogame," said Jim. "PlayPlace!" "PlayStation, PlayPlace — whatever, Jim. You know what I'm talking about, right?" Jim nodded. "Okay, in the PlayPlace, they have one of those netted-off areas with all the plastic balls inside. You know what I'm talking about?" "Sure," said Jim. "The pool of plastic balls." "You know it?" asked Karen. "I know it," said Jim. "So I go to the bathroom, I come out, I happen to look through the door to the PlayPlace — something catches my eye. I stop, I look. It's Janine Gorjanc." "What do you mean, it's Janine?" said Jim. "In the pool of plastic balls," said Karen. "What do you mean, *in* it?" "She's *inside* with the balls," said Karen. "Just sitting inside it. The balls up to here." "What are you saying," said Jim, "she's sitting inside the pool of plastic balls?" "*Inside* it," said Karen, "yes, with the balls up to here." "What was she doing in there?" "Sitting." "Right, but why?" "You're asking me?" said Karen. "How should I know?" "Are you sure it was her?" "It was Janine Gorjanc," said Karen. "She was sitting inside the pool of plastic balls."

The following day Karen convinced Jim to follow her to McDonald's. They ordered lunch — Karen finally got her fish sandwich — and then had a seat at a booth toward the front. Before even taking a bite, Karen said, "Be right back." When she returned, she said, "Go look."

"Is she in there?"

"Go look," said Karen.

When Jim got to the bathroom, he stared through the door to the PlayPlace but saw nothing. Nervous, he rushed inside the men's room. When he came out, however, he realized that he had all the time in the world. He stared through the door and then through the loose black netting into the darkened space where ordinarily one found children flopping around, tossing balls at one another, and grabbing hold of the netting for balance as they stalked along the ever-shifting surface of hundreds of balls. But all that wild activity had been replaced by the still, mournful presence of Janine, the same heavy and muted presence she carried with her everywhere around in the office. Jim felt it palpably even through the glass door. Not one ball stirred. Not one happy child banged about. She was not submerged, as Karen had described it for him the day before. Her legs, to the knee, were merely lost beneath the balls. It looked as if she were resting poolside, which she was, in a manner of speaking, though her motionless slump revealed none of the delight or relaxation that phrase conjured. Her elbows rested on her knees as her downcast head and rounded shoulders bent forlornly into the collection of balls gathered around her, and her grim expression made it seem that she was spilling jewel-colored tears. Jim guessed she had taken off her shoes before going in because a small black pair of women's pumps sat in front of the child-sized stairs leading up to the pool.

Jim returned to the booth and slid into his seat.

"I saw her," he said.

Karen said, "Is it not the weirdest thing you've ever seen?"

"I don't know," he said, nodding slowly. "I'm still just trying to believe it."

The next day Karen and Jim convinced Benny Shassburger to go to the McDonald's with them. They didn't tell him why, they just said there was something there that he'd want to see. They all ordered lunch. "So why am I here?" asked Benny when they sat down. "Because Janine Gorjanc —" Jim began, only to be immediately cut off by Karen. "Don't tell him!" she cried, slapping his hand. "It won't have the same impact if he hears about it before he sees it." "What am I seeing?" said Benny. "Okay," said Karen, "I want you to go to the bathroom, and on your way there, I want you to look through the door to the play area. You know what the play area is, right? Don't stare, don't open the door. Just peek through. Got it?" Benny came back and said, "What the hell is it?" "It's Janine Gorjanc," said Karen. "Yeah, I know that," said Benny. "But what is she doing in there?" Jim and Karen shrugged speechlessly. "I gotta see it again," said Benny, rising again from the booth.

He lingered at the men's room. Janine sat hunched over the colored balls with her legs submerged. She had hold of a ball and she was tossing it slowly between her hands. She dropped it and picked up another one. Then she scooped up several balls at once and spilled them out upon her lap, and some of them remained caught there as she laced her arms under her thighs and hugged herself.

Benny returned to the booth. "It's like she's a five-year-old," he said.

"Is it not the *weirdest* thing you've ever seen?" asked Karen.

On the third day they brought Marcia Dwyer with them. They went through the procedure with Marcia and when Marcia returned from the restroom she said, "Yeah, that is a little strange." "A *little* strange?" said Karen. "It's a little more than a little strange, Marcia." "You dumbasses," said Marcia, looking around at the collection of morons some random lottery had stuck her with. "She's *mourning.*" "Mourning?" said Jim. "Yeah, mourning," said Marcia. "Grieving. Ever hear of it?" "Is that what she's doing?" asked Jim. "She's mourning?" "Of *course* she's mourning," said Karen. "But who mourns like that?" Marcia replied sensibly that different people mourned in different ways. "Some people don't even cry," she said. "Some people can't stop crying. It all depends." "Yeah, but you don't seem to be getting it, Marcia," said Karen. "She's in a pool of plastic balls in the middle of a McDonald's. That's just fucking weird."

Jim begged off the next day, and so did Benny, but Karen managed to convince Amber Ludwig to eat at McDonald's with her, and with Amber came Larry Novotny. When Amber returned to the booth she was in tears. The day after that, Dan Wisdom accompanied Karen to the McDonald's. Then the weekend passed, and on Monday it was Chris Yop. On Tuesday, Reiser limped over there. No one really wanted to go. It was McDonald's, after all, and lunch with Karen was always an earful. But she was so persistent, people went just to get her off their backs. Then there was Janine, sitting in the pool of plastic balls, and everyone knew why they had come.

Over the course of the next few weeks, practically everyone made it over to the McDonald's. If Karen couldn't go, they went without her. That is to say, *we* went without her. You see, everyone was talking about it. It wasn't something you could afford to miss. You *had* to go. First you heard about it, then you had to witness it for yourself. You stood in front of the bathroom as if you had every intention of going inside, but instead you stared through the door, through the netting, and spied the unmistakable, hunched figure of Janine Gorjanc — sometimes staring off at nothing, other times addressing the balls in some way, holding them or tossing them or skimming her hands over their undulating surface. You went so that when you got back to the office, you, too, could testify that you had seen it — Janine Gorjanc in the pool of plastic balls — and what a peculiar sight it was.

JOE POPE CAME UP the elevator with his bicycle and walked it down the hall to his office where he found Mike Boroshansky, dressed in a navy blue suit coat, leaning his butt against the back credenza, and Benny's friend Roland standing with his back against the wall, waiting for him to arrive. The laptop, which had gone missing the week prior, sat on top of Joe's uncluttered desk, as did the office curios which had proven thin enough to slip between his wall and bookshelf: green license plates from Vermont, a frame of Burt Lancaster and Frank Sinatra in navy-issued uniforms gathered with others in a bar. People passing by recognized those things because they were accustomed to seeing them in different offices.

"Why don't you close the door, Joe?" Mike Boroshansky suggested. "Lynn should be down here any minute."

The whole thing was cleared up in half an hour. Not long after Lynn entered, Genevieve Latko-Devine was seen knocking at Joe's door. The usual suspect was brought in — this was several months before Tom was sacked, but he was always riding on thin ice. We could hear his muffled protestations through the paper-thin walls. They were interrupted by Benny Shassburger. To Benny's credit, he went in there of his own accord. He didn't have to go in; he could have stayed out of it. Roland never said it was he who had first suggested Joe Pope's office might be one of interest. Lynn Mason wanted to know who was responsible. "Give me a name, Benny," she said. Benny deflected her request. "It wasn't any one person, I don't think," he said. "It was more of like a zeitgeist." " 'Zeitgeist'? What's that, what's a 'zeitgeist,' Benny?" "You know," he said. "No, I don't know," countered Lynn. "All due respect, Benny, I think art directors should avoid using fancy words. If you have a name for me of who's responsible for this, I'd like you to say it." "I don't have a name for you," he said. "It was just something going around, a lot of people were talking about it. It was a joke, I thought." "Sounds like you must have a whole bunch of names for me, then," replied Lynn. "Yeah, but not one specific name," said Benny. "Honest — I don't know whose idea it was, and I don't know who did it. But I can tell you that it wasn't Tom." "I swear to god I'm not guilty of this one," said Tom. Lynn ignored him. "Next time," Lynn said, "that you tap into a 'zeitgeist' around here, Benny? The first person I'd like you to come talk to is me. Otherwise, I'll come up with a name myself, and I don't think you'll like the name I come up with. Understood?" "I understand," he said. As he was leaving, he heard her say, "Jesus Christ, these people do the stupidest shit."

"Nice to have your laptop back, anyway," said Mike Boroshansky.

"Joe," she said. "I'm sorry about this."

Joe waved it away. "What are you going to do?" he asked.

"How about we fire every fucking one of them," she said.

At noon that day, Benny said to Roland, "Man, I *told* you not to go in there anymore, didn't I? Didn't I say he wasn't your guy?" "You did," said Roland. "So why'd you have to go in there?" "It gets boring doing a night shift, Benny," Roland replied defensively. "You ever work a night shift? You do whatever you can to kill time. I didn't expect to find anything. But there it all was! What was I supposed to do then?" "Yeah, but if you would have just stayed out of there," said Benny, "none of this would have happened, and I wouldn't be in trouble with Lynn." "How was I supposed to know they were setting the guy up, Benny?"

We respected the fact that Benny hadn't named any names. It was nice to know that if one of *us* did something stupid, he would probably keep that to himself, too.

Later that afternoon we saw Joe Pope walking in the direction of the coffee bar, which is to say, our direction — there were a few of us down there enjoying a break — and we were curious: what would he order? What does the inscrutable Joe Pope have for a pick-me-up? But then he walked past the ordering place and kept coming. He stopped directly in the middle of our conversation, halting it, and we thought, Oh, shit — here it comes. He'd reached a breaking point. Our hearts started beating in our chests. We wondered in a flash — how defensive should we be? How dissembling? It was our custom to dissemble shamelessly to Joe Pope, usually in matters of whose fault this was, or what had gone wrong with that, and then after he'd leave and our sensors relocated their moral north, we'd likely feel a tinge of regret for our dishonesty. Of course he would return soon enough and, born into sin, forgetful and unreformed, we dissembled once more. But maybe we wouldn't dissemble this time. Maybe in fact we owed him an apology. The guy had been railroaded, after all — he had every reason to be pissed off. And when he began to speak, in a steady quiet voice, looking each of us in the eye, each according to our turn, and for the same length of time — "I have tried my best," he began, "not to let certain things get to me, and to deal with each of you on an individual basis, as fairly as I know how" — we couldn't argue with what he said and thought he probably did deserve an apology, though it was still far from certain that he'd get one. We'd already been upbraided by Lynn and made to feel small by Genevieve, who said, as she had on other occasions, that she was done with us forever. "My fairness comes to an end, however," Joe continued, "the minute you turn Janine Gorjanc into one of your games."

"Janine Gorjanc?" said Hank Neary, just as surprised as the rest of us to hear Joe speak her name. "Who would do a thing to Janine?"

Joe just stood there with the prepossessing silence that made us monumentally uneasy. He didn't look an inch too short just then. He didn't offer an explanation or make any threats. He wasn't there to seek redress for the wrong done to him. He just said: "No more. Don't bother her on her lunch hour. Don't stand in front of the bathroom so you can gawk. Just let the woman be."

Tom Mota had gone to Joe and told him what we were up to at

the McDonald's. Tom Mota, of all people! We couldn't believe it. Then we heard that he'd gone to Janine and told her too. After that, we had to file in there one after the other in order to apologize. Amber Ludwig, Larry Novotny, Benny and Jim. Don Blattner said something to her at a print station. Genevieve Latko-Devine called her at home. Monday came around again, and we apologized on Monday, too.

"It *is* odd," Janine admitted to us.

We told Janine that she didn't need to explain a single thing to any of us.

"No, it *is,*" she insisted. "I know it's odd. But it was one of her places. She was only nine, you know. She had her places. I still go to the Toys 'R' Us, and the Gymboree. They think I'm crazy there, too. The McDonald's people think I'm just nuts. But those are my places now, too. They became my places. I was with her when she was in those places. And I just don't know how to give them up yet. I would be there anyway, right, had she lived?"

We felt like hell. We apologized some more. We had made a spectacle of Janine's life, and of her grief, and we made a solemn vow — most of us did, anyway — that there would be no new spectacles.

— — —

TOM CLIMBED THE ROTTING RUNGS, keeping careful hold of the wooden pole's rusted handrails. The ladder's disrepair was one sign of the inattention the billboard had suffered in its remote, abandoned location so far west, where the traffic lanes narrowed from eight to four and the distance between exits stretched out to miles. But it would have been a mistake to attribute the shoddy decrepitude of the element-battered billboard to location alone. Other billboards that far west, especially those advertising the casino boats, were sturdy new metal constructions without a speck of chipped paint, some lit by twenty-four-hour spotlights. It was the goddamn vendor who deserved a lot of the blame for letting the thing go, and as he climbed, Tom puzzled over the mystery of why more wasn't made of the space. Some hustle could always be found. That Jessica Gorjanc's fourth-grade picture blown up to inhuman dimensions had been left to languish long after her actual body was put underground wasn't just cruel disregard for human suffering. It was bad business practice.

Dawn hadn't broken when he nosed his aging Miata deep into the off-road recess where a small woods grew up a hundred yards from the highway. His climb up the ladder was slow and cumbersome owing to all the supplies he carried in his backpack, including, importantly, a Thermos half-full of martinis which he had shaken briefly with ice cubes before closing the trunk and following his flashlight's lead. Crickets chirped in the sleepy dark. Survivalist tactics had taught him a nifty trick: masking tape on the base of the powerful yet compact light allowed him to hold the thing comfortably between his front teeth while he climbed, illuminating the path above him while freeing up his hands, one of which he needed to hold on to the roller. This he placed first on the scaffold once he reached the top. He lifted himself up and removed the capacious hiker's pack from his shoulders and set it next to the roller. Passing the light down the length of the scaffold, he saw the thing for what it was: three graying wooden planks affording him no more room than what was given a window washer hanging outside his window on sixty-two. Before the first pink in the sky, he unscrewed the Thermos and poured himself a drink, his bartending aided immeasurably by the Maglite in his mouth. He removed the light and took a sip.

He unpacked his supplies — two cans of white house paint, a

deep-well roller tray, two roller heads, and a telescoping extension pole. He sipped from the Thermos lid as he mixed and poured out the paint and the fumes rose up to greet him. The faint sun barely touched on him as he walked the length of the scaffold, running the roller up and down the face of the billboard, working efficiently and thoroughly to cover the girl's fading image. It had been up there a number of months, all through the bad midwestern winter and the start of the spring rains, puckered in places, bubbles of paint cracked in half. Thanks to the extension pole, he covered more than he thought he would, but he still had a good bit to go yet, so he set the roller down and finished the martini and took out a paintball gun from the backpack. He poured a second martini and then loaded the gun. From his position on the scaffold, he could see the girl's face only at a steep angle, which prevented him from knowing exactly how to aim. But he had brought with him plenty of white pellets which he had chosen to match the house paint, and as he sipped the second martini and the sky announced the beginning of another empty, interminable weekend, he walked back and forth along the planks loading and shooting, covering over the dead girl's image one bitter blot at a time, because his complaints to Jane Trimble had gotten him nowhere — and because in conversation the previous morning, Janine said she couldn't bear to look at it one day longer.

4

CARL'S EXTRACURRICULAR ACTIVITIES — AN ADMISSION TO LYNN — TOM'S CALL GETS RETURNED QUICKLY — DOUBLE AND RED — A NEW LOW — TEAM-TALK BULLSHIT — THE SOURCE — A CONVERSATION WITH CARL — LYNN IN — A CONVERSATION WITH SANDY — DEIRDRE'S NEW DOOR — LEAVE ROBBIE STOKES OUT OF IT — WILL MARCIA PLEASE JUST CALL? — KNOCK IT OFF

ONE DAY CARL GARBEDIAN lifted his computer monitor and placed it on the other side of his desk. He didn't like it there, so by the end of the day he had returned it. But in the interim he noticed how dusty the desk was, so the following morning he brought cleaning supplies from home and dusted his desk, his credenza, and his bookshelves. He stayed late and dusted the furniture in offices down the hall from his own. Marilynn was working late, of course, and he had nothing better to do, and, surprisingly, he found pleasure in the task. The next night he did the desks and credenzas in offices on other floors until Hank Neary, working late one night on his failed novel, returned from the bathroom and found Carl inside his office, dusting the legs of his chair. "What are you doing to my chair, Carl?" he asked.

Earlier Carl had taken to shielding his eyes with a legal pad during input meetings. He came into the conference room, plopped the legal pad down on the table, and squinted under the sudden light. "Jesus Christ, that's bright," he said, bringing his hand up to where the legal pad had been. He was blinking and squinting, trying to adjust, but eventually he had to resume the use of the legal pad. "Christ, it's bright in here. Can't we turn that light off?" Out of the corners of our own dimmed and puzzled eyes, we looked around at one another. Finally Tom Mota said to him, "Carl, man. It is off." And it was true — sometimes, sunlight coming in from the windows convinced us to keep the overhead lights off. Yet he kept squinting and hovering under the legal pad throughout the entire meeting.

Some time later he ran down the hall. He ran down the hall a second time. The third time it was like he was doing laps or something. A few of us were in Benny Shassburger's doorway, standing around chatting to Benny on the inside. When Carl came around again, Tom shouted out at him. "Carl! What the hell, man — what are you doing?"

Carl stopped, shaking his head breathlessly at Tom. Then, like a cat you can't reason with, he darted off again.

"What's up with him?" Benny asked.

Tom shrugged. "How should I know?"

Within the week, Carl had blacked out his windows with construction paper. The paper, if not exactly sanctioned by management or the office coordinator, was the sort of thing usually tolerated in our office, on the basis that we should enjoy a creative environment and have our quirks indulged, so that we might continue to think up clever headlines and catchy designs. On the other hand, Carl was questioned about it, and he explained that out of nowhere he had acquired an extreme sensitivity to light, producing as proof a pair of the boxy black sunglasses one typically sees only on the elderly, which he claimed he wore everywhere nowadays, including, sometimes, in the office itself. The specter of a worker's comp claim seemed to hover over the handling of Carl's delicate eyes, so Lynn Mason instructed the office coordinator to tell Carl he could keep the paper up. Then, when she had two minutes to think, Lynn went down to Carl's office.

"A sudden sensitivity to light doesn't sound healthy," she said, standing in Carl's doorway. "Maybe you need to see an ophthalmologist."

"Oh, no," said Carl.

"I don't mean to pry, Carl, but when was the last time you had a physical?"

"Oh, I don't need a physical," said Carl.

He went on to explain that if it weren't for his sensitivity to light and the occasional excruciating headache, and some dizziness and uncommon sweating, he had never felt better his entire life. "It has cleared up," he said to her, "all my thoughts of suicide."

Lynn was too taken aback by Carl's frank admission of thoughts of suicide to stop and say, What's *it?* What's cleared it up? Instead she moved from the doorway into Carl's office, shut the door halfway, and said to him, "Carl, you were having thoughts of suicide?"

"Oh, yeah," Carl said. "Oh, big time. I had done research, Lynn. I knew . . . well, I seriously doubt you want to hear all the details. But I'm here to tell you, I was prepared."

Lynn listened to him as she sometimes can, like a person being paid by the hour to do so. She took a seat on one corner of his desk and her brow was furrowed with concern as Carl told her the story of his long nights when Marilynn worked late and he was alone, how envious he was of her career choice compared to his own, and how all activity had at once lost its luster. And then he said something that gave her a sense of the depth, the incomprehensible depth of his onetime despair.

"Don't be alarmed when I tell you this," he said, "because I can promise you it has all passed, but one of the reasons — and I feel so ashamed of this — but one of the reasons I wanted to kill myself was so that she would find my body." Abruptly Carl burst into tears. "My wife," he said. "My beautiful wife! She is so loving, so good," he said, as the force of his tears began to quell. "I cannot tell you how good she is, Lynn, and how much she loves me. And you know, she has the hardest job? She sees the sickest people. They die on her constantly. But she loves them, and she loves me, and I wanted to do this terrible thing to her."

By then Lynn had come closer and put her hand on Carl's shoulder. She moved her hand gently over his shoulder and all that could be heard was his soft crying and the friction of the fabric under her hand.

"Why would I want to do that?" he asked. "For attention? How shameful. I'm terrible," he said. "A terrible person." She continued to comfort him, and after a moment, he wheeled back in his swivel chair, stood, and hugged her — he needed someone to hug. Lynn hugged back without hesitation, and likely without any regard for who passed by and saw them hugging because the door, after all, was only half-closed. They stood in his office hugging.

Lynn said, "Oh, Carl," patting him gently on the back, and by the time they parted, he had stopped crying and started to clear the tears from his eyes.

They talked a little longer, and that's when she asked him what had changed that he no longer felt the way he had, and he told her that he was finally taking medication. He didn't mention whose medication he was taking, but no matter. When she left, no doubt she realized how little she knew about the individual lives of the people who worked for her, how impossible it was to get to know them despite little efforts here and there, and she probably also felt the slightest, just the very smallest discomfort for how it seemed

Carl had hugged her for an uncommonly long time, as he had hugged so many of us during those berserk and unpredictable days.

When Tom Mota saw Carl's blacked-out windows, he knew the day had come and gone when he should have said something to someone about what he knew. He didn't want to say anything. First of all, another man's business was none of his own. Second, Carl had confided in him, and Tom had no desire to betray that confidence. And then there was a third thing, something slimy and unpleasant: a familiar, expectorant, implacable hatred. Carl had told Tom that he didn't want his wife to know that he was depressed because his wife had told him he was depressed and he didn't want her to know that she was right. Tom had had a wife who was right all the time, too, and so he could understand Carl's desire to deprive the person who loves him most the righteousness of confirmed knowledge. Tom was standing outside Carl's office gazing at the blacked-out windows when a cry came from within.

It was a howl, really, a grumbling cry of pain that erupted into a throttle. Had it not been a slow day at lunch hour, this terrible noise would have brought people out into the halls.

Tom had assumed Carl's office was empty. From where he stood, he could see no one inside. "Carl?" he said, stepping in.

Carl was laid out across the hard corporate carpet behind his desk, gripping his hair. Fists full of hair, almost yanking it from its roots, and even in the dim light, Tom could see how pinched and red the poor man's face had become. Carl did not open his eyes at Tom's approach.

Tom went back to his office, picked up the receiver, and, before putting it to his ear, as the dial tone hummed in the air, he shook his head and whispered, "Fuck."

He left his name and number for Carl's wife, who worked in the oncology department of Northwestern Memorial next door.

Then he remembered that before being sidetracked by Carl, he had been taking work down to Joe Pope, so he got up again, but before he could darken his doorway, the phone rang.

"Goddamn," he said to Marilynn, "I never had a doctor return a call so fast in my life."

"I'm worried about Carl," she explained.

"So if I was just a regular patient," Tom wondered aloud, "how long would you have kept me waiting?"

"Please tell me what's going on," she said.

He explained everything he knew — the day he'd gone into Carl's office with the book, Carl's admission that he was taking Janine's meds, the bottle with the three-month supply, everything. He told her that Hank had walked in on him dusting his chair, that he had been shielding his eyes with a legal pad during inputs, that he had jogged a half-dozen laps around the far perimeter of the sixtieth floor, and that once not long ago, he came across Carl at his desk staring with a pensive, almost scientific expression at one of his hands, turning it slowly, turning and staring at the hand as if it were a rare find or a foreign object. Then Tom said, "He's currently lying on the floor of his office, he's blacked out all his windows with construction paper. I think he needs medical attention."

Marilynn was most certainly a doctor in that she didn't waste time before grilling him on specifics. What was the medication? How long had he been taking it? Tom didn't have too many answers. The questions he liked least came last, back to back, so he didn't have a chance to answer them — they sounded rhetorical and accusatory. "How long have you known about this? How could you possibly, possibly not have said something sooner?"

"You want to know why I didn't tell you sooner?" he said. "Because I hate my wife, that's why."

Marilynn was incredulous; he could tell even over the phone.

"Because you hate your wife?" she said. "What kind of answer is that?"

Tom, ever the logician, replied, "Because she's a fucking bitch — and if you were a man doctor, I'd call her even worse."

Marilynn, understandably, must not have known how to respond to that, as a period of silence ensued.

"Look," Tom said finally, "I'm not proud of it, but when he said he was doing this without your knowledge because he hated when you were right, I could relate, because my bitch of an ex-wife is another one who's *always* right, a lot of the goddamn time, anyway — except for her taking the KIDS to fucking PHOENIX and letting them call some FUCKING PILOT FOR FUCKING UNITED *DADDY BOB,* AS IF THEY HAVE *TWO* DADDIES, *WHEN I'M THEIR ONLY FUCKING DADDY! SO THAT'S WHY! SUE ME!*"

He hung up. He collected himself. She called back.

"I just need to know," she said, "if you think he'll come in on his own, or if I need to get somebody."

"Like to restrain him?"

"He hasn't been home for two days," she told him. "I've been calling and calling. I have no idea where his head is at."

"He doesn't need restraining," said Tom. "He needs somebody to help him off the ground."

Tom went down to Carl's office and asked him if he wouldn't mind accompanying him next door to the hospital. When Carl said nothing, Tom got him to his feet and walked him over.

He was diagnosed with toxic poisoning. When we visited him, his lips were chapped and his skin looked windburned. Last we had all been together in a hospital was for Brizz. "Hope you don't end up like him, Carl," said Jim Jackers.

"Jim," said Marcia. "If you're going to make bad jokes, at least make them half-funny." She turned back to Carl. "Just ignore that idiot," she said to him. "How are you feeling?" Carl had several big white pillows behind him and he was hooked up to an IV.

"Everything looks double," he replied, "and red."

We found that exceedingly hard to respond to. Everything looks double and red? Oh, well, that'll go away, Carl. That's just a temporary side effect of *permanent brain damage.*

"Carl," said Benny, "you're going to be back on your feet in no time."

"Will I be able to play the piano?" Carl asked tiredly.

It was a measure of how odd he had been acting, and how strange some of his comments had been, that this old joke did not register, and someone replied in all sincerity, "Oh, of course you will, Carl. Of course you'll play the piano again."

"I was joking," said Carl, lifting his hands lethargically — an indication, maybe, that those hands didn't play the piano. "Hey, is Janine here?" he asked.

Everyone knew by now that Carl had stolen Janine's drugs.

"She isn't here right now, Carl," said Genevieve, who was standing across the bed from Marcia. "But she wanted me to tell you that she sends you her best."

In reality, Janine was back at the office, trying to take stock of just how many bottles Carl had gotten into. It seemed that the three-month supply of whatever he first took had not been enough for Carl, that he had diverted from the instructions on the label, and that over the course of several weeks he had returned to Janine's desk late at night, taking other drugs, and conducting an incautious and unregulated experiment on himself.

As you can witness a child who has just banged his head pause before his face slowly transforms into a sad mask of pain, we watched Carl register the news that Janine was not among us, and struggle not to cry.

"Carl, would you like us to come back later?" Genevieve asked softly. As she was bending down to him, her ear lost its hold on her hair and a strand of it spilled over and she had to put it behind her ear again with that unself-conscious grace she possessed when dealing on an everyday basis with her unearthly hair. "Carl," she said, "should we come back?"

"I wanted to tell her something," Carl said, biting his upper lip.

"Would you like me to give her a message?" she asked.

"I wanted to sing her a song."

"You wanted to sing her a song?" said Genevieve.

"I wanted to sing her a song," said Carl.

Out in the hallway we reported to Carl's doctor that he'd been saying and doing a number of peculiar things for a matter of weeks. "I have no doubt," the doctor said. "He was all over the board with those drugs and the dosages were incredibly high." He turned back to reassure Marilynn that they were getting Carl cleaned out, and that he foresaw no permanent damage. Once Carl was detoxified, they'd put him on the right medication with the right dosage, and he'd be back to his better self.

We thought that was like saying Carl would play the piano again. Did he have a better self to begin with?

Marilynn, also lab-coated and pinned with ID — she was an attractive woman with short blond hair — thanked the doctor by name. He smiled and gently squeezed her shoulder.

After he left, Marilynn turned to Tom Mota and said, "Thank you for your help."

"I won't apologize for not helping sooner," he said. "And I won't apologize for yelling at you over the phone." He was like a child in that he wouldn't look her in the eye as he addressed her. "I can't apologize for something I don't feel sorry for."

"I wasn't asking for an apology," Marilynn said, tall enough to look down on him. "I just wanted to thank you." She started to walk away.

"Do you mind if I ask you a question?" Tom said. She turned back. Tom moved toward her and got, we thought, a little close, cocking his shaved head as he tended to do when exercised. He was wearing a tan trench coat, which he must have thought made him look taller. The loose belt was hanging down. "Just out of curiosity," he said, and he made that terrible smirk. It was creepy how he insisted on staring only at her neck. "Why is it that he finds it necessary to medicate himself nearly to death? You have an answer for that, as a medical practitioner? What one person does to drive the other person to *poison* himself?" Marilynn was stunned into silence. "Just out of idle curiosity," he said, lifting his shoulders. Finally he looked her in the eye.

We couldn't believe how out of line he was. He had hit an all-time low.

"You are . . . extremely rude," she said at last, her lips trembling, "at a time my husband is very sick —"

"Oh, go fuck yourself," he said, turning away, dismissing her with both hands.

"— when all I've done —" She struggled not to break down. "— is try to help him. I *tried* to help him," she said.

"Hey, I'm just trying to understand," he said, turning around and pointing at her, "why you hate us. And why *we* hate you."

We went in to say a final good-bye to Carl — all except Tom. Lynn Mason arrived. That was surprising. "I didn't think you did hospitals," said Benny, in reference to her phobia.

"I don't do them when I'm the subject under investigation," Lynn replied. "When it's somebody else, I do hospitals." She turned to the man in the bed. "Carl, what the hell? Just what the hell?"

Her words sounded accusatory but her tone was one of tender confusion.

"I fucked up," Carl said.

He seemed to become more coherent with her arrival. It was a delicate time, given that layoffs were happening all around us, but business appeared to be set aside for the moment, and for ten minutes there we were almost a healthy functioning team again. Someone even said something to that effect — Dan Wisdom, painter of fish, who had positioned himself against the wall so as to be out of people's way. He said Carl needed to feel better soon because he was a vital member of the team. Lynn looked over at him and shook her head.

"No, let's not have any of that team-talk bullshit right now," she said. "Let's leave team-talk bullshit at the office for now and just talk about the fact that you guys, if you guys are in need of something — whatever it is, I don't care — Christ, come see me before you do something like this. Carl, for Christ's sake."

"I fucked up," he repeated.

"You gonna get better?"

"Gonna try."

"I bought you these crummy flowers," she said. It was in fact a pretty pathetic bouquet. We all thought, *Shit! We forgot flowers!* Lynn turned to Genevieve. "In-house florists at a hospital, and this is all they had."

After she left, we asked Dan if he was offended by how she had responded to his innocuous remark about the team.

"Are you kidding me?" he said. "I thought that was terrific."

SIX MONTHS LATER, Carl had recovered from toxic poisoning and was now on a regimen of antidepressants tailored personally to him. None of us could say we had noticed much of a change. Perhaps it was a victory just to see him stable. He wasn't cleaning other people's offices during his downtime, or doing laps around the hall. But on the other hand he still wore off-brand blue jeans and bad shoes and spent his lunch hour behind a closed door eating the same meal.

"Sorry to interrupt, Carl," said Amber. A few of us had come with her, and now we were standing behind her in Carl's doorway. We had elected Amber as our spokeswoman.

"That's okay," he said. "What's up?"

Amber took a step inside the office. She grabbed the back of a chair and paused. She looked back at us. We were like, "Go on. Go on!"

Finally she told Carl that Karen Woo had informed everyone that he was the source.

Carl wiped his mouth with his napkin. He shrugged. "The source of what?" he replied.

ON THE DAY LYNN MASON was scheduled for surgery, she showed up at the office.

Karen saw her first. Karen was always the first to know everything. We expected her to know everything first, just as we expected Jim Jackers to be the last to know anything. This time was no different — Lynn Mason was in the office, and Karen had been the first to see her. She had come across her in the women's room.

Genevieve was next. On her way to Marissa Lopchek's in HR, she saw Lynn standing at the window in the Michigan Room. "At first I didn't think it was her," she said, "because how could it be her? She's supposed to be in surgery. But on my way back from Marissa's, she was still at the window. She'd been there for, I don't know, twenty minutes? She must have felt me staring or something because she turned, and just as she turned I started to walk away real quick because I didn't want her to catch me staring, but she saw me anyway and said hello, but by then I was halfway down the hall, so I had to go all the way back to the doorway to say hi because I didn't want to seem rude, but by then she had turned back to the window and — oh, it was *so* awkward. What is she doing here?" she asked.

Dan Wisdom saw Lynn cleaning her office. She and the office coordinator were boxing things up in there. We asked him what kind of things and he started to list them: stock-photo books, outdated computers, long-dead advertising magazines, half-empty soda bottles. . . . It was your right and privilege as a partner to keep as cluttered an office as you wanted, and we had all grown accustomed to shifting things to the floor whenever we went into Lynn's office for a meeting. "You wouldn't recognize it," said Dan. "One of the custodians came up with a cart. He took down . . . I can't even *tell* you how many boxes full of old crap." We asked him why she was cleaning. "I have no idea why," he said. "I thought she was supposed to be in surgery."

Benny had seen her, too. Certain pockets of office space had been unoccupied for some time, workstations vacated by those who had walked Spanish down the hall. Benny found Lynn at a desk in one of the more fallow clusters of our formerly occupied cubicles.

"You know the place," he asked us, "on fifty-nine?"

We knew it by heart: all the cubicle walls barren, no radio playing, the printers off-line, and the only hope for corporate revitalization the fact that no one had yet turned off the overhead lights — we, too, had been victimized by the dot-coms. None of us liked it down there; it was too naked a reminder of the times we lived in. But if you needed someplace where you could hear yourself think and weren't likely to be disturbed, there was no better place than that deserted section of fifty-nine.

"She was sitting on top of one of the cubicle desks," said Benny, "with her legs hanging down. It was funny to see her like that. What was she doing sitting inside a cubicle? I was so surprised to see someone in there I almost jumped back. But then to look closer and see it was her? Way strange. I would have said something but, man, she was all spaced out. She was just *zonked out.* She had to have heard me, but she didn't look up. So you know what I did. I got the hell out of there."

Marcia Dwyer found her at a print station. She was standing against the wall, next to the recycling bin and the stacks of boxes holding copy paper. Marcia was there to photocopy something for the rest of us, a list of interesting facts about breast cancer found on the Internet. She greeted Lynn, and the greeting seemed to wrench the older woman out from underwater.

"What was that?" Lynn asked.

"Oh," said Marcia, "I was just saying hello."

"Oh. Hi."

Marcia advanced toward the copier. Lynn was just standing there against the wall. "Oh, do you need to use this?" Marcia asked suddenly.

Lynn shook her head.

"Oh. Okay."

She made her copies. "Bye," said Marcia, when she had finished.

Lynn looked up. "All done?"

"Yeah."

"Okay."

"I don't think I've ever had a more awkward exchange my entire life," Marcia told us. We were discussing these run-ins in Marcia's office. "What was she doing just standing there against the wall?"

"Maybe all this happened yesterday," someone suggested.

It wasn't as absurd a notion as it might sound. Some days, time passed way too slowly here, other days far too quickly, so that what happened in the morning could seem like eons ago while what took place six months earlier was as fresh in our minds as if an hour had yet to pass. It was only natural that on occasion we confused the two.

"No, it was this morning," Karen assured us. "Trust me. I saw her. Lynn's in."

"What probably happened," Amber suggested, "was that she stopped by the office to finish up some last-minute business, and then she walked over to the hospital. So she's not *in* in. She just stopped by on her way."

"Cleaning her office?" said Larry. "Standing in the Michigan Room for half an hour? That's last-minute business?"

"Maybe."

"Or maybe," said Larry, "there never was an operation."

"What do you mean, there never was an operation? Of course there was an operation."

"Because," Larry continued, "she doesn't have cancer."

"How can you say that, Larry? Of course she has cancer."

"How do you know it's not just a rumor, Amber?"

"Because I just *know*."

"Anyway," said Karen, "her operation was scheduled for nine. She couldn't have recovered in that time, so she must have missed it."

"It was scheduled for nine?" said Genevieve. "I thought nobody knew when it was scheduled for. Where are you getting nine from, Karen?"

"I always get my information directly from the source," Karen said.

— — —

WE DIDN'T HAVE much else to do, you see. We had the pro bono fund-raiser ads, sure — but what were they when compared to our workload of yore? We had already made headway on them; they would be finished in no time. The more pressing matter that morning seemed to be discovering why Lynn had chosen to come into work instead of dealing with a life-threatening illness. And so when Karen Woo told us who her source was, naturally we went in search of answers.

"I'm not the source of that information," said Carl in front of his *penne alla vodka*. He denied knowing anything about Lynn Mason going into surgery at nine. And if he had known, he wouldn't have said anything — certainly not to Karen Woo.

"But Lynn did receive a diagnosis of cancer, did she not?" asked Amber, inside his office.

"As far as I know she did," he said. "But I'm not the source of that information, either, and I don't know why Karen's saying I am — unless it's because Marilynn's an oncologist at Northwestern. But what Karen doesn't know is that I moved out six weeks ago, and besides, Marilynn wouldn't tell me anything — not if Lynn were a patient."

It was the first we had heard of Carl and Marilynn's separation. We didn't inquire further because we didn't care to pry. We asked in the most general way how he was holding up, and he replied clinically that it was the best decision for both parties. We deduced from that that Carl had probably not been the prime mover.

"I don't mean to change the subject," said Amber.

"Please do," said Carl.

"But then so you're not the source."

"The source of what?" he repeated, a little edgier this time.

"Of the fact that she has cancer."

Carl shook his head. "I first heard that from Sandy Green," he said.

— — —

SOME OF US THOUGHT Sandy Green in payroll was the second coming, others the devil incarnate — it all depended on what you were getting paid. Her office was a firetrap of put-off filing. Sandy had gray hair and wore one of those ribbed finger condoms that gives one speed in the sport of accounting. Off a remote corridor at the far end of sixty-one, her windowless office was known as the Bat Cave for its general darkness and inaccessibility. "I talked to Carl a couple days ago for about five minutes about FICA withholdings," said Sandy. "I doubt very seriously that in five minutes I would have said something to him about Lynn's cancer."

"Okay," said Genevieve, "but what we're trying to determine is if Lynn even has cancer, and if you happen to be the one who knows that for a fact."

Sandy looked genuinely perplexed — then suddenly her face ironed out and she raised her plastic finger in the air and gave it a three-time shake. "I remember now," she said. "I said something to him like, 'I would take this issue up with Lynn,' and he said, 'Okay, I'll talk to Lynn about it,' and I said, 'But you had better do it today, because . . .' But I didn't say anything more. I waited for *him* to say something. And he did, he said, 'Oh, right, I'll do it today, right.' So *that's* when I said, 'Poor Lynn,' and he said, 'Yes, it's too bad.' So he already knew. He got his information from someone else."

"But how did you get *your* information?" asked Genevieve.

"How did I get my information?"

"Yes, that's what we're trying to find out."

Sandy put her elbow on her desk, and her cheek in her palm, and there was silence as she tried to remember. "Hold on," she said. She picked up the phone. "Deirdre, was it you who told me about Lynn's cancer? Or did Michelle tell the two of us, I can't remember. Are you sure? All right, honey." There was a long pause. Sandy startled us with a wicked cackle. "Leave your mirror at home next time, honey! Okay, bye-bye." She hung up the phone and turned to us. "Deirdre tells me she told me."

— — —

DEIRDRE INFORMED US that she received her information about Lynn's cancer from Account Executive Robbie Stokes. "Oh, good," said Deirdre, "my new door's here."

With that, the building guys came in with her new door and everyone got out of their way.

— — —

ROBBIE STOKES' office was empty. He was in Account Management, and, strange for any account person, he had hung something non-Monet on the wall: a neon Yuengling sign, intended for a bar window. It hummed and flickered in the deafening silence.

Someone from inside a cubicle cried out, "Bring me the world!"

— — —

ON THEIR WAY OUT of the building, Amber and Larry ran into Robbie. "I hear you guys have been looking for me," he said. "I didn't start that rumor. I got that rumor from Doug Dion."

Larry assured Robbie that nobody was saying he started anything. We were just trying to get to the bottom of it.

"Well, just do me a favor," said Robbie, "and don't say I started it, okay? Because I don't want this to get me into trouble with Lynn."

Amber assured him we were being discreet.

"No, just leave me out of it," he demanded. "Don't even say the name Robbie Stokes."

SOME OF US RETURNED to Marcia's office and explained what we thought she needed to do.

"Are you *out,*" she said, "of your fucking minds?"

Benny happened to fall by.

"Benny," said Marcia, "listen to what these yahoos want me to do."

Dan Wisdom, painter of fish, showed up and insisted on interrupting. He said he had come across Chris Yop at a print station and told him that Lynn Mason was in fact in the office that day.

"We were just standing there," said Dan, "and he's got about fifty resumes coming out on the heavy bonded stuff, you know, the really good stuff, when I tell him that Lynn's not in surgery after all. And immediately he's like, 'But I been walking the halls this whole time!' You should have seen his face. So I ask him, 'Weren't you at least afraid security would see you?' And he says, 'Security? Security's a joke. Security never comes up here.' He makes a good point."

We all agreed he did.

"But now that he knows that Lynn's in? You should have seen how scared he was leaving the print station. Checking both ways down the hall like he was in some parody of a spy movie. It was the funniest thing I've ever seen."

"Have you ever seen *Top Secret,* with Val Kilmer?" Don Blattner asked. "Now *that's* funny."

"Hank," Marcia called out. She rolled to the side of her desk in the chair that once belonged to Tom Mota, to better see into the hallway. "Hank!"

Hank reversed in his tracks to stand just outside Marcia's office. He straightened his bulky glasses, a nervous tic of his, and they fell right back down his nose.

"Listen to what these yahoos want me to do, Hank," she said. "They want me to call the hospital, right — listen to this — and *pretend* that I'm Lynn, and say, 'Oh, I'm a little confused — something — blah blah blah — and I was wondering, was I scheduled to be in surgery today?' Yeah, I'm supposed to call up and impersonate my boss while, excuse me, we're not just going through layoffs — *and I happen to have the wrong chair* — but this is a woman who might be really sick. And they want me to call up and say, 'Oh, can you tell me, do you happen to know if I have cancer?' "

"That sounds like a bad idea," said Hank.

We tried to explain to him why it was really our only option, if we were going to know one way or another with absolute certainty.

"Under normal circumstances," said Amber, who had returned with Larry to the office and was now eating a Cobb salad from her lap, "I wouldn't think it's such a good idea, either. But if she had an appointment this morning and she didn't go, don't you think we should be worried about her?"

"Well, then, *you* make the call," said Marcia.

"I don't think —" said Hank.

"It wasn't my —" said Amber.

"No way that would —" said Don.

". . . be trafficking in rumors," said Larry. "And you'd be doing everyone a big —"

"STOP IT," said Joe Pope.

He was standing right behind Hank in Marcia's doorway and no one had noticed. Everyone turned and some got to their feet as he moved to stand just inside the office and the room went cold. "I can hear you guys from *inside the elevator,*" he said. There was a new command in his tone and his brow was menaced with possible disdain. "Now, please," he said. "Just knock it off."

5

THE UNBELIEVABLE REPORT — ON NOT KNOWING SOMETHING — CHAIRS — FURTHER DEBATE — BENNY'S OPTIONS — THINKING ABOUT BRIZZ — THE U-STOR-IT — THE YOPANWOO INDIANS — THE TRIPLE MEETING — CHANGES TO THE PROJECT — JIM ALWAYS THE LAST TO KNOW — TOM'S MOTHER DIES — SCREWY ASSIGNMENT — UNCLE MAX — JIM TAPPED — YOP'S REQUEST — WE STAND UP TO KAREN

SOMEONE PASSED AROUND a link once to a news article posted on a reputable website that we all read and talked about for days. A man working at an office much like ours had a heart attack at his desk, and for the rest of the day people passing by his workstation failed to notice. That wasn't the newsworthy bit — there are, what, a hundred and fifty million of us in the workplace? It was bound to happen to somebody. What we couldn't wrap our heads around, what made this man's commonplace death national news, was the unlikely information provided in the first sentence of the dispatch: "A man working in an Arlington, Virginia, insurance firm died of a heart attack at his desk recently and wasn't discovered until four days later, when coworkers complained of a bad-fruit smell."

The article went on to explain that Friday had passed, and then the weekend, and no one had discovered this man fallen in his cubicle. Not a coworker, not a building guy, not someone collecting the trash. Then we were supposed to believe that *Monday* came around, Monday with its meetings and returned phone calls, its resumption of routine and reinstatement of duty, *Monday* came and went, and they didn't find him then, either. It wasn't until Tuesday, Tuesday afternoon, when they all went in search of a rotten banana, that they saw one of their own dead on the floor by his desk, obscured by his chair. We kept asking ourselves how could that be possible? Surely *someone* had to come by with a request for a meeting. Someone had to come by to inquire why a meeting was missed. But no — this poor jerk was the subject of not so much as a morning greeting from one of his cube neighbors. We didn't know how that could happen.

We hated not knowing something. We hated not knowing who was next to walk Spanish down the hall. How would our bills get paid? And where would we find new work? We knew the power of the credit card companies and the collection agencies and the consequences of bankruptcy. Those institutions were without appeal. They put your name into a system, and from that point forward vital parts of the American dream were foreclosed upon. A backyard swimming pool. A long weekend in Vegas. A low-end BMW. These were not Jeffersonian ideals, perhaps, on par with life and liberty, but at this advanced stage, with the West won and the Cold War over, they, too, seemed among our inalienable rights. This was just before the fall of the dollar, before the stormy debate about corporate outsourcing, and the specter of a juggernaut of Chinese and Indian youths overtaking our advantages in broadband.

Marcia hated not knowing what might come of being caught with Tom Mota's chair, with its serial numbers that would not match up with the office coordinator's master list. So she swapped Tom's chair for Ernie's and left Tom's in Tom's old office. Even so, she was still scared that the office coordinator would look for Ernie's chair in Ernie's old office — from which Chris Yop had taken it, swapping it with his own lesser chair when Ernie retired — and discover not Ernie's serial numbers but Chris Yop's, and upon that discovery, go in search of Ernie's chair, which Marcia was presently sitting on. Sooner or later, Marcia feared, the office coordinator was bound to find out what she had done. So she felt the need to get her original chair back from Karen Woo, who had received it some months prior when Marcia took Reiser's chair when Reiser offered it to her after taking Sean Smith's chair after Sean got canned. She went to Karen to ask for her chair back, but Karen didn't want to part with her chair, which she claimed wasn't the one Marcia had given her at all, but was Bob Yagley's chair, which she had swapped with Marcia's late one night after gentle, soft-spoken Bob was let go. Bob's old office was currently occupied by a woman named Dana Rettig who had made the leap from cubicle to office less by virtue of merit than by management's perception that so many vacated offices looked bad to potential visitors. When Dana made that leap, she brought along her own chair, which had once belonged to someone in Account Management and was a better chair than Bob's, which was really Marcia's. "What was wrong with my chair?" Marcia asked her. Dana replied that nothing was wrong with it per se; she had just gotten attached to the Account Management person's chair. "So where is my chair, then?" asked Marcia. Dana told her it was probably in the same place she left it, Dana's old cubicle, but when she and Marcia walked down to that particular workstation, they found some production person fresh out of college — he looked all of fifteen — where Dana used to sit, who told them that somebody a few months back had passed down the hall only to return, pull rank, and take his chair, which was replaced by the cheap plastic thing he had been sitting on ever since. All attempts to get the fresh-faced peon to pony up a little information on who had strong-armed him out of his chair were for naught until Marcia asked him point-blank how he expected to get out of production hell and make it to Assistant Art Director if he couldn't even sketch a face on a legal pad. So the production kid made a rough sketch from memory of the man who took his chair, and when he was through filling in the hair and putting the final touches on the eyes, Marcia and Dana examined it and determined it was a dead ringer for Chris Yop. Was it possible that Yop had grown bored with Ernie Kessler's chair, walked past a chair he liked better and bullied it out from under a production nobody, and walked away with Marcia's chair, which he sat on until the office coordinator came around giving him heat and he found himself without any alternative but to take it down to Tom's office and pretend it was Tom's, so that when Marcia went in to swap Tom's real chair with Ernie Kessler's, it wasn't Ernie's chair at all but Marcia's original one that she took back with her? Did Marcia have her own chair again? "Are you absolutely sure that this is the guy who took your chair?" she asked the production peon. The production peon said no, he wasn't sure of that at all. Marcia had no idea whose chair she had. It might have been hers, it might have been Ernie Kessler's, or it might have been the chair of some indeterminate third party. The only person who knew for certain was the office coordinator, who owned the master list. Marcia returned to her office beset by the high anxiety typical of the time.

Larry Novotny hated not knowing if Amber Ludwig could be convinced that it was in both of their best interests for her to have the abortion, because he hated not knowing what his wife might do to him if the affair came to light, while Amber hated not knowing what God would do to her if she were to go through with it. Amber was a Catholic who hated not knowing a lot of the mysterious ways in which God worked. Was it possible, for instance, that God could send Tom Mota back into the office with all of God's wrath to rectify the sins Amber had committed there on desks we hoped to god were not ours?

We, too, hated not knowing the specifics of Tom's intentions to change history. Most of us thought Tom Mota was not a psychopath, and that if he had wanted to return he would have done it a day or two after being let go. He had had time to cool off now and collect his wits. But some of us remembered the way he treated Marilynn Garbedian in the hospital the day her husband was admitted for a serious illness, remembered how he smirked in his trench coat and stared at her neck, as if he were about to land a blow in that delicate place, and couldn't help thinking that that was perfectly psychopathic behavior. But to others that was just good old-fashioned misogyny. Tom was just confusing Marilynn Garbedian for Barb Mota, his ex-wife, and was taking out on Marilynn what he wanted to take out on Barb. But if that were the case, some of us argued, who was he going to take it out on next? Tom subscribed to *Guns and Ammo.* He had a sizable collection of firearms in his possession. Most of those guns, however, were collectors' items and probably couldn't even fire anymore. Well, some of us thought, what's stopping Tom from going out and buying new guns? How easy it was to visit a gun show and three days later find yourself in possession of the assault weapons ideal for a situation like the one we were envisioning. We had to remind ourselves that because of Barb's restraining order, he'd probably have to wait more like ninety days. Besides, he was on record saying those items were unsportsmanlike. "Automatic rifles, man — where's the sport in that?" he used to say. That was little relief to some. It would be unsportsmanlike to kill us with anything more than old-fashioned handguns, therefore Tom won't kill us? That was not a winning argument. Tom could have easily had a change of heart with respect to those heavier items, owing to the more recent setbacks of his failed life, and after some less-than-truthful data entry, using a shady Internet dealer, he might be taking possession of those unsportsmanlike items from a UPS man even as our debate raged. Some of us said that was absurd. Tom was not coming back. Tom was trying to move on. But others pointed out that we had had the very same conviction that Lynn Mason wouldn't show up for work on the day she was scheduled for surgery, and look how that turned out.

We hated not knowing what Lynn Mason was doing showing up for work on the day she was scheduled for surgery.

JIM JACKERS SPENT his lunch hour in the waiting room of the oncology ward at Rush-Presbyterian surrounded by some very sick people. Present also were a number of robust family members, either staring off into the distance with their arms folded, or retrieving water for their loved ones. Jim waited and waited for the doctor with whom his father had put him in touch. Jim's father sold medical equipment, and when Jim told him of his recent project, he contacted an oncologist on his son's behalf and told Jim the doctor was willing to speak with him. Jim wanted to talk to the doctor in the hopes of gaining the insight necessary to arrive at the winning concept for the fund-raiser, but at that particular hour the doctor proved too busy to spare any time, so Jim thanked the nurse and returned to the office.

He was taking the elevator up to sixty, where his cubicle was located, when at fifty-nine the elevator came to a stop and Lynn Mason got on. They greeted each other and talked briefly about Jim's shirt, which Lynn said she liked. Jim turned around and showed her his favorite feature, the hula dancer stitched on back. The dress code of any creative department will always be casual; they may reserve the right to take our jobs away, but never our Hawaiian shirts, our jean jackets, our flip-flops. Lynn said she liked the hula dancer's skirt, which Jim could make shimmy back and forth by moving his shoulders up and down. He turned around once again and demonstrated.

"I used to be a hula girl," said Lynn. "In college."

Jim turned back to her. "Serious?" he said.

Lynn smiled at him and shook her head. "Kidding."

"Oh." Jim smiled. "I thought you were serious."

"From time to time I do kid, Jim."

The elevator bell rang and Jim stepped off. He walked down the hall to his cubicle, thinking how stupid it was to ask Lynn if she had really been a hula girl.

When he got back to his desk, he began to stress out about his lack of insight into the fund-raiser ads. He was disappointed he hadn't been able to speak to the oncologist, whom he hoped would give him inspiration. He sat down but didn't know where to start. He checked his e-mail, he got up and ate a stale cookie from a communal plate in the kitchen. He came back and there it was, the same ogle-eyed computer screen. There was a quotation pinned to Jim's cube wall that read, "The Blank Page Fears Me." Everyone knew it had been mounted up there out of insecurity and self-doubt, and that there was nothing more true than that statement's opposite. But whenever Jim found himself in the position he was currently in, staring helplessly at the blank page with a deadline and a complete lack of inspiration, he looked up and read that quotation and took comfort. The blank page fears me, he thought. Then he thought, What was Lynn Mason doing in the elevator with me on the day she was scheduled for surgery?

He went down to Benny Shassburger's office. Benny was the first guy Jim went to when he had something. We all had someone like that, someone we took our best stuff to, who then typically took that information somewhere else. Benny was on the phone.

Jim went in and sat down and started listening to Benny's end of the conversation. Benny was saying something about renegotiated prices — he was trying to get the person on the other end to come down a little. He said over and over again he couldn't afford it. Jim wondered momentarily what that was all about, but then he returned to the fact that he had just shared the elevator with Lynn Mason on the day she was scheduled — and it wasn't just surgery, was it? A mastectomy, that wasn't like an outpatient sort of thing, thought Jim, where you go in in the morning and they patch you up and you're back at work by one. An operation like that takes days to recover from. He didn't know much about breast cancer but he knew that much. He wanted Benny off the phone. We accumulated days and days in other people's offices, waiting for them to get off the phone.

"That was the U-Stor-It," said Benny once he was off. "They're jacking up my fees."

"Oh, man," said Jim. "To what?"

Jim's red eyes bugged out when Benny told him the price. "Steep, huh?" said Benny. "But I don't know what else to do, man. I gotta keep it somewhere."

When we found out Benny had received a totem pole from Old Brizz, we told him he had a few easy options. Leave it for the future owners of Brizz's house to deal with — that would probably be the easiest. Or he could find a collector and they'd probably come and take it away for free. Chris Yop suggested he leave it on the corner of Clark and Addison and watch until one of the homeless carried it away in a shopping cart. Karen Woo said he should hire a stump-grinding company to go over to Brizz's and turn that totem pole into multicolored wood chips. Tom Mota liked the idea of sawing it into pieces and giving each one of us a head to decorate our offices with in remembrance of Brizz.

"Are you guys not in the least curious why Brizz had it in his backyard to begin with?" Benny asked.

Sure we were curious. But there was probably a simple explanation for it. Brizz himself had inherited the thing from those who sold him the house, or something along those lines.

"So why did he leave it to me in his will," asked Benny, "if he just found it in his backyard when he bought the place? Why deliberately leave it to me?"

One night we had drinks after work at this nearby underground sports bar. We brought together several checkerboard-cloth tables and talked around pitchers of beer in various stages of consumption. We were getting buzzed on that airless bunker's dank fumes more powerfully than on the watered-down swill they served, when Karen Woo asked if we knew what Benny was doing with his totem pole. We ran through Benny's options for her. "No," she insisted, "no, that's not what I'm asking. I'm asking if you know what he's actually doing with it."

We did not.

"He's visiting it," she said.

We asked her what she meant by that.

"He's going down to Brizz's," she said, "and spending time with it."

There were several plausible answers for why Benny would do a thing like that. It was a novelty item, and Benny got a kick out of owning a novelty item. Or he was measuring it for removal. Or he was meeting with someone to appraise it. Maybe it was worth some money.

"No, you guys don't understand," Karen said, "this isn't a onetime deal. He's been down there . . . Jim," she said, just as Jim returned to his seat after tending to some business with Mr. B. "Tell them how many times Benny's been down there to see that totem pole."

"I don't know," said Jim, shrugging his shoulders.

"You do too know, Jim — how many times?" Jim was reluctant to give up his friend. "Ten times!" cried Karen. "In a month! Isn't that right, Jim?"

We asked Jim what Benny was doing down there.

"He's just looking at it," said Jim. "It's something to look at. I got goosebumps the first time I saw it."

"The Art Institute has things in it that'll give you goosebumps, too," Karen replied. "Not many people go there ten times a month, Jim."

The following day we asked Benny if he was really going down to Brizz's to visit the totem pole. If so, we asked, why? We said Jim Jackers mentioned he'd been down there ten times in the past month. Was that true?

"I don't know, I don't count," Benny said. "What's with the third degree?"

We asked if he was going down there to meet with someone to appraise it because maybe it was worth money. Or if he was measuring it for its eventual removal. Or if he got a kick out of owning a novelty item.

"What does it matter?" he replied. "I go down there. What's the big deal?"

We didn't understand, that was the big deal. Because soon we found out that he wasn't just going down there. He was leaving direct from work. In other words, he was driving down there during rush hour. We asked him why he would brave traffic just to look at a totem pole. He mumbled something evasive and wouldn't commit to an answer. Had he given any more thought, we asked him, to what he was going to do with it when Bizarro Brizz put Old Brizz's house on the market? The sensible thing was to leave it for the future owners. Benny replied he didn't think he would do that. In that case, we wondered, what were his plans for it? Somebody mentioned there might be some real Indians out there who'd like to have their totem pole back, who would know what to do with it better than he would. Benny's response?

"Brizz gave that totem pole to me," he said. "He didn't give it to a real Indian."

That was the stupidest thing we ever heard. A month earlier, there had been no totem pole. The idea of owning a totem pole would have probably seemed totally absurd to Benny. Then Brizz leaves him a totem pole, and he's braving traffic to go visit the thing. We just wanted to know why.

"You guys need to get a life," he said.

We asked a favor of Dan Wisdom. He lived in Brizz's neighborhood. We asked Dan to take a few hours off one night from his fish paintings, drive by Old Brizz's, and find out what Benny was doing — you know, how he spent his time.

"He told us how he spends his time," said Dan. "He looks at the thing."

Yes, but it had to be more complicated than that. Get out of the car, we told Dan, and look at it with him, and then ask him what's going through his head.

"Who knows what's going through his head?" said Dan. "What's going through his head is his own business. Besides," he added, "I don't really live in Brizz's neighborhood. I do live on the South Side, but the South Side, you know, it's a big place."

We told Marcia Dwyer that Benny had had a crush on her for a long time. Just ask to go down there with him, we urged her. Tell him you want to see it. He would be thrilled to have you join him. Then ask him why he's become so obsessed with the thing.

"Okay, first of all," Marcia said, "you guys are losers. And second of all, I don't really care what he's doing down there. Maybe he's finding out something about himself. Maybe — and I know, this sounds crazy to you guys — but maybe he's looking for something. A signal from Brizz. Some sort of sign."

We had forgotten that Marcia was into Buddhism in a big, sloppy way — reincarnation, the laws of karma. Religious fancies she probably didn't know the first authentic thing about.

"And third," she said, "Benny Shassburger has a crush on me?"

We're not sure what you may or may not know, we said one day when, happily, we stumbled upon Benny's father, waiting for Benny in the main lobby. Some of us recognized him from the picture in Benny's office, an imposing man with beard and skullcap. But about a month ago, we said to him, his son was given an odd little bequest by a guy who used to work here. Did he know what we were referring to?

"The totem pole?" his father asked.

Yes, the totem pole. And did he also know that during the past six weeks, Benny had gone to the guy's house a dozen or more times? After work, when he had to sit in traffic, he went all the way down to 115th Street to look at the totem pole. We asked him if he was aware of that.

"I knew he went down there." His father nodded. "I didn't know it was that many times, but I knew he went down there, sure. I've been down there with him."

He had been down there with him?

"Sure."

And what did the two of them do while down there?

"We looked at it," said Benny's father.

That was it? All the two of them did was look at it?

"Well, then we put on our headdresses and prayed for corn. Is that what you're looking for?"

No doubt we had the right man. That was a response that

would have come from Benny Shassburger's own mouth in the days before he clammed up and refused to say a word about why the totem pole had such a hold on him and drove us crazy with his secrecy. We asked Benny's father if he was at all curious about why someone Jewish like Benny would become obsessed with a pagan artifact like a totem pole.

"If you're asking me, does my son pray to it," his father replied, with a change in tone, "I don't think he prays to it. I just think he likes it."

Yes, we said to Benny the next day, we had a conversation with his father. No, we never asked him if Benny prayed to it. We didn't mean to offend anybody. We just want to know, we said to Benny, honestly, we just want to know why you go down there to look at the totem pole so often, and what you're thinking about when you're down there.

"I go down there," he replied simply, "to think about Brizz."

So it was funny. While Benny was thinking about Brizz, we were thinking about Benny. What could Benny be doing down there in Brizz's backyard, what is he thinking about standing in front of the totem pole — that's what we were wondering. And Benny, he was wondering — well, what, exactly? What was there to think about with respect to Brizz? His cigarettes, his sweater vest, his conversation with the building guy, and all the unmemorable days he spent in our company. That takes about ten seconds. Where do you go after that? What more was there to think about?

"Look," said Benny, reaching the limits of his patience. "I didn't purchase the thing. I didn't put it in my backyard. I'm just visiting it. What would you have done to Brizz if you'd found out he had a totem pole in his backyard, and when you asked him why, he refused to tell you?"

Hound him, threaten him, torture him, kill him. Whatever it took.

But the point wasn't Brizz. We weren't going to get any answers from Brizz. Brizz was gone. Benny, on the other hand, was still alive. Benny could tell us what we wanted to know.

"I'll never tell you," he said. "It's a secret I share with Brizz and you scumbags can't know about it."

"Has Benny gone insane?" Karen asked Jim.

Inexplicably Benny gave us all ten dollars. He went from office to office, cube to cube, handing out ten-dollar bills. What's this for? we asked him.

"A refund," he said. "I don't want your blood money."

Turns out he was returning the ten bucks he'd won from each of us when he put Brizz on his Celebrity Death Watch.

"He's gone insane," said Jim.

Bizarro Brizz finally put Brizz's house on the market, and now the situation, we thought, had to change. There would be no backyard for Benny to visit anymore. There was no — what would you call it? — memorial site, or whatever, to spend time at, and to reflect upon the recently departed, and all the mysteries Brizz left behind, or whatever else Benny was chewing on down there. Naturally we thought he would give it up. He would either leave it for the future owners, or give it away, or have it appraised, or hire a stump-grinding company to dispose of it. Instead, he hired a moving company to transfer it out of the backyard into the largest unit available at the U-Stor-It facility at North and Clybourn, where he kept it in bubble wrap horizontally upon the cement floor, because it was too big to fit inside his apartment.

When we heard Benny was not getting rid of the totem pole but had chosen to keep it, even going so far as to store it at great personal expense, we kept asking him why. Why, Benny? Why? Benny, why? When he continued to refuse to tell us — or perhaps he just found himself unable to explain his reasons even to himself — we let the full force of our dissatisfaction be known. We did not like not knowing something. We could not abide being left in the dark. And we thought it was the height of hypocrisy for Benny, who was always telling everyone about everyone else, to try and keep a secret from us. So we took up squawking at him. We did mockeries of ceremonial dances in his doorway. The worst thing we did was take scissors to this old toupee Chris Yop had in his basement, and put the mangled thing on Benny's desk, which Karen Woo doused with a bottle of fake blood she kept in her office, so that what lay on the desk looked like a fresh scalping. Someone suggested we find a yarmulke to put on top, but we all sort of agreed that to marry those two atrocities together would be stepping over a line.

In our defense, it was Chris Yop and Karen Woo's idea, the fake scalping, and they were really the ones who went in and executed it. Hank Neary said it best when he said, "Yeah, that was really just a Yop and Woo production." We picked up on that, and afterward, it became the name of the tribe Benny belonged to, the Yopanwoo tribe. We said, Hey, Benny, how do you and the Yopanwoo stay warm in the winter? Have you and the Yopanwoo received restitution from the U.S. government, Benny? Your fellow tribesmen, Benny, do they consume firewater to excess? Benny just smiled at these jibes and nodded his head amiably and returned to his desk, and without a word of explanation, continued to store Brizz's totem pole for three hundred and nineteen dollars a month.

On the afternoon Lynn Mason should have been recovering from surgery, Benny discovered they were raising the price of his storage unit by thirty bucks. That in and of itself was not outrageous, but compounded with the rest, he was shelling out a preposterous monthly sum.

"It's time I get rid of it," he said to Jim. "It's not doing anything except sitting in there."

Jim was chomping at the bit to tell Benny his news of riding the elevator with Lynn Mason when she should have been at the hospital. But he was surprised to hear that Benny was thinking of giving up the totem pole.

"You've always said that Brizz gave that totem pole to you for a reason," he said. "Now you're talking about giving it up?"

"What choice do I have?" Benny replied. "I can't spend three hundred and fifty bucks a month on a totem pole. That's insane."

"It wasn't insane at three-nineteen?"

"No, it was insane then, too," said Benny. "By the way, you want to know how much it's worth? I had an appraiser look at it. On the antiques market, this guy tells me, it could sell for as much as sixty thousand dollars."

Jim's jaw dropped. He let out a few choked grunts of disbelief.

"Oh, and here's another thing," said Benny. "Lynn Mason's in the office today."

Jim's expression turned from incredulity over the worth of the totem pole to disappointment at hearing from Benny the very news he had been waiting patiently to reveal himself.

"Aw, man!" he cried. "I wanted to tell you that!"

Joe Pope suddenly appeared in Benny's doorway carrying his leather day planner.

"Guys," he said, "we're meeting down at the couches in ten minutes."

———

A TRIPLE MEETING was bad news. Especially if it came so quickly on the heels of a double meeting. The announcement of a triple meeting could only mean the project had been canceled or postponed, or changed. We had ten minutes to ruminate on which was the worst fate. If canceled or postponed, our only project went away, and with it, all hope of looking busy. Looking busy was essential to our feeling vital to the agency, to mention nothing of being perceived as such by the partners, who would conclude by our labors that it was impossible to lay us off. (No need to look too closely here at the underlying fact that our sole project was pro bono, and so something we weren't getting paid for.) If the project was changed, the work we had put in so far on our concepts would all be for naught. That was always a pain in the ass. As much as we loved a double meeting, we always approached a triple meeting with trepidation and discomfort.

And for good reason this time. After detours to the restroom, to the coffee bar for a pick-me-up, to the cafeteria for a can of pop, we shuffled down to the couches to hear the bad news. We were no longer developing ads for a fund-raiser.

Joe sat on a sofa and tried to explain. "Okay, here's the thing," he said. "It's not really an ad for anything anymore." He immediately retracted that and said of course it was an ad for something. Or rather it was an ad for *someone.* But no, in the traditional sense of an ad, it wasn't really an ad. Of course it was an *ad,* but more in the spirit of a public service announcement.

"I'm not doing a very good job of explaining this," he said. "Let me start over. What the client wants from us now is an ad specifically targeted to the person diagnosed with breast cancer. We're no longer reaching out to the potential donor with a request for money. We're talking directly to the sick person. And our objective," he said, "is to make them laugh."

"Make them laugh?" said Benny. "I don't understand."

"Neither do I," said Jim, from the floor.

"You come up with an ad," said Joe, "that makes the cancer patient laugh. It's that simple."

"What are we selling?"

"We're not selling anything."

"So what's the point?"

"Think of it — okay," he said, sitting forward and putting his elbows on his knees. "Think of it as an awareness campaign, okay? Only you're not making the target audience aware of anything, you're just making them laugh." When that still made little sense, he added, "Okay, if we're selling something, we're selling comfort and hope to the cancer patient through the power of laughter. How's that?"

"That's an unusual product," Genevieve remarked.

"It is an unusual product," he agreed. "We have no product. We have no features or benefits, we have no call-to-action, we have no competition in the marketplace. We also have no guidelines on design, format, color, type styles, images, or copy."

"What *do* we have?" she asked.

"We have a target audience — women suffering from breast cancer — and an objective — to make them laugh."

"Why did the project change?"

"I don't know," he said. "Lynn just forwarded me the e-mail with the changes and asked me to pass them on to you."

"Who's paying for the ad now that it's no longer for a fundraiser?" asked Dan Wisdom.

"Good question. Same people, I think. The Alliance Against Breast Cancer."

"Joe," said Karen, "how come I can't find any presence for this 'Alliance Against Breast Cancer' on the Internet?"

"I don't know," he replied. "Can't you?"

Karen shook her head. "There are charities, institutes, research centers, and about a thousand alliances, but none with the name 'Alliance Against Breast Cancer.' "

Joe suggested that Alliance Against Breast Cancer might be some kind of umbrella group of regional organizations, each of which had their own website.

"So what are we supposed to do now with the fund-raiser concepts that we already have?"

"Shelve them."

"Well, that blows," said Karen.

"It's not like we had anything good anyway," said Larry.

"We did, too, Larry. We had 'Loved Ones,' okay? Joe, when did this change occur?"

"Like I said, Lynn just forwarded me the e-mail."

"I thought Lynn was off today."

"Change of plans, I guess."

"So everybody knows that Lynn's in today?" said Jim, looking around at us. "How come I was the last to know?"

"Because you're an idiot," said Marcia.

"Okay, guys," said Joe. "Let's get to work."

— — —

HEADING BACK FROM the couches, knowing we had to toss out our ad concepts for the fund-raiser and start over again in the disagreeable hours of the afternoon — which tended to stretch on and on — we felt a little fatigued. All that work for nothing. And if we happened to cast back, in search of edification, to days past and jobs completed — oh, what a bad idea, for what had all that amounted to? And anticipating future work just made the present moment even more miserable. There was so much unpleasantness in the workaday world. The last thing you ever wanted to do at night was go home and do the dishes. And just the idea that part of the weekend had to be dedicated to getting the oil changed and doing the laundry was enough to make those of us still full from lunch want to lie down in the hallway and force anyone dumb enough to remain committed to walk around us. It might not be so bad. They could drop food down to us, or if that was not possible, crumbs from their PowerBars and bags of microwave popcorn would surely end up within an arm's length sooner or later. The cleaning crews, needing to vacuum, would inevitably turn us on our sides, preventing bedsores, and we could make little toys out of runs in the carpet, which, in moments of extreme regression, we might suck on for comfort.

But enough daydreaming. Our desks were waiting, we had work to do. And work was everything. We liked to think it was family, it was God, it was following football on Sundays, it was shopping with the girls or a strong drink on Saturday night, that it was love, that it was sex, that it was keeping our eye on retirement. But at two in the afternoon with bills to pay and layoffs hovering over us, it was all about the work.

— — —

YET SOMETHING HAPPENED that afternoon that made it hard to concentrate. Benny Shassburger called Joe into his office to inform him he had received an e-mail from Tom Mota. The subject line read, "Jim tells me you're doing some pro bono cancer ad."

"So he's been in touch with Jim, too?" asked Joe, taking a seat across the desk.

"Apparently. Like I said, I only got this a few minutes ago."

"Read it to me."

Benny turned to his computer. "It's kinda long."

"That's okay. Read it."

"Okay. He starts off, 'So Jim tells me you're doing some pro bono cancer ad over there. YEEE-HOOO! I'm free!!! But as you aren't, for what it's worth, I thought I'd tell you the story of my mother's cancer, and you can use it if you want. My mother was one mean bitch. When she wasn't being a mean bitch, she was being deaf and mute. And when she wasn't being deaf and mute, she was crying in the bathtub. And when she wasn't crying in the bathtub, she was sharing a bottle with Mr. Hughes. Let me tell you, that there was one slimy glass-eyed fuck, Mr. Hughes. Anyway, those are my four memories of my mom. She looked like Rosie the Riveter — you know the woman I'm talking about, who wears the bandana and says "We Can Do It!"? It was the unsmiling face they shared. But that's where the similarity stopped because my mom couldn't do anything and she had Xs over her eyes like in a cartoon of someone dead. I never bought her a Mother's Day card but I'm sure they never wrote one for her either. Can you imagine? "Happy Depressive's Day, Ma. Love, Tommy." But then she started to die. None of us wanted a THING to do with her. I got one brother on a ranch in Omaha, he didn't want her. I got another brother in Newport Beach in Orange County, California — they only want their red convertibles and their yachts out that way, rich fucks. Anyway, my sister, she was doing my mom one better in the Tenderloin. That's a little piece of paradise full of whores and drunks in San Francisco. No way SHE could have taken the old lady in. (My sister's a whole different story. I'll tell you about her sometime.) So anyway, my mom was still in the same apartment we grew up in — imagine living your whole goddamn life in the same two rooms in Romeoville. Me being about six miles from there, I had to be the one to go pick her up and bring her over to the house. BUT NOT

THOSE FUCKING CATS! NO WAY. NO CATS. Barb couldn't believe that my mom was on her deathbed and I didn't want a thing to do with her. But that's because she never knew the woman when she was throwing dishes at the wall in her goddamn robe. The point I'm trying to make here is that it was Barb who convinced me to go over there and get her, and man, just between you and me, Benny, I REALLY, REALLY fucked things up, to be honest with you. With Barb, I mean. Don't you think you and I should get together and have a beer? I miss her and I'd like to talk about it. Anyway, we put my mom up in the attic until she died and eventually she did die and it was even painful to watch. She absolutely refused to go to the hospital and then she refused to sit up for the home nurse we hired. But then, I couldn't believe THIS. She asked for a priest. I had no idea she had a religious bone in her body. So we brought in a priest and if I could only tell you what it was like to watch my mom hold a priest's hand. She was pretty out of it by then, without her dentures and looking like HELL. I felt sorry for whatever Higher Power was about to receive her but I also have to admit that I felt some envy for how God or whatever could convince her to hold the hand of His servant when I couldn't even recall the last time she'd held MY hand, if ever. And that's because she was a mean bitch, but also because her father was a drunk and an abusive son-of-a-bitch and all of THAT daytime talk-show psychology. Anyway, I'm getting ahead of myself, because before she asked for the priest, between the time I picked her up in Romeoville (WITHOUT CATS) and the time she lay dying in the attic, I sat with her after I got home from work and we would watch Wheel of Fortune together. And while we were silent and just watching TV, it was more than I remember us ever doing together when I was a kid. We'd watch Wheel of Fortune while Barb made dinner downstairs, and over four or five months I saw how no matter what kind of a mean bitch you have for a mother, it's tough to watch her die, because ovarian cancer is a much meaner bitch than any bitch it ever consumes. It just WASTED her, Benny. I did not even recognize her. She looked more like the skeleton in your office than my mom. Man did I cry when she died. I kept asking Barbara WHY, WHY was I crying? And she kept saying, of course you're crying, she's your mom. But WHY? I hadn't talked to her in ten years. And I didn't give one fuck about her. But then you see someone just WASTE like that. And if there is ONE THING I wish I could take back, ONE THING in my entire life I wish I could do differently, it would be when we were going through all that shit during the divorce when I REALLY lost it one time and I just screamed at Barb, I HOPE OVARIAN CANCER EATS YOUR CUNT! I didn't mean it. I'm ashamed of it now. No, that doesn't even half describe it. You're the only one I've told that to. Can you tell me WHAT THE FUCK I WAS THINKING? Man oh man oh man. Anyway. Use any of this in your ads if you want, and hello to all those fucks. Tom.'"

That e-mail got forwarded around pretty quickly, and some of us felt vindicated. He was talking about having a beer with Benny, and how he regretted the awful thing he had said to Barb. Those weren't the ravings of an imminently homicidal former employee seeking to even a score. Even Amber, though horrified by practically everything he had written, reluctantly agreed that it might have indicated a more stable person than the one she had imagined moving in and out of Tinley Park gun stores since the day he walked Spanish. One thing she couldn't let go of, however, was wanting to know just exactly what Tom had done with his mother's cats.

"Did he just leave them behind when he went to pick her up?" she asked. "He didn't just leave the cats in the apartment, did he?"

She wanted Benny to e-mail him back to inquire about the fate of the abandoned animals, but nobody else thought that was a good idea. "But what happened to them?" she persisted.

"Oh, will you just shut the fuck up about the goddamn cats, Amber?" said Larry.

We knew there was some domestic tension between the two, owing to the ongoing abortion debate, but nothing on the order of that. Trouble in paradise, folks. Those of us in Amber's office at the time departed it hastily.

— — —

JOE WENT DOWN TO Jim's cubicle to ask what he'd heard from Tom. "Building security asked us to relay to them any communications that we might get from Tom," he told Jim.

"I didn't know that," said Jim. "Nobody told me that."

"Don't sweat it. Just be sure to forward the message to Mike Boroshansky."

"Why am I always the last person to know anything around here?" he asked Joe. Joe didn't have an answer for him. Jim squared himself to his computer and opened Tom's e-mail. "You really want me to read this to you?"

"Please," said Joe. "First tell me what the subject line says."

"The subject line," said Jim. "It says, 'I Need a Wetter Mare.'"

"I'm sorry. It says what?"

"That's what he wrote. 'I Need a Wetter Mare.'"

"Is that some private thing between you and Tom?"

"'I Need a Wetter Mare'? No, I don't know what the hell that means. What could that mean? How the hell should I know?"

"Jim, relax. Go ahead and read me the e-mail," said Joe.

"'Smalls — remember when we shot that laundry detergent commercial? I'm talking about the one of all the guys playing a game of football, and bringing home their grass-stained clothes to their loving wives? Well, they weren't really landing on the grass when they were tackled, were they? They were actors. We laid mattresses down for them. They were landing on mattresses! Gotcha, TV America! But anyway, my question to YOU, JIMBO, is this: when Captain Murdoch throws his grenades at the BAD GUYS, and the BAD GUYS go leaping up, do those BAD GUYS have mattresses, too? Wouldn't it hurt, JIMBO, to have a grenade explode and to be NOWHERE NEAR a mattress?' "

When *that* got forwarded, we just thought Tom was having a good time with his old friend Smalls. Convincing Amber of that, of course, was impossible. It sent us right back to square one with her. She even pressed and pressed until we were forced to agree that at the very least, the variance in tone between the two e-mails indicated that Tom Mota had his bad hours along with his good.

AFTER LEARNING OF THE CHANGE to the project, Genevieve stepped out of the office and walked down Michigan Avenue to the Borders near the Water Tower, where she purchased a few books. She came back to the office and started reading. Halfway through a breast cancer survivor's memoir, she was interrupted by Joe. "Hey," he said, knocking on her open door.

"Oh, this stuff is just *way* too emotional," she said. "Oh, I have to stop reading it." She put the book down. She stretched her face out and ran her fingers under her eyes to dry them. "Oh," she said. She took a deep breath and sighed.

"You okay?" he asked.

"Yes. I'm okay."

"I just stopped by to make sure you were clear on what we're doing."

They were a team, Joe and Genevieve, copywriter and art director, and they worked together in greater harmony than the majority of other teams. "I guess so," she said finally. "Although to be honest, I can't imagine coming up with anything."

He moved inside and sat down across from her. "Why not?"

"So I'm reading this memoir, right?" she said, lifting the book off her desk and setting it down again. "And basically it's all sadness. It's panic, fear, anguish, a lot of bravery. There's some crying. Everyone in the family is wonderful. The woman's brother quits his job to take care of his sister. He's a saint. The woman is a hero. Because there's nothing but bad news for her, and then more bad news. But every once in a while there's a little dollop of humor. Without it, trust me, you'd kill yourself reading it. Like the brother comes in, right. The woman has just found out like two pages earlier that her cancer's not responding to the treatments. Then the brother comes in — he's shaved his head so she won't be the only one who's bald. He comes in wearing a big, bushy blond wig, and the woman just dies laughing for how ridiculous he looks. And you die, too, it's such a relief. But of course midway through laughing, she breaks down into tears for how much she loves him, how good he is to her — I mean, he's just her *brother,* for god's sake. He isn't required to, to . . . oh, and here I go again," said Genevieve, returning her fingers to just below her eyes. She let out a long sigh. "The point I'm trying to make," she said, grabbing a tissue forcefully from a box on the desk, "is that there is really very little humor in a diagnosis of cancer. And what humor there is, is humorous only in the context of a whole lot of sadness. Now, how can we be expected to do that with a stock photo and a ten-word headline?"

Joe sat back in the chair. "Yeah," he said. "I agree."

"You do?"

No one ever expected Joe Pope to say something was hard because, when it came to thinking up ads, the guy was something of a savant.

"Make the cancer patient laugh," he said, and his voice got quiet. "Isn't this assignment a little screwy?"

THE IMPORTANT THING was that it was *our* screwy assignment, and it was all we had. By late afternoon Genevieve had finished her memoir, while Hank Neary, combing carefully through Internet sites, could soon pass himself off as a practicing oncologist. Benny Shassburger took the opposite approach. He found a stock photo of a beautiful woman draping herself across the red felt of a pool table. He doctored it in Photoshop by covering her breasts with surgical masks. That, he thought, was a brilliant image. The cancer patient would really laugh once he had the right headline in place. Two hours went by before he condemned the brilliant image to the dustbin of bad ideas and moved himself down to the coffee bar for a late-afternoon latte.

Jim Jackers got on the phone and started calling people. With no inspiration and frightened by the blank page, his only recourse was the imaginations of other people. He caught his mother, a librarian, at the checkout desk of the Woodridge Public Library.

"Let's say you have breast cancer," he began.

"Oh, Jim," she whispered, "please let's not even think about it."

She quickly changed subjects, asking him what he wanted for dinner. His mother was a sensitive and superstitious woman who believed even the most casual mention of disease was a morbid flirtation with death that conjured bad luck and evil spirits and should be avoided at all costs. He should have known better than to call her first.

"Let's say you have breast cancer," he said next to his father. "What's funny about it? How do you want to be cheered up?"

His father gave it a second's thought. "Call me up with a scenario where I have breast cancer and you ask what's funny about it," he replied. "That should do the trick."

"I'm serious, Dad," Jim urged him. "What's funny about breast cancer?"

"What's funny about it? Son," he said. "Very little."

He tried to explain the assignment to his father but his description was a muddled briefing of the morphing project, and it ended with Jim saying he'd have to get back to him with certain details. "Sounds to me like you need to figure out what the hell's going on over there," said his father.

"Well, it's a confusing assignment."

"Talk to your great-uncle about this," his father suggested. "I imagine he'd be a good resource."

Everyone knew that Jim's creative coup d'état came from a suggestion from his great-uncle Max, who lived on a farm in Iowa. According to Jim, his uncle had Mexicans running the farm while his days were spent in the farmhouse basement reconstructing a real train car from scratch, which was the only thing he had shown any interest in since the passing of his wife. He traveled to old train yards collecting the parts. When someone asked him at a family function why he was doing it, his answer was so that no one could remove the train car from the basement after he died. When it was pointed out to him that the boxcar could be removed by dismantling it, reversing the process by which he had constructed it, Jim's great-uncle replied that no Jackers alive was willing to work that hard at anything. Picturing this ornery farmer at his lunatic task, lost in the rural delusions of grief and old age, we probably laughed a little too hard, spurring Jim to defend his uncle's singular hobby.

"What?" he said. "It's like Legos, but for adults."

That only made us laugh harder.

"The man lost his wife," he said.

Jim was so desperate one day to come up with inspiration for an ad, he exhausted his traditional list of people, broke down, and called his uncle Max. "You know how when you buy a new car," he began — and immediately Max interrupted him.

"I haven't bought a new car in thirty-five years," said Max.

Jim suspected then that this was probably not a man with his finger on the pulse of the buying public. Patiently he tried explaining his assignment. When people buy a new car, he said, they usually have an image of themselves that corresponds to the car they buy. Jim wanted to know from Max how Max would want to perceive himself when purchasing a new ink cartridge.

"Ink cartridge?"

"Yeah," said Jim. "You know, for your printer."

"Uh-huh," said Max.

We had a client at the time whose marketing objective was to make their customers feel like heroes when purchasing one of their ink cartridges. Our charge in every communication was to inspire the potential buyer with the heroic possibilities of man-using-ink-cartridge.

"I want to see myself as Shakespeare," Max said. "What's this for, anyway?"

Shakespeare, thought Jim. Shakespeare. That's not bad.

"It's for a client of ours," he said. "They make printers and ink cartridges and that sort of thing. I'm trying to come up with an ad that makes you want to buy our specific ink cartridge after you see our ad because it inspires you and makes you feel like a hero. Will you tell me more about wanting to feel like Shakespeare?"

"So you're trying to sell ink cartridges?"

"That's right."

Another long pause. "Do you have a pen?" his uncle asked. He began to quote: " 'It was the best of times, it was the worst of times, it was the age of wisdom, it was the age of foolishness, it was the epoch of belief, it was the epoch of incredulity . . .' "

Finally Jim reached out for a pen. He tried to keep up with him. At a certain point, Max stopped quoting and told Jim the lines should start to fade out, gradually at first, eventually disappearing altogether. Then he suggested the headline: "A Great Writer Needs a Great Ink Cartridge." The small print could explain how, if ink cartridges had been used throughout time, the history of literature might have been at stake using a cheap ink cartridge.

Not only was Jim startled that his uncle could quote what he thought was Shakespeare seemingly off the top of his head; he was floored by the speed and ingenuity of his advertising abilities. Who was a greater hero than Shakespeare? And the person encountering the ad that his uncle had just pulled out of his ass could immediately put himself in Shakespeare's shoes. Max had just made a million Americans feel exactly like Shakespeare. He told Max he'd missed his calling. "You should have been a creative," he said.

"A creative?" said Max.

Jim explained that in the advertising industry, art directors and copywriters alike were called *creatives.*

"That's the stupidest use of an English word I ever encountered," said Max.

Jim also told him that the advertising product, whether it was a

TV commercial, a print ad, a billboard, or a radio spot, was called *the creative.* Before he hung up Jim asked Max for two more examples of great pieces of literature, suspecting that an entire campaign could be generated from Max's concept. He went down to Hank Neary's office — Hank was just then engrossed in a printer manual. "'The best of times, the worst of times,'" he said. "That's Shakespeare, right?"

"Dickens," said Hank. *"A Tale of Two Cities."*

"And what about 'To be or not to be'? Shakespeare?"

"Shakespeare," said Hank. *"Hamlet."*

"That's what I thought," said Jim.

Sometime later that afternoon, Max Jackers surprised Jim by calling him back. "You folks over there," said Max, "you say you call yourselves *creatives,* is that what you're telling me? And the work you do, you call that *the creative,* is that what you said?" Jim said that was correct. "And I suppose you think of yourselves as pretty creative over there, I bet."

"I suppose so," said Jim, wondering what Max was driving at.

"And the work you do, you probably think that's pretty creative work."

"What are you asking me, Uncle Max?"

"Well, if all that's true," said the old man, "that would make you creative creatives creating creative creative." There was silence as Max allowed Jim to take this in. "And that right there," he concluded, "is why I didn't miss my calling. That's a use of the English language just too absurd to even contemplate."

With that, Max hung up.

JIM TOOK HIS FATHER'S advice and called Max about the breast cancer ads. When Max picked up, Jim asked him to imagine that he was a woman recently diagnosed with the disease. As the words "breast cancer" escaped his mouth, Jim had the conviction once again that he'd called the wrong man. Max had come through for him in the past, but what did a man who'd spent his entire life working a farm in rural Iowa know about a predominantly female disease? Still Jim persevered while Max remained silent on the other end. He wanted to know what Max, as a woman with breast cancer, might find funny if he were, say, flipping through a magazine at a doctor's office. Still more silence from Max, so Jim explained further that this woman was probably impatient for her name to be called, her mind was probably half on other things, but when she came across the ad, she stopped and read it and it made her laugh. "What we're looking for is what's funny about it," he said. Then he stopped talking and put the ball in Max's court.

"What's funny about what?" Max finally said.

"What's funny about breast cancer," said Jim. "Not breast cancer per se, you know, but what's funny to somebody with breast cancer flipping through a magazine."

Max cleared his throat. "Jim," he said, "do you recall a sweet old gal, just the salt of the earth, probably the sweetest woman you ever met in your life, by the name of Edna?"

"Edna," said Jim. "Edna . . . Edna. . . . No, I don't think so, Uncle Max."

"You don't remember your aunt Edna?"

"Oh, *Aunt* Edna. Of course I remember Aunt Edna, Uncle Max."

"Edna died of breast cancer," said Max.

"She did? Aunt Edna?"

Now Jim realized why his dad had suggested he call Max. It wasn't because of Max's marketing wit. It was because Max's wife had died of the disease. Suddenly Jim realized he should have approached things differently. His phrasing might have been a little cavalier. "Uncle Max, I'm sorry," he said. "I guess I didn't remember how Aunt Edna died."

"It sounds to me," said Max, "that you don't know much of anything on the subject."

"I remember the funeral," said Jim. "I was seventeen."

"They don't typically sit in the waiting room flipping through magazines," said Max. "Their minds aren't *half* on something else."

"You see, we're . . . we're doing this, uh, a pro bono campaign," Jim stuttered.

"But there ain't nothing funny about it," said Max, "that I ever saw."

"And what we're trying to do is, we're just trying to lift their spirits a little."

"And there ain't nothing left to say in this conversation."

— — —

"WELL, I'M TAPPED," said Jim, when he made it down to the coffee bar.

"It's an impossible assignment," Benny agreed, pulling a stool out for him.

"I got a few ideas," said Marcia, taking possession of a chai latte from the barista. "Thanks," she said, handing off a dollar. "But they're all tired and stale."

"I have one thing that's funny," said Larry. "One thing. But I think it's funny only if you're already dead."

"There are two things you just can't advertise," said Hank matter-of-factly. "Fat people and dead people."

"Is that a quote, Hank?"

"They're not dead, Hank," said Amber. "They're just sick."

"Fat people and dying people, then."

"Suicides are tough," added Larry.

Chris Yop showed up looking furtive and unwell, vigilant despite familiar surroundings, carrying some rough layouts on sketch paper. Significant sweat blots under the arms of his Hawaiian shirt indicated a higher level of vascular dysfunction than we were accustomed to. He had evidently been hard at work. "I need someone to take these in to Lynn," he announced, setting his layouts on the coffee bar. We asked him what they were. "My concepts for the fund-raiser ads," he said. "I think they're pretty good."

"Humbly you submit," said Larry, picking them off the coffee bar.

It was obviously just plain wrong that the man was still in the building a full day after being laid off. But to have concepts, too? Some nerve system crucial to an understanding of the agreement one enters into when engaging in the capitalist system had obviously gone haywire in him, along with the rest of his ailing networks.

"The problem I'm having," he said, glancing back as if spooked, "is I can't get credit for them because, well, you know, officially . . ."

"You're insane?" said Marcia.

"No, *Marcia,*" he said, "not because I'm insane. Because officially I don't work here anymore."

"Oh, right," said Marcia, taking a sip of her latte. "Forgot that detail. But I wouldn't worry, Chris. I've seen your resume. They're going to scoop you right up."

"Why are you being mean to me, Marcia?"

"Because you called me Karen!"

"Chris," said Benny, "listen. The project's changed."

Yop's attention was suddenly focused on the opening elevator doors.

"Chris? Are you listening to me?"

"Sorry," said Yop, snapping back. "Benny, is Lynn really in today? Or was Dan Wisdom just fucking with me?"

"Chris, listen. It's no longer an ad for the fund-raiser. It's this other thing now."

"What other thing?"

"The project's changed," he repeated.

"But I've been working on fund-raiser ads," said Yop. "I was hoping you guys could take these in to Lynn and, you know, let it slip I came up with them."

"I don't think you want credit for these," said Larry, setting the ads back down on the coffee bar.

"Now you're telling me the project's changed? — Go screw, Larry. — Benny, I spent a lot of time on these. I worked *hard,* man. I'm trying to get my job back here."

He paused to order a decaf from the barista.

"Chris," said Benny. "Shouldn't you go home? Shouldn't you stop worrying about these ads and go home and talk to your wife?"

Yop looked away, distant and pensive. He removed a napkin from the dispenser on the coffee bar and wiped sweat from his brow. Then he set his head down on the bar, losing it inside his arms. He stayed that way for a while. When he looked up again, nudged by the barista holding his coffee out to him, his eyes were bloodshot and veiny. "Thanks," he said, taking the cup. He handed off his dollar. "Will somebody do me a favor, please," he asked. "Will somebody please e-mail me with details on how the job has changed? Will someone do that for me, please?"

Before departing, he turned back to Marcia. "I'm sorry I called you Karen this morning," he said. "I know you're Marcia. My brain is fried, I just got confused."

He hurried off down the hall, staying close to the walls.

"'Tomorrow morning there'll be laundry,'" said Hank. "'But he'll be somewhere else to hear the call.'"

Karen Woo came toward us from the opposite direction.

"Everybody come with me," she said.

She reversed in her tracks and headed back to her office.

When we got down there she was sitting behind her desk holding the phone to her ear. She said to the person on the other end that she wished to speak with a nurse in the oncology department. As she waited to be transferred, no one spoke. We couldn't believe it — she was making the call. Her cool composure was astounding, preternatural, and somewhat sinister. When the nurse came on, she remained confident and in character. We held her in awe.

But as we waited, it was almost as if something swept the room and a collective epiphany dawned upon all of us at once and we knew for certain how wrong we had been about everything. No one would just miss a crucial operation. A crucial operation must have never been scheduled. Why had we not bowed to the eminently more reasonable likelihood that there was no cancer? That it was just a rumor, as Larry had suggested. Or if Lynn *did* have cancer and an operation had been scheduled, there were a thousand very simple explanations for why she might have missed it. Some scheduling conflict with the doctor, some clarification was needed in the diagnosis, more tests had to be taken, blood drawn, the doctor was sick, the hospital had lost power. All today's intrigue was just cheap talk to better dramatize our lives. Why had we not seen it *before* Karen got on the phone with the nurse? Oh, to be seduced by that meddling, insensitive woman! To play along in her deception just to have our craven tabloid hysterias confirmed or denied. It was despicable. *We* were despicable. We should have stood up immediately, denounced her actions with one voice, and demanded that she —

She hung up the phone. "Her operation was scheduled for nine," she said. "The doctor was prepped and waiting. They called her at home, they called her at work. The nurse sounded irritated. She wanted to know when I wanted to reschedule."

The Thing to Do and the Place to Be

THE NIGHT BEFORE THE OPERATION she has no association dinners to go to, no awards ceremonies, no networking functions. A plan comes to her impromptu in the back of the cab as she steps in and instructs the driver to take the Inner Drive. She envisions her sofa, her two cats, something good ordered in, and a bottle of wine she's been saving. They ask you not to eat anything twelve hours before, but honestly, that's unreasonable, isn't it — your last chance at a normal meal for how long?

She brought no work home with her, not tonight, because work would not be an appropriate way to spend the evening. Yet whenever she's without it, even for the duration of a cab ride, she starts to feel anxious. Luckily it's a short ride. She pays the cabbie and steps out in front of some serious real estate. She lives in the top-floor condo overlooking the winding coastal edge of Lake Michigan.

The doorman stands at his post in the lobby; they exchange greetings and she heads up the elevator. Inside the condominium, she slips off one heel while hanging her keys on the hook. She slips off the other one, and with two heels in one hand, walks down the hall to where her pajamas await. Getting into pajamas — now that's appropriate. Here is a good place to be, she tells herself, right here in this apartment, and getting into her pink hospital scrubs and jersey zip-up — that's the right thing to be doing.

At the kitchen table she pours herself a glass of wine. She reflects on the day, it can't be helped. Chris Yop broke down when she delivered the news. If Martin were here, she'd say to him, A grown man crying! Would *you* do that? Of course you wouldn't! Let me tell you something, I think I've grown immune to the emotion involved. His crying? It didn't faze me one bit. You want to know when I feel something? It's the person who says to me, Lynn, you've been terrific to work for, and I understand you're just doing what you have to do — *that's* who I feel sorry for. Those people kill me. A grown man crying? Uh, no. And listen to this! An hour later, he shows up for a meeting. I come in, he's sitting in my office. I *just* fired him, he's sitting in my office. I said to him, Chris, you have to leave. God knows I can't have them sticking around!

Wait — did she just say that last part out loud? A hazard of living alone. One of the cats is looking at her from the floor. Or is it just a look of hunger? She reminds herself — Martin's not *actually* here, Lynn. "But you are, aren't you, Friday," she says, bending to scruff up the cat's black coat. The cat bow-backs and asks for more. "Yes, you are," she says, "and so am I, and so who needs him?" She straightens up and takes another sip of wine. Look at all of the chairs! A total of *four* chairs at the kitchen table! Why do I need four chairs? It's important that she not second-guess anything, now that she's home. She's home, she's in for good. Stop thinking, stop thinking, stop thinking.

She wonders where Martin is. Is he at work? What time is it? Six-forty-five, of course he's at work. Stop thinking. He'll be at work for hours. Stop it. Lynn Mason, on the other hand, knocked off early today. Two very important new business pitches, absolutely crucial to the agency's future, and strategies for both still need to be worked out with the account people, but Lynn left the office at a reasonable hour, to come home to her cats, to spend the evening before her operation in a relaxing manner, unwinding with a little television, going to bed early and getting a good night's sleep. What could be better, more desirable than that? Don't think about Martin. And if she's tempted, remember — it's Martin *at work.* Just a man at his desk, grumpy, nasty with the day's odors, engaged in some dull legal matter. Consider how undesirable his company would be right now. How could she want that, with all she's got going on right here — the Chinese food on its way, and so many chairs to choose from.

The doorman calls up from the lobby. Her delivery has arrived. Thank god, send him up. If he's cute, she's going to seduce him. No joke. It's done, it's decided. Think she has time to play games *tonight?* No, if he's in the least way cute, she's going down on him in the hallway. Well, not *in* the hallway. Why don't you come inside? Will you shut the door for me, please? Delivery boys must dream of this. Maybe choose different pajamas? The pink scrubs and zip-up — not very mistress-of-the-night. She needs a robe, nothing underneath. Because it all sounds like a joke until you understand that someone has to be the last one to hold her breast in his mouth — tonight's *it* — and she'd really rather it not be Martin.

But he comes and goes. Young Asian, has his charms, but she loses the nerve. She takes the food over to the couch. The initial comfort of a seat on the sofa — yes, this *is* the right place to be, right here, and turning on the TV the right thing to be doing. She eats her dinner and drinks her wine while watching an episode of

The Simpsons, and a half hour later her conviction is still nearly intact.

On her third glass of wine, she repeats it to herself: Here is a good place to be, right here, and this thing the right thing to be . . . wonder what Martin's doing? He's working. Lynn, you know this. He'll be there for hours. Think about something else. Wonder . . . wonder what movies are playing. She likes to see a movie when she has the time. Always better to see them *with* someone, though. Alone, there is that awkward ten minutes between the time you arrive and the time they dim the lights for the previews when against all reason you believe everyone in the theater is staring at you because you are a woman alone at the movies. It's probably a good thing she's here on the sofa, rather than waiting self-consciously for a movie to begin. This *is* the right place to be. Unless the alternative was a movie theater with Martin.

Television isn't working out. She turns it off, gets up, makes the cold transition from carpet to tile — but what is there in the kitchen for someone looking to indulge? No food for twelve hours my ass. This could be *it.* Let's see — some freezer-burned ice cream. What's in the cupboard? A third of a bag of mini marshmallows. For the life of her she can't remember buying those. She's not interested in any of it — though when she turns her attention to cleaning the bedroom closet, she does take the ice cream with her. It's a spoon-bender. What compels her to do *that,* to clean? She stabs at the tub after every new pile of mess she drags from the closet out into the tidy room. It will be nice, she thinks, to have a nice clean closet during my recovery.

Fifteen minutes later she does not want to be cleaning the closet. On this night of all nights, cleaning the closet? Does she have such a deficient imagination, that's all she can come up with?

Imagine if one night in a lifetime were looked upon as a scientist might look upon it, or some other life form studying our species, and from that one night, the worth of the entire life were derived. Well, she'd rather hers not be evaluated by the TV she's watched or the closet she hasn't cleaned. Besides, that goddamn ice cream requires a pickax. Abandoning everything, she returns to the kitchen and finishes the bottle of wine.

— — —

MARTIN IS FORTY-FIVE and has never been married. His parents divorced when he was young and he never forgave the institution for any of its false comforts. He goes on and on about it, until finally she tells him, "Okay, I got it the first eight hundred times, you're not the marrying type." Still, he needed someone to go to Maui with. His firm kept a luxury box at Wrigley, there wasn't a restaurant in the city he couldn't afford — he wasn't about to sit in them alone. He needed companionship, he needed sex. But perhaps that paints too one-sided a portrait of Martin. He could have dated only younger women, girls practically, paralegals and secretaries without a brain in their heads, attracted to his partnership, his money, the broad chest under his starched shirts. Instead he was with her, someone his own age, someone whose professional achievements he respected. And last August, he spent a week in Florida, an entire week in Cocoa Beach, taking her old dad around. Eating at five-thirty, speaking loud so he could hear — the whole routine. He never complained. That was something, wasn't it — giving of his vacation time, meeting her family? And once in a while, he would show up with flowers, he would come up behind her and kiss her neck, and that would be enough to look past the birthday he forgot, or the dates he'd have to cancer because of work.

Cancel. The word she wants is *cancel.*

But what would commonly happen was that he would call at the last possible minute. "Deposition . . . judge moved up the court date . . . important conference." Whatever it was would leave her alone, looking down the long double-barrel of Saturday and Sunday when it should have been three bottles of Merlot on Mackinaw Island and bedsheets warm with body heat. "Oh, fuck, Martin, not again." "Hey, I'm sorry," he'd offer. "But this is work, Lynn. This is what I do." "Yeah, but you know what? Fuck you, because this was planned. We planned this thing, you and me — and what, I'm going to call Sherry *now?* I'm going to call Diane and say, Martin stood me up again, the asshole, want to rent a movie?" "Does it even count," he'd ask, "does it even matter that I'm sorry?" The sorry part was how well she knew that Sherry, with twin ten-year-olds, was not in a position just to drop things and listen to another Martin story, and the other sorry part was how loathsome it sounded, renting a movie with sad, fat Diane. Sometimes she almost wished Martin were married and that she were fucking another woman's husband so it could all be simpler — easier to deal with a cliché than Martin's overriding obsessions. He wasn't *just* not the marrying type. He was pathologically noncommittal. "I can't do this," she'd say. And there was silence on the other end. "Can't do what?" "*This,*" she'd say. And that was it, they were off again.

Then a night would come along — hey, not unlike this one — when enough time had passed that the specifics of their last conversation grew vague, when Lynn discovered that in the intervening days her anger at Martin had shifted toward understanding, which had spilled over, that night, into regret for how she had reacted when he canceled their plans. It had always been an understanding we share, the thought went, how important work is, and when we get together it's what we talk about — this frustration of mine, that fascinating case of his, how we're succeeding and failing and working hard. She would reflect back and think how selfish she had been, and slightly childish, too — and she would call. Or a few days would pass and *he* would call. "You were right, I fucked up, we had it planned," he'd say. "Can we do it this weekend?" How good it was to have her hands on his chest again, how good to trip over his shoes again on the way to the bathroom.

But not this night — no calling him this night. Not after their last conversation. No way to shift any of that emotional content. That back-and-forth is frozen like a mastodon in ice, and the rider on top, with his spear and animal urges, he is their year together, suspended forever with his mouth gaping wide, his whoop and howl finally silenced.

— — —

WHOA — SUDDENLY it's like something in a science fiction movie: how'd she get *here?* Just a second ago, she was sitting on the sofa with the cats, eating Chinese. There was television, and the last of the ice cream. Next she knows, she's dressed and sitting in a public place, seeing and being seen. A delicately lit wood-paneled wine bar new in the neighborhood. She feels on display for being the only one actually sitting at the bar. The crowd's in back. What was that she kept repeating to herself? Here is the right place to be, alone at this bar, and this thing I'm doing, having my, what, fourth? my fourth or fifth glass of wine for the night, what a wise and prudent thing to be doing. Not any more convincing here than it was back home. She can't even work up a conversation with the bartender, who seems fixated on the contents of his wallet. Jeez, don't let me distract you. No need for a little conversation, what they used to call the human touch. By all means, keep looking through your ATM receipts. She'll just content herself with mulling it over again: the fact that there *is* some place — she's absolutely certain of it — one place that is the *right* place to be tonight, and *one* thing that is the right thing to be doing. Is it really sitting in Martin's office, under very familiar fluorescent lights, amid all those oppressive document boxes, watching Martin read Westlaw downloads, just so she can be in the presence of Martin? No, goddamn it, no — that is bullshit. There is something else, something that is Lynn Mason's, that belongs to her and to her alone and is not contingent upon the existence of Martin Grant. But what? Only thing she can say for sure, *it's probably not here.* Amazing how quickly a glass of wine goes when you're the only one at the bar. Ladies and gentlemen, I'll be saying good night now, you won't be seeing me tomorrow. "Another one?" asks the bartender. "Just the tab," she says.

One day she said to him — they were on again — "Hey, come here, will you, and feel this for me?" She was in the shower. It was a workday, one of the rare occasions Martin slept over during the week. He came to the shower door. "Hey, I'm going now," he said. "Have to get home to shower." He was standing behind the opaque glass. "Did you not just hear me?" she asked him. "What?" he said. "I asked you to feel something." He didn't move. "What is it? I'll get wet." And instantly, she had a thought. More like a suspicion. It was when he said, "I'll get wet" — what sort of thing was that to say? *Roll up your fucking sleeve then, you jerk!* It led her to believe he *had* heard her, heard her all too well. It can't be helped, when a woman is in the shower and says, *come here and feel this,* that a tone creeps in. Not fear, not just yet. Concern, and she's looking to unburden some of it. She's looking for somebody to say, *that feels to me like it's nothing.* But Martin, Martin was quick. Martin would immediately grasp the implications of a request like *come here and feel this,* and he would pick up on the tone, too — and knowing what that tone implied, all it might lead to and all it might require of him, he came to the shower door with his own agenda. *Have to go home, have to shower.* Was it true, or was it just her suspicious mind? "What is it, Lynn?" he said. "What is it you want me to feel?" "Never mind," she said. "No, what *is* it?" he said, with an impatience intended now to make her believe that he was eager for it, really wanting the opportunity. "It's nothing, forget it, get out of here," she said. He opened the shower door, startling her. She slammed it shut. "Get out of here! Go home and shower." He already had his keys in his hand. They jangled as he spun them around on his finger. "Okay," he said — and that was the extent of his protest. She hated the disappointment she felt when, with the water off, she heard the front door slam.

He spent the next month in California on a case. He left messages but she didn't return them, and then he stopped calling. It was two weeks after his return that they next saw each other, and they should have been thick in a fight before even taking a step inside the restaurant — about the calls put in and not returned, the monthlong silence, the insult of the two additional weeks. But being across from him again was where she wanted to be. She had missed his conversation. God — had she not realized how much? It was always the same thing — pissed-off judges and incompetent prosecutors and legal issues she needed explained. But the way he talked, his mannerisms, his inimitable masculine mannerisms — she had missed them. And he had missed her company, too, it seemed. He listened to her talk about the difficulties the agency was facing and the miserable experience of laying people off. Later that night they went back to her place and it was even better having him inside her than it was having him across the table from her. She had to interrupt it briefly to tell him not to touch there, not the left breast, to spend his attention on the right breast but not to touch the other one, and he guessed appropriately that it would not be the time to ask, "How come?" and so said nothing.

But at breakfast the next morning, at a place in the neighborhood where they sat in a courtyard on a wrought-iron table under the new spring sun, he surprised her. "I'm putting two and two together," he said, "and it may come to equal five, but I thought I might ask. How are you feeling, healthwise?" "Why are you asking me that?" she said. "Because last time we were together you asked me to feel something. And this time you tell me not to feel something. Is it just a monthly . . . a matter of bad timing? Or is there something else going on?"

Martin, who cared only to talk about the law. And when it wasn't the law it was jazz — the history of jazz, how to listen to jazz, this one particular recording that changed jazz forever. "Everybody would disagree with me, but it was Louis Armstrong's 'St. Louis Blues.' There had never been anything like it." She knew it by heart by now. Oh, god — had she misread him? Had her decision not to return his phone calls when he went to California been based on a presumption that when he came to the shower door, he thought, *Reach in, and I'm doomed.* Two minutes of sexless inspection of the thing he lavished his attention upon at certain convenient hours and he was in it for months, maybe years. He was in for meeting the doctors and learning the terminology and driving her back and forth and holding her head as she retched. If he wasn't likely to commit to something that included security, love, protection, how eager was he for a commitment like that? But was it possible *he had in fact simply not heard her?* "I have a lump in my breast," she said. "I found a lump." He raised his eyebrows. "A lump," he said, looking down, suddenly toying with an empty cream container. "What's . . . what's a lump?" *What's a lump?* He hadn't expected that answer, had he, even if it was the obvious one — not here, not at breakfast in the sun. "Why don't you just forget about it?" she said. "No, I mean, of course I know what a lump is," he said. "But what have you done about it? That's what I mean to ask. What do the doctors say?" "I'm doing fine," she said. "Is that what they say?" "Martin," she said, "I'm fine." "Were you ever going to tell me?" "I told you last night," she said. On a dime he turned into the litigator. "No, you didn't tell me last night. You told me not to touch last night. You didn't tell me you found a lump." "Why don't you not worry about it, Martin — because I think you'd rather not worry about it than worry about it." "I brought it up, didn't I? Wasn't I the one who brought it up?" Well, she thought — wasn't he? Just where did Martin stand? Who was this man she had been fucking for the past year *really,* and how would he react with his back up against the wall? Let's find out. "Okay," she said, "go to the doctor's with me." He returned to futzing with the creamer. He didn't look up for some time. "So you *haven't* seen a doctor?" "I just asked you to go with me," she said. "So obviously I haven't." "Why not?" he asked. "Because I need someone to go with me," she said. He returned his attention to the creamer. "Sure," he said, not looking at her. "I'll go with you. Of course." She smiled at him. He looked up. "What?" he said. "I'm fine," she said.

— — —

BETTER THAN BEFORE, anyway, because here is a good place to be, not a half-bad place, anyway, and this thing she's doing may be a little uninspired, but certainly better than getting blotto at a wine bar. She parks in the underground garage and goes up by elevator and steps lightly into the bright and soothing atmosphere. Home, then bar, and now, a half hour before closing time, a department store — not a very fertile imagination on me, she concludes. She wishes to god she could think of the thing she knows is right. It probably isn't shopping, but as she told herself on the way over, shopping's not a bad interlude. And would you look at all the shoes? She wanders around the displays. Pumps, heels, sneakers, sandals — you know (thinking back on all those shoes she pulled from her closet when eons ago it sounded like a good idea to be cleaning), I don't really need any more shoes. She doesn't really need any more anything. But will you just look at all the hard work these good folks have put in to make you feel like nothing could ever be wrong when there's so many pairs of shoes to buy! She hasn't even gone into the main body of the store yet, it's all so lovely and pleasant already.

And all of it soured by the lack of the one thing she wants: not likely to find Martin here in the women's shoe department, is she? In any department of Nordstrom or anywhere else at this hour of the night. Nine-thirty — right now Martin's walking the hallway toward some associate's office. Is she really longing to be a part of *that?* She would replace these bright and open spaces full of the world's best footwear, fashions, perfumes, and accessories — and for everything else, there's MasterCard — just to join Martin in a hallway of bare walls and ugly carpet as he moves toward an associate's office on some inconsequential item of business? Come on, be reasonable. So it is Martin, it is Martin's body — he's still standing in some boring jerk's doorway talking about document production and privileged materials. Shop, for god's sake! Buy something! Make this night memorable in shopping's extremely cheap way. What she has in mind is something extravagant, something outrageously expensive. You wear it once and put it away forever. No, not *that,* not a wedding gown. She doesn't want to marry Martin, believe it or not. She just wants to follow him around the corridors of his office, stepping into the supply closet with him to pick up some file tabs, or whatever. That's a far cry from vows. It's *not* not having Martin forever that makes her momentarily wacko for Martin; it's not having him *tonight.*

She passes the man at the piano. What's he playing? Can't name it. She drifts around the perfume and makeup counters, fending off the lab-coated jackals that want to spray her and paint her and make her look her best. Just looking, thanks. Which is what she's been doing, for twenty years more or less, with respect to men. She doesn't mind finding herself unmarried, it's just how things turned out, and she's not eager to marry *just* to marry. Only those with the most dull and conventional pieties, looking in at her from the outside, would suspect or pity her for being forty-three and still unmarried. Would they pity a man? They would *envy* the man. She heads up the escalators. That's not to say that when she sees her friends marry, she doesn't have moments of, not jealousy, but envy, though not envy of the friend for getting married but rather of that conviction both the bride and bridegroom seem to share that, well, this thing they're doing is the right thing. Where does that come from? She did think for a time that she and Douglas would marry, and when instead it went in the opposite direction, because Douglas was not, in the end, what she wanted, she woke up one morning and thought, not unlike finding herself all of a sudden in that wine bar, "Whoa, I'm thirty-eight! Who's playing tricks on me here?" And for a moment she thought along the conventional line herself, reflecting on what a loss it might be if she never married, and if she did, how old would she be by then — no younger than forty, if she got lucky — and so maybe too old to have children, and what a loss that might be, too. But do let it be known — what floor is she on? — let it be known in Women's

Apparel, at nine-thirty-five PM — dinner is probably being delivered to his office about now — on the night before she's scheduled for major surgery and at the age of forty-three, that her marital status has not been, for whatever reason — because she is "cerebral," because she is "cold," because she is "ambitious" — it has *not* been the focus of her life. If she had spent a tenth of the energy finding the right man as she has building the agency she started with the other partners, she would be living in Oak Park right now putting dinner plates into the dishwasher. *Have you finished with your homework? Should I take the car in tomorrow?* With some circumspection, with some healthy amount of doubt, she can say that right here is a better place to be, in Nordstrom, and this thing she's doing a better thing than loading up the dishwasher in Oak Park. And those people who think, Oh woman, oh sister, oh girl you have no idea what you're missing out on, we just have to part ways, me and them, because I have made a good life for myself. I know what to do with my life. I just don't know what to do with *this one night.*

— — —

SHE ENDS UP in the lingerie section. If it's invasive, and they think it is, and if a couple of other factors are in play, she's agreed to have a mastectomy. Basically they put it to her this way: if we go in there and we find this and we find that, we don't see how you have much of a choice. And if she's going to have a mastectomy, she needs to start thinking about breast reconstruction. They're going to save as much as they can, and they've asked that she come in tomorrow with a favorite bra, which they will use to measure where the incision line should be. They will cut just inside the bra line so that the plastic surgeon can do his thing after she has completed her six months of chemo and radiation, should they be necessary, which they likely will be. *There's nothing but bad news for her, and then there's more bad news.* So come in, they told her, with a special bra, and with that in mind, she gravitates toward Intimate Apparel. Her choices are endless — slinky, padded, sheer, cotton, rhinestoned, patterned, leopard-printed, silky, hot pink. This is what makes the country great, isn't it? And it's what's made her life in advertising possible, the opportunity afforded by this glut to market one particular offering in a way that allows it to stand alone as the leader in the marketplace. She would know exactly what to do with any one of these brands, if they were fortunate enough to win that account. But marketing one for her particular needs tonight? Picking the one bra in this haystack of bras that will define where they make the incision and that will, somehow, when all this is over, make her feel sexy again — even she admits there's not likely to be one bra here that can fill an order like that. She takes one off the rack. Maybe this one. Another one — maybe. Soon she has ten bras in her hands, she has twelve, fifteen. She takes them to the fitting room and despite the pain caused by the chafing tries a few of them on. She looks at herself in the mirror. The idea is to look sexy again. *And for whom exactly?* Yourself, of course. Yes, well, that's all wonderfully self-affirming and very strong-minded as any decent woman should be these days, but let's just face facts here and say that when a woman — no, when a *person* is thinking about feeling sexy, it is always with the idea of someone else in mind. Someone in the back of the mind who says, "I can't believe how sexy you look in that." And just who is that person for her? Unfortunately the timing is such that it can't be anybody other than you-know-fucking-well-who, and that is not an option. Sexiness with Martin in mind is no longer an option. And sexiness *after* Martin? That's where it gets complicated, because first she'll have the stitches. Those will scar up quickly, and for six months, while the post-op treatments are doing their tricks, she'll wear the prosthesis. Then the plastic surgeon does the breast reconstruction in stages — who knows how long that takes. So what is she looking at here? A year, a year and a half? How is she going to feel sexy during any of that? Who's going to look at her scars, at her prosthesis, and say, "I can't believe how sexy you look in that." You see, there *is* no man after Martin, not for a long, long time, and before she can help it, she's screaming. She's in the tiny dressing room with a thousand bras screaming as loud as she can. It sounds like AAAAAAAARRRRRRRRRRRRRRHHHHHHHH!!! When she stops she feels the pulse of her blood pumping in that part of her breast that is sore to the touch, and a rawness in her throat. She has a terrible head rush from the wine and the scream. She sits down on the bench. Salesclerks come running. "WHAT'S WRONG IN THERE? DO YOU NEED SECURITY?" She will not cry. No. She stands up and starts handing bras over the door. "I don't want these!" she says. "Take them!" At first she offers a few at a time, then she scoops them up and tosses them all over. "I don't want any of them! I just want out of here!" What a stupid place to be, this dressing room, and trying on bras, trying to look sexy, what a ridiculous thing to be doing.

— — —

AFTER HE FOUND OUT, he left long voice mails for her at work. Who knows what effect he intended by them. Typically she picked up the phone and listened to them thirty seconds after he had left them, and carried on a dialogue with his recorded voice. "What I don't understand," he said in an early one, "is how an intelligent, reasonable person could possibly wait, despite knowing that something was wrong, feeling sick, and still refuse to see a doctor. I don't get that, I don't understand that behavior coming from an intelligent person." "That's because," she said into the phone, as the message unfurled, "intelligent people are not *always* guided by their intelligence. Sometimes, Martin, something called fear is a little more powerful." He would know that basic fact of human psychology, she thought, if he were in marketing, but as a practitioner of the law, he believed that the decision that was most rational, or at least most shrewd, would always triumph if it determined one's own self-survival. "Yes, I should have shown an interest earlier," he said in a later voice mail. "I was wrapped up in my work, I wasn't paying attention. But now," he said, "now that I know, I can't *not* know anymore, Lynn, I can't just unlearn it, and now that I know and can't not know, I feel . . . you know . . . a certain obligation . . ." "Obligation?" she said out loud. ". . . concern for you, Lynn, and your well-being . . ." "Oh, Martin, be still my beating heart." ". . . that I can't just — well, what is it you want me to do exactly, huh?" he asked. "Just forget about it? Is it one of those things, you know — we do this together, we do that, but this is one of those things we just don't talk about, it's off-limits, when frankly, Lynn, you could be very, very — uh, yeah, I'll be with you in a minute, okay?" he said to someone who must have just shown up in his doorway. Returning to the message, he continued, ". . . that you should, uh . . ." He had lost his train of thought. "Look, the point is, you *have* to see a doctor," he said. "Okay? Look, I have to go. I should have said all of this to you in person but you won't pick up your goddamn phone. Please call me back."

In one of the last messages he said, "There's something I've been thinking about and wondering about and I'm very curious: am I the only one who knows? Have you told your father, or any of your friends? Because if you haven't, and I'm the only one, you can see how I might feel a great deal of responsibility. In fact you could see how it's just a little unfair of you, even . . ." "Oh?" she said. "I'm curious to see how this works." "... because now I know," he continued, "and you won't take my advice to see a doctor, and that leaves me to worry about you ..." "Oh, poor Martin!" "... but without any recourse to remedy that worry. Now that's unfair, Lynn ..." *Then you should have kept your fucking hands off me!* she thought. *You shouldn't have crawled into my bed and tried to bite my nipple!* "... I'm not complaining about it, I don't want you to think I'm complaining. I'm just trying to plead my case here, that you should go to the doctor. If you don't want to do it for yourself, for fuck's sake, Lynn, do it for me."

He convinced her at last, or she simply yielded — after a week's time it was tough to determine if she agreed because she had found some reserve of strength, or because she was hopelessly weak and he had worn her down with his voice mails. He would go with her, that was the condition. In the car on the way to her appointment, she tried putting into words her fear of doctors, hospitals, procedures — but there was no articulating it. "I spent a lot of time in hospitals when my mother was dying," she said. "I was just a kid. Maybe that's when it started."

"What did she die of?"

"Give you one guess," she said.

There was silence. Then he talked in general about the amazing advances they'd made in medicine over the years, with the same optimism that marked every conversation of its type, and she could only think how naive he was to think she would be responsive when she had always been immune to that sort of hopefulness. Technology would never advance past primal fear. It would never trump human instinct.

He parked in the hospital parking lot and for a half hour tried to coax her from the car. She wanted him inside the room during the exam, would that be okay? He said it would be. She didn't want him to leave her side, was that understood? He said he had understood that from the first time she had asked, and the second time, and the third. "Why are you stalling?" he asked. When had Martin become so . . . committed? Had she misjudged him from the beginning? Or was this what was required for that commitment to take hold, that she be sent to hell and back? For she was in hell, in that car in the hospital parking lot, and not one cold hand had yet been laid upon her. After three or four attempts to articulate her fear on the ride over she had finally given up, but now she said to him, "I think I can finally explain it," she said. "It comes down to this. And it's so simple, Martin, I can't believe I didn't think of it before." "Well," he said, "so tell me." "I cannot physically enter that building," she said. "I cannot get out of this car and enter that building. See that building? I can't. I won't." There was silence. Then he said, "Well, sounds like fear to me." But he said he still didn't understand. "What is it fear *of*, exactly?" he said. "Fear of death? No, you tell me that's not it. You don't fear death. Is it that they might tell you something's wrong? You know something's wrong. It's not that either. So what is it? Most people, Lynn, they feel something ain't right, they get scared. That's natural. But the next step is getting it fixed. They're *eager* to get it fixed. You," he said, "you have all that reversed. You know something's wrong — that doesn't scare you. You go weeks letting it get worse! The idea of getting it fixed? *That's* what scares you. Am I right? Isn't that how it works with you?" That's why he made partner, she thought. Good insight, good reasoning skills. "Yes," she said. "I never thought about how fucked up it is until you put it like that, but yes, that's it." There was silence. "Do you think there's a word for that?" she asked. "I could think of a few choice words," he said. A moment of levity. After that he stared through the windshield, thinking. "Look," he said, turning to her. "I'll be right back. You stay here, okay?" "Where are you going?" she asked. "You said you wouldn't leave me." "Once we got *inside,*" he said. "We're still in the parking lot." He reached out and took her hand. "Trust me," he said. So she let him go and he went inside the building. Ten minutes later he came out again and told her that her appointment had been rescheduled. The wave of relief that came crashing over her quickly receded again into a sea's depth of despair when he said it was only rescheduled for later that day. "What time?" she asked. "Don't worry about what time," he said. "Just put this on." "What is it?" "What's it look like?" he asked. "It's a handkerchief." "But how am I supposed to 'put it on'?" He started the car and placed it in reverse. "Like you're a pirate's captive," he said, "and you've just been told to walk the plank."

— — —

SHE WALKED INTO THE FIRST BUILDING holding his hand. They took an elevator that made her ears pop. She felt ridiculous because the elevator was full and what the hell was she doing in this blindfold? At one point she heard Martin say, "Stop staring." "I'm not," she said. "How could I be?" "I wasn't talking to you," he said. After what seemed like an eternity the elevator stopped and everyone got off. He led her by the hand. When he brought her to a halt he undid the blindfold and she knew instantly where she was: on the viewing deck of the John Hancock building, overlooking the city. She was surprised and delighted. "What is it you're up to, Martin?" she asked, cocking an eye at him. He shrugged innocently and gestured at the view. "I'm showing you the city," he said. There was the Sears Tower ahead of them and Lake Michigan to the left and to the right the grand and gaudy suburbs. They pointed out where they worked and where they lived and identified the buildings they knew by name. They put money into the viewfinder and looked out at Wrigley Field. They cast their eyes west as far as they would go and they still couldn't exhaust that endless metropolis. When they were through, Martin put the blindfold back on her. They took the elevator down, walked back to the car, and climbed in again. They drove. Again he parked and led her by the hand. This time they walked up some stairs and she knew there were no stairs in a hospital entrance and so they had to be some other place, and when he held the door open for her and guided her in, she couldn't see a thing but she could still smell, and she knew right away where they were. She heard a man say, "Two?" "Two," replied Martin, who made her walk all the way to their table in the blindfold. "All right, take it off," he said. "I knew it!" she cried out. "I knew just where we were!" They waited twenty minutes for a deep-dish pizza in a back booth under the dim light of Gino's East, where the black planks above them made them feel as if they were eating under the main deck of a creaky old pirate ship. Those planks had been mercilessly graffitied and dollar bills had been stapled to them. When they stepped out again into the bright shock of daylight, he put the blindfold back on her. She wondered now if her luck had run out.

But they drove what she thought was too short a distance to be back at the hospital and when he took the blindfold off again, she said, "I should have known." They were at the Jazz Record Mart on East Illinois. "Yes," he said, full of an irony she loved, "an aficionado like you deserves to be indulged on a day like today." "Please," she said, "here's my credit card, buy what you want — *just take your time.*" He spent almost twenty minutes looking through the dusty bins for his obscure recordings. "Not long enough," she said, when he was through. Then it was back to the blindfold and the car, parking the car and being led by the hand. Stairs again, and not just six or seven of them — three long flights, almost enough to make her winded. She couldn't believe what he was doing, holding her hand and guiding her along, devising this scheme so uncharacteristic of him, or at least uncharacteristic of that understanding she had arrived at long ago of the living breathing man — a Martin who was without whim or fancy, who drove home only the nail of hard truth, or chose to avoid the issue altogether. What the day had proven more than anything, she thought, was her haste to judge, and the rigidity of those judgments once made. They were inside now — the place had an airy, echoic atmosphere, rumbling low with hushed voices, and footsteps on marble stairs she could pick out one by one. He took the blindfold off and they spent an hour guiding themselves through all the highlights of the Art Institute. "I thought you weren't an art fan, Martin," she said. "I'm not a fan of any of the bullshit," he replied, "but at this level, there are things I enjoy." "Is that right?" "Sure," he said. "Point one out to me," she said skeptically, "when we come upon it, will you?" "This one here, for instance," he said. "This one?" "Yes, this is a fine piece," he said. "Care to argue?" They were standing in front of Georges Seurat's giant *Sunday Afternoon on the Island of La Grand Jatte.* "No," she said. She didn't care to argue.

It was three in the afternoon by the time they left and she knew now, getting out of the car, walking with him, that her luck had finally run out. "Don't take it off," he said. "Martin," she said, and her voice trembled. They were walking across a parking lot that was unmistakably the parking lot of a hospital. "Lynn," he said, "do not take it off." Her hands began to shake as they had in the car earlier in the day. "Just keep walking," he said. And she managed to because she could trick herself: *maybe not, maybe not just yet. . . .* But there were no stairs, and when he opened the door and the slightly warmer air from inside hit her and the light coming in above the blindfold got lighter, more fluorescent, she knew for an absolute fact where they were and she was terrified. "Just keep walking," he said. He brought her to a stop and made her sit, and the chair beneath her was hard and plastic like a chair in a hospital waiting room, and she was terrified. "I'm not leaving your side," he said. "I'm just going about ten feet away for a couple of seconds to talk to someone, then I'll be back." He returned. "I'm right here," he said. They sat there a long time. After a while, he said, "Why don't you take the blindfold off now." "No way," she said. "Trust me," he said. "Take it off." "I'd really rather not," she said. "Come on," he said, "you can do it." She did as she was told, squinting a little as she looked around. Clerks stood behind glass. There were digitized numbers on the walls. "The DMV?" she said. "You bastard!" She swung at him with the blindfold. "You see!" he cried. "You can do the hard part!" She sighed with relief. "But now you might as well resign yourself," he said. "You'll never know when we're actually there."

THIS IS PROBABLY not the right place to be, probably the *wrong* place, actually. Matter of fact, if the wrong place could be identified on a map — "You Are Here" — this would probably be it. And this thing she might do, enter the building and have the night guard call up and inform him who he had waiting for him in the lobby? *Not* the right thing to be doing. But she's been driving around for half a gas tank now and lo and behold she ends up here. The street where his firm's office is located is one block east of Michigan Avenue. The Mag Mile is deserted like always this time of night. She's parked illegally, but the only vehicle to drive past in twenty minutes is a cabbie with his light off. Going home, probably. That's the wise choice, cabbie — big day tomorrow, take yourself home and rest your weary bones. Why can't she have a cabbie's good sense? Lynn Mason in her Saab outside Martin Grant's office building doesn't feel forty-three so much as fourteen, unhinged by strong affections. "Wait wait wait wait wait wait wait wait wait wait wait wait wait wait *wait!*" she says out loud, pounding the steering wheel and grabbing onto it, shaking it. She can't *actually* be where she is! How did the night, starting at the top of the mountain with Chinese and TV, run like a landslide of shit down to this low ravine here? Does she really want to go up there and just *be* in an office? There is no mystery, no attraction, no reward, no surprise in the empty corridors of an office at ten at night — she knows from firsthand experience. Spending her last night in an office, that's insane. But the thing is, in that office *up there?* There is Martin. There is *Martin.* And the universal truth is, it matters not where he is, if he is drowning in the ocean or burning in a fire — that's where his lover wants to be. So it doesn't matter if he's an unshowered, crabby, gaseous, overworked, eye-twitching, mind-dulled man under the purgatorial light, walking the barren halls with their unringing phones and bad art. She wants to be up there. How could she help but find herself parked here, regardless of what she told herself earlier in the evening — that there would be no calling Martin tonight, no talking to Martin? A foolish consistency is the hobgoblin of little minds, and at this hour, she has thrown all consistency to the wind.

And yet, something stops her from going in. She sits in the car for twenty minutes and doesn't move. If you're the night guardsman, and you're listening carefully, after a while through the glass you can even hear the car start up again. She drew your attention because she just sat out there for twenty minutes. Then you saw her bang really hard on the steering wheel, she looked like a crazy! You had to ask yourself, What's she up to? And then to just leave!

Almost a peel-out. Sit in your car twenty minutes, just to leave again? Wonder what that was all about.

It was about coming to your goddamn senses, she thinks, driving off. And here's why: Martin has made it clear to her what the terms are, and she can't accept the terms. It's as simple as that. He did all those wonderful things — he took her to the top of the Hancock building, to Gino's, to the Art Institute, and then when the time came he took her back to the hospital, and she thought she knew they had arrived but because of his canards she was able to think *but maybe it's another DMV,* which was all she needed, that and the blindfold, to follow him in and sit next to him and deal with being in the hell she was in. And he didn't leave her. And when the doctor said, in essence, things are bad, by using words like "advanced," "aggressive," "better for chances of recovery," Martin was the one, because she was too stunned, to ask the questions. He *was* good to her, she *had* reason to be parked outside his building. But he had also done something terribly, terribly unexpected, something truly surprising, revealing of his true character — something terribly *honest.*

The doctor's visit was on a Friday, and after the trauma of it, the night followed in a deep funk, and it was a godsend to have Martin next to her in her bed. Saturday she woke up and found the funk replaced by a burning need to know a thousand things. All the questions she would have asked the doctor, had she had the power to the day before, came to her all at once. Martin had to remind her of many of the things the doctor had said. He practically took her through the entire prognosis again, the options that were available and the consequences that followed from them. But his expertise was limited, so midmorning, he went out for breakfast and stopped at a local bookstore, where he picked up a book that took a breast cancer patient step by step from discovery and diagnosis all the way through remission. He returned with it and together they ate and they read and they debated, and they came to conclusions: the goal was to do whatever gave her the best chance of a complete recovery. It would not be without its consequences.

"You think I should have the mastectomy," she said.

"No, I think you have to wait until the doctors get in there," he said, "and let them decide that, but yeah, I think you should give them permission beforehand, that if they think they should do it, they do it."

"And what do I do without my breasts," she said, "such as they are?"

"You . . . I don't know," he said. "You don't do any nursing for a while."

He must have seen it on her face. *Don't do any nursing?* Was he not aware that the prospect of having children was becoming dimmer and dimmer, and was he so insensitive that he didn't think in advance that she might be bothered by that? Not that she was bothered — she was fine with it — but to be reminded like that? What was wrong with him?

"No, that was a bad joke," he said quickly. "That was a terrible joke. I'm sorry I said that. I was trying for a little humor."

"I think you should stick to reasoning," she said.

What she had wanted him to say, of course, was, *What do you do without breasts? I don't know. I won't mind.* But they weren't talking about the two of them at the moment. They were talking only about her, getting her to a place where she could admit these difficult circumstances to herself so she could make the right decisions. Somehow, by the end of Saturday night, they had gotten there, more or less. She looked past the bad humor. She thanked him many times. He went home. She wanted it that way. It had been an exhausting two days.

It wasn't until Sunday — or three days before the scheduled operation — that they got around to talking about the two of them. He came over early and was standing in his spring overcoat and wouldn't sit down. She came out from the kitchen and said, "Why are you still standing?" "I've been thinking about something," he said, "and I think you should know what it is." She knew not to like the sound of that. For all the things she had had to worry about since her diagnosis, she had not forgotten that a busy man, a workaholic, a sworn bachelor would probably not find it in his best interest to play nursemaid to a sometime girlfriend. He had acquitted himself the past two days like a gentleman — a king, really — but it was going to happen sooner or later, something like this: I wish you the very best of luck, Lynn, but I'm not equipped for it. I do hope you call me when all of this is through. "Will you at least take your coat off?" she asked. "Of course," he said. When that was done, she handed him his cup of coffee. "Let's take this over by the sofa," she said.

And there he laid it all out for her: he was hers. Entirely. Whatever she needed from him, she had it. He would take days off work. He would be by her side at every appointment. He would see her through the entire thing. "From start to finish," he said. "If you'd rather have Sherry or Diane or whoever, that's fine. I'm just making myself available." "Thank you, Martin," she said. She was stunned again, speechless — what a surprise. "I'm touched," she said. "I won't know what I'm *doing,*" he said, "but I'm willing to try — whatever it takes." "I'm pleased," she said. "Really, I'm very touched." "But there's one thing I have to make clear," he said. "It's a condition, I guess. And I know it's terrible timing, but I can't . . . you see, I watched you, the past couple of days, Lynn. You surprised me — especially yesterday. Yesterday, it was like you came alive. You wanted to know everything. And you dealt with these hard . . . these goddamn hard facts. I was so impressed. And that got me thinking last night, when I went home, got me thinking that you could handle anything. Anything."

"Why don't you tell me what it is you have to tell me," she said.

He set his coffee down on the table and took her hands. "It's something I've been thinking about for a while now. It predates all . . . *this*," he said. "And it is bad timing, but it's not the time to be dishonest. Not now. And so I'll just say it — I've been thinking for a while now that you and I are not right for each other. In the long term, I mean. And I would hate to go through this with you and the whole time you're thinking . . . well, I don't know what — that I'm doing it because I'm in for the long haul. I *am* in for the long haul to make you better, but not because —"

"Yeah, I get it, I know!" she cried, cutting him short. "You're not the marrying type, I get it!"

"No, it's not just that," he said. "It's that, you and I . . . I'm just being honest here. I am totally committed to seeing you through this. But as a friend," he said. "Only as a friend."

Well, wasn't that something? Martin Grant *was* honest. He was an honest man. Of course he had had to give her a swift kick in the ass before she could realize it. He had had to knock the wind out of her to show her just how honest he was. Tending to her, nursing her — he'd take that. Breast cancer, that part was fine. It was the sum of her parts that was not, in the end, what he wanted. She told him she couldn't do it that way, impose on him that way if he . . . and he tried to object by saying . . . but she said I'm sorry, I just can't . . . and he said will you think it over . . . and she said no. He left soon after. She spent a sad Sunday afternoon alone.

And now, maybe she should ease off the gas a little. Doing ninety down Lake Shore Drive — that's a suicide mission, which can sometimes be a dream of rescue. They don't fix the potholes this far south. There are longer spells between working streetlights, too, when the black sky descends through the open sunroof, blotting her out again — until, first hood, then dash, then her hand on the wheel, she is lit all too brightly once more. She's avoiding her face in the mirror and all the lachrymose self-pity etched there. Fuck that. And for those of you who think Lynn Mason in addition to cancer suffers from the disease the talk shows diagnose as Needing the Man, if you think that's why she was parked outside Martin's office building, then you haven't yet understood the special circumstances of this Tuesday night, the forces at play that make her desperate and wanting in a way that is wholly unlike her. She has never — or not often — suffered from Needing the Man. Self-sufficiency has always been her first and last commandment. And not because she was of a generation of girls taught to reject the dependency suffered by their mothers and grandmothers. It wasn't a *man* she was afraid of losing herself to. It was a person, another person. It wasn't political, this headstrong determination to answer to no one, to achieve, to be the boss, to earn and sock it away, to use foul language whenever she goddamn well pleased, to eat rich, to fuck who she wanted to fuck and to fire who needed to be fired even if they broke into tears. It was *personal.* She did not care to hitch her wagon to anyone else, because she knew truth, happiness, success, all of what was deep and holy, was already present in the car with her. She just didn't have access to any of it tonight and wanted someone with her in the passenger seat.

Because fear of death, boy, that has a way of menacing your

convictions and making you feel lonely. Death has a way of ruining your plans and sending you on a tailspin on what should be a work night. Really, Lynn, better slow down, she tells herself. If not for your life, at least for the price of a ticket. She looks at the clock in the dash: midnight. She *loves* the Saab. What will happen to the Saab if she does, in fact, die? Better question: just where is she headed in the Saab at midnight at ninety miles an hour down Lake Shore Drive? Well, it's probably not the ideal place to be, this club she knows on the South Side — this club Martin introduced her to, where they spent some time together, called the Velvet Lounge. And the thing she plans on doing, catching the midnight set — is not something she's doing out of a genuine love of jazz, she admits that. She's going there for Martin, to remember Martin, to mourn Martin. She's going for nostalgia's sake. So isn't it just perfectly appropriate that the Velvet Lounge should be closed on Tuesdays? She sits in her car outside the bar, listening to "St. Louis Blues" on a CD Martin had left behind. *Got the St. Louis Blues! / Blue as I can be! / Man's got a heart like a rock cast in the sea!* Appropriately, it's a very short song. These stupid enduring artifacts — a bar, a song — that stick around after the lover has cast his heart into the sea, they are solace and agony both. She is drawn toward them for the promise of renewal, but the main experience is a deepening of the woe.

It's past midnight. She's miles from him. *Home.* The word she wants is *home.* She doesn't believe she will have the strength to submit herself to the doctors tomorrow without him. In a moment of clarity, she asks herself, is she really in love with Martin, with *Martin,* or is her broken heart circumstantial? Would she feel such emotion for him if she were not going into the hospital tomorrow, if he hadn't arranged her first trip to the doctor with such compassion, if he were not the last man to know her body intimately before it would be grievously altered? And then the answer comes to her: *all* broken hearts are circumstantial. Every lovelorn jerk is the victim of bad timing, good intentions, and someone else's poor decision making. She might as well admit it — yes, she's in love with Martin, and she's discovered it at the worst possible time, *after* he's broken her heart. In a sudden reversal of all that conviction she had when peeling away from the curb that Martin's office was the worst place to be, and contacting Martin the worst thing she could do, she goes in search of a pay phone. She has her cell phone, but if she calls on the cell she won't have the option of hanging up at the last minute without Caller ID informing him who was calling.

She calls from the pay phone of a closed gas station. It isn't unreasonable to expect to catch him at his desk. In fact, despite the late hour, it doesn't even cross her mind that he could be anywhere else. The familiar ring, the familiar voice mail — speak now or forever hold on to your self-respect. She hangs up. Wise choice. She calls back. "Martin, I'm at this number, it's —" She gives him the number. "Can you call me here when you get back to your desk, please? It's urgent." She peers about as she waits. There is a dark orange light cast above the gas pumps that is almost supernatural in its hazy Halloween glow, illuminating, though that's not the right word — *animating* the pumps and the oil stains and the pockmarks and the overflowing garbage pails into something ugly and vaguely menacing, and when a man pushing a shopping cart rattles his way across the pavement in the dark, the noise unnerves her, and she looks around. Great, now she's frightened of being attacked, too, of rapists and murderers and of all men lurking this late at night. Talk about a landslide of shit. At this eerie-ass gas station at the witching hour, folks, she has officially been buried in it. All she needs now is the start of rain, the motor failing to turn over, a car with tinted windows to stop at an uncomfortable distance, and a plague of locusts. Wouldn't that make the night complete? A football field's distance away the highway looms. She hears the faint whir of whizzing cars. Has it been two minutes, or four hours, since she called? She tries again. "Martin," she says. "I need to talk, please call me back." "Martin," she says, on her third try. "Are you at *home?*"

He *is* at home, sleeping. "What time is it?" he says, after the sixth ring. Oh, *no* — how long has he been at home? *Why* is he home? *How could he be home?* Now in the time before her reply, the entire evening requires rethinking. She envisioned him in familiar surroundings — refilling his coffee and pulling out a file and popping aspirin and readjusting his trousers after sitting down. She took comfort knowing where he was, even if she wasn't with him. Finding him at home, however, waking him up, she realizes she knows nothing of where he might have been or what he was doing, and that's very, very unsettling. She thinks the worst — a drink with someone new, fresh conversation, the beginning of what he *does* want. She's lost him. "What are you doing home?" she asks. "What am I doing?" he says. "I'm sleeping." "When did you leave work?" she asks. "I don't know," he says. "Seven?" *Seven?* She doesn't say it aloud but inside it's a scream as loud as that in the dressing room. Seven? She's been picturing him for five hours in a place she thought she knew and now she knows nothing. What she badly needs is a step-by-step explanation of everything he's done tonight. But she can't ask for that. Better come to the business at hand before she says something pathetic. Too late: "What have you been doing at home since seven?" she asks. "I mean, isn't it unlike you, to go home at seven?" "I was tired," he explains. "I wanted to come home." "So you went home at seven?" "Yes, Lynn," he says. "I came home at seven. I ordered food, I watched TV — what's going on?" So nothing out of the ordinary, she thinks. Nothing social. No *dates.* He's honest with her, she knows that by now — at last, tell the man why you're calling.

"I've changed my mind," she says. "I need you to go with me. I don't know what I was thinking. I won't be able to do it without you."

There's silence on his end. "But I thought . . ." he begins. "Okay," he resumes, a second later. "I'll go with you."

"You don't have to worry," she says. "I understand the conditions. I fully accept the conditions."

"Okay, but . . . what's changed? Because on Sunday you said —"

"I'm scared," she says simply. He doesn't reply. "It's just that I'm scared."

"Okay," he says. "What time do you need me to pick you up?"

— — —

HEADING BACK ON LAKE SHORE DRIVE, she is calm as a dove in a cage. No music, just the wind coming in from the sunroof and the Saab's faithful trill. To her right is the quiet lake. She remembers the time the car went kapooey. As she drove along someone might have been strapped to the underbelly banging on it with a monkey wrench. It jerked and tottered, and the strange movement and the clanking filled her with anxiety, as if she were the extension of consciousness of the machine she loved. She took it in and when she got it back three days later, all had been returned — the familiar purr of the motor, the smooth palpable glide of the tires on the street. She feels like that now: steady, quiet, functioning, recovered. No longer gadding, flitting like a pinball. Those hours are behind her, and only now can she see it: at twelve-forty-eight AM enveloped by the sturdy Saab and moving north at a reasonable speed she knows exactly where it is, the right place that has eluded her all evening, and what she should have been doing all along.

The night's drama had muddled her, obscuring her rightful destination, and within fifteen minutes she arrives. She enters the building and greets the man who watches over it at night. He knows her by name. "Surprised to see you here this late!" he says, and with these words she knows instantly that her biggest mistake was ever leaving to begin with. It was climbing into that cab and heading home. She takes the elevator to sixty and walks down to her office. Has anyone but her yet recognized the critical importance to the agency's future of these two new business pitches? And the strategies haven't even been worked out yet! They have two weeks until presentation. It's insane to think she even has a moment to spare. She sits down at her desk. Here is a good place to be, right here, thinking, What must be done? What must I do first? Amazing how energized she feels, given these last few months of everyday fatigue. No different than waking up after a long night's rest, and she is ready to start the morning. She reaches out to her mouse, disrupting the screensaver. The clock says it's just after one. Just a very early morning, that's all. She works until six.

She's exhausted. She rises off her chair and goes to the window. Just now the sun is coming up, the city dot-matrixing into life again, one dark spot at a time turning into light, brightening the buildings and the streets and distant highways. The stippling reminds her of the giant Seurat painting in the Art Institute, the one Martin liked. Not that Chicago, with its hard charm and gray surfaces — practically still with inactivity at this hour — is anything like Seurat's colorful sprawling picnic. But watching the sky open at her window, it is magnificent, especially after all the work she's put in, and a minor epiphany hits. We've got it all wrong. Normal business hours should be from nine p.m. to five a.m. so that we're greeted by the sun when work is through. All that was despairing and hopeless the night before has evaporated, and all that talk about the transformative power of the light of day has come true for her. She is strong again, on firm ground again. She has done things as best as she could imagine doing them, and if her imagination is an impoverished one, if it lacks in some fundamental way and the result has been a default to working harder, working longer, her life defaulted to the American dream — hasn't it been a pursuit of happiness all the same? *Her* pursuit of happiness. And no one, not Martin, not anyone, can take that away from her. It can be taken away only by death. And because of these new business opportunities, death, she's afraid, will have to wait.

She picks up the phone. She just wants to let him know that last night she went a little crazy — who knows why. But with the light of day, her senses have returned, and she doesn't need him to take her to the hospital after all.

"What are you talking about?" he says. "I was just about to leave to pick you up."

"No," she says. "That's not necessary."

"Lynn," he says, "I'm picking you up."

"Martin, I'm already at work. I'm a block away from the hospital. I don't need to be picked up."

"Lynn, why are you doing this?"

She promises to call when she's out of surgery. He protests again, but she insists. She hangs up and staggers over to the white leather sofa. It's cluttered with free samples of former client products — cans of motor oil, boxes of lightbulbs — and accordion file folders full of documents. Moving all this to the floor she lies down and, just before falling asleep, resolves that when she wakes up, the first thing she will do tomorrow — today — is clean this shameful office, and make a new start of things.

Returns and Departures

1

ON NOT GETTING IT — BENNY SPOTS CARL — HOSING THE ALLEYWAY — MARCIA'S HAIRCUT — AN INADVERTENT OFFENSE — THE NEW BUSINESS — A REQUEST FOR GENEVIEVE — THE CAFETERIA — GOING UNDER — THE DIFFERENCE BETWEEN JOE AND THE REST OF US — "THESE PEOPLE" — AN ELITIST — THE WATER TOWER — WHY IT WASN'T CYNICISM — THE GARDEN HOSES — JOE MAKES A DECISION

IN THE MORNING WE CAME in and hung our spring coats on the back of the door and sat down at our desks and sifted through last night's e-mail for something good. We sipped our first cups of coffee and cleared our voice mails and checked our bookmarked websites. It might have been a day like any other, and we should have been grateful, ecstatic even, to find no declaration of bankruptcy waiting for us in our in-boxes and no officewide memo announcing eviction from the building. We had every reason to believe that payroll management still acknowledged our existence, that Aetna had been paid and remained committed to our well-being, and that no one had been granted a seizure order to repossess our chairs.

Why, then, did discomfort pervade the hallways and offices? What made this morning different from others like it?

The unfinished pro bono ads that had eluded us the day before. We had been asked — was it possible? — to create an ad that made breast cancer patients laugh, a strange and vexing assignment. What was the point of it? No matter. Our job wasn't to ask what the point was. If that *had* been our job, nothing articulated to prospective clients in our capabilities brochure and on our website would have escaped our rolled eyes. The point of another billboard outside O'Hare? Another mass mailer on your kitchen table? Good luck mustering an argument for more of that glut. If we had to call into question the point, we'd have fallen into an existential crisis that would have quickly led us to question the entire American enterprise. We had to keep telling ourselves to forget about the point and keep our noses down and focus on the fractured and isolated task at hand. What was funny about breast cancer?

We didn't have an answer, and it was making us nervous. Jim Jackers, fearing the blank page and searching for direction among the hoi polloi, was not the only one who suffered anxiety about turning in crap work. One crap ad could make the difference between the person they kept on and the one they let go. No one could say that was the criterion, but no one could say it wasn't.

But it wasn't just our jobs at stake, was it? When we had trouble nailing an ad, our reputations were on the line. A good deal of our self-esteem was predicated on the belief that we were good marketers, that we understood what made the world tick — that in fact, we *told* the world how to tick. We got it, we got it better than others, we got it so well we could teach it to them. Using a wide variety of media, we could demonstrate for our fellow Americans their anxieties, desires, insufficiencies, and frustrations — and how to assuage them all. We informed you in six seconds that you needed something you didn't know you lacked. We made you want anything that anyone willing to pay us wanted you to want. We were hired guns of the human soul. We pulled the strings on the people across the land and by god they got to their feet and they danced for us.

What, then, were we to make of an empty sketch pad or blank

computer screen? How could we understand our failure as anything but an indictment of us as benighted, disconnected frauds? We were unhip, off-brand. We had no real clue how to tap basic human desire. We lacked a fundamental understanding of how to motivate the low sleepwalking hordes. We couldn't even play upon that simple instrument, embedded within the country's collective primal cortex, that generates fear — a crude and single-note song. Our souls were as screwy and in need of guidance as all the rest. What were we but sheep like them? We *were* them. We were all *we* — whereas for so long we had believed ourselves to be just a little bit above the others. One unfinished ad could throw us into these paroxysms of self-doubt and intimations of averageness, and for these reasons — not the promise of gossip or the need for caffeine — we found ourselves driven out of our individual offices that morning and into the company of others.

"I could *not* believe it," said Benny Shassburger, leaving his office just as we had settled in. This was an old trick of Benny's — to abandon us at the moment we needed him most, so that we knew never to take him for granted. He stopped briefly in the doorway and turned back. "Hold on a sec while I fill up my coffee and I'll tell you the whole story."

We talked among ourselves until he returned. "Okay," he said, coming into the room with a full mug and a trailing odor of stale coffee grounds. He sat down and the delicately webbed seat sank for him a little more than it did for the rest of us. He squared himself to his desk and said, "So who did I see this morning parked right outside the building but — what?" He stopped midsentence. He had something — "Where?" It was on his other cheek — we hoped to god he'd find it fast. He wiped his whiskerless face and looked down. "Doughnut glaze," he said.

There were doughnuts? Benny's story would have to wait for those of us wanting doughnuts. Those of us who'd already eaten, or who were watching their weight, or Amber Ludwig, who had just split open a brown banana and was already halfway through it, filling Benny's office with its singular ripe musk — we sat tight.

Benny proceeded to tell us that he'd seen Carl Garbedian parked in the drop-off zone just outside the building, Marilynn in the driver's seat beside him. Was it possible? Our understanding was that Carl and Marilynn were separated. "Of course they're separated," he said impatiently. "But if you'll just let me tell you my story . . ."

CARL SAT IN THE PASSENGER SEAT of the car looking out upon the day. There was his building, up ahead, with the beggar he knew so well sitting cross-legged near the revolving doors, tired this hour of the morning, it seemed, as he hardly had the energy to shake his Dunkin' Donuts cup at all those entering. As Carl glanced around, he recognized people from the office converging upon the building, but nobody he cared to talk to.

Directly to his right, something curious was going on. Two men in tan uniforms were hosing down the alleyway — a small dead-end loading dock between our building and the one next to it. Carl watched them at their work. White water shot from their hoses. They moved the spray around the asphalt. The pressure looked mighty, for the men gripped their slender black guns, the kind seen at a manual car wash, with both hands. They lifted the guns up and sprayed the Dumpster and the brick walls as well. They spot cleaned, they moved refuse around with the stream. For all intents and purposes, they were cleaning an alleyway. An alleyway! Cleaning it! Carl was mesmerized. It was the sort of thing, six months ago, that would have sent him right over the edge, seeing these men, these first-generation Americans without much choice in the matter, spend their morning in the dark recess of a loading dock power-spraying the asphalt and the Dumpster — good god, was work so meaningless? Was *life* so meaningless? It reminded him of when an ad got watered down by a client, and watered down, until everything interesting about the ad disappeared. Carl still had to write the copy for it. The art director still had to put the drop shadow where the drop shadow belonged and the logo in its proper place. That was the process known as *polishing the turd.* Those two poor saps hosing down the alleyway were just doing the same thing. All over America, in fact, people were up and out of their beds today in a continuing effort to polish turds. Sure, for the sake of survival, but more immediately, for the sake of some sadistic manager or shit-brained client whose small imagination and numbingly dumb ideas were bleaching the world of all relevancy and hope. And meanwhile, that mad-bearded fellow there with his crossed legs could hardly lift his grease-caked hands to make it a little easier for someone to flip him a quarter.

"Well, we have to find some way of getting her in," Marilynn was saying into her cell.

Carl turned his attention back to the noble fools scouring the bricks. Another thing that would have sent him spiraling was how quickly he could come up with the advertising copy designed to sell power sprayers to those shit-brained managers. "Uniform liquid distribution guarantees remarkable scouring intensity for maximum coverage and time efficiency," he thought to himself as he watched the men work, "while the high impact of our spray angles makes cleaning any surface a snap!" His quick command of that cloying and unctuous language, that false-speak, while his wife was next to him talking to Susan about mammography results or negative drug reactions, whatever — it would have been all too much to bear.

But not so much this morning, not so much somehow. Oh, he was still clear-eyed and sober about the day's dim prospects. He knew he had affixed himself, by some accursed fate, to this massive, mind-boggling effort — to *work,* to the polishing of the turds. And yet, he was changed. For Marilynn was beside him talking on the phone, and he felt no need to call her and leave a voice mail. He was not inclined to undress in the car. Marilynn had picked up the cell phone, and this was a delicate morning — the first morning after the first night they had shared together in six weeks. She might have had the good sense to ignore its ring until he had gotten out of the car. But no, she answered it as she always did, despite its being a delicate morning — yet when Carl searched himself, he did not feel ignored or preempted, at least not cripplingly so. Why was that? Because Marilynn had a job to do. Was it not that simple? Just as those men had to power-wash an alleyway, just as he had to polish the turd of an ad, Marilynn had to pick up the phone at inconvenient times and discuss estrogen receptors with goddamn Susan. Realizing this, he did not sit in the passenger seat pouting and devising schemes to draw her attention toward him. That, as he measured things, was progress. That was the promise of those little pink pills in their proper dosage. That was some kind of miracle. And when Benny shambled up and banged on the car window, it wasn't Carl's first instinct to dismiss him irritably, but to half-smile and offer a little wave. Benny being Benny, he went over to watch the unexpected pair from the drop box.

"No," his wife said, "I don't feel comfortable bringing him into this."

Just then Carl noticed a woman crossing the street. She looked familiar, even if he had a hard time placing who it was right away. Suddenly it dawned on him. Unbelievable! — she was completely transformed. Into a vision. A genuine beauty. No Genevieve Latko-Devine, but my god, thought Carl, who could have guessed such a thing were possible? It was Marcia Dwyer, and she had cut her hair. Gone was that flap that crested just above her forehead like a hard black wave, gone was that wall of glossy curls that hung between her shoulder blades like a cheap curtain of beads. In its place was now a delicate and textured cut, short in the back, curving under her chin in front and free to move in the wind. Its color was no longer tar black but a rich chestnut brown. She looked as fashionable as a model in a shampoo commercial. Carl was overcome by the change. "I cannot — will you — Marilynn," he said, tapping his wife, "Marilynn, will you look at that?" He was pointing through the windshield. "Do you see what I see?"

Marilynn was preoccupied at the moment, but Carl's excitement was alarming. "Susan?" she said. "Susan, can I ask you to hold, please?"

"Marilynn," he continued, "do you see that girl there, that woman?" He was pointing through the windshield. "Look right there, the one that just stepped up on the sidewalk, you see her?"

"The one carrying the denim purse?"

"Yes," he said. "But — ignore that for a minute, if you can. And look at her! *See* her!"

"What am I looking at?" she asked.

"That's Marcia!" he cried. "Marcia Dwyer! Marcia cut her hair!"

"Oh," said Marilynn.

The two of them watched Marcia enter the building. Marilynn peered over at her husband, waiting for him to say something more. But he was still watching the building, lost to his thoughts. Marilynn waited another beat before resuming her conversation with Susan, just in case there was something more Carl wanted to say.

With some maneuvering to obscure the fact that he had been spying, Benny came around again to the Garbedian car. Benny dropped to a squat, and Carl rolled down the window.

"Did you just see Marcia Dwyer?" asked Benny.

"She looks terrific!" cried Carl.

Benny looked toward the building as if to catch a final glimpse. "She does look terrific," he agreed.

"If I had had to place odds," said Carl, "I would have said Marcia Dwyer would have gone to her *grave* with that old haircut. I never would have thought, not in a million years, that she would wake up out of it and realize how crappy she's looked all this time."

Benny looked back at Carl, who was not really paying any attention to him while he spoke.

"Would you really call her crappy-looking?"

"Not in a million years!" cried Carl, ignoring the question. "But she *did!* She woke up, looked at herself, and said no, this is not working out."

"She has a cute face, don't you think?" said Benny.

"And who cares," said Carl, "if it was some stylist who suggested it. She *went* with it. She said yes! She said let's make a change. Benny, it's inspiring! It inspires me to want to lose some of this weight — I mean, look at this thing," he said, looking down at his belly as if it were something quite independent of himself. When he looked up, he found that Benny had stood and was walking away.

A second later, Carl got out of the car and tried catching up with him. "Hey, man, wait up!" he called out. He forgot entirely about Marilynn. The good-bye kiss that at one time had been so important to him — not in and of itself, of course, but as a gauge of Marilynn's morning attentiveness to him, of her willingness to put him before the phone call — must not have mattered much now, because without even saying so much as a good-bye, he abandoned his wife to catch up with his coworker. Marilynn, surprised by this, thought who-knows-what about Carl's sudden departure. She asked Susan to hold on again and honked the horn. Carl looked back, realized that he had forgotten about his wife — she had just slipped his mind! — and halfway between the two, asked Benny to please wait while he said good-bye to Marilynn real quick. Being curious about what Carl had to say, as much as he was about what might happen back at the Garbedian car, Benny put a foot on the first stair leading up to the building and turned back to watch. Carl leaned through the passenger-side window, a few words were exchanged, and then the separated couple kissed each other good-bye. When Carl emerged from the car and headed toward Benny, he did so almost at a gallop, as if skipping a step for the sake of urgency — and that, Benny said, *that* he had never seen before.

"Carl hurrying?" he said. "I've never seen that before."

That's where Benny ended the story. But we sensed there was more to it. So at lunch hour, finding Carl's door open for the first time in eons, a few of us went in. He was at his desk eating a low-cal Subway sandwich and drinking a diet iced tea. It was astonishing. We asked him for his version of events.

"I had completely forgotten about his crush on Marcia," he told us, sitting back in his chair, "and I had just called her crappy-looking. What an idiot. So I told him, I said, 'Benny, I'm sorry if I offended you back there.' But he just shrugged it off. 'You didn't offend me,' he said. 'You offended Marcia, I think, but not me.' So I said, 'I completely forgot about your crush, man, I'm sorry.' And he said, 'My what?' "

It didn't take long before Benny was spilling his guts down by the lake, which was only a few blocks east of us. The two men climbed over the breakers and stood at the edge of the runners' path that dropped off into the water, where Benny admitted to Carl a love for Marcia that he called paralyzing. It was taking away his nights, he said. It was starting to hurt just seeing her in the halls. Sitting across from her in a meeting, that was torture. And coming upon her alone in the kitchen took his speech away. "And you know me," he said to Carl. "I never lack for something to say. But now, I'm starting not to enjoy this." "So what are you going to do about it?" asked Carl. Benny said what he always said, the same thing he had said to all of us: his love for Marcia was complicated because Marcia was not Jewish, and it was important to him — for reasons heathens like us couldn't understand — that he marry a Jew. Stores a totem pole for three-nineteen a month and calls *us* heathens — that was rich, we thought. And what's more, everyone knew it was just an excuse in case Marcia found out about the crush and didn't like him back.

Benny's crush wasn't news. He had told each and every one of us about it at one point or another, and in great detail. The news wasn't even Marcia's haircut. Marcia had finally crawled her way out of her Megadeth-and-Marlboros origins and staggered into the fashionable reality of a new century, and her looks had improved for it. She was no longer reliving the smoke-and-screw glory days of George Washington High. Her haircut was a jump up in three income levels, it was a move to Paris, it was the opening of some seventh seal on the South Side, and if Benny's encounters with her in the hall had smarted before, he was in for a world of hurt now.

Carl leaving the car without a kiss good-bye, that was interesting, too. Carl engaged with the world — when did that happen? After stealing Janine's drugs, overdosing, poisoning himself into the hospital, and being released under a psychiatrist's supervision, Carl had gone from reproachful insolence to mild indifference. But when did he go from indifference to galloping and gossiping and chasing after Benny? Had *we* been forced to lay down odds, all our money would have been on the unlikely haircut long before Carl leaving the car without a kiss from Marilynn.

But that wasn't the news.

The news was delivered by Joe Pope, who came by Benny's office to announce that in a few days, we would start work on two important new business pitches. A beverage company was about to launch their first caffeinated bottled water, and a popular brand of running shoe had seen their market share dip over the previous few years. Both were looking for new agencies and had graciously invited us to pitch them ideas. The next step was to present them with creative that would bowl them over. Joe didn't have to tell us how important winning new business was, but he did anyway. "So we need to clear our plates of this pro bono project as quickly as possible," he said. "You'll be presenting concepts on what makes a breast cancer patient laugh first thing in the morning."

"As in tomorrow morning?" said Benny. "I thought we had till next week."

"Priorities have changed," said Joe. "Now it's tomorrow morning."

"Christ, Joe," said Larry. "You serious?"

It was like a fire alarm we weren't even getting paid for.

"Is she in today?" asked Amber Ludwig. Her tone of voice and downcast eyes might have indicated she was inquiring of someone trying to pull out of critical condition.

"Is who in?" replied Joe. He knew who she meant. We all knew.

"Listen," he said, moving more fully into Benny's office. "Does anyone have anything to show her?"

Ordinarily we would have taken this question, coming from Joe, as a kind of accusation. But the reality was that no one had a thing, and so what was the point of dissembling? We just sort of stared at him.

"I don't have anything, either," he admitted. "Not a damn thing, and I've been thinking about it all night."

It was good to hear that even he was struggling. He went on to offer us a few modest strategies he had come up with, general directions we might consider, which was kind of him. But that still didn't help cushion the blow of his bad news, and in the end it didn't get us any closer to figuring out what was funny about breast cancer.

— — —

GENEVIEVE WAS AT HER DESK, reading the breast cancer companion guide that had absorbed her attention yesterday evening after she'd finished the survivor's memoir, when Amber came to her doorway. Genevieve put the book down and moved her blond hair behind an ear. "What's up?" she said. Amber walked in and sat down, tucking one of her thick legs under the thigh of the other. "You don't know about Karen's phone call to the hospital yesterday, do you?" Genevieve shook her head and took a sip of her diet pop. She had not been with us during the call. "Then let me fill you in," said Amber.

Amber spoke. Both women turned to look at Larry in the doorway when he appeared in his Cubs cap, popping M&M's into his mouth one at a time. Amber turned back to Genevieve and continued talking while Larry moved inside and stood directly behind her.

"And remind her of her fear," he said, interrupting. Larry had been convinced by Karen's call to the hospital that Lynn's cancer wasn't a rumor after all.

Amber ignored him for the moment, but eventually came around to his point — Lynn's aversion to hospitals. It would be extremely hard for someone in the grip of a fear of hospitals to willingly admit herself to one.

Benny Shassburger came to the doorway and in a low voice said, "Are you guys talking about Lynn?" Genevieve nodded, and Benny, his khakis rustling, moved through the office to the back credenza, where he placed a haunch on the sharp wood corner. "Here's what I keep coming back to," he said. And he went on to remind her that the pro bono ads, which concerned themselves with breast cancer awareness, arrived at the same time that she was going into the hospital. "Was that just a coincidence?" he asked.

"What are you trying to say?" asked Genevieve.

"That she definitely has breast cancer," said Jim Jackers, who had been listening from the doorway. "And that she wants us to know about it."

"Why would she want us to know?"

"I don't know," said Jim. "Maybe just subconsciously."

Chewing on the last of his M&M's, Larry Novotny now began to rub Amber's shoulders with his free hands. Genevieve had turned in her chair to better talk with Benny, but her attention was pulled back to Amber when Amber abruptly stood and moved over to the chair closer to the wall. Larry, whose hands were still in the massage position, watched her go. Amber looked straight ahead at Genevieve, who looked at Larry, who lifted his cap in the air and smoothed back his hair. He left the office, passing Jim standing in the doorway.

Jim moved into the office and sat down in Amber's old chair. Hank Neary came into the room and, looking around, squatted down with his back against the wall. He put his elbow patches on his knees, pulling tight the sleeves of his corduroy coat, and then adjusted his glasses. Benny continued, and Genevieve refocused her attention on him. "As a matter of fact," he said, moving a finger between Hank and himself, "Hank and I don't even think there *is* a fund-raiser."

"Of course there's a fund-raiser," said Genevieve.

Hank elaborated. There could very well be a fund-raiser. We just didn't think Lynn had donated our time to it. We didn't think there was a committee chair pestering her. In fact, crazy as it sounded, we thought there was no client at all — unless that client was Lynn Mason herself.

"Yeah, I totally don't follow," said Genevieve, shaking her head at Hank.

Dan Wisdom showed up, taking one step inside the office to stand flush against the door, his hand on the doorknob. Hank explained that "the client" had chosen to move away from the fund-raiser ad, with its specific purpose and call to action, toward a nebulous public service announcement intended to make the cancer patient laugh for some vague reason that had nothing to do with raising money or finding a cure.

"Laughter," said Hank. "One thing Lynn might be in short supply of right now."

"So you're saying," said Genevieve, smiling mockingly at Hank, "that she made the whole thing up just so she could get a laugh?"

"That's exactly what we're saying," said Karen Woo, moving from the doorway to stand directly in front of Genevieve's cheap silver bookshelf. "Which is why nobody can find anything on the Web for the 'Alliance Against Breast Cancer.' You have to admit, Genevieve. It's a little weird that nobody's ever heard of this so-called Alliance. I mean, what kind of alliance is that?"

"I don't care," said Genevieve. "This just doesn't sound like something Lynn would do."

"Maybe she did it to keep us busy, too," said Dan Wisdom. "It's not like we had anything else going on."

"Don't you think Lynn would do that?" Amber asked her. "Keep us preoccupied during the downtime, to protect her team?"

"So which is it, then? Did she do it for herself, or did she do it for us?"

We debated which was the most likely answer.

"You guys gotta get your stories straight," said Genevieve.

Even Carl Garbedian showed up. Here was an amazing turn of events. First running after Benny, and now this. He stood next to Dan Wisdom in the doorway. "I'll tell you what I think," he said. He wanted to claim that Lynn had made up the assignment because Lynn's life was so much about marketing, the only way she could come to terms with her diagnosis was to see it presented to her in an ad. In a time of personal upheaval she fell back on the familiar language of advertising. She had to have it sold to her.

We immediately tried to distance ourselves from that theory. You steal prescription drugs from Janine Gorjanc and almost die of toxic poisoning, and six months into your recovery you're an expert on the DSM-IV? Not likely. Carl's psychologizing dampened the credibility of the argument we were trying to make — though Genevieve didn't know yet about any argument.

Marcia, with her smart new bob, slid between Carl and Dan in the doorway. "What's going on?" she asked, looking around.

We told her we were trying to convince Genevieve to talk to Joe.

"Talk to Joe?" Genevieve replied, suddenly aware that we weren't there just to shoot the shit. "What am I talking to Joe about?"

Everyone knew that Lynn and Joe were tight. We saw them talking at night on our way out — the door cracked, one leaning into the other across the desk. She told him about client problems and whatnot and he expressed to her his impressions of us. It didn't go in Joe's favor to be seen in there like that because it was widely believed that he exerted influence on who walked Spanish and who didn't. But that wasn't the point right now; the point was, if any of us had any sway with Lynn Mason, it was Joe Pope. If anyone was going to confront her with what we suspected, if someone was going to *help* her, it would have to be Joe.

"And what do I have to do with that?" asked Genevieve.

If any of us had any sway with Joe Pope, it was Genevieve.

"No," she said, shaking her head. "Nuh-uh." She shook her head and set her pop down on the desk and said, "No way. This entire conversation is ridiculous."

"Genevieve," said Amber. "She might be dying."

— — —

IT DIDN'T TAKE HER long to come around. After Karen's phone call the evidence was on our side, the argument was too compelling, and Genevieve was too compassionate. If Lynn was really sick, Genevieve didn't have it in her to sit back and do nothing. She talked it over some more with Marcia; she went back to Amber; she went in to Benny's. By eleven that morning she was as convinced as the rest of us that the risk of doing nothing outweighed the risk of being wrong, and when she went in search of Joe twenty minutes later, she had the conviction of the newly converted, which wouldn't last forever, but would for the moment brook no discouragement or allow for second-guessing. She approached him in the cafeteria on fifty-nine, where he was dropping coins into a vending machine.

Seven tables and three vending machines under a dismal light — that was our cafeteria. We'd call it a break room but "break room" might imply something to look forward to. On our rare trips to the cafeteria, we got what we needed from the vending machines and then we got the hell out. Eating there was never an option because the lights, the chairs — it was as depressing as a hospital waiting room, but absent any magazines or lifesaving devices. No one ever took comfort in the cafeteria. The perfect place to await your self-help group's arrival — that was the kindest description we could give to it.

And so the deterrents to congregation guaranteed them a level of privacy. He opened his pop at one of the tables and she told him what she knew. He listened, and when she made her request, he declined. They talked about it awhile longer and he declined again. They got up from the table and he placed his empty can in the recycle bin just as the Bible group folks, carrying their floppy, shiny-edged books, began to shuffle in for their Thursday lunch.

We wanted to know from Genevieve his reasons for declining to get involved. "He said it was none of his business," she told us. But why wouldn't he want to help her? we asked. If she was unwell, and terrified? Karen's phone call was very compelling evidence that something was not right. Was he heartless? Did he not see a distinction between sticking your nose in where it didn't belong, and answering a cry for help? "I don't think he sees it quite like that," she replied. Well, then, how does he see it? "Differently," she said.

Twenty minutes after their talk in the cafeteria, he was seen entering Genevieve's office. She set her pencil down and took off her glasses, which she used only when looking at the computer. He shut the door. He moved inside and sat down. He scooted the chair forward and placed his arms on her desk. He looked at her from under his thick brows and said, "Look, it's not because it's none of my business. It isn't, but if I knew for a fact that she needed help —"

"You would do it."

"Yes," he said. "I would help. I just can't say I'm convinced she's sick. I will admit," he added, "that it was weird that she said she would be out the entire week, and then she showed up and never explained why. And she's been preoccupied, no doubt about it. But okay, so what? That means she has cancer? Maybe she's just worried about winning the new business."

Genevieve stopped biting her pinkie nail. "Or maybe she's really sick."

"And you want me to be the one to go in and ask her which it is."

"Hard to think of anyone better."

"Why? This, by the way, is not the reason I refuse, either," he said, "but try to see it from my perspective. I'm a man. Women's issues — not something Lynn and I talk much about. But I'm supposed to go in there and talk to her about an incredibly personal matter. Whereas," he said, gesturing as if to present Genevieve to herself, "you are a woman — much more suited to the topic. But you're asking me to be the one."

"Joe, I wasn't asking you to go in there alone," she said. She lifted herself up using the armrests of her chair, crossed her legs, and sat back down again Indian-style. "I'll be with you."

"So why do you need me in there at all?"

"I need you . . ." she said. She bit her nail again while thinking and then said, "I don't need you, to be honest. I'll go in there on my own, if I have to. I'd *like* you in there because I think you can make the difference. Everyone knows Lynn's opinion of you."

He was skeptical. "What does everyone think they know about Lynn's opinion of me?"

"That she respects you," she said. "That you're a voice of reason. That she listens to your suggestions and delegates to you and even defers to you. She doesn't do that with the rest of us."

"I think," said Joe, "that what most of them see is Lynn and me talking, they see me in her office at night and they think whatever it is they want to think."

"Well," she said, "what should they think? Don't you talk privately with her?"

"But about *what,* Genevieve? It isn't . . . is Larry screwing Amber? It's not what pathetic thing did Carl do today. We're not talking personal matters, we're discussing business. We're talking about ways to keep this place from going under."

She left it at that. He had said no. Not out of any lack of sympathy, but for his own perhaps valid reasons, and better to stay friends than to push too hard. And besides, she was startled to hear him say so baldly, *We're trying to keep this place from going under.* Such an admission momentarily distracted her from the question of Lynn's health. When it got around, it distracted us, too.

But the first thing he did when he got back to his desk was call Genevieve on the phone.

"So if it's so important to them," he said, "if they're so concerned, why don't *they* go in and talk to her? What's stopping them?"

"She's an intimidating person."

"So they're cowards."

"That's a little harsh," she said. "Haven't you ever been intimidated?"

"Of course," he said. "But if I feel strongly about something, I go in with my knees knocking and try to get the job done."

"And that's why you are where you are," she said, "and they are where they are. That's the difference between you and them, Joe."

He hung up the phone, no change in his decision. Within fifteen minutes he knocked again and shut the door and sat down. His seat was practically still warm from their earlier conversation. "So because Karen Woo makes a telephone call, Lynn has cancer?" he said. "Do you know who we're talking about here? These people get things very, very wrong, Genevieve. It's the same group that's absolutely convinced that Tom Mota's coming back here to blow everyone to pieces."

"Hold on," she said. "That's unfair. There are only a few people who actually believe that. And then maybe just Amber. Most of them don't think that."

"But they sure do talk about it. And talk, and talk, and talk. But okay, forget that. One time, I overheard Jim Jackers saying that he believes Freemasons rule the world. Jim Jackers doesn't even know what a Freemason *is*."

"Jim Jackers is only one of many," she said.

"I listened to Karen Woo give an explanation of photosynthesis once," he said. "God only knows why they were discussing photosynthesis. They hung on her every word, like she was a PBS special. *Her explanation didn't even involve sunlight.* These people will believe anything. They will *say* anything."

"Joe —"

"Genevieve, you know the way things work here. One person says something at lunch, and next you know they're all walking into Lynn's office as one big mob to carry her over to the hospital for a disease she might not have. These people — you can't trust anything they say."

"I had no idea you were such a cynic, Joe."

"No," he said, "it's not cynicism." He leaned back in his chair. "Trust me. Not just yet it's not."

He left, and that really should have been the end of it. But as she sat trying to concentrate on her work, bits and pieces of their conversation kept nagging at her, objections she had been too slow to consider came to her suddenly, subtleties she had let pass now demanded she speak for them.

She found him on the phone. She waited for him to get off without taking a seat. "'These people,'" she said, when his call ended. "You kept saying that. You said it several times — 'these people.' I want to know what you meant by it."

"What do you mean," he said, "what did I mean by it?"

"When somebody says 'these people,'" she said, "you can hear it, can't you, Joe? A little condescension? I'm just wondering what sort of opinion you have of the people who work for you."

He leaned back in his chair and clasped his hands together behind the back of his head. "They don't work for me," he said. "They work for Lynn."

"Oh, you know what I mean," she said.

"Genevieve, I'm not really their boss. I'm not Lynn. But I'm not really one of them, either. I'm caught somewhere between being a partner, and being the guy in the cubicle, and they know that, so they come to me for certain things if it's in their interest, but on the other hand, if they don't like something, I'm usually the one they blame."

"And for that," said Genevieve, and she began to count off on her fingers, "you have a better title than the rest of us, you make more money, and you have a lot more job security."

She had yet to sit down. Neither of them spoke. You didn't talk about money or job security during a time of layoffs, not in the tone she had taken, and not when you were friends. The silence extended into awkward territory.

"You're right," he said at last. He let his hands fall from his head to the padded armrests of his chair. "I have advantages others don't, and I shouldn't complain about the price I might have to pay for those advantages. I'm sorry if I came across as some kind of martyr or something."

"And I wasn't trying to be snide just then," she said, finally sitting down, reaching out to touch the edge of his desk as if it were a surrogate for his hand. "You do get mistreated here. I don't blame you if you're frustrated. But you kept saying 'these people,'" she said, "lumping everyone together, and that didn't sound fair to me, Joe. Because some of them happen to be good people."

"I agree," he said.

"But then you lump them all together as 'these people' who will 'say anything' and 'believe anything,' and it just makes you sound like an elitist."

Which was the criticism we made of Joe most often — that he was aloof, that he held himself apart, that he held himself *above.* More than the juvenile speculation over his sexual orientation, more than the exaggerated claim of his social awkwardness, it was his elitism we kept coming back to time and again, like the stereotype that must have some truth to it if it gains such traction. "An elitist," he said, as if hearing the word for the first time.

"I'm not saying you are one," she said. "I'm just saying that I'm one of 'those people' this time, because I happen to think they're right — I think something's wrong with her. So when you lump me in with a guy who believes Freemasons rule the world — which I'm not sure he actually does, by the way. I think he might just think he's being funny. Jim's very desperate to be funny. He's very desperate to be liked. But, anyway, you can't dismiss all of us just because of Jim Jackers."

He looked at her. He swiveled almost imperceptibly in his chair. "An elitist," he said again — not defensively, but with a tone of curiosity, as if Genevieve had just introduced him to a new word. "What *is* an elitist?" he asked.

The guilelessness of the question caught her off-guard, as if a child had asked it, and it was her duty to explain. "Well," she said, "I don't know the dictionary definition, but I would define it as someone who thought of himself as better, or superior, to other people — someone who looked down on them and maybe deep down didn't like them all that much."

"Then I'm not an elitist," he replied quickly. "I like people a lot."

"I know you do — which is why I like *you,*" she said. "And it's *me* asking you to talk to her. Not Jim Jackers. Not Karen Woo, or Amber, or Marcia. Me. Because I'm convinced there's something wrong and that she might be scared and she might need help."

She hung forward, waiting for a reply. His eyes never wavered from hers, her incredible blue eyes, persuasive just by their sheer force of clarity and beauty. He merely said, "Let me think it over."

He was standing in her doorway ten minutes later. "Want to get some lunch?" he asked.

It was a cool day for late May, with a crisp lake breeze. Postage-stamp gardens lined Michigan Avenue all the way to the Water Tower. Red and yellow tulips were hanging on in the last days of spring. The sky was bright but the sun had peaked — it was just past one. They headed north, moving in and out of the city's large swaths of sunlight and shade created by the tall buildings and the streets that ran between them. They stopped for sandwiches on the way. They sometimes had lunch together on the benches in the courtyard of the Water Tower where the pigeons pecked at the ground and the man in gold paint stood on a milk crate still as a statue in hope of donations, and the tourists shopping at the department stores along the Magnificent Mile stopped to consult guidebooks or take pictures. They had eaten there so often, apparently, that they didn't need to ask each other where they were headed, which revealed a familiarity between them that was frankly a little surprising.

He was accustomed to the men catching sight of her and staring as she walked past. She was magnetic even in blue jeans and a simple cotton brown sweater, walking with her hands tucked deep into her back pockets. She would remove a hand from time to time to resettle a wind-whipped strand of hair.

They sat at one of the benches and ate their sandwiches. Once they were finished and he had returned from the trash bin, he said, "I looked the word *elitist* up in the dictionary. Do you think I'm a dork or what?"

"You're a copywriter," she said. "All copywriters are dorks."

" 'Resembling someone with the belief —' . . . how did it go?" he asked himself.

"You really looked it up?"

" '. . . the belief of being a part of a superior or privileged group —' . . . something like that. 'Part of a superior or privileged group' — I know that's right."

"You really looked it up," she said. She was turned to him with her legs crossed, one hand holding her hair flat while her elbow rested on her knee. The gold tips of her hair wavered in the wind.

"Well, first you said you thought they had made me into a cynic," he said. "But I'm not a cynic, and I can prove it. I came back to your office, remember? Twice. I came back to argue it. I was a skeptic — there's a big difference between that and a cynic. And the difference," he said, "was you. If it was just them saying she had cancer, I'd be a cynic, you bet. But because you were saying it, too, I was willing to give it some credit. But you have to admit that most of what they say is bullshit, which I try to avoid. And because I avoid it, people think I'm an elitist. I personally never gave any credence to that, but when you said it, I had to wonder. But your definition didn't sound right to me — that an elitist was somebody who probably didn't like other people. That's a misanthrope," he said.

"So you looked it up."

"Yes, and I'm happy to report back that I'm not an elitist."

"It really bothered you."

"It did," he said.

"Just to clarify," she said. "I never said you *were* an elitist. Just that you sounded like one."

"Okay, but listen. I'm not an elitist by the definition I just gave you, either, Genevieve, the dictionary one, because I'm not a part of the group. I refuse to be a part of any group."

"Everybody's a part of a group," she said.

"In the group photo, maybe. In the Directory of Services. But not in spirit."

"So what does that make you?" she asked. "A loner?"

"That sounds like somebody wandering at night down a highway."

"So you're not a loner. You're not an elitist, you're not a cynic. What's left, Joe? You're a saint."

"Yes, a saint," he said. "I'm a saint. No, there is no word for it. Okay, listen," he said, straightening on the bench and looking away from her. "So I have a story for you."

She took the lid off her fountain drink and pulled out an ice cube. She put it in her mouth, fastened the lid back on, and, shivering, resumed holding her hair against the wind.

"How can you eat that?" he asked. "Aren't you cold?"

She rattled the cube around in her mouth. "Tell me your story."

He paused, looking down at the pigeons pecking nearby, and at people walking past. There was an art exhibit within the Water Tower and groups of two and three kept passing in and out. "So I started running with this clique in high school," he began. He had turned away again and wasn't looking at her while he spoke. "I found myself doing a lot of stupid shit. Going along with the flow, you know. I smoked a lot of pot with people who were . . . Christ, they were all fucked up. Did you know I went to high school in Downers Grove?"

"I thought you were from Maine," she said.

"We lived in Maine until my dad got laid off. Then we moved here. I didn't want to move. Who wants to move when you're just about to start high school? Starting over again with new people, it sucked. The first couple of years sucked. But by the time I was a junior I had made some friends. Poor fuckers from bad homes. It was actually a great year. More fun than I'd had as a freshman for sure. So the year goes by, school's about to let out for the summer, and me and my friends are going to kick the shit out of this kid because he's been calling up this girl who goes out with a friend of ours. Calling her up to ask her out, and bad-mouthing my friend while he's at it. Bad-mouthing his parents, too, because these people . . ." He trailed off and shook his head. "This friend of ours, his parents were serious drunks. All I remember is going over to his house and all the dogs everywhere, and bottles of whiskey stacked along one wall in the kitchen. Dog shit just lying around the house and nobody ever picked it up. Anyway, it got back to my friend that his parents were being bad-mouthed, and naturally we decided that this little shit had to get his ass kicked. The shit's name was Henry. Henry Jenkins. Henry Jenkins of Downers Grove North. He had been a friend of ours for like a month, until he annoyed somebody and we got rid of him. Henry was a scrawny little dude, almost looked stunted, like he never got any bigger than eighth grade, even though he was the same year as us. *Anybody* could kick the shit out of this kid. Our friend didn't need our help. But we all agreed that because he bad-mouthed his parents and tried to steal his girl that we needed to get in on it, too."

"Boys," she said.

"No, I wouldn't call us boys," he said, shaking his head. "Some of those guys were already big pituitary dudes. Not boys. And I remember thinking, nobody needs anybody's help kicking Henry's ass. Henry could walk past a shoe store and be bruised for weeks. So the day it's supposed to happen, after school, I have terrible butterflies in my stomach, because I'm nervous — was I really going to do this thing? There are six of us, right, six — and then little scrawny Henry. It's not my fight. I know I should step away. But even that isn't enough — that's just cowardly. What I really need to do is object. To my friends. What, am I crazy, right? They're my friends. You only have so many friends in high school, and I had gone a long time without any. You don't object. You do what they do. So when I tell them it isn't my fight —"

"So you did object?"

"Eventually. I said I wouldn't do it, and even went so far as to say it wasn't their fight, either. They looked at me like I was worse than Henry, because at least Henry wasn't a friend. I was a friend. So they tell me, go home then, if that's how it is with me. Leave, you pussy, go home. But I couldn't leave. They were my friends. And I was scared for Henry, too, and I figured it would be better for him that I stay in case . . . I don't know what. If it got out of hand, there'd be somebody to step in and help him. So what do you think I ended up doing? I ended up watching while they held Henry down and took these garden hoses — we'd planned all this out, you know. We had wonderful imaginations. We had stolen some garden hoses from the neighborhood, and my friends wrapped Henry up in them real tight, using them like rope. And when his hands and legs were bound with garden hose — trust me, he couldn't move. Then they stuffed his mouth with somebody's shirt so nobody could hear him cry. He was squirming around on the lawn of his backyard, his eyes real big, you know, and everybody was laughing. They stood him up, and then they started kicking him. Kick, and he'd tip over. They'd stand him up again and — kick. He'd fall, but without his arms to catch him. They did that over and over again. Lift him up, kick him, watch him fall down. Lift him up, kick him over. Every time he hit with a thud. He was crying like hell. And I just watched. I couldn't stop them, but I couldn't leave, either, in case they wanted to do something like toss rocks on his head, which they debated for a while. But they didn't do that. Eventually they left him for his parents to find in the backyard — *we* left him, I mean. I ran away with everybody else. And when the police came to my door and showed my parents the Polaroids of Henry's bruises, there was no way I could say, Oh, but I wasn't really a part of that, I was just watching, or, I was really there just to protect Henry. Because that was as much of a lie as it was the truth, and for my participation I was sent to juvenile court, and I spent my last year in high school at one miserable fucking place."

"You never told me this," she said.

"I never tell anybody," he said. "And not because I'm ashamed. I am ashamed, trust me. But that's not why I never tell it. It's over, it's done, it's history. I spent a year in hell, and then I went to college. I never joined a fraternity. I didn't want a thing to do with fraternities. But I'll tell you what else I never did. I never joined that loose association of counterfraternities, either. That was every bit as much of a club. I never bad-mouthed the frat boys because I knew guys in fraternities and I liked those guys, individually, some of them I liked very well, and if I was ever tempted to bad-mouth them, I could feel it coming over me again. Joining the club, losing control. Losing my convictions. That's what I'm guilty of, Genevieve. Believing I'm better than the group. No better than anyone individually. Worse, because I stood by and watched Henry get wrapped up in garden hose and kicked over. There is no word for me. Someone better, smarter, more humane than any group. The opposite of an elitist, in a way. But that's not to say," he added, "that I'm not good and fucked up. And full of shame."

GOOD THING WE NEVER invited Joe Pope to join the agency softball team. Didn't like groups — well, what did he think he was doing working at an advertising agency? We had news for him. He was one of us whether he liked it or not. He came in at the same time every morning, he was expected at the same meetings, he had the same deadlines as the rest of us. And what an odd profession for him, advertising, where the whole point was to seduce a better portion of the people into buying your product, wearing your brand, driving your car, joining your group. Talk about a guy who just didn't get it.

We took it personally, his reluctance to speak on our behalf. That old joke by Groucho Marx had been inverted: he'd never want to belong to a club that would have *us* as members. Well, if that wasn't arrogance, if that wasn't elitism, we didn't know what was. And what did that attitude leave him with? Probably a very boring existence. He could attend civilized concert recitals though never himself join a quartet. He was allowed to read novels so long as he didn't participate in any book club. He could walk his dog but his dog was forbidden from entering a dog park where he might be forced to commingle with other pet owners. He didn't engage in political debate. That would demand he join in. No religion, either, for what was religion but one group seeking a richer dividend than the others? His was a joyless, lonely, principled life. Was it any wonder none of us ever asked him to lunch?

Well, there was nothing more we could do about it. Although we didn't know what Genevieve was waiting for, since she had agreed to speak with Lynn without him, if it came to it. Really, we didn't have much time. But when we pressed her to act, she said she was waiting. We asked her what for? "He's still debating it," she replied. We told her to give up. Joe Pope was a lost cause.

He came in and sat down across the desk from her. "They're very convincing people," he said finally. "That's the whole problem, of course. They can convince you of anything."

"Are you convinced?"

He took a moment to respond. "From the moment I came in here yesterday," he said, "and said to you, what a screwy assignment — you remember? I was more or less convinced. It's how convincing *they* are that gives me pause. Convinced and convincing," he added. "They're two different things."

She waited, sensing a tip in the scales, not wanting to say anything for fear the least word might carry some counterweight.

"But then she might actually be sick," he said.

"Yes."

"And then I wouldn't be doing it for them, would I?"

"No," she said.

"My duty isn't to them."

"Not to them," she said. "No."

He bent forward, closed his eyes, and held his steepled hands at his forehead. He stayed in that position for a long time before looking up again.

"Well, then," he said. "No time like the present."

2

PROOF OF LIFE — THE STORY OF TOM MOTA'S CHAIR, PART III — THE DIFFERENCE BETWEEN A SOCKET WRENCH AND AN ALLEN WRENCH — ON THE WAY TO THE LAKE — THE IDIOT — MARCIA HAS A PANG OF CONSCIENCE — THREE-FIFTEEN — THE TOY CHEESEBURGER — THE GRANDFATHER CLOCK — AN UNCOMFORTABLE DEVELOPMENT — THE REAL YOPANWOO INDIANS — AN UNINTENTIONAL INSULT — KAREN PASSES BENNY — JOE KEEPS AT IT — GENEVIEVE'S E-MAIL — HOW IT WORKS, HERE AND ELSEWHERE

FIFTY-NINE WAS A GHOST TOWN. We needed to gather up the payroll staff still occupying a quarter of that floor and find room for them among the rest of us and close down fifty-nine, seal it off like a contamination site. Odds were we were contractually bound to pay rent on that floor through the year, shelling out cash we didn't have for real estate we didn't need. But who knows — maybe we were keeping those abandoned cubicles and offices in hopes of a turnaround. It wasn't always about ledger work at the corporate level. Sometimes, like with real people, it was about faith, hope, and delusion.

While Genevieve and Joe were debating approaching Lynn Mason about her missed appointment, Jim Jackers went down to fifty-nine to find the inspiration eluding him at his desk. Sometimes it was necessary to physically relocate if nothing was coming. Jim left everything behind, including the blank page that feared him, and went down to fifty-nine just to think. What was funny about cancer? What was *funny* about it?

In the anonymous cubicle where he ended up, the carpet was gray and the ceiling was white. The fabric walls were orange, and there was a desk with no chair. One edge of the desk was chipped, or whittled — it almost looked gnawed — revealing the cheap permaboard inside. Otherwise there was nothing else to it — and nothing to do but figure out how cancer was funny. The room hummed with a canny stillness, which should have aided his concentration, but instead distracted him. Maybe it was the sound of the overhead lights. It was as if the blank page had followed him and morphed through a miracle of physics into a pure sound. All fifty-nine was a blank page, separated by cubicle partitions. The floor's lonesome eeriness surrounded him in its silence and blankness like an all-consuming void, and once he was sucked in, he would lose not only his job, but his mind as well. To distance himself from these bleak thoughts, he started to ruminate on more pleasant matters, like what he would have for lunch. He was pleased to find a Styrofoam coffee cup on the floor under the desk, a cigarette butt curled at the bottom like a dead tequila worm. Proof of life! Nothing funny coming to him, he shook the coffee cup and watched the butt bounce around until that activity brought out stale and unpleasant fumes, which reminded him of Old Brizz. Could it have been, he wondered, Brizz's own snuffed cigarette? Had one winter day been simply too much for him, so that he snuck down to fifty-nine, where he enjoyed three or four illicit puffs in the climate-controlled comfort of the indoors? Jim thought how grand it would be if the butt was Brizz's — a memento mori from a moment's stolen pleasure, perhaps all that was necessary to validate an entire lifetime. But the find also got him thinking again: Brizz had died of cancer. How could anything be funny about dying a miserable death and leaving nothing behind but a cigarette butt? Not proof of life — proof of death.

Jim was further afield than ever. Suddenly the silence on fifty-nine felt less like the blank page and more like the silence of catacombs. Each of the empty cubicles was a chamber waiting for its coffin.

A tinkling sound distracted him. What a great relief. He pricked up his ears. Silence. Enduring silence. Then — *clink clink — clink. Clink. "Urfff,"* someone said. Thank god — proof of life. He got up and entered the hallway. He looked in both directions, waiting. More silence. Then the dull sound of something heavy hitting carpet — *thump.* It seemed to come from further down — that honeycomb of cubicles over there, nearest the windows. Then, the cacophony of many tools being stirred about. That led him the rest of the way. He came to the doorway of a cubicle where he found Chris Yop on his knees taking a wrench to an upended chair.

When Yop looked up and saw Jim standing in the cubicle doorway, he said nothing. He simply went back to work. "Yop," said Jim, "what's that you're doing down there?" Yop didn't reply. The base of the chair consisted of six spokes, each of which ordinarily had a wheel attached to its end. The spokes were facing in Jim's direction, and looked like the dangling legs of an upturned bug. Yop was kneeling at one side of the chair and removing the sixth and final wheel. Done with that, he placed the wheel in with the others. He had with him a large black suitcase — the kind one rolls through airports — which lay next to Reiser's toolbox in the crowded little workstation. Everyone knew Reiser kept tools in his office, and Yop had evidently borrowed them. He had tucked his tie between the two middle buttons of his dress shirt, so it wouldn't hang down and interfere. Jim said he looked like a copy-machine technician, but a confused one, operating on a chair. "Whose chair is that, Chris?" Jim asked. Again Yop didn't reply.

We got this story from Marcia Dwyer, who heard it from Benny. When Jim first related it to Benny, inside Benny's office,

Benny asked him, "Weren't you worried about being seen with him, doing what he was doing?" Predictably, Jim said he hadn't even thought about it. "From the minute I saw him, I knew what he was up to," he said to Benny, "but I didn't think *I'd* get in trouble for it. Besides, it was something to watch. You ever seen a chair get taken apart like that?" At one point, after several minutes of continuous work, Yop stood and took his suit coat off, folding it neatly over a cube wall. Then he unbuttoned his cuffs and rolled up his sleeves and wiped his brow with the backs of his hairy wrists. "How come you're so dressed up, Chris?" Jim asked him. Again, no reply. Not so much as a glance in Jim's direction. Strange behavior coming from Chris Yop, who yammered on and on about whatever the fuck. It made standing there awkward for Jim. It occurred to him for the first time that the silence might be deliberate, that Yop was upset with him for some reason.

"What would he have to be upset with you for?" asked Benny. "You didn't do anything to him." "I didn't think I had," Jim said. "But I was standing in the doorway talking to the guy and he wasn't answering. So I started wondering if I had pissed him off somehow." Later, when Marcia related the story to us after hearing it from Benny, we thought that that was exactly how insecure Jim Jackers would react. There was Chris Yop, no longer an employee, told to leave the building *two days ago* under threat of arrest and currently destroying agency property, and still Jim wanted to be his friend.

He asked Yop if he had done something wrong. Yop didn't even bother to look up from the chair. "You didn't e-mail me about the changes to the project," he finally replied. According to Jim, this was said as if Yop were Jim's boss, and that serious consequences would follow from Jim's oversight. At the same time, Yop sounded hurt. Jim had to remind himself that he hadn't done anything wrong and had no reason to feel guilty. "Was I supposed to e-mail you?" he asked. "I asked somebody to," said Yop. "Do you not remember me asking?" "You mean yesterday at the coffee bar?" "Nobody e-mailed me," said Yop, who was now working a set of bolts connected to the base of the chair. "Which is okay," he added. "I am not unaware, Jim, that I have been shitcanned. Everyone thinks I'm unaware of that — I am not unaware. I am not unaware that I'm an old man and that this is a young man's game." Jim told him he didn't think forty-eight was so old, and that he'd probably have a new job in no time. Then he tried to explain to Yop that the change to the project was so bewildering — he was really struggling to arrive at even a single concept — that he wouldn't have felt confident e-mailing anyone about it. "Hey, Jim," said Yop, looking at Jim for the first time since he appeared in the doorway, and what Jim saw was the flushed, perspiring, dejected expression of someone trying to conceal the anger that made his voice quiver. "You don't have to explain to me, okay? It would have been stupid of you to e-mail me. Any of you. You don't think I know that? Hey," he added, his hands shaking as he opened his arms wide, "I'm not stupid. I know I've been shitcanned. I know no one wants to be caught exchanging e-mails with me. I just didn't expect to be treated the way I was treated yesterday at the coffee bar."

Upon hearing that, Benny demanded to know, "How did we treat him yesterday at the coffee bar?" Jim said he couldn't remember. When he related the story to Marcia, Benny asked her, "Do you remember treating him any particular way yesterday at the coffee bar?" Marcia stood in Benny's doorway next to the skeleton, hands on her hips, wrists turned inward. "I think I called him insane," she said.

Jim, standing in the cubicle doorway on fifty-nine, wanted to know from Yop how we had upset him yesterday at the coffee bar.

Yop didn't answer him directly. "I'm not getting paid for being here anymore, Jim," he said, on his knees in his nice pleated dress slacks and working the wrench. "Do you understand what that means? I'm hanging around of my own free will. I'm here because I want to be here. You think I want to be here? No way I want to be here, Jim. But I hung around for a couple extra hours yesterday, waiting for an e-mail that never came. Not from you, not from Marcia, not from Amber — nobody. At least when I got shitcanned, Lynn Mason gave me severance, you know what I'm saying, Jim? At least the agency said, Chris Yop, we have a parting gift for you. You guys at the coffee bar? You couldn't even send me an e-mail."

Yop finished removing the last of the bolts, which allowed him to slide the wheel base off the hydraulic lift bar. He placed the base in the suitcase — now the chair looked like nothing more than a silver pole attached lollipop-style to a seat and backrest. "I *heard* you," said Yop, out of the blue, on his knees and glowering at Jim. It startled Jim because he had been watching him remove the base of the chair, and next he knew Yop was pointing a screwdriver at him and staring angrily, and he hadn't even seen him pick that screwdriver up. "Every *one* of you," he added.

"You heard us what?" said Jim.

Yop refused to elaborate. He just replaced the screwdriver for a wrench and went back to the chair.

Marcia moved from the doorway into Benny's office because the story just got interesting. She sat down across the desk from him. "What did he mean by that," she asked, " 'I heard you'? That's a weird thing to say, isn't it?" "I asked Jim the same thing," Benny said. "He had no idea what he meant. What *could* he have meant by it? What did we say that he might have overheard and took offense at?" " 'I heard you,' " said Marcia, sitting back in the chair to better puzzle it out. " 'Every one of you.' What could that mean?" "Something about him crying, maybe, breaking down in front of Lynn?" "Maybe," said Marcia.

It took Yop a total of about a half hour to get the chair down to its component parts. The only time he wasted was locating a tool and then making sure the size was right. After that it was just a matter of loosening and turning. "And nobody disturbed you that whole time?" Benny asked Jim. "It's fifty-nine," Jim stated plainly. "No one even walked by." The payroll people and the bathrooms being on the other side of the floor, Benny didn't doubt it. Yop went steadily and methodically at his work while Jim continued to look on, impressed by Yop's command of tools and their function. "What's that thing called," Jim asked Benny, "where you have several pieces, all different sizes, and you attach them to the main tool depending on which size you need?" "You're asking me?" said Benny. "I'm no expert with tools." "I think it's called an Allen wrench," said Jim. When Benny told Marcia that nobody was sure what Yop was using to dismantle the chair, Marcia replied, "You guys don't know what an Allen wrench is?" When Marcia told *us* that, we knew right away that Benny must have felt a real pang of masculine insufficiency for not knowing his tools in front of Marcia, who could probably take apart a motorcycle blindfolded for all the years she spent on the South Side with her four brothers. "They're called sockets," she said, "and that's a socket wrench, not an Allen wrench. An Allen wrench removes an Allen screw, which has a hole in it that fits the wrench — oh, it's hard to explain. Haven't you ever put a table together? Or a bookshelf?" "Once, I did," said Benny. "In college."

Unlike Jim or Benny, Yop was very proficient. "Where did you learn to work with your hands?" Jim asked him. Yop wouldn't say. The one thing he did do was start to whistle a little. Being a bad whistler he soon gave it up. "In all honesty," he said to Jim, taking small steps on his knees to reposition himself with respect to the chair. "I'm glad nobody e-mailed me. I for one wouldn't want to work on a team where the other team members don't have any respect for me, Jim. That's just me personally. But you, you do what you need to do. Hold this for me, will you?" Yop went into the toolbox and picked up what seemed to Jim like a random tool and held it out before him.

Benny wanted to know if he took it. "Yeah, I took it," said Jim. "Jim!" cried Benny. "So what if it's fifty-nine, man! If somebody had walked by and seen you holding a tool while Yop was taking that chair apart, you think they would have understood you were just holding a tool for him?" "I got distracted!" cried Jim. "I didn't know why he was saying what he was saying. He said he wouldn't want to work on a team where nobody had any respect for him, but that I needed to do what I needed to do. What did he mean by that, Benny? Do the other people on the team not have any respect for me? Is that what he was trying to tell me? I mean, I know Marcia doesn't like me —"

Marcia bolted forward in the chair across from Benny. "He said that?" she asked with squeamish alarm. "He said he knows I don't like him?"

"— but what about all the others?" asked Jim.

At last Yop had finished. He stood up and dusted off his pants. He put his suit coat back on. Then he bent down and placed the rest of the items inside the suitcase — all the nuts and bolts, the armrests, the levers, the lift bar, and the webbed seat. But he had underestimated the size of the backrest, and no matter how he turned it or how hard he pushed, it was always an inch or two too big, preventing him from zipping the luggage closed. "Fuck," he said, looking up at Jim. So Jim carried it out for him wrapped in packing paper, which we kept in the mount room.

"Jim, what in the hell!" cried Benny. "Why would you help that guy out?"

"I felt bad for how he thought we had mistreated him at the coffee bar," said Jim.

"Oh my god," Marcia said to Benny. "I wish you wouldn't have just told me that."

Benny wanted to know why it bothered Marcia to hear of Jim's misplaced goodwill toward Chris Yop. "Because I am *so* mean to that guy." "To Yop?" "No," she replied. "Well, yeah, to Yop, but to Jim especially. I am mean to *everybody,* Benny — but especially to Jim. And the guy — he just wants to be liked!" "You're not so mean to him," Benny tried to reassure her. "Not any meaner than anybody else." "Yes, I am," said Marcia. "I'm terrible." She looked visibly upset. One hand was up by her furrowed brow, as if she were trying to cover her eyes and disappear from her shame. But, boy, thought Benny, did the new haircut make her look good.

"So tell me honestly, Benny, do they have any respect for me or not?" Jim had asked him.

"And how did you answer him?" Marcia wanted to know.

"I danced around it," said Benny. "I didn't exactly lie to him, but I didn't exactly tell him the truth, either." Marcia told Benny she just wanted him to move on and finish the rest of the story.

Yop walked out of the building rolling his black suitcase along the marble floor. In his suit and tie, he looked like any other businessman headed out to the airport. Nobody at the lobby desk confused him for Hawaiian-shirt-wearing Chris Yop from the creative department. His premeditated sprucing-up revealed a criminal canniness that frankly should have been a little alarming, but this was a more innocent time, and so we weren't too bothered by it after it came to light. A little later, Jim walked out with the backrest wrapped in brown paper — just a man taking an oversized package to the post office. In fact, he had slapped an address label on it for the sake of appearance.

"Jim," said Benny, shaking his head sadly.

They met in front of a corner convenience store and Jim followed Yop down to the lake. When the urge overtook Yop, which was often, he turned abruptly on the sidewalk and told Jim what was on his mind. "No more offending them," he said, the first time he swung around, stopping Jim in his tracks. "Be sure to go back there and tell them that, Jim, that Chris Yop is no longer in the building to offend them with his presence. And I will *never* return. How pleased they'll be, I'm sure. Karen Woo. And that fucking Marcia."

"Why single me out?" asked Marcia. "What did I ever do?"

"He's obviously unhinged," said Benny. "I wouldn't take it personally."

Given the chance, Jim would have responded by saying he didn't think anybody was offended that Chris was still in the building, just a little unsure why, given that Lynn Mason had let him go two days earlier. But it was clear that Yop wasn't soliciting replies. He turned quickly and walked on, leaving Jim to catch up. Holding the chair's backrest before him prevented Jim from seeing the ground and he almost tripped over an irregularity in the sidewalk. The next time Yop turned, it was just as abruptly, and Jim recoiled a little. "Thank god, Jim, thank god for the love of a devoted woman." Jim thought Yop might try to stab him in the eye with his pointing finger. "It's the only thing that's worth a damn. Without Terry," he concluded, "this whole world would be for shit."

He turned and marched on. The wheels of his suitcase drummed the sidewalk partitions at regular intervals. He turned a third time, but only to say, "Your so-called friends. What a joke." Jim anticipated more, but Yop, smiling humorlessly and shaking his head slowly, said nothing. He paused long enough for Jim to reply — it almost seemed he wanted him to — but Jim was at a loss for words. When Yop turned back again he let out a smirking, hostile laugh. Two blocks from the lake, they were caught at a red light and had to stand next to each other as the traffic moved past. "Not even to catch up," said Yop, turning to him. "You hear that? Be sure you tell them that. *Not even to catch up.*" "Catch up?" said Jim. "What do you mean, not even to catch up?" "Not that they would care if I keeled over tomorrow," he added.

"Oh my god, so I tore up his resume and threw it in his face," said Marcia. "It doesn't mean I want the man to die."

"I don't know," said Benny, "maybe we should have just e-mailed him."

At that time of day, the promenade alongside Lake Michigan was fairly empty. Most people didn't make it all the way down to the southern terminus anyway, where the land doglegged out into the water and the promenade ended at a little beach. Despite the lingering chill, there was plenty of sunlight, and in the distance to their right a few robust bathers were lending the lake its first signs of summer life. Otherwise, it was just Jim and Yop and the occasional elderly speed-walker. Yop brought the suitcase to rest just behind the breaker, unzipped it and took two of the chair wheels from inside, climbed over the breaker, and approached the water. Just as he wound back, a great May wind rose up. Yop flung the first of the wheels into Lake Michigan while his tie fluttered in the opposite direction. On his return to the suitcase the tie was still flung over one shoulder. "You guys think I *wanted* to cry?" he asked Jim. "I wasn't crying for me," he said. "I was crying for Terry. I was crying for Terry *and* me." By that point, Jim knew not to respond. He watched as Yop tossed the remainder of the wheels and the armrests out into the water. The armrests floated, as did the webbed seat and backrest — which Yop tossed out Frisbee-style, brown paper and all — but the silver pole sank quickly. He stood over the water shaking the suitcase upside down. Every nut and bolt plopped down into the lake. Then he zipped up the suitcase and returned to where Jim had stood watching him, just on the other side of the breaker. He lifted the suitcase and climbed over the breaker one leg at a time and set the wheels of the suitcase back on the ground and began to walk away, but then stopped and turned back to address Jim. "I would thank you for your help, Jim," he said, "but I've always considered you an idiot."

Yop's final remark to Jim Jackers sent Marcia over the edge. She burrowed into her seat, squirming herself into a ball of shame and regret, and cried, "Please tell me he did not!" She vowed never to be mean to Jim again. She vowed never to be mean to anyone again. "How could he say that to him?" she asked. "You said it to him just the other day," said Benny. "But how could he say it and *mean* it?" she asked. Marcia was the rare one among us who used the occasion of other people's cruelty to be reminded of her own, and to feel bad about both. She made a vow like the one she now made to Benny — never to be mean again — every two or three weeks, until something Jim said or did had her sniping again, telling him to shut up and leave her office. What was refreshing about Marcia was that she said these things to his face, but unlike Yop, they weren't eternal damnations. They were just momentary expressions of her exasperation — things we wanted to say, but we lacked the courage — and they always resulted in mad fits of compunction.

"Jim didn't seem all that upset about it, believe it or not," Benny assured her. "He just wanted to know if *I* thought he was an idiot."

"And you said no, right?" said Marcia. "Benny, tell me you didn't dance around that one."

"I told him of course he was an idiot," Benny said. "I had to, Marcia. If I had told him he *wasn't* an idiot, he would have known I thought he was one."

"This place is so fucked up," she said.

We were outraged for Jim, too. The poor guy had gone to great lengths to help Yop seek his revenge against the office coordinator and her system of serial numbers, and then he was left with an insult. We rallied to Jim's side. We told him not to sweat that remark. Then we tried to understand what Yop could possibly have against *us*. Why was he directing all his outrage toward us, we asked Jim, when, having dismantled Tom Mota's chair and having tossed it into the lake, the object of his bitterness was so obviously one specific person, i.e., the office coordinator? Jim didn't know, except to say that Yop was hurt that we hadn't e-mailed him with instructions about the changes to the project. But just what was he planning to do once he got those instructions? Salvage his job? We felt maligned.

"At least I understand Tom Mota," Marcia told Benny. "Tom's just full of frustration for how his life turned out. But Chris Yop? Chris Yop I just don't get."

In the end we had to understand that of course Yop would hate us. We were still employed, and he wasn't. He was working on out-of-date fund-raiser ads while we knew the project had changed. We had been together at the coffee bar, and he was on the outs.

"But Chris Yop wasn't what I came in here for, was it?" said Marcia.

"I don't think so," said Benny.

"What was it?" she asked herself. "Why'd I stop by?"

"I don't know," he replied, intrigued, hopeful.

"Oh my god," she said out of the blue. "Can you believe it's only three-fifteen?"

SOME DAYS FELT LONGER than other days. Some days felt like two whole days. Unfortunately those days were never weekend days. Our Saturdays and Sundays passed in half the time of a normal workday. In other words, some weeks it felt like we worked ten straight days and had only one day off. We could hardly complain. Time was being added to our lives. But then it wasn't easy to rejoice, exactly, realizing that time just wasn't moving fast enough. We had any number of clocks surrounding us, and every one of them at one time or another exhibited a lively sense of humor. We found ourselves wanting to hurry time along, which was not in the long run good for our health. Everybody was trapped in this contradiction but nobody ever dared to articulate it. They just said, "Can you believe it's only three-fifteen?"

"Can you believe it's only three-fifteen?" Amber asked Larry Novotny. You bet Larry could believe it was three-fifteen. Larry could believe it was eleven-fifty-nine and the clock was about to strike midnight and the governor had yet to call. Time was seriously running out for Larry. Was she or was she not going to have the abortion? It wasn't something he could ask every fifteen minutes, certainly not every five minutes, though time moved for him now in five-minute intervals, at the end of which he debated asking her once again if she was going to do it or what. He usually decided against asking her again, having asked only twelve five-minute intervals ago, which, before all this started, was only an hour, but which now felt more like twelve or even fourteen hours. Amber had made it clear that she did not want to be asked every hour if she was going to have an abortion.

"Are they still down there?" she asked Larry. "What do you think they're doing down there?"

Larry got up and peeked his head down the hall to Lynn Mason's office where the door remained closed. They had seen Genevieve and Joe enter ten minutes ago, or nearly two hours ago, according to Larry's new clock, and during those ten minutes Larry had debated seriously with himself, twice, whether or not to bring the matter up again with Amber. On his return he slapped his cap on his jeans three times and then screwed it on his head, nodding in the affirmative. They were still down there.

"What do you think they're talking about?" she asked.

Larry thought they were probably talking about whether or not Amber should have the abortion. They were probably discussing the misfortune Larry was facing, and how little desired it was that he tell his wife not only that he was having an affair but that the woman was pregnant and intended to keep the baby. There was no way to put a good spin on that, no way of saying cheerfully, "Charlie's going to have a half brother!"

"How long have they been in there?" asked Amber. "Ten minutes? It feels more like twenty."

"It feels more like two hours," said Larry.

It was disappointing and a little irritating that Amber was fixated on a crisis unraveling in some other office when the more significant crisis was taking place right here. "Have you, uh . . ." he began, "thought any more about, uh —"

She had been working the little white lever on a windup toy. It was a kid's toy from a Happy Meal, a cheeseburger with a sesame seed bun and all the fixings painted on. It also had a pair of enormous white feet. At last the toy could be wound no further and she leaned over in her chair and set the cheeseburger down on the carpeting. Some slight imperfection in the feet made it go in a gradual circle, which it did over and over again until finally it died and the room went silent again.

When she looked him in the eye at last he noticed her eyes had reddened. Oh, no, he thought. Not this again. He removed his cap once more and smoothed back his hair. Then he put the cap back on.

"I go back and forth," she said.

JIM JACKERS WAS HARD at work on the pro bono ads and had been working on them steadily for a few hours, since his return from helping Chris Yop throw his chair into Lake Michigan. Looking up from the blank page to the blinking clock, he discovered it was only three-fifteen. He decided that today was perhaps the longest day of his life. Not only had he been called an idiot to his face, but he could do nothing to counter that opinion, because he couldn't come up with even a single funny thing to say about breast cancer.

"WHAT TIME IS IT, JOE?" asked Lynn Mason.

Joe glanced down at his watch. "Three-fifteen," he answered.

She reached up to set the hands of a grandfather clock. It was standing against the far wall, to the left of the white leather sofa, and it was a testament to how cluttered that office had been before she and the office coordinator cleared everything away that none of us had any memory of a grandfather clock. It had blended into the background along with everything else, or had perhaps been obscured by lawyers' boxes full of old files. Or perhaps we were just not very perceptive people. But now that the layers of old magazines, dead files, and the like had been removed, it was possible to discern an attempt to make her office look like a proper one. The desk was located farthest from the door, so that when she sat at it, she could see everything before her — the door itself, the glass-top table to the left, the bookshelves and antique armchair against the right wall, and the sofa and the grandfather clock looking back at her from the far wall.

Ten minutes earlier, Genevieve and Joe's knock had interrupted her at her cleaning. Most of the work had been done the day before, but that afternoon she had been called away by meetings with the other partners to discuss strategy for the two upcoming new business pitches. Now she was putting the final touches on what was essentially a brand-new office. She answered the knock on the door by calling out and Joe put his head in. "I'm here with Genevieve," he said. "Do you have a minute?" She motioned them inside with a quick whip of a dirty rag. When Genevieve walked in behind Joe, she said, "Hi, Lynn." "Come in," said Lynn, "have a seat." How odd to see Lynn Mason with a can of polish and a rag, bending in her skirt and buffing the wood to the side of her desk. They did as they were told and sat down in the twin chairs placed directly in front of her desk. Immediately they had to turn to their left as she moved on to polish the bookshelves and then the wood inlays on her antique armchair. While she worked, she told Joe that she had asked Mike Boroshansky to dedicate one of his guys full-time to their five floors.

"A security guy?" said Joe. "How come?"

"Because we just can't take any chances," she replied.

Genevieve thought she dusted the way she did everything else, with great gusto and command. It was the first time she had ever been intimidated by someone else's dusting. She sat quietly.

"But Lynn," he said, "there are only one or two people who genuinely believe he poses a threat. Most of it is just idle chatter."

"It's not just me, Joe. It's the other partners," she said.

She moved from the armchair over to the leather sofa behind them and began to wipe that down as well. Joe twisted in the chair to keep her in his sights and talked to her over the backrest. Genevieve chose to keep staring straight ahead.

"These recent e-mails to Benny and Jim," Lynn was saying, "the way he left this place, his behavior toward his wife — the man destroyed all his belongings with a baseball bat. Now, I'm not saying I definitely think he's on his way back here," she said, looking at Joe during a brief interlude in her dusting, "but when he's swept up in something, he doesn't act right, not like a normal person, and I don't think we can take the chance."

She returned her attention to the sofa. "But how is one guy from security going to stop him if he does come back?" asked Joe. Genevieve was surprised by his contrariness, and had new insight into the openness of dialogue that passed between them when the rest of the team was out of the room.

But that wasn't the real news. The real news was that Lynn Mason now entertained the notion of Tom Mota planning a return. That point of view had had only one serious spokesperson until then — Amber Ludwig, who worried about everything. Security had posted his picture at the lobby desk, but they were screwball comedies down there. Lynn Mason's concern legitimized the idea. That was a new and uncomfortable development.

"We're working on getting an order keeping him from the premises," she said, "but in the meantime, Mike's giving us a guy, and we're putting him outside your office."

"Why my office?" Joe asked.

"Because your office looks directly onto the elevators, and if he comes back here, this is the floor I think he'd visit first, and to be honest with you, Joe, I think the biggest grudge he has might be against you. With maybe me being the exception."

"I disagree," said Joe. "It's true he didn't care for me in the beginning, but by the time he left, for whatever reason, I think I'd earned his respect. And to be honest with you, Lynn, I think we're blowing this whole thing way out of proportion."

"Well," she said, with her back to him. "There's still going to be a man outside your office."

Through with her cleaning at last, she opened the door to the grandfather clock. When Joe informed her of the time, she set the hands accordingly and wound the clock with a key. She set the brass pendulum in motion and then shut the door and watched it swing. In the intervening silence Genevieve glanced back to see what she was doing, found her standing before the clock, and once again realized how small she was in real life. Joe could probably lift her off the ground. He was no muscleman but he was no slouch, either, and he could probably take her by her two arms and lift her, maybe all the way until his own arms were extended, and at the very thought of Joe holding Lynn Mason up in the air like that, like a child, and with a little extra effort, even spinning her around, Genevieve had to choke back the laughter rising in her throat, because Lynn was just then coming around to her desk and pulling her chair out to have a seat. All at once she loomed larger and more intimidating than ever before.

"Now," she said, "what did you want to talk about?"

"NOW I REMEMBER WHAT IT WAS!" cried Marcia.

It had finally come to her. She had heard Benny was selling the totem pole and she wanted to stop him. "Who told you I was doing that?" he asked. It was making the rounds — the rise in rental rates and his reluctance to pay the difference. "But who ever said I was selling it?" he asked. "Don't do it," Marcia pleaded. "Please, Benny. Do you want to see them win?" "Who's 'they'?" he asked cautiously. "Every single one of those motherfuckers," she replied. She had momentarily forgotten her vow never to be mean again. "If you sell it, Benny, you will be handing a victory to every ignorant motherfucker on the payroll. You don't want to do that, Benny, you don't. And I don't want to see it happen." "What I *want* to do," he said with sincerity, "is I want to stop giving three hundred bucks a month that I don't have to that storage place — that's what I really want." "I'll pay the difference," she said. "You'll do what?" "The difference between what you're paying right now and the rise in rates," she said. "What is it? I'll pay it. I'll write you a check every month." "Why would you do that?" he asked.

Part of it, she explained, was to help rectify every despicable, hateful thing she had done since that happy day she had been hired. It was an effort to restore the balance, to reclaim her right to raise her head and stand up proudly. Benny did not need reminding that Marcia was a dabbler in Asian religions. In fact he had been reading up on them. He had been studying the Four Sights, the Eightfold Path, and the Ten Perfections in the hope that one of them might come up in conversation. He was slipping allusions to the Bo tree into many of the stories he told. Marcia hadn't responded to any of them as he had hoped she would, either because she wasn't paying attention, or because the allusions meant nothing to her. We said nothing because Benny was Jewish, and we assumed he, as a Jew, knew more about religion than the rest of us. But in fact he had mistakenly been studying Buddhism, while Marcia considered herself more of a student of the Hindu religion. The only thing he got right was a copy of the Bhagavad

Gita sitting on his desk, on top of some papers, with the spine facing conspicuously in her direction.

"So let me see if I get it," he said. "You want to help your karma."

"Yes," she said.

"From good must come good," he said, "and from evil, evil. Is that what you're saying?"

"Yes!" she cried. "That's *exactly* what I'm saying. How'd you even know that?"

"I've been reading about it lately," he said.

But it was not as simple as cutting him a check, she explained to the novice. Karma did not take if an offer was made only in the anticipation of a return. A genuine and pure impulse had to precede the selfless act. "So what's your impulse?" he asked. "Not to see those bastards win," she replied simply. Benny said he was just hazarding a guess here, but that didn't sound very pure to him. Marcia reminded him of the Yopanwoo Indians. The Yopanwoo Indians had made a mockery of every real Native American tribe ever to suffer an injustice. The practical joking had turned a tragedy into a farce. She promised Benny it was as pure as they came. "I'm from Bridgeport, I never met an Indian in my life," she said. "But I was still offended. And I thought what you were doing with it — with Brizz's totem pole, I mean. To be honest, I didn't know what you were doing with it, but I thought whatever it was was . . . was —" "Weird?" he said. "No," she said, shaking her head and its all-too-lovely new contoured hair. "No, not weird. Noble." "Noble?" he said. "You thought it was noble?" He wondered briefly where she had been with this talk of nobility when they were hooting at him from the hallway and bloodying that skinned toupee on his desk — though he said nothing about that and took the compliment with pleasure. Her good opinion was well worth three-nineteen a month — though that wasn't why he had done it. "So to stick up for the Indians," she said, "and to see that those bastards don't win, and to help you do whatever it is you think you need to do with Old Brizz's totem pole, you tell me the difference and I'll write you a check." There was a fourth reason, too, of course, which was that it might help Marcia improve her karma, but she left that off the litany.

"Marcia," he said, "that won't be necessary."

"I know it's not *necessary,*" she said. "I want to do it."

"I'm afraid I've already gotten rid of it," he said.

The appraiser who had come out to the U-Stor-It had informed Benny not only of the totem pole's market value but also a thing or two of its origins. He believed it to be the work of a tribe whose descendants were still living in southeastern Arizona. Their onetime woodworking skills were unsurpassed, producing some of the most virtuosic and dazzling Indian art in the world — that is, until the number of tribesmen declined and survival became more difficult and their craftsmanship suffered. That morning, Benny had received a call from the appraiser, who had sent snapshots of the totem pole taken at the storage facility to members of the tribe in Arizona. He informed Benny that the chief of the tribe had confirmed with near-absolute certainty that the pole was theirs. "And there are like . . . ten of these Indians left in the world," said Benny. "I'm exaggerating, but just barely. And they can't make these things anymore — not like how they used to. Which explains the hefty price tag. It's irreplaceable." "How on earth," said Marcia, "did Brizz ever get ahold of it?" "The sixty-thousand-dollar question," replied Benny. "Or why didn't he sell it when he needed the money? I have no idea — and I have no idea why he gave it to me and not somebody else. So not knowing why, I hung on to it. But now, I don't see I have much of a choice but to give it back to them, knowing how few of them there are left." "Maybe that's *why* he gave it to you, Benny — because he knew you'd find the right guys to give it to." "Maybe," said Benny. "But one thing I told those Indians, I'm not paying the shipping and handling. That's up to you guys." "You spoke to them?" "On the phone," he said. "By the way, I meant to tell you. I like your new haircut."

Immediately she turned away from him and her hand rose up to greet her hair in a tentative and self-conscious manner, as if she were trying to hide it from him. "Don't talk about my hair right now," she said.

"Why not?"

"Because it's stupid. We're talking about something else."

"Don't you like it?" he asked.

She turned to the opposite wall, as if expecting a mirror there, something reflective to see herself in. "I don't know," she said. "Let's not talk about it."

"I think it's a great update," he said.

She turned back to him. "Update?" she said. "What the hell does that mean?"

"No, I just meant —"

"That's a pretty shitty thing to say," she said.

"No —"

"I have no idea what the hell it means," she said, "but it sounds pretty shitty."

"No, I was just saying I liked it."

"Update," she said. "You don't say 'update,' Benny. That's the wrong word."

No! NO! He had tried to say it just right! He had considered other options, alternative phrases, but he thought what he had settled on was perfect. He had rehearsed it over and over again, practicing a nonchalance in his voice, then waited for the exact right moment — *and still he flubbed it!* He probably should have run it by a copywriter.

Even with the best of intentions, it was impossible not to offend one another. We fretted over the many insignificant exchanges we found ourselves in from day to day. We weren't thinking, words just flew from our mouths — unfettered, un-thought-out — and next we knew, we had offended someone with an offhand and innocent remark. We might have implied someone was fat, or intellectually simple, or hideously ugly. Most of the time we probably felt it was true. We worked with some fat, simple people, and the hideously ugly walked among us as well. But by god we wanted to keep quiet about it. If in large part we were concerned only with making it through another day without getting laid off, there was a smaller part just hoping to leave for the night without contributing to someone's lifetime of hurt. And then there were those, like Marcia, who had the ability to turn even a compliment into an insult, bringing us (Benny especially) to our knees so that the only way to win was to remain silent, absolutely silent — unless, of course, the opportunity presented itself to bloody a scalp and leave it on Benny's desk.

"I'm sorry if I offended you," said Benny. "I was just trying to say it looked nice."

"No, I'm sorry," she said. "I don't take compliments very well. Was I mean to you just then?"

"No, no, not at all," he assured her.

Suddenly Genevieve was standing in his doorway. Benny went quiet. Marcia saw his attention diverted and turned and saw Genevieve, too.

"Marcia, can I talk to you?"

Like that, Genevieve was gone. Marcia looked back at Benny. "Sure," she called out after her, rising quickly. Benny had never seen Marcia's eyes so wide.

"Benny," she whispered.

"Go," he said.

When Marcia left, Benny called Jim to tell him the news but Jim wasn't picking up. He stood and walked out into the hallway. Things were quiet. He went back inside and put another call in to Jim. Again no answer. He went back out into the hallway. Everything was calm and empty. The large fake plants stood unstirred at both ends of the hall, and on the walls between the doorways hung all of the agency's past advertising awards, collecting dust. He returned and called Jim a third time. Then he e-mailed him to tell him to listen to his voice mails. He spent two minutes waiting for a reply at his desk before deciding to hunt Jim down. He went back out into the hallway, but he stopped when he saw Karen Woo approaching. He had no desire to be the one to let Karen know that Genevieve had emerged from Lynn's office. She would only spread the news around. So he casually lifted his arms and grabbed ahold of the top of the doorway, as if he were just hanging out, having a stretch. Karen grew closer, and he thought they might just greet each other and nothing more. And in fact, she seemed to have no intention of stopping and chatting, which was a relief. She just said, "Turns out Lynn doesn't have cancer after all," and then she passed by and disappeared down the hall.

MARCIA STOOD WITH HER BACK against the closed door of Genevieve's office while Genevieve paced behind her desk, occasionally stopping to grab the back of her chair, as if to throttle it.

It was very simple. Lynn sat down at her desk and the question of where to start, how to broach the subject, eluded Genevieve entirely. Luckily, Joe began to speak. She couldn't remember what he said, exactly, but he was very direct. Genevieve was nervous. She had to keep reminding herself of why she was there. This person who could so thoroughly dominate every other aspect of life — who *dusted* with domination — was really very sick inside, and weak, and in need of intervention, even if that intervention came from a cowed underling sitting mutely beside Joe. If she had not kept that in mind, she would have had to excuse herself for being so nervous. Joe said, basically, that a rumor had emerged, he did not know from where, that she had been diagnosed with cancer. Normally he didn't put much stock in rumors, but he hoped she would understand why he'd give second thought to one that claimed she wasn't well. There was the conviction among certain individuals that an important operation had been scheduled for yesterday, but that she had missed it. Perhaps deliberately. Her aversion to hospitals — something of a well-known fact — might explain why. He was there — and then he remembered Genevieve and turned to her. "The two of us are here," he said, turning back to Lynn, "to let you know that these rumors are out there, they're floating around, I don't know to what degree of truth, but if there is something we can do for you, if we can help you in any way —"

"Joe, have they suckered you into it at last?" she asked him.

It? What was she referring to specifically, Genevieve wondered. While Joe was speaking, the tricky smile Lynn sometimes wore to express disbelief or bemusement appeared on her face. Joe must have seen it, too. Yet he persevered. Genevieve didn't know where he found the will to continue with Lynn Mason looking at him like that. He stopped briefly when she interrupted to ask if he'd been suckered in, but then something truly remarkable happened. He kept at it.

"No, I don't think I've been suckered into anything," he replied. "I'm not here on their behalf. I'm here for myself — and Genevieve — because I believe there might be something wrong with you."

"There's nothing wrong with me," she said simply, drawing into her hands a silver letter opener in the shape of a stiletto.

"That maybe you're sick," he continued — Genevieve did not know how or why and wanted him to stop — "but because of your fear, you aren't letting yourself get looked after properly."

"There is nothing wrong with me," she repeated.

Joe was silent. Genevieve was ready to leave. Okay, Joe, she's okay — let's go. "A person with a genuine fear," he continued, slowly, not apprehensively but patiently, as if trying to coax something out of her, "somebody incapacitated by fear, *would* say she wasn't sick, if it meant she could continue with her life and not face that fear."

Lynn offered a grudging, humorless chuckle. "I'm sorry, Joe," she said. "Do you have access to my medical file?"

"No."

"No," she said, "no, I didn't think so."

"No, this is pure speculation, Lynn," he continued, and by then, Genevieve felt the definite need to distance herself from Joe somehow. Not sick, Joe! *Please* stop talking! "Speculation that is probably not justifiable," he continued. "But if you are sick, and scared, and keeping yourself from medical attention —"

"It was a mole," she said.

All look of disbelief drained from her face. Now she wore a deadpan, ice-cold, *corporate* expression that said, simply, this is none of your business. "It was a mole they feared was cancerous, and I had the appointment rescheduled, if you must know, because of the urgency of the new business pitches. Genevieve," she said, glancing down at the letter opener which she had been fingering while Joe spoke, "will you excuse Joe and me, please?" When she looked up at Genevieve, Genevieve said of course and left the silent office and closed the door behind her.

"A mole?" said Marcia. "This whole time it was only a mole?"

After Marcia left we heard Genevieve talking on the phone to her husband, *screaming* at him, though he had done nothing, poor guy. But that someone somewhere had done something terribly wrong, she was dead certain. She knew she was angry. She knew something had to be done to someone. She just didn't know exactly what.

"Who was it?" she demanded of us. "Who was the first to say it was cancer?" We tried to tell her, Genevieve, no one knows who. No one will probably ever know who. "Well, who spread it then?" she hollered. "Who was responsible for spreading it?" She was with us yesterday when we tried figuring that one out, we reminded her, and she knew as well as we did that it was almost impossible to say who spread it. "Then whose idea was it to send Joe in there?" she asked. "Was this just some elaborate hoax to get Joe?" Well, that was just crazy talk, and we told her so — delicately, and not in so many words, because by then she had worked herself up into a fury. "Why did *I* get involved?" she asked. "How could I have let myself get wrapped up in this?" Now she was addressing herself, and we had no answers for her. She threw up her hands and left our offices.

We thought Joe Pope handled the whole thing with equanimity. At one point, Jim Jackers called out as Joe passed by his cube. They didn't say a word about Lynn Mason. Jim just wanted to know if it was true that the ads for the breast cancer patient were now running in Spanish. "Does that mean we should be gearing our message toward a Latino market?" he asked.

"That's the first I've heard of that," replied Joe. "I would be very surprised if that were true. Who gave you that information?"

"I think they're playing a joke on me," said Jim.

"I would have to assume it's a joke," Joe said. It was just about the funniest joke ever.

Late in the afternoon, Genevieve sent us a group e-mail — the address list was a foot long — that denounced our "tactics," our "sham sentiments." We were "pathetic" and "dumb." We had been "led by the nose" to "set Joe up." That was ridiculous — for who would we have allowed to take us by the nose? What an elaborate and fainthearted conspiracy she envisioned. She never used the word, but it was hard not to read between the lines. How could it be a conspiracy? Was someone — say, Karen Woo — so diabolical, so shrewd, so capable of manipulating circumstance, that she could pull off with such delicacy the very subtlest of conspiracies, by spreading an outlandish yet eminently *believable* rumor, and then distorting the conversation she had had on the phone with the nurse at Northwestern to seal the veracity of her lies and set the fall guy up? Wasn't that a little far-fetched, even if none of us had actually heard what the nurse had said — or could confirm that there was even a nurse on the other end? And what real damage could she have hoped to achieve? This was not, as only Hank could put it, "the sweaty Moor's murder of Desdemona." No way, we thought, no way it was Karen Woo. If she really wanted to stick it to Joe, we gave her enough credit to bleed the fucker dry. Besides, Genevieve had to face facts. A conspiracy was an impossible thing to prove. The most anyone could say was that this was how these things worked, here and elsewhere. Mistakes were made. Accountability got lost.

"I am DONE," she concluded in her e-mail, and went on to list all the things she would no longer be doing with us in the future. Lunch and after-work drinks, mainly. We had heard it before. We wondered how long it would last this time.

3

ORDERING CABLE — LYNN FORGETS — BACK TO THE FUND-RAISER — ROLAND CALLS BENNY — AN INDETERMINATE FATE — ANDY SMEEJACK'S LUNCH — WHAT'S GREAT ABOUT A SILENCER — AMBER FREAKS — CARL SINGS — A QUESTION OF COURAGE — LARRY'S REVELATION — CARL GETS WEIRDED-OUT — A CONVERSATION ABOUT WORK — THE MELEE BEGINS — CHICAGO'S FINEST

THE FACT THAT LYNN MASON did indeed have breast cancer came out eventually. By then it was no longer a subject of our speculation. We had moved on, or regressed, rather, back to the question of who would be the next to go. For the morning following Genevieve's freak-out, when we woke up all across the city and the greater metropolitan area, we still had no concepts for the pro bono project.

We didn't give up entirely. If nothing came to us in the hour between waking and leaving, we still had the commute to work and the ride up the elevator. We had coffee at our desks and the alchemical kick of insight it promised. What would make them laugh? The ailing, the nauseous, the prepped and stitched and scarred, the toxic, the irradiated — what would make them laugh? What was funny about frailty and bad luck, about limping home to await the bad news, about wheeling around an IV pole? What was ticklish about the possibility of death — a perfectly ordinary and thus utterly baffling death?

We met at Lynn's office at the appointed time. The dread was palpable. We found her office clean and orderly. She was sitting behind the desk, inspecting her middle drawer for things that could be tossed into the trash. She gestured silently for us to enter, as she was on the phone. She tested a Bic that gave her nothing and so she threw it out. We took our seats, criminals on the trundle cart awaiting their turn at the gallows.

"I can't believe how hard it is to arrange for a cable guy to come to your house," she said, after hanging up. "It's astonishing that anyone has cable at all. Do you guys have cable?" she asked.

We all said we did.

"So somebody had to stay home one day," she said, "and wait for the cable guy to come?"

We weren't sure how to answer that one. An honest response would reveal that there had been a day in our dark pasts when we had taken a morning off and stayed home to await the cable guy instead of coming in to work. We didn't want her to think we'd ever choose cable over work. Work was what allowed us to afford cable. On the other hand, there were times when we came home and really needed to veg out with some cable, and those nights reminded us that we'd have feigned the flu for an entire week if that's what it took to get cable.

"I'm just saying there has to be an easier way," she said. "They can't expect you to wait home on a Tuesday from ten to two for the cable guy to come, can they?"

"They got you by the balls," said Jim Jackers.

To Lynn he said that. It was awful. We winced terribly.

"They do got you by the balls," Lynn agreed.

"You don't have cable already, Lynn?" asked Benny Shassburger.

"Rabbit ears," she said. "Pathetic, I know. But I do get *The Simpsons* on rerun."

We were amazed that Lynn watched *The Simpsons*. Nobody was more amazed than Benny, who asked her what her favorite episode was. She had an answer for him right away. It was different from Benny's, although each of them knew and respected the other's favorite episode. Soon they were reciting lines. To hear Lynn Mason quote Homer Simpson was shocking. More shocking, though, was the remark Amber made when she interrupted them.

"I'll stay home for you and wait for the cable guy," she said.

Lynn looked at her. "I'm sorry?"

"If you need me to," she said. "I'll come over and wait for him."

Lynn laughed, but not in a mocking way. It was a gentle expression of surprise. "That's okay," she said. "I'll manage it somehow. Maybe my doorman can let him in."

Amber's sympathy for Lynn during the days we believed she had cancer had permeated so deeply into her psyche that even now, when the rumor had been retired, she still looked upon Lynn as ailing and in need of help. It was absurd and touching. Lynn changed subjects.

"Sorry, what are you guys here for again?" she asked. "Did we have a meeting?"

We all turned to Joe Pope. He reminded her that she had asked to see concepts for the pro bono ad —

"Oh, shit," she interrupted. "That was today, wasn't it?"

He nodded.

Lynn placed fingertips at her temples. "Joe, it completely slipped my mind." She shook her head. She looked around. "I'm sorry, guys. My mind is entirely on this new business."

"Should we come back?" he asked.

Simultaneously we all fell to the hard carpet and began to pray. We prostrated ourselves before her, our pathetic and undeserving selves, and pleaded for mercy. *More time — please give us more time!* It must be said: we were a small, scared, spineless people. In reality we sat perfectly still, silently holding our breath.

"No no," she said. "Show me what you got."

"Well," he said, "after the change came in from the client —"

"Change?" she said. "What change?"

"The e-mail you forwarded me?"

"Oh, right," she said. "Remind me?"

Remind me? What the hell was going on here? We had spent hours and hours speculating on the nature of this pro bono project, and she didn't seem to recall the first thing about it. So Joe explained the change, as well as the difficulties we had been encountering. He went so far as to suggest that what the client now requested might be impossible to achieve, but if we were to achieve it, we'd certainly need more time.

"Well, that's the one thing we no longer have," she said. "Our first priority is to win this new business for the agency. We can't waste any more time on charity work."

She asked us if we had generated concepts for the fund-raiser. We all said we did.

"Then bring them to me," she said. "That's what they wanted initially, that's what they're getting."

So we left her office to retrieve our fund-raiser concepts. When we returned, she looked through them and, in the end, chose Karen Woo's "Loved Ones" campaign. It was disgusting to look over and see Karen's face just then. Lynn asked Karen to forward them to her. She would PDF them over to the client herself. "And if they don't like them," she concluded, "they can find a new agency. Because right now, we have bigger fish to fry."

"Lynn," said Karen. "How come I can't find any presence for this Alliance Against Breast Cancer on the Internet?"

"Karen," said Joe.

"Thank you for your hard work, everyone," said Lynn.

And with that, our pro bono project came to an end.

— — —

BECAUSE OF THE NEW BUSINESS, we didn't have much of a chance to talk over this unexpected development. We had an input meeting midmorning during which we discussed the caffeinated water client and their needs. Directly after that we had another input meeting to go over the creative needs of the running shoe manufacturer. We all knew the importance of winning new business, so after these meetings we returned to our desks and started to brainstorm.

And so it was a full office when, near noon, Benny got a call from Roland. Roland was manning the front desk of the downstairs lobby, midway through a double shift. Benny had noticed that on days Roland worked a double shift, his eyes were glassy and red and stuck at half mast, that he yawned every thirty seconds, throwing his oblong, open-mouthed face up like a wolf howling at the moon, and that he sometimes stole away to fifty-nine for a twenty-minute nap. This was a postretirement gig for Roland so he could supplement his Social Security. Who was going to begrudge the man twenty minutes? According to Benny, the naps were badly needed. "One Friday," Benny told us once, "he kept calling me Brice. I didn't say anything to him because I knew he knew my name and I didn't want to embarrass him, but Brice? Why Brice?" Jim Jackers suggested "Lenny" would have been more likely, or even "Timmy." "Timmy makes more sense than Brice," said Jim. "At least it rhymes with Benny." "Jim, *Nancy* makes more sense than Brice," said Benny. "Who calls somebody Brice? Anyway, I didn't say anything to him, and by Monday he was calling me Benny again. It's those double shifts, man. They muddle his brain."

When Benny picked up the phone, Roland told him that he believed Tom Mota might be in the building. "And maybe he just got on the express elevator," he added. "What do you mean maybe?" asked Benny. Later, when recounting the story, Benny thought it was perfectly possible the man was hallucinating, given that it was a Friday and he was on the tail end of a double shift. "What makes you think it was even Tom?" he asked. But instead of listening to Roland's response, in his head, Benny heard Amber. Again he dismissed her prognostications of Tom's return as the anxieties of a worrying homebody. He trusted in Tom's better instincts and wasn't inclined to think that anyone was in any immediate danger. But regardless of how he felt, if Tom really was back, some people would definitely want to know. There was also the possibility that Benny knew nothing about Tom's better instincts. "Why are you calling *me* about this?" Benny suddenly interrupted Roland in midspeech.

". . . and said he had a package to deliver," Roland continued, "so I sent him up on the express elevator. Because I can't get ahold of Boroshansky," Roland added, belatedly answering Benny's question, "and I thought somebody up there should know about this."

"Wait, Roland — you mean to say he approached you, and you looked at him, and you still can't be sure it was him?"

"Because of the makeup!" cried Roland, exasperated.

"What makeup?"

"Haven't you been listening to me?"

Benny hadn't heard a word he'd said. "No," he said. "What are you talking about, makeup?"

"Hold on a second," said Roland. "That's Mike on the Motorola."

Benny waited. What was he waiting for? Instructions from a bleary-eyed, untrained security guard with scant natural aptitude for his post, debilitated by a double shift. The smart thing would be to hang up. He waited. Roland came back on.

"Benny? Yeah, it's Roland."

"Well, who else would you be?" Benny replied impatiently.

"Mike thinks you should warn people."

Benny hung up. He walked out into the hallway. To his left he caught sight of Marcia, who at that instant had reached the end of the hallway, turned left, and disappeared, leaving nothing but the dusty leaves of the fake potted tree to quiver in her wake. He thought of running after her, but he was distracted by movement to his right. Hank had rounded the opposite corner in perfect synchronization with Marcia and then he, too, disappeared, into his office. Benny was left to stare at the other potted tree, the mirror image of the one he just turned away from. For the briefest moment he stood frozen, equidistant from both trees, uncertain what to do.

Roland couldn't say for sure that the man he had seen was Tom, so Benny couldn't say for sure that it was Tom coming up on the express elevator. Even if it was him, Benny couldn't say that Tom intended anyone any harm. He had no instinct for what to do with the limited information he did have. Should he start to scream? Cower under his desk? Or should he go stand by the elevator and be the first to greet Tom? During that brief moment, the empty hallway felt possessed of a haunted tranquillity that gave the impression that all down the hall, and down the other hallways and offshoots of hallways and the passageways between cubicle partitions, the offices and workstations had been suddenly and irrevocably vacated, and that all the corporate, animating, human life that once burbled and cackled and Xeroxed and inputted had ended with an inextricable filing away, and that all the days spent here, the time served, the camaraderie enjoyed, were now casualties of some unhappy, indeterminate fate.

In the next instant, there was a flurry of activity. Hank reemerged from his office and disappeared around the same corner he had lately come from, Marcia returned around the same corner where she had lately disappeared, and Reiser, in need of a hallway break, limped out of his office to the right of Benny. Reiser gripped the Louisville Slugger he kept in one corner of his office and tapped it on the heel of his shoe, as if approaching home plate. Larry and Amber, on the other side of Benny, suddenly spilled out into the hallway too, trying to contain a quiet, fierce disagreement just as Marcia approached, forcing her to pass tenderly between the two lovers as if trying to avoid a land mine. She was preparing to pass Benny with nothing more than a grimace of discomfort for having to walk past such office awkwardness. Benny thought it wiser to whisper than to wail, so very casually he reached out and took Marcia's arm. She was wearing the pink cotton hoodie she wore whenever she complained of being cold. Beneath it, her arm was soft and thin and felt good in his hand.

"Marcia," he said. "Tom Mota might be back in the building."

--- --- ---

TOM MOTA TOOK THE EXPRESS elevator past sixty all the way up to sixty-two. Sixty, sixty-one, and sixty-two were connected by interior stairs, so anyone could move freely between them. No one saw Tom as he stepped from the elevator.

He must have walked straight and then taken a right at the wall that dead-ended at the print station. He walked on until he reached the hallway juncture, allowing him to go in either direction. He chose to proceed left, passing the men's and women's restrooms to his right, turned left again, and walked down that hallway, flanked on one side by beige cubicle walls and on the other by the windowed offices coveted by those inside the beige cubicles. Overhead the ceiling panels alternated, two white tiles for every panel of fluorescent light. Tom proceeded to walk on the beige carpet beneath them.

Andy Smeejack was sitting behind his desk in one of the

windowed offices, trying with his stubby, maladroit fingers to crack a hard-boiled egg. Andy was in Account Management. Cracking it was easy — he held the egg like a polished stone and tapped it softly against the edge of his desk. He had laid a napkin down where he planned to collect the bits of shell, but that particular egg clung to each and every piece like a stubborn, protective motherland, and Andy was forced to get surgical on it — probably a comical sight, this hulking, dieting giant patiently picking off the shell of his desperately meager, entirely unsatisfying lunch. He was loath to yield even a fraction of rubbery egg white to the smallest bit of shell. Unfortunately, his clumsy fingers were much more spry at grabbing juicy Italian beef sandwiches and greasy fat cheeseburgers, and now large swaths of his lunch were being ripped off in his haste, leaving him with a moon-cratered egg darkened by the gray yolk inside. When he finally looked up, taking half the egg in his mouth, he saw the clown standing in eerie, carnivalesque incongruity in his doorway. The clown's face was painted bright red, with a broad white band encircling his mouth. A fat red ball made of foam was attached to his nose. The clown's head was a carrot-colored mass of jubilant curls, and his oversized bow tie was red and white striped. He wore suspenders and baggy blue pants. Andy, halted from chewing and unable to say much with his mouth full, looked closer at the clown. He was holding a backpack in one hand, and in the other . . .

Tom and Andy once got into a shouting match over a miscommunication that resulted in the missing of an important deadline, and neither of them had ever forgotten it.

"You know what's so great about a silencer, Smeejack?" Tom asked, raising the gun. He pulled the trigger. "It silences," he said.

"OH MY GOD, OH MY GOD," Amber kept saying. She placed her hands on her still-flat belly and all that was just then growing inside. Her plump knees buckled a little, and Larry had to reach out for her. "Amber," he said. "Amber, we should move. We should move, Amber." Benny and Marcia exchanged a look.

"Amber," Benny repeated, "I don't know for sure that he's even in the building, do you understand?"

"Oh my god, oh my god."

Larry was holding her up by her arms. "Amber, let's just move, okay? Let's not stay here."

"She might be hyperventilating," said Benny.

"Benny," said Marcia, "there's Joe."

Benny looked down the hall just as Joe was entering his office at the far end, near the elevators.

"Oh my god, oh my god."

Her panicky, tear-inflected singsong quavered as if she had already been witness to unspeakable violence.

"Larry, Marcia and I are going down to tell Joe," said Benny, "so it's up to you to get her to calm down."

"What do you think I'm trying to do here?" asked Larry. "Amber, are you listening to Benny? You have to calm down. We're going to take the emergency stairs, okay? Let's just take the emergency stairs."

But Amber didn't want to take the emergency stairs. She didn't want to take the elevator because he was coming up in the elevator. She didn't want to go back into her office because he was coming for her in her office. To go anywhere at all she had to walk the hall, and the hall was the worst place of all, exposed and defenseless and easily targeted, so she remained frozen, trying not to collapse, saying over and over, "Oh my god, oh my god," as copious and automatic tears flowed easily from her eyes and Larry tried to coax her, convince her, wake her, budge her — something, anything, before Tom Mota showed his face.

Benny and Marcia hurried down to Joe's office. While they had been wasting time with Amber, Joe had left it again.

SMEEJACK LOOKED DOWN at his classic oxford and tie at the place where he had been shot and was astonished by the bright red color and how quickly it had appeared and how smartly he stung beneath it, and randomly it came back to him, the vivid memory of shopping for the shirt at the big-and-tall store in the Fox Valley Mall, the Muzak and burbling fountain, and the popcorn and the hot pretzel he ate, and he couldn't repress the thought, "My last meal was an egg." Then out loud he said, "Ow. Fuck." And a little yolk flew from his mouth.

He called 911 and realized that he couldn't speak. He spit the egg violently from his mouth. "Please send an ambulance," he said. Then he began to cry.

By then Tom had moved on.

CARL GARBEDIAN WAS SINGING. Genevieve Latko-Devine was sure of it. Sure that *someone* was singing, anyway, and from where she sat in her office on sixty-one, she believed it was coming from next door — yes, from Carl's office. Singing! Really it was more like an atonal mumble, and she hadn't picked up on it immediately, as all her energy and attention were dedicated to coming up with caffeinated water concepts. But at some point the warble reached the outer limit of her radar, and she thought, "Is Carl singing?" So she got up from her desk and entered the hallway and crept along the few feet of wall separating her doorway from Carl's, and sure enough, he was singing. He had a mirthless, workaday voice, half the words were unknown to him, and he kept repeating the same stanza over and over again — but it was in fact a song:

"He got himself a homemade special
Something something full of sand
And it feels just like a something
The way it fits into his hand . . ."

Carl Garbedian was singing! He was offering hellos in the morning, he was saying good evenings at night, and now at midday, he was singing. And it wasn't the mad loud caterwauling spontaneously indulged during his whacked-out days of popping Janine Gorjanc's pills. No, this was regular old passing-the-time, happy-to-be-alive singing. She thought this surprising show of life might have something to do with the possibility that Carl and his wife were reconciling. If Carl had only known how delighted his simple singing made her! She wouldn't do something so stupid as interrupt and explain — that would only ruin the moment, and make them both feel awkward. But if she could have communicated to him how his singing was a simple reinforcement of something essential, which commonly went missing on a day-to-day basis — that his singing was to her what Marcia's haircut had been to him — he might have organized a talent show and performed a number from *A Chorus Line* with gold-spangled top hat and cane.

REALLY THE SONG WAS just stuck in Carl's head, and the motivation to sing purely mechanical. The work he had before him, this new business, it was just more of the same, really. Not something that would cause him to break out into song. And the recent developments with Marilynn, they were positive, but the two of them had a long way to go — she was still picking up her phone when they were saying good-bye, and he was still living alone in the suburban town house they had been unable to rent for months. The medication was working, no doubt about it, but his life still seemed empty, at least when he compared it to his wife's, and he still puzzled over how one could be thirty-six and still not know what to do with one's life. Which is not to say he wasn't, strictly speaking, in a song-singing mood. Because he did have a little something to fantasize about, as he sat working methodically and joylessly at the tedious, somewhat anxiety-producing task of winning new business.

"Why not quit?" Tom Mota had asked him in an e-mail sent earlier that day. "I'm sure you've had this thought a million times, and probably answered yourself with a million good reasons why not. Can I guess at a few? You have no other training. You've let too many years go by to start a new profession or return to school. And how could you let your wife be the main breadwinner? Etc etc etc. But have I got the answer for you! (Two weeks after being jerked off by Lynn Mason and I still can't stop sounding like a goddamn ad.) Anyway, I was thinking the other day, what am I going to do with myself? What do I got? I got no wife. I got no kids. I do have a dead-end, routinized, enervating, obsequious, numbingly dull — oops! Nope, don't even got a job anymore, do I? A small amount of money left over from the sale of my house — that's it. When that's gone, what will I do? Get another job in advertising? First of all, not given the current job climate. Second of all, NO FUCKING WAY, NOT IN THIS LIFETIME! So what am I suggesting? I'll tell you what I'm suggesting. I'm suggesting starting my own landscaping business. And I want you,

Carl, to join me. I think that some communion with nature, even if it is just the goddamn lawns of suburban yokels, and the pathetic green postage stamps in the industrial parks of Hoffman Estates or Elk Grove Village, I think it might be exactly what's missing in your life, Carl — what you lack without knowing you lack it. Think of it. The sun on the back of your neck. The taste of cold water after you've worked up a genuine thirst. The pleasures of a well-groomed lawn. And the sleep you will enjoy when every bone and muscle in your body has been thoroughly exhausted. I plan on being in the office later today to talk to Joe Pope. I'll stop by your office. THINK ABOUT IT. Peace, Tom."

— — —

ONCE SHE HAD DETERMINED that Carl Garbedian was actually singing, Genevieve snuck away from his door and walked in the direction of the kitchen. In the cupboards we had an endless supply of individually packaged, calorie-free powders that we kept next to the cup-o-soups and the silver bags of coffee grounds, and all you had to do for a fruit punch was add cold water from the cooler. On her way down the hall, she passed a man dressed as a clown. She tried not to look. It was obviously someone hired for a singing telegram or some other professional service and he was probably sick of being stared at in office buildings. "Genevieve," said the clown as he went by, as if he were tipping his hat to her on a dusty street of the Old West. It startled her, halted her abruptly, turned her around in her tracks. The clown continued on without an explanation or even a backward glance. "Who is that?" she asked. But whoever it was didn't answer, and entered Carl Garbedian's office without so much as a knock.

— — —

WHEN BENNY AND MARCIA WALKED into Joe's office and discovered he wasn't there, Marcia, who had not left Benny's side since he reached out and took her arm, looked at him and asked, "What do we do now?"

He had no immediate answer. "We don't even know that Tom's in the building," he said. "We could be totally overreacting. Roland's not the sharpest knife in the drawer."

"But what if he *is* here?"

"What if?" said Benny. "Maybe he's just come to say hello."

"What if not?" said Marcia.

Gone, suddenly, was her spunk, her sass, her strutting and calling out how she saw things without softening or accounting for feeling. Replacing all that now in Joe's office was someone much smaller — a hundred and ten pounds with a very thin, pale neck and bright Irish eyes, spooked by Amber's hysterical reaction. And now she was asking him, Benny Shassburger, the boy-faced and slightly overweight Jew from Skokie who, despite the Jews' well-documented historical peril, had grown up in the northwest suburbs of Chicago knowing no greater danger than a wild curveball thrown at his head during a pony league game. Marcia Dwyer, who had laughed at him yesterday for not knowing the difference between an Allen wrench and a socket wrench. Marcia, who he was madly in love with. She was asking him to take charge. Do something! Save lives, if lives need saving! See me to safety! He nearly collapsed under the weight of it. But then he rose to the occasion. Recalling suddenly that they were standing in Joe's office, and the ongoing antagonism between Joe and Tom in their day, he said, "We leave this office, that's the first thing we do."

As they departed, for a brief second, in the midst of confusion and fear, he felt flattered. My love Marcia, looking to me for guidance!

In the next instant, pure, blood-chilling fear snapped him out of it. The doors to the elevator opposite them suddenly flew open.

It was only that clueless goober Roland, finally making his way up from the ground floor.

"Have you seen him yet?"

"You're not even sure it *is* him!" cried Benny.

"I know," said Roland, "I know." He shook his head, deeply disappointed with himself. "But Mike wants everybody to evacuate anyway," he said, "just to be on the safe side. He told me to tell everyone to take the emergency stairs."

"Why not the elevators?" asked Benny.

"Because Mike said," said Roland.

So Benny and Marcia hurried to the emergency stairs. As they started their descent in the cold echoing stairwell, Benny could not stop himself from thinking — much as he couldn't help feeling flattered in Joe's office when she had turned to him for help — that in its way, this was romantic. Taking the stairs with Marcia, their hearts racing, fleeing death together. He had to consciously stop himself from turning to her on one of the landings and grabbing both of her doe-like arms and finally declaring his love for her. It would have been a poorly timed moment, and much more likely that she would have replied not by saying, "You like me, Benny?" but "Are you *out* of your fucking mind, telling me this right now?" Better to tell her after all this was over, which he promised himself he would do. Finally he would get up the courage. That whole business about Marcia not being Jewish, that was only to protect himself from the humility of rejection if it turned out Marcia didn't feel the same way. As long as Marcia would agree to raise the children as Jews, he really didn't give a damn what his aunt Rachel on her West Bank settlement thought of his apostasy.

They took the stairs quickly. They said nothing, but it was still good to be the one accompanying her from the building. He was glad it was him and not somebody else, and the only thing that could have improved matters was if he had had the nerve to take her by the hand. But that was the same nerve he needed to admit his crush, a nerve he didn't seem to possess. Nerve, he thought — and the next thing he knew, he was seized with a thought as inappropriate as confessing his love: when all was said and done, would she think he was a coward for having fled with her down the stairs, when what he *should* have done was stay with Roland and tell the others to evacuate? He wanted nothing more right then than to share the experience of fleeing the building with Marcia. What couple could say they had done that together? But was it more important than letting her know that he wasn't a coward? He regretted his next thought even more: wasn't it *in fact* more important not to be a coward than to flee the building? Without considering his duty or the question of his courage, he had followed Roland's instructions from Mike Boroshansky and hurried out the heavy gray door. Was it the right thing to have done? To leave everyone's fate in the hands of Roland — that was dicey business. Suddenly the final, most inappropriate thought of all came to him, and he forgot Marcia entirely. Grabbing hold of the rail to halt his momentum, he stopped abruptly in the middle of a flight of stairs. Marcia made it to the bottom before turning back, and on the landing between the forty-eighth and forty-seventh floors, she looked up at him and saw that he had stopped, and the expression on his face was full of reticence and uncertainty. "What did you forget?" she asked. He just stood there, not looking at her, but not *not* looking at her, either, staring indeterminately with eyes glassy and faraway. He focused finally just as the fleeing footsteps of others began to descend upon them.

"Jim," he said.

LARRY HAD FINALLY MANAGED to coax Amber into the server closet on sixty, which felt more like a walk-in refrigerator. The small room was bright, well insulated, and maintained at a steady temperature so the elaborate machines didn't overheat. Larry and Amber went to the back and hid behind the black metal shelving that supported the hardware, while Larry tried to calm her hyperventilating tears by saying, "Shh." "Shh," he kept saying, as she clung to him in their contorted, half-fallen position in the far corner behind the massive wire coils spilling from the well-spaced servers humming like fans on their shelves. "Shh," he said, as she buried her face into his chest and wept as soundlessly as she possibly could, heaving in his arms with her great waves of irrepressible fear, until his T-shirt had soaked up so many of her tears that he felt them cooling on his skin in the intemperate air. "Shh," he said, even as a malignant, hopeful thought crept over him, as sinister and troll-like as an evil wish in a fairy tale doomed to end badly: rather than killing them, maybe Tom Mota was actually saving Larry's life by traumatizing Amber so thoroughly that she would have a miscarriage. Wouldn't that be a great turn of events. Because if the trauma wasn't sufficient to rid them of the problem at hand, and if she fell on the wrong divide of the debate, which seemed more and more likely as the days progressed — to put it plainly, if that baby didn't disappear, Larry Novotny might as well throw open the door and holler at Tom wherever he may be to please come spray them with automatic fire because his life was over.

Over. His wife had given birth to a child herself just a little over a year ago, and their marriage was too fragile, too young, too troubled already to withstand the revelation of an infidelity, even a little workday one that had meant nothing, Susanna, swear to god it meant nothing. "Shh," he kept saying, as he grew more and more angry with Amber and her crying. She was always concentrating on crises happening elsewhere, while paying little attention to the one growing and dividing, dividing and growing within her very body, the body of the woman he had once desperately desired but now had come to mildly hate, the woman he held in his arms as she wept and trembled like a child but as only an adult can tremble, fully aware of the possibilities of violence and death. "Shh," he said, when what he wanted to say was, "Listen, I really need you to tell me once and for all that you're having this abortion." Because if she wanted to avoid carnage and annihilation, if she cared a whit about limiting the destruction, she would do something about those cells activating and organs maturing right there inside of her — otherwise his marriage was in bloody fucking tatters. "Shh," he said, and this time he added, "Amber, shh. Why are you so hysterical?" She lifted her head off his chest and looked at him. The raw rims of her nose were bright red and her pale cheeks were wet and puffy. "Because I'm scared," she whispered breathlessly between sobs. "But we don't even know that he's out there." "I'm not scared for *me,*" she said. "Can we please stop talking?" But he didn't want to stop talking. "Who are you scared for?" he asked, with a creeping concern. "Me?" he suggested. "Are you scared for me?" She put her head back on his chest and resumed trembling. "Lynn Mason?" he asked. She wouldn't reply. He went down the list. Was it Marcia? Benny? Joe Pope? How could any of them be the cause of such emotion?

And then the scales fell from his eyes. The day she had decided to keep the baby had come and gone and he had not known it. Hers were the tears of a mother, her fear a mother's fear.

TOM WALKED INTO CARL GARBEDIAN'S OFFICE without so much as a knock and sat down across from him. He stared at Carl without saying a word, relishing with a smug smile the confused expression on Carl's face at the sudden sight of a clown, resolving to say nothing until he spoke. Carl looked, and then looked closer. "Tom?" he said.

"You guessed it," said Tom.

Carl leaned back warily in his chair and reconnoitered the full scope of Tom's appearance with a skeptical and hesitant eye. "Tom, why are you dressed like that?" he asked with a quiet temerity.

"Carl, of all people, I would think that *you* would see the humor in this," Tom said. "Why aren't you laughing? Why aren't you shitting your pants with laughter right now?"

If Carl was tempted right then to shit his pants, the cause was probably not laughter.

"Don't you think this is funny?" asked Tom. "I come back here dressed as a clown! It's my homecoming, and look at me! I would think you would think this was funny, Carl."

Carl managed to make something like a smile and agreed with Tom that it was funny. "It's just the meds," he added, by way of explaining the delayed hilarity. "They tend to even me out."

Tom looked away in perfect disappointment. He turned back and asked, with a petulant and exasperated tone, "Doesn't anybody have a sense of humor around here?" He was offended once again by our failures of character. " 'TOM, THAT YOU, TOM? YOU COME TO BLOW US ALL AWAY IN A CLOWN OUTFIT, TOM?' Is that all I get from you guys? Why do you see me dressed like this and take it so goddamn seriously?"

"Because clowns are kind of scary, I guess," Carl ventured. "To me, at least. And especially when you don't know why somebody would be dressed up like one."

"Well, maybe I got me a job as a clown," said Tom, widening his eyes so their whites really popped amid all that red makeup. "Ever think of that?"

"Is it true?" asked Carl hopefully.

He wanted to call his wife. From the moment the clown came in and sat down Carl knew something was wrong and wanted the opportunity to speak to Marilynn one last time. She was so good. She had the hardest job. She had loved him very much.

Tom situated his backpack on the chair next to him and leaned forward, interlocking his fingers and placing his folded hands on the edge of Carl's desk. "Let me ask you a serious question, Carl, and you be honest with me, okay? You tell me the truth. You fucks thought I was coming back here for target practice, didn't you? Honestly — everybody was predicting it, weren't they?"

Weirded-out, and reluctant to say just about anything, Carl didn't know the prudent answer.

"Just answer the question, Carl. It's a simple question."

"Well," Carl began, "a few people —"

"I knew it!" cried Tom, jolting out of his chair and looming over Carl's desk. "I fucking knew it!" He was pointing at Carl as if Carl were the spokesman for all the fucks in the world.

"You didn't let me finish," said Carl.

"You fucks *actually* thought I was coming back here to blow people to bits," said Tom, shaking his orange curls in grave, exaggerated disappointment and violently tapping Carl's desk three times. "Unbelievable."

"Why *are* you back here, Tom — isn't that a fair question? And why the clown outfit?"

Tom sat back down again and struck a less aggressive perch on his seat. Carl was grateful for it. Since walking in, Tom seemed to be right up in his face. "I'll tell you why I'm back here," he said. "I came to ask Joe Pope to lunch, that's why. That's right — Joe. But then this other idea came to me, and it sort of took on a life of its own. So now I'm dressed like a clown. Why? I'll tell you why I'm dressed like a clown," he said, reaching over and unzipping his backpack, from which he removed his gun.

Carl wheeled back hastily, all the way to the credenza, and hoisted his clammy palms in the air. "Hey, Tom," he said, just as tears sprang instinctively to his eyes.

He wanted so badly to talk to his wife. He was reminded of that distant, phantasmagoric episode in his life when he had stood at the pawn shop fingering a Luger. He recalled all the pills he had hoarded, and the time he sat in the garage with the key in the ignition, towels plugging every gap where the exhaust might escape, so that once he had the nerve to turn over the engine, it would be done. Who was that person? Not him, not any longer. He wanted to live! He wanted to *landscape!* He wanted more than anything just to call his wife.

"Oh, put your hands down, Carl," said Tom. "I'm not going to shoot *you,* you fuck."

"I thought you wanted to start a landscaping company," said Carl. "I've been thinking about it all morning. The sun on my neck, remember? You and me — I could come up with some money, I love the idea. Why would you want to do something stupid?" He clattered unthinkingly, hoping to say the right thing.

"Listen to me, Carl," said Tom. "Carl, shut up! Listen to me. I'm dressed like a clown because every single one of you fucks in this office at one time or another thought that Tom Mota was nothing but a clown, am I right? Be honest with me, Carl. Am I right?"

"To be honest with you, Tom, it's hard to be honest with you when you've got a gun pointed at me."

"I'm not going to shoot you, Carl! Just be honest. Everybody thought I was a clown, didn't they?"

"I think," Carl began, trying to breathe, to contain his fear, to gauge what action he might need to take, "I think everyone knew you were going through a tough time, Tom . . . and that you probably . . . you weren't behaving like your normal self. I think that's —"

"In other words," said Tom, "a clown."

"I never once heard anyone use that particular expression," replied Carl, who still had his hands up.

"Carl, will you relax, please, Jesus. It's not a real gun. Doesn't anybody know the difference? Here, watch —"

Tom pointed the gun at one corner of the office and pulled the trigger. *Splat!* went the pellet, and a dousing of red paint coated the corner walls in a comic-book-like blot. Carl looked in wild-eyed astonishment, yet still refused to put his hands down. His shirt was dusted with red blowback from the pellet. He looked back at Tom.

"Are you fucking crazy?" he asked.

"No, I'm a clown," said Tom. "And you know what clowns do, don't you, Carl?"

"No, you fucking maniac!"

"Careful, Carl," said Tom, motioning with the gun to the backpack in the seat beside him. "I might have a real one in there."

"What do clowns do?" asked Carl, a little more mildly.

Tom warped his mouth into a severe hangdog frown and raised his brows to complete a picture of melancholy. "We're such sad creatures at heart, us clowns," said Tom. "Down-and-out and full of woe. So to make ourselves feel better —" Tom's face blossomed into a smile like a flower drawn from his sleeve — "we pull pranks!"

JOE NEEDED A NICKEL. He could have sworn that when he left his office he had had every coin he needed to get a pop from the machine but he was shy a nickel and had to return. He took it from the mug where he kept spare change and left the office again, spying Benny and Marcia and Amber and Larry in the hallway engaged in some new drama, not exactly working on winning the new business. The elevator doors had yet to close again and he raced to catch them. If he had lingered in the hall to speculate why they were all in hysterics, they would have silently accused him of scolding them from afar, and that was a tired accusation — though on this occasion it would have been correct. Because Jesus Christ, did they not understand? We had to win the new business!

He returned to the cafeteria on fifty-nine to buy his pop and was about to leave when he saw Lynn sitting in the far back at one of the round tables under the bright and appalling fluorescence. "What are you doing down here?" he asked, approaching her. She was alone and, despite all the noise he had made, the dropping coins and the falling can, she seemed to be taking notice of him for the first time.

She watched him draw closer, two fingers at her temple.

He set the pop on the table. She kicked out a chair for him. He sat down and opened the pop and the thing hissed and spit and he hunched over to slurp up the fizzing soda before it spilled over.

They sat in silence. Then she spoke to him again of things they had gone over yesterday after Genevieve had left the office — which partner would oversee the effort to secure the new business, and the ways in which he, Joe, would need to step up and assume more responsibility.

"Can I ask you a question?" he said.

"Of course."

"Why did you lie about it to Genevieve yesterday, and then tell me the truth after she left?"

She removed her two fingers from her temple and turned them into a kind of shrug and then returned them to her temple. "I just don't want them to know about it until the last possible second," she replied. "I want to be in the hospital under anesthesia before they start talking."

He nodded. "Understandable."

"And I know I can trust you to keep it to yourself."

They sat in silence, the only sound the refrigerated hum from the vending machines in the distance.

"Not that I believe I'll be able to escape it," she said. "I'll be way, way under and their voices will probably still penetrate."

He smiled. "Probably," he said.

"But until they carry me kicking and screaming toward the operating room in one of those terrible green gowns, I'd prefer to keep them in the dark. Or at the very least, second-guessing."

She sat up and placed her feet back inside her heels. She glanced over at him as she did so. "It's very quick," she said, "from what they tell me. A day or two and they have you out of there."

"Is it next door?" he asked.

"Yes. Carl's wife, actually."

"No kidding."

"She scares me."

"Is that why you missed your first appointment?"

She nodded.

"What's changed?"

"I have a friend," she said. "He isn't letting me get away with it this time."

"You have a friend," he said. He smiled.

"Is that so hard to believe?"

"No."

"It isn't a boyfriend," she said.

"I'm happy to hear you have a friend," he said. There was silence, then he said, "Do you feel sick, Lynn?"

"Do I feel sick," she said. She thought about it. "Yes. I feel sick."

"Would you like me to be there during the operation? Or is there something I can do for you afterward?"

"You can win this new business," she said.

"For you, I mean."

"That would be for me," she said. "This is it, Joe. This is my life."

He was silent. "You've worked hard."

"Yes," she agreed. She had finished putting on her shoes and was now sitting perpendicular to the table with her hands holding her knees. "Too hard?"

There was a note of vulnerability in the question that he wasn't expecting. But it was also clear, the way she was looking at him, that she wanted him to answer truthfully. "I don't know," he said. "What's too hard?"

"All these other people have so much going on in their lives. Their nights, their weekends. Vacations, activities. I've never been able to do that."

"Which is why you're a partner."

"But what am I missing? What have I missed?"

"Have you been happy doing it?"

"Happy?"

"Content. Has it been worthwhile? The work."

"Yes," she said. "Maybe. I suppose."

"Then you may be better off than they are. Many of them would prefer not to be here, and yet this is where they spend most of their time. Percentagewise, maybe you're the happiest."

"Is that how you judge it?" she asked. "It's a percentage game?"

"I don't know."

"But what do they know," she asked, "that I don't know? That if I knew, I would prefer not to be here, too?"

"Maybe nothing," he said.

Was she thinking of Martin, a home with Martin in Oak Park, a Volvo in the driveway and a bottle of wine breathing on the French tiles of the kitchen counter, while her child plays with a friend in the backyard? Was she thinking, Then I would be healthy? No one dies in Oak Park. Everyone in Oak Park is happy and no one ever dies.

"Or maybe everything," he said. "I work about as much as you do. I don't know what they know, either."

They sat in silence.

"When should I tell them?" he asked.

"I'm rescheduled for Thursday," she said. "You can tell them then." She paused. "But this is the important thing," she added. "I mean this. Above all else, Joe. Win this new business."

TOM MOTA LEFT CARL'S OFFICE and proceeded down the interior stairs to sixty, where most of the good people he wanted to take the piss out of were located in their tidy workstations, like that fuck Jim Jackers who had always been an idiot, and Benny Shassburger who still hadn't responded to the heartfelt e-mail Tom had sent him in which he recounted his mother's painful, ugly death. He would have liked to pump Karen Woo full of red pellets, and Dan Wisdom, painter of fish, that movie-quoting fuck Don Blattner, and the agency's real ballbuster, Marcia Dwyer. Unfortunately for Tom, many of us were already marching down sixty flights of emergency stairs, owing to the good work of Roland. Unfortunately for the rest of us, any given floor was a circuitous blueprint of cubicle clusters, hallway offshoots, print stations, mount rooms — spaces easily overlooked — and Roland, as Benny predicted, missed many of them in his haste to reach the other floors. Tom had a fair share of unfortunate souls to shoot at once his melee began, and the bullets that came from his gun were every bit as real to us as those in the guns of the Chicago police who had just arrived outside our building, pulling up along the curb with their sirens blaring.

"'It came into him, life,'" Tom declaimed to the fleeing backside of Doug Dion, "'it went out from him, truth.'" He shot Doug in the back and Doug went down, bringing several of us out into the halls with his cries of traumatic certainty. Like Andy Smeejack before him, Doug confused a sting for the real thing. Tom merely needed to turn to find a new target. "'It came to him, business,'" he trumpeted preposterously before shooting someone new, "'it went from him, poetry.'" And also, "'The day is always his, who works in it with serenity and great aims.'" And with a smile, he let go of another round.

They *actually* believed he could shoot at someone and intend them harm. That's how little those fucks ever really knew him. He stopped midhallway to load more pellets into the gun.

We behaved as you might expect. We recoiled, hovering under our timberstick desks, collecting under conference room tables like game hens in a shooting gallery, and generally scampering for our lives. Amber Ludwig in the server closet heard shrieking from outside and went into overdrive trembling and hyperventilating, just as Larry, who had abandoned her there, disgusted by his revelation that Amber planned to carry the baby to term and convinced that her crying was baseless, backed away from the door he was tempted to open. He made no attempt to reattach himself to her. She wouldn't have had him anyway. Instead, he took position behind the nearest of the metal shelves and prepared to push it over on Tom and beat him with wired hardware should he enter the server closet.

Benny found Jim exactly where he had predicted he would, listening to music through headphones and working on the new business. The two men tried to avoid the shrill and fearsome noises coming from unseen parts of their familiar floor by heading in the opposite direction. They had just rounded the corner past the potted tree nearest Joe Pope's office when they ran into Genevieve, who had been frantically searching for Joe ever since the clown's spooky greeting sent her back to Carl's doorway and she overheard Tom telling Carl that he wasn't going to shoot *him.* She worried that Joe was an obvious target and wanted to warn him, but when she couldn't find him and people started screaming she turned distraught and now she was in tears.

"Shh, calm down," Benny told her.

"Let's take the elevator," said Jim, since they were right there.

"No, we can't," Benny replied. "We have to take the emergency stairs."

"Why?"

"Because Mike Boroshansky said so."

So the three of them started off in the direction of the other potted tree and the emergency stairs on that side of the hallway, and had almost reached Benny's office at the midway point when

Tom's voice rose up behind them in the hall and Jim suddenly went down.

"'I content myself with the fact that the general system of our trade —'" Tom thundered, as he advanced toward them at a steady though not particularly fast pace down the hall.

"I've been shot!" cried Jim. "I've been shot!"

Benny pulled Genevieve into his office and pushed her behind the desk.

"'— is a system of selfishness —'"

"It hurts!" cried Jim, writhing on his back. "Oh, it hurts!"

Hovering low in his doorway, Benny reached out to grab one of Jim's hands to pull him inside the office.

"'— is not dictated by the high sentiments of human nature —'"

Tom's stentorian, little big man voice was growing closer. Benny pulled Jim in further as Tom shot him twice more, once in the torso and once in the leg. The skeleton with the Buck Rogers gun looked on helplessly from inside Benny's office.

"Ow!" cried Jim. "Oh!" His eyes were as wide and fearful as a wounded dog's.

"'— much less by the sentiments of love and heroism —'"

Benny paused to get a closer look. That wasn't blood. That was —

"'— but is a system of distrust —'"

Benny stood up and entered the hallway. "Tom," he said, "are those just fucking paintballs?"

"'— not of giving, but of taking advantage,'" concluded Tom, standing but two feet from Benny and taking aim at his chest.

Just at that moment, Lynn and Joe stepped off the elevator and stopped abruptly in front of Joe's office, peering down the hall. Seeing the clown with the gun, Lynn shouted, "What's going on? Hey — what do you think you're doing down there?"

Tom swiveled around to face them.

"Joe," he said, resting the gun at his side. "I've come to take you to lunch."

It was too late. A shirtless, shrieking Andy Smeejack had rounded the opposite corner, barreling down the hallway with bouncing man breasts and a belly white as a whale's, leaping over Jim just as Benny turned to make room for him, and landing with crushing severity upon Tom's absurdly festooned smallness. Both men careened into the wall and bounced off, landing with hard, nearly soundless thuds on the carpet, Smeejack on top, pinning with his tub of guts Tom's body to the floor while pummeling him madly with sidewinders and haymakers until Joe and Benny pried him from his determination to kill the bastard with his bitter, fat, paint-flecked hands, and then the police swarmed in.

4

THE AMERICAN DREAM AND WHY WE DESERVE IT — WHO SHOULD BE DEAD — "GARBEDIAN AND SON" — USELESS SHIT — THE END OF AN ERA — WE URGE BENNY TO SAY SOMETHING — ROLAND TRICKED — A NOTE TO JIM — D.O.C. — JOE AND WHERE HE'S AT ("UP *HERE*") — TOM IN LOVE — A VISIT TO THE HOSPITAL — DERIVATIVE CONCEPTS — DEPARTURES

WE BOUNCED BACK. Or we quit. Or we took a vacation. For two or three weeks there we had a tough time resisting the urge to replay events. Everyone had a version. Conflicting accounts never diminished one side or the other, they only made the matter richer. We were blowing the whole thing way out of proportion, because nobody had died, but we talked about it as if death imagined were as good as real. We stayed later than normal to talk about it or we took days off or else we called it quits. Someone from Project Services sued us, citing negligence. It was a little awkward because we still had to work with her. She approached us at the coffeemaker and the microwave to make sure we knew it was nothing personal. She was suing the building, too, along with Tom Mota and the paintball gun manufacturer. She was out of the building and two blocks down when the shooting began, but who were we to say what damages this individual or that deserved? That would be up to a jury of our peers. We had all been deposed before and would likely be deposed for this. In the meantime we had our conflicting accounts to perfect and our insatiable appetite to revisit them.

The bottled water and the running shoe were no competition against Tom Mota's shenanigans. Something as exciting as this had not struck us since the premiere season of *The Sopranos*. Before that, we had to stretch back to the Clinton impeachment and the summer of Monica. But those things couldn't hold a candle. This happened to *us*. And the great thing was, we could talk and talk without any of the casualties or long-term psychological damage of a Columbine or an Oklahoma City. We pretended to know something about what they had gone through. Maybe we did, who knows. Probably not.

All that week and the week following we played at the game of corporate win-win-win but our real occupation was replaying events and reflecting on the consequences of still being alive. India reentered our horizons. Again we took stock of our ultimate purpose. The idea of self-sacrifice, of unsung dedication and of dying a noble death, again reached the innermost sanctum where ordinarily resided our bank account numbers and retirement summaries. Maybe there was an alternative to wealth and success as the fulfillment of the American dream. Or maybe that was the dream of a different nation, in some future world order, and we were stuck in the dark ages of luxury and comfort. How could we be expected to break out of it, we who were overpaid, well insured, and bonanza'd with credit, we who were untrained in the enlightened practice of putting ourselves second? As Tom Mota was taking aim at our lives, we felt for a split second the ambiguous, foreign, confounding certainty that maybe we were getting what we deserved. Luckily that feeling soon passed, and when we rose up alive and returned to our desks and, later, to our lofts and condos and suburban sprawls, the feeling was that of course we deserved all that we had, we had worked long, hard hours for it all, and how dare that fucker even pretend to take it away? How grateful we were to be around to enjoy everything we deserved.

We speculated about who should be dead. Who should be in

critical condition right now and who in stable condition and who would have been paralyzed for life? If Amber Ludwig had been there she would have objected to such morbid games, but Amber had been diagnosed with post-traumatic stress disorder and given time off. She retreated to her mother's house in Cleveland where she could revisit her stuffed animals and reflect on Larry's behavior in the server closet. The rest of us would have liked some time off. They only gave us that Friday afternoon, which we took gladly, but we, too, suffered from stress and all sorts of disorders and would have liked more than an afternoon. Some of us said Friday afternoon, wow, behold the generosity. But others tried to see it from their perspective. If they didn't win the new business, they were screwed. And who did they screw when they got screwed? You betcha. So we hustled back Monday morning and pretended to work while carrying on the conversation that started Friday after Tom's arrest and continued unflagging through the weekend, over the phone and at brunch, with relatives and news reporters, and the central message we wanted to convey, the moral of the story and the kernel of truth, was how relieved we were not to have died at work. The last thing we wanted was to expire between cubicle partitions or in the doorways of the offices where we spent our days. Hank Neary had a quote and we told him politely to shove the quote up his ass. "When death comes, let it find me at my work." He said he couldn't remember if it was Ovid or Horace who said that and we replied we could give a good goddamn what Ovid the Horse said. Ovid the Horse got it wrong about death and work. We wanted to die on a boat. We wanted to die on an island, or in a log cabin on a mountainside, or on a ten-acre farm with an open window and a gentle breeze.

Carl Garbedian, god bless him, turned in his letter of resignation. If you must know the very end of our story, a story set in the pages of an Office Depot catalog, of lives not nearly as interesting as an old man and the sea, or watery-world dwellers dispelling the hypos with a maniacal peg leg, then this is its conclusion: Carl Garbedian was the only one of us who got out of advertising for good. The rest of us didn't have the luxury of concluding like the hero of a Don Blattner screenplay, shaking off the ennui with a Himalayan trek in search of emeralds and gurus. We had our bills to pay and our limitations to consider. We had our families to support and our weekends to distract us. We suffered failures of imagination just like everyone else, our daring was wanting, and our daily contentment too nearly adequate for us to give it up. It was only Carl who got out. And wait until you hear the nail-biting adventure he embarked upon. He tendered his resignation the Monday after the shooting, and when his two weeks expired, he began implementing a business plan for the creation of a suburban landscaping company. Daredeviling to put every Blattnerian hero to shame! But good for him, we thought. If that's really what he wants. You'd have to be a fool to give up a climate-controlled office for the Chicago heat in July, but good for him. We asked him what he planned to do in the winter. "Shovel snow for the city," he said. We said good for you, Carl. Great Jesus! we thought. Shoveling snow? In a truck at three in the morning in a freezing February blizzard? And how much payola would he have to part with to get a snow-shoveling contract from the city? We asked him what he planned to call his landscaping company. "Garbedian and Son," he replied. No shit? He was entering into business with his father? "No, no," he grinned. "That's just a little trick I picked up in advertising."

The trick was to play loose with words. Eventually, if everything went well, "Garbedian and Son" meant three Hispanics would come to your home and manicure your lawn. When we said,

"Don't miss out on these great savings!" we really meant we gotta unload these fuckers fast. "No-Fee Rewards" meant prepare to pay out the ass. Words and meaning were almost always at odds with us. We knew it, you knew it, they knew it, we all knew it. The only words that ever meant a goddamn were, "We're really very sorry about this, but we're going to have to let you go."

— — —

THEY LET GO OF MARCIA DWYER. They came for her even before the building people had finished removing the splatters of paint from the walls and carpet. Jim Jackers had seemed the next logical choice. Who in their right minds would choose Marcia over Jim? But for reasons that would remain ever obscure, they took Marcia. "Restructuring," they said. "Lost clients." How many times had we heard that? It still said nothing about why Marcia and not Jim. We might as well have been inquiring about the random and inscrutable selection process of fatal diseases.

They gave her a half hour in which to collect her personal items. It was part of a new protocol for the physical removal of former employees that Roland had to stand against the wall with his hands folded, mutely watching her pack. They were treating Marcia like an inmate at the Joliet Correctional Center. Perhaps it had to be that way after Tom's arrest, but the only dangerous thing about Marcia was her glower. Did he really have to just stand there like that, as if vigilant against sudden movement? We'd seen firsthand how the man handled a crisis. If Marcia decided suddenly to brandish a stapler in a half-threatening manner, he'd fumble with his Motorola and forget his name. The least he could do was offer to help. Failing that, he could take a seat and relax.

Marcia picked her way across the desk, the credenza, and the bookshelves, removing a clock, a figurine, a cluster of books. She unplugged her radio and wound the cord around its brown plastic body and placed it in a box. Then she went through the desk drawers one redundant item at a time, investigating every matchbook, business card, hairband, Band-Aid, aspirin container, lotion bottle, bendy straw, multivitamin, magazine, nail file, nail polish, lip balm, and cough drop that had languished in her desk for who knows how long. Did it belong in a box or in the trash? She unpinned from her corkboard a collage of photographs, receipts, coupons, utility bills, personal reminders, wisdom quotes, greeting cards, ticket stubs, and drawings in her hand and in the hands of professional artists she admired, and those, too, she either threw away or put into a box. Marcia's office reverted back to the anonymous — nothing on the desk but a computer and telephone, the walls blank, the divot-ridden corkboard bereft of all sign of her two thousand days among us. It was a swift and stultifying transformation, depressing to watch.

Genevieve Latko-Devine arrived in her doorway looking ashen and out of breath. "I just heard," she said.

"Roland, you're annoying me," said Benny. "Do you really have to stand against the wall like that?"

"Sorry, Benny. It's part of the new rules."

The mood in the office was solemn and wistful until Jim Jackers showed up and asked Marcia if she was planning to return dressed as a clown to terrorize us all with a paintball gun. Any other day, Marcia would have shut him up with a quick put-down, but his inappropriateness could no longer touch her. What clung to us because of Jim no longer clung to her.

"I have been a total bitch for a year now," she said, taking a seat for the last time in Ernie Kessler's chair. "I hated everybody, you know why? Because I thought no way they deserved to stay on if I was going to be laid off. But all that time, I didn't get laid off. I only got laid off today. I was thinking ahead, and hating everybody for it. Now I can finally stop being a bitch. You know how good that makes me feel? Why didn't they do this a year ago?" she asked.

This was one of several possible responses — the silver-lining response. Marcia had found a spin clever enough to carry her out of the building with her head up. We had no desire to expose it for what it was, and so we all agreed it was a good thing that she could finally stop being a bitch. If Amber had been there, there would have been tears.

"Do you know that since layoffs began," she continued, "I haven't been able to enjoy a single cup of coffee at the coffee bar? I was always too worried someone might come along and see me and think I should be working and not at the coffee bar enjoying a cup of coffee. I can enjoy coffee again," she said.

Not enjoying your coffee at the coffee bar was far better than no coffee bar at all. Twenty minutes earlier, Marcia herself would have said the same thing. Now a great distance had grown between us. She had fallen into the dark abyss, while the rest of us still stood at the brink, watching her plummet. Soon we would lose sight of her completely. It was tough to behold, but there she was — no longer one of us. An era was coming to an end. The era of browbeating, sarcasm, belittlement, and berating. The era of bad ballads from eighties hair bands issuing from her office. The era of conscience-riddled insults followed by profuse apologies to anyone but the insulted. We would not have Marcia's new haircut to look forward to anymore. To be honest, we had already grown pretty much accustomed to it.

"Can I take these boxes home for you in my car?" asked Genevieve. "I'd be happy to drop them off." We didn't think

Genevieve had a clue what she was asking. Genevieve lived in a gorgeous loft in Lincoln Park with her lawyer husband. Did she know how far Bridgeport was? Was she even aware there was a South Side?

"Why you?" Benny said to Marcia. "What bullshit. Why not Jim here?"

"Hey!" said Jim.

"Do you remember last week," Marcia continued, with a conviction that would have impressed the biggest cynic, "when I ran into Chris Yop at the print station? And do you remember how worked up I was over having Tom Mota's chair, with the wrong serial numbers? You guys told me to go in and replace Tom's chair with Yop's chair, that used to be Ernie's chair, remember? Because it would be better to be caught with Ernie's chair than to be caught with Tom's? Do you remember that?" she asked. "Do you realize how insane we've all become?"

She got off the chair and stood before the partially filled boxes on her desk with her hands on her hips, wrists turned inward. She looked around a final time at what remained to be done and found there was nothing. "Wow," she said.

"Are you ready?" asked Roland.

She didn't even look at him. She didn't look at us, either. She looked through us, to the dusty surfaces where her things had been, to the barren walls between which for six straight years she had completed the work that had earned her a living. Was this it, then? Was there to be no ceremony, beyond Roland's aid out the door?

"I'll help you down with those boxes," said Benny.

"You know what?" she said. "Hold on." She opened them up again and peered inside each one for a full minute or two. "I don't want any of this shit," she concluded at last. "Will you look at this? What is this?" She pulled out a cheap die-cast statuette of Lady Liberty. Next she held up a small book entitled *50 Tips for the Direct-Mail Marketer.* "Roland," she said, "can you just have these boxes thrown out for me?"

"Wait a minute, hold on," said Benny.

"You don't want your stuff?" said Roland.

"Marcia," said Genevieve.

"It's called useless shit, Roland," said Benny. "And of course she wants it."

It was madness to leave without your useless shit. You came in with it, you left with it — that was how it worked. What would you use to clutter a new office with if not your useless shit? We could remember Old Brizz with his box of useless shit, shifting the box from arm to arm as he talked with the building guy. Of course, Old Brizz never had an office again. His useless shit really was useless. He had cause to leave his useless shit behind. But his was a rare case. All things considered, it was better to take your useless shit with you.

"Marcia, take it with you," said Benny.

"I'm happy to drive it over to your house tonight," said Genevieve.

"But I don't want any of it," said Marcia.

It was how we knew to feel sorry for them. Before their terminations, we knew them by their tics, their whines, their crap superiorities, and just one day earlier, we thought that if all that were to disappear suddenly, so much the better. Then we saw them carrying a box full of useless shit to the elevator, and they were pitiable and human again.

But Marcia refused, and after hugs and good-byes walked

toward the elevator with Roland, carrying nothing but that denim bag that served as her purse. She probably hadn't even reached the lobby floor before Jim Jackers began to scavenge the useless shit she had left behind.

Nobody could believe Benny was just going to let Marcia leave without admitting he had a crush. He had promised himself he would and stupidly spread word of that promise to the rest of us, but every time the timing was right, he had a new excuse. The Monday after Tom's spree, he was too busy accumulating conflicting versions of events and offering his own to tear himself away. That continued through Tuesday, and on Wednesday he claimed he was too busy working on the new business. On Thursday Joe told us Lynn was in the hospital, and we got wrapped up debating whether or not it was a good idea for us to visit her. But now it was Friday, and suddenly Marcia was leaving forever, and still Benny had said nothing. It was a mystery to us how he could be such a confident and lively raconteur and yet such a bashful lover. Jim came out of Marcia's office holding the souvenir of the Statue of Liberty Marcia had disparaged on her way out, along with a shot glass and a copy of *Vogue.*

"Benny," he said, "are you really going to let her leave without saying something to her?"

It happened all the time. Maybe someone had a legitimate gripe that deserved airing. Maybe someone had a compliment that shouldn't go unspoken. No one said a thing. So long and stay in touch, that's usually all we said. Take care of yourself, good luck. We said nothing about affection, appreciation, admiration. But neither did we say don't let the door hit your ass on the way out.

"She's coming with us tomorrow to see Lynn, isn't she?" he

asked. "So I'll see her tomorrow. I'll say something then. What's the big deal?"

But Saturday came and went, we paid our visit, and still he said nothing. The following Monday, Marcia showed up in the building lobby, as if taking a page out of Tom Mota's book.

Roland was at the front desk and wouldn't let her go up, not even as a visitor.

"I'm sorry," he said. "After the incident, we can't let former employees back in the building. You're not even supposed to be in the lobby," he said.

She convinced him to call Benny. "Send her up here!" Benny hollered at Roland into the phone. "What's wrong with you?"

"I can't do that, Benny," Roland said helplessly as Marcia stared at him across the lobby post. "It's against the new rules."

"Well, then tell her to hold on," Benny replied, standing up. "I'll come down to her."

He fixed up his corkscrew curls in the cloudy brass of the elevator. When he reached the lobby floor he sucked in his gut and stepped out with several others. It was lunchtime. People were coming and going through the revolving doors.

"Come on, man!" he said as he approached Roland. "Does she look like a threat to you?"

"It's the new rules, Benny!"

"Don't give him a hard time," said Marcia. "He's just doing his job."

"What are you doing back here?" Benny asked.

She had returned, she said, in order to take apart Chris Yop's chair, that used to be Ernie Kessler's, so she could toss it piece by piece into the lake.

"Of course you have," said Benny. "Let's go outside and talk."

Which is how it came to pass that we saw them conversing outside the building on our way to lunch. We spent that hour speculating on what Marcia was doing back at the office and what the two of them were discussing. Perhaps she liked *him.* Perhaps Roland, at his post in the lobby, was wondering the same thing, because despite the hard time Benny gave him about keeping Marcia in the lobby according to the new rules, we knew the two men were friends, and that Benny had talked to him just as he talked to the rest of us about his paralyzing and unrequited crush. "So what are you going to do about it, Benny?" he'd ask. "I'm going to tell her," Benny announced at last, after Tom's spree. "I promised myself I would and I will." Maybe, thought Roland, that confession was happening right now, right outside the building. He returned his attention to his small amount of daily paperwork. When he looked up again ten minutes later to see how things were progressing, Benny and Marcia were gone.

— — —

ROLAND HAD APPEARED TO LOOK right at them as they walked past, but they were sheltered within a group of incoming lawyers from the firm below us and eventually he looked away again. They passed by freely, and after stepping off the elevator on sixty, walked together in the direction of Jim's cubicle.

Marcia wanted Benny's reassurance that Jim wasn't there. Benny explained that he had sent Jim out to pick up sandwiches at the Potbelly, where the line was always atrocious.

"I'm telling you," he said. "He won't be back for hours."

"If you tell anybody about this," said Marcia, with a familiar, scolding, clawing tone. How he loved that tone!

"I wouldn't be threatening me right now if I were you," he said to her. "One call down to Roland and I could have you arrested."

They made it down to Jim's cube and Marcia set the envelope upright between two rows of keys on his keyboard before noticing the souvenir she had purchased during a visit with her family to the Statue of Liberty. "Hey, what's this doing here?" she asked. Then she noticed that Jim also had her Fighting Illini shot glass, several magazines, and her Scorpio keychain, which listed the attributes of her personality. After his initial pillaging, he'd gone back for more. "What the fuck?" she said.

"Well," replied Benny, sheepishly. "You did leave them behind."

Jim wasn't the only one with Marcia's things. If she had stayed and scoured more workstations, she would have found them divvied up among us and scattered across the office. The only items we left behind were her unused tampons and marketing textbooks. Within two hours of her departure, her boxes had been picked clean. Don Blattner took her radio. Karen Woo swept down on her bookends. Someone of remarkable stealth stole in and took Chris Yop's chair, which used to be Ernie's, which Marcia had replaced with Tom Mota's, which Chris Yop had tossed in the lake. Now someone else had the burden of possessing the wrong serial numbers but the pleasures of an ergonomic masterpiece.

"I don't even feel like giving it to him now," she said, reaching for the envelope.

"Don't do that," said Benny.

She left the envelope where it was.

Those of us who didn't go to lunch that day saw them talking by the elevators. That was most of us, because of the pressing demands of the new business. We wondered the same thing those of us who'd gone to lunch wondered. After Marcia slipped past Roland on her way out — coming off a full elevator, ingeniously disguised as one of us — we all went down to Benny's office and asked him what they had been talking about. He refused to say.

"Never mind," he said, dismissing us outright. We had to think that could only forebode bad news. Someone as loquacious as Benny Shassburger reduced to "Never mind"? No doubt that meant he had been rejected. We asked him a second time and a third. We came back fifteen minutes later and asked the same question in a different way. We sent him e-mails. "Never mind," he wrote back. Not wanting to rub it in, we let it drop.

When he returned to his cube, after dropping Benny's sandwich off, Jim puzzled over the white envelope on his keyboard. On the cover of the card, a cheap generic Hallmark item made of recycled paper, a hound dog's fat snout and heavy ears rested on a pair of crisscrossed paws, while his blubbery furry body floated in a background of blue. Above his cocked and woeful head, a cumulus-shaped thought bubble announced, "I feel so blue . . ." And on the inside, "For the way I treated you." There was no note, no revisiting specific slights. Only her name to inform him who had left it. *Marcia.* It was scrawled reluctantly. He pinned the card to his cube wall.

— — —

TOM WAS BEING HELD TEMPORARILY in a central holding cell near the city courthouse. At his initial hearing, his bail was set at twenty thousand dollars, which some of us thought was a little much, and others considered much too little. In the end it didn't matter because no one would post it for him, and he didn't want to part with any of the little money he had saved from the sale of his Naperville house. Or so he told Joe Pope, who went to visit him. Tom labored under idiosyncratic and stubborn notions, but even he must have known that the court costs, lawyers' fees, and criminal fines that he'd have to pay for pulling his little stunt were going to tap him dry forever. We had no doubt that his inclination to stick around the jail cell was influenced by the fact that he had been processed on a Friday, and that by posting bail, he'd have nothing but another aimless weekend to muddle his way through, getting drunk and harassing the groundskeepers of his apartment complex, and composing e-mails to people who never wrote him back. So he decided to stick around and have a few hot meals on the state until his arraignment, when he would be charged with five counts of aggravated assault and battery, destruction of private property, and trespassing.

When we heard Joe Pope went to visit him, we were beside ourselves with disbelief. We were surprised, confused, angry, curious, tickled, and dumbfounded. It took everything in us not to dismiss the rumor as an absurd invention. But no, it was true, Joe himself admitted it before commencing a meeting in the Michigan Room. We were there to discuss details of the caffeinated bottled water, and everyone was fearful of a long night. Comparing conflicting accounts and trying to win the new business at the same time was taking it out of us. It would only prolong things to talk about anything but the work, but we couldn't help ourselves, and someone asked Joe as he walked in if it was really true. Had he become Tom Mota's prison wife?

Joe smiled. He set down his leather day planner and pulled out a seat at the head of the conference room table.

"No, seriously," said Benny. "Did you go visit him?"

"I did."

"How come?"

Joe sat down and scooted in. "I was curious," he said.

"Curious about what?"

Joe looked around the room. We were quiet. "Do you remember what he said to me?" he asked us. "He was standing in the hallway, holding the gun, which I thought was real at the time. And he says, remember what he said? He said, 'Joe, I came to take you to lunch.'"

Some of us recalled hearing Tom say that and some of us were hearing it for the first time. What we remembered most clearly was Tom unfurling some lunatic gibberish as he wheeled and aimed and pulled the trigger — crazy talk that announced we were in the hands of a madman.

"No, after all that," said Joe. "The last thing he said before Andy tackled him."

"I don't remember him saying he wanted to take you to lunch," said Larry Novotny.

"Maybe because at the time, Larry," said Karen Woo, "you were cowering with Amber in the server closet."

According to Joe, Tom said it so calmly and matter-of-factly that it was almost as shocking as finding him there at all. Or rather, it was the juxtaposition between what he said — "I've come to take you to lunch" — and what he was doing — dressed as a clown and holding a gun — that was so odd. What did it mean? he wondered. Was it a euphemism? Did Tom actually intend to kill him and that was his clever way of saying it? If so, why did he point the gun at the ground just as he said it? Joe did not yet know it was a paintball gun. When he found that out, it seemed Tom might have legitimately wanted to take him to lunch.

"Where do you think he wanted to take you?" asked Jim Jackers.

"The Sherwin-Williams café," quipped Benny.

"Jim," said Karen, shaking her head across the table at him, "where he wanted to take him is not the point."

"After he was arrested," Joe continued, "Carl came to my office and showed me an e-mail Tom had sent him. It said that Tom was stopping by the office that day because he wanted to talk to me. I went to see him because I was curious. What did he want to talk about?"

"And what was it?" asked Benny.

"Ralph Waldo Emerson," said Joe.

"Ralph Waldo Emerson?"

"Is he the guy with the pond?" asked Jim.

"You're thinking of Henry David Thoreau," said Hank.

"Jim is thinking of the Budweiser frogs," said Karen.

We recalled the book Tom had purchased for Carl Garbedian, and what he had said to Benny on the day he was terminated. Tom Mota, ladies and gentlemen — martini addict, gonzo e-mailer, sometime wielder of an aluminum bat, great garden enthusiast, paintball terrorist, and our own in-house Emerson scholar. He had the annoying tic during his time with us of pinning aphorisms to the wall. We liked nothing less than people quoting at us from their corkboards. Hank Neary was the only one who could quote at us with impunity because he rarely made any sense, so we knew the quotation must add up somehow and we marveled at the obscurity. Quotations that tried to instruct us or rehabilitate our ways, like those Tom favored — we didn't like those quotations. We were especially put off by Tom's because it seemed a great irony that Tom Mota was trying to reveal to us a better way to live, when just look at the guy! What a fuckup. His quotations were never allowed to stay pinned up for very long. It would take him days to notice and then he would holler out into the hall, in his inimitable and eloquent manner, "Who the fuck's been stealing my quotes?"

He and Joe were sequestered in a small, windowless room. We expected something different: a booth, some bulletproof glass, a pair of red phones. But according to Joe it was a room no bigger than the average office on sixty. It was almost possible to imagine their unlikely conversation unfolding where conversations always unfolded for us, only this time, the door locked from the inside, and Tom wasn't allowed any thumbtacks with which to pin up his ludicrous and heartfelt quotations. Joe was sitting at the table when Tom was escorted in by two guards. He was wearing a tan jumpsuit with D.O.C. stenciled on the back, and he was shackled with handcuffs. The guards told them they had fifteen minutes.

"Being treated okay, Tom?"

"How are those fucks?" asked Tom. "Recovering?"

Joe gave Tom the general rundown of events after he was arrested. Tom said he was happy we got Friday afternoon off. They talked about Tom's situation, what his lawyers were saying they could do for him if he pled guilty and acted penitent. Then Joe asked him what he had come there to ask him.

"I just said, 'What did you want to talk to me about that day, Tom?' " Joe said to us. "And finally he admitted that he was the one who had Sharpied *FAG* on my wall."

"No shit," said Benny.

"I thought you did that to yourself," said Jim Jackers.

"No," said Joe.

"Jim, think about it," said Karen. "Why would Joe do that to his own office? God."

"I can't tell you how many times I asked him, Joe," said Benny. "I said, 'Tom, come on, man, tell me the truth. Did you do that to Joe's wall?' Every time he denied it."

Tom tried to explain himself. "I refused to conform," he said to Joe. "When somebody said something stupid, everybody smiled and simpered and shook their heads. But me, I told them it was stupid. Everyone listened to the same goddamn radio station.

Fuck that. I stayed late and went by everybody's desk and spun the dial. I wore three polos on top of each other for a month, Joe, because I wasn't being fooled and I wanted people to know it. I learned all that from reading Emerson. To conform is to lose your soul. So I dissented every chance I got and I told them fuck you and eventually they fired me for it, but I thought, Ralph Waldo Emerson would be proud of Tom Mota."

Genevieve spoke up from down the conference room table. "He's pleased with himself?"

"No, he's not pleased with himself," said Joe. "Hang on."

"But what I didn't know for a long time, Joe," Tom had continued, "was that I was down here." Joe demonstrated in order to explain what Tom meant. Tom had rattled his handcuffs in a sudden vortex whipped up by his spinning hands, which hovered just above the table. "Down here, resenting everything. The rut I was in. My never-enough salary. The people. I stormed around. I poked my nose into everyone's business. When there was an insult to be made, I made it. When I could disparage someone, I took the opportunity. I Sharpied *FAG* on your wall. And I thought, it's because I refuse to conform. If they don't like it, they can fire me, because I can't live like everybody else. But then you walked in and found what I'd written, Joe, and what did you do? Do you remember?"

"I couldn't remember exactly," Joe said to us. "I remember I called Mike Boroshansky and told him that someone had vandalized my office. But that wasn't what Tom meant. After that, he said. After the official notification and all that. Did I remember what I did then? And I told him I couldn't remember specifically."

"You left it up there," said Tom. "*You left it up there.* The building people and the office coordinator, who knows what those fucks had going on, but whatever it was, it must have had them by the balls, because it wasn't until the following day — don't you remember? — that they got around to removing it."

We asked Joe if that was right. Did it really take them until the following day to remove *FAG* from his wall?

"Maybe," he replied. "I remember it took them a while. But to be honest, I'm just going on what Tom told me."

"I'm telling you," said Tom, "it wasn't until the next day. Whenever I'd walk by, the first thing I'd do is look in at you. I expected to see you all up in arms, screaming into the phone at someone about why it was still up there. But what did I find you doing instead? *You were working.* You were . . . I don't know what. If it had been me, I'd have been hollering at someone every five minutes until they came with a goddamn can of paint and covered over that fucker, because who likes to be called a fag? But you? You didn't care. It couldn't touch you. Because you're up *here,* Joe," said Tom.

Joe demonstrated once again. Tom had lifted one of his manacled hands as high as it would go to demonstrate where he thought Joe was, the second hand having no choice but to follow.

"I thought *I* was up there, but no, that whole time, I was down *here,* with everybody else — churning, spinning, talking, lying, circling, whipping myself up into a frenzy. I was doing everything they were doing, just in my own way. But you," he said, "you stay here, Joe. You're up here." His hand delineated Joe's place with such vigor it made the second hand jerk back and forth.

"I tried to tell him that wasn't necessarily true," said Joe. "I could be way down here for all he knew," he said, bending his chin down to the conference room table so he could touch the floor. "But Tom had made up his mind. I was up here." Joe extended his arm in the air once more.

"I thought I was the one living right," said Tom. "I was the one saying fuck you to the miseries of office life. Nobody could resist conforming in the corporate setting, but I managed it. Making it a point every day to show how different I was from everybody else. Proving I was better, smarter, funnier. Then I saw you sitting side by side with the word *FAG* on the wall — working — *at peace* — and I knew — *you* were the one. Not me. I used to think it was just because you were arrogant. But then I knew it wasn't arrogance. It was just your nature. And I hated you for it. You had it, and I didn't, and I hated you."

We asked Joe if he had really been at peace the day he found *FAG* on his wall.

"At peace?" he said. "I'm not sure that describes it. Tom thinks he knows me, but he doesn't. And I tried to tell him that, I said, 'Tom, finding my office vandalized like that, you have no idea how that made me feel. Maybe I was mortified. Maybe I wanted to kill myself. Maybe I went into the bathroom and cried. Don't assume you know.' But he wouldn't listen."

"Did you cry, Joe?" asked Jim.

"Jim, he's not going to tell us if he cried," said Karen.

"I didn't cry," said Joe.

"I know you didn't cry, Joe," said Tom. "Because you weren't bothered. And I had no choice but to respect you for it, even though I hated you. I still hated you the day they let me go, and probably the day after, but on the third day, it disappeared, all of it . . . just . . . *poof,* I don't know why. Probably because I wasn't working there anymore. I had distance, suddenly. And what I was left feeling toward you was admiration. More than admiration. It was love —"

We couldn't help it, it was so absurd, Tom saying that he loved Joe — we just cracked up.

"Don't laugh," said Joe sternly. "You wanted to hear it. Let me finish."

The table got quiet again.

"I had wanted to smash your face in," said Tom. "I couldn't stomach the sight of you. I wanted to apologize for that. That's why I wanted to take you to lunch," he said. "I really did want to take you to lunch. But as that fuck so eloquently puts it, 'Character teaches above our wills.' And before I knew it, I had the paintball gun thing all worked out in my head and I just couldn't stop myself."

The two guards came into the room just then and announced that Joe's time was up. He looked at his watch and couldn't believe that fifteen minutes had passed. Joe stood, but the guard immediately told him to sit down again. "There was a whole procedure to it," he explained to us. "Tom would be led out by the first guard, and I would be led out by the second one. I had to remain seated until Tom was out of sight."

"Thanks for coming, Joe," Tom said, as the guard approached and took his arm. "I appreciate it."

"Is there anything I can do for you, Tom?"

"Yeah." Tom raised his manacled hands abruptly. "Stay up here, you fuck," he said.

Immediately the guard reacted and Tom put his hands back down.

With that, Joe began to pass handouts around the table. "Like I said," he added, not looking at any of us. "Tom Mota thinks he knows me, but he doesn't. Not really."

We each took a handout.

"Okay," he said. He straightened in his chair, and the meeting began.

— — —

OUR VISIT TO LYNN in the hospital was a rough twenty minutes. We shared oblique glances and sweaty palms and the crippling fear of pauses in the conversation. There was no easy breathing from the moment we arrived. She was sitting up in her hospital bed, swimming in her blue cotton gown, a plastic ID bracelet around her child's wrist. It was a well-known phenomenon that she was a small woman physically who loomed in our imaginations as a towering and indomitable giant. She looked even smaller now, lost in all the blankets and pillows of the hospital bed, and her arms, which we had never seen so much of before, looked as undefined and reedy as a little girl's.

We had nothing in common with the dying and so never knew what to say to them. Our presence seemed a vague and threatening insult, something that could easily spill over into cruel laughter, and so we chose our words carefully and moved with caution gathering around the bed and restricted our jokes and bantering. It would not be appropriate to storm in and be our full flush selves, encouraging her with loud voices to return to us because, just beneath the spoken words, the real truth ran fast as a current: she may never be one of us again. So we minced and pussyfooted and swallowed our words, mumbled and deflected and softened our voices, and she saw right through it. "Come in," she said when we first arrived. "Get in here. What are you all being so shy for?" One after the other we filed in. Her hair was back in a ponytail, she wasn't wearing any makeup, and there was no sign of a single pair of designer shoes. She had just undergone a grievous surgery and was suffering from unspecified complications. Yet she still generated the greatest energy in the room. It was a private room about the size of her office and so it felt a little like entering that enervating space to receive dreaded news about some irrevocable and costly error we had committed at the agency's expense. We greeted her. We presented her with flowers. "Will you look at all your funeral faces," she said, looking toward the foot of the bed, and to the right of her and to the left. "You'd think I was dead already. Would it have killed you to practice your expression in the mirror before coming in here, Benny?" Benny smiled and apologized. She looked next at Genevieve. "And you," she said. "Did you have a conversation with my doctors I should know about?" Genevieve also smiled and shook her head. "Well, so what's next, then?" she asked. "A reading from the Bible?" We tried to explain that we had been ambivalent about coming. We thought maybe she would have preferred her privacy. "I would have preferred never to have stepped foot in this dreary hell," she said. "But if I have to be here, it's nice to see some familiar faces. But somebody start acting like a jackass or I'll hardly know you."

"I do a mean imitation of James Brown doing an imitation of Clint Eastwood," offered Benny. "Want to see it?"

"I can't picture that," said Lynn.

"Believe it or not, it's true," said Jim.

So Benny did his imitation of James Brown doing Clint Eastwood, which defied description to anyone who hadn't seen it, but had us laughing within a few seconds, and that finally broke the ice.

We talked about Tom Mota and the incident, and Joe told of seeing him in jail. And we talked about Carl's resignation, which came as a surprise to Lynn. "You're leaving us, Carl?" "I am," he said. "Well, I think that is terrific news," Lynn said. We were shocked to hear how in favor she was of Carl's departure until she elaborated. "Advertising isn't your thing," she explained. "It doesn't make you happy." Carl agreed and told her of his ambitions for Garbedian and Son. She said the same thing we said: "Good for you, Carl." Though she was probably thinking, Who wants to be twirling a weedwhacker around a subdivision in the middle of a heatstroke summer? Give me my chair over that any day of the week. Oh, what I'd give to be back in my chair — she was probably thinking that, too.

After a while we could tell she was starting to flag, so we told her we'd better let her get some sleep. But first Jim Jackers had a presentation to make.

We thought it was a terrible idea from the very beginning. Lynn had asked us to do a pro bono project for a breast cancer awareness fund-raiser, claiming to know some committee chair who had pestered her. The next day, the project morphs from a fund-raiser into a public service announcement, with the baffling mandate to inspire laughter in the breast cancer patient. What happened to the fund-raiser? No one knows. Is there really a pestering committee chair? No word on that, either. Just Joe Pope instructing us on the changes. We say okay, whatever. We get down to work. We read books, we do research. We come up with squat. We file into Lynn's office at the eleventh hour — she's forgotten about it entirely. We unload the "Loved Ones" campaign on the "client." The project ends. Tom comes in and shoots us with paintballs.

But then we found out Lynn did in fact have cancer. When that came to light, Jim Jackers suggested we revive the ads we failed at so miserably and present them to her in the hospital, in order to cheer her up.

"Because what if she did make up that assignment?" he asked. "Don't you think she'd like to see those ads more than ever, now that she's actually in the hospital?"

"Don't be an idiot, Jim," said Karen Woo. "Of course she didn't make up that assignment."

"Well, that's a different tune you're singing all of a sudden, Karen."

"Oh, Jim, don't be so dense."

"How am I being dense?" he asked. "I'm just saying — what if?"

He claimed to have a concept. We thought he must have reconciled with his uncle. "No, I came up with this on my own," he said. When we heard that, we let out a collective groan. Jim's original concepts were usually worse than Chris Yop's.

"But it's really not a bad concept," Benny said to us. "I think she'd get a big kick out of it."

We asked him to explain the concept to us, but Jim had sworn him to secrecy until they talked to Joe. They went in, and Joe purportedly said, "I couldn't have come up with this. Whose idea was this?"

"Jim's," said Benny.

After they got out of their meeting, we asked Benny if Jim had been reconciled with his uncle.

"You guys already asked me that," Jim cut in. "I told you I came up with these ads on my own." He showed us one. We thought it was derivative, full of borrowed interest, and rather unoriginal. "But that's the whole point," Jim argued. "That's what *makes* them original." We had to agree to disagree, and immediately began devising ways of escaping before Jim unveiled them.

But it was hard to distance ourselves from him inside Lynn's hospital room when he announced that "we" had a presentation for her. Lynn herself looked at him from her ocean of bed with an expression somewhere between surprise and skepticism. We all held our breath for fear of what inappropriate preamble might escape Jim's mouth. He reminded her of what the pro bono project had once asked of us — to present the breast cancer patient with something funny in her hour of need. For the first time in his life, he didn't call it the "pro boner" project.

"And so without further ado," he said, with embarrassing grandiosity, as he unzipped the black portfolio and pulled out the first ad. What choice did we have but to stick around?

From the foot of her bed, he held the ad high so everyone could see. Each concept had been glued to black mount board with two-inch borders, which made the thing really pop. "As you can see," he said, "this visual shows the familiar sight of a laminated placard you might see hanging in a hospital or a gynecologist's office, of the featureless female form giving herself a breast exam. One arm is raised in the air and bent at the elbow, while the hand of the other arm probes her left breast." Somebody snickered. Jim paused, evidently irritated. "Juxtaposed with this image," he continued, "is the famous 'Miss Clairol' headline. 'Does she . . . or doesn't she?' And our subhead reads, 'A tumor so small only her oncologist knows for sure!' "

We watched Lynn's face for some sort of reaction. "Let me have a closer look," she said. Jim handed the ad to her. She took it and we felt no different than we did when sitting in her office waiting for her to assess and judge and deliver her verdict on real ads.

"This is funny," she said.

"But you're not laughing," said Jim.

"I never laugh, Jim," she replied. Which was true, she never laughed. She only said, "This is funny." And then you knew she liked it.

"Here's the next one," he said, pulling the second ad from the portfolio and holding it before her. "You recognize this famous shot," he began, "of a man dressed all in black, gripping the armrests of a black leather armchair while the speaker in front of him is blowing back his hair, his tie, his martini glass, and the lampshade next to him. It's from the old Maxell tape ad. Except in ours, the stereo speaker has been replaced by the profile of a giant breast emerging from the margin on the left, which we scanned from an old *Playboy* of Benny's. The headline reads, 'No Other Disease Delivers Higher Recovery Rates.' The word *Maxell* has been replaced with the word *Mammary* in the bottom right-hand corner, and the small print reads, 'Get blown away by your fast recovery.' This," Jim concluded, "combines a little humor with a little hope."

"Let me see it, Jim," she said. We watched her reaction. "I like it," she said, tapping it. Which was enthusiasm we hadn't seen or heard since Joe and Genevieve unveiled Cold Sore Guy.

"This next one," said Jim, "shows the extreme close-up of a man in a surgical mask and scrubs, holding up near his face a scalpel and a pair of operating scissors. It's an unfamiliar image, but in the upper right-hand corner we've placed a subtle Nike Swoosh," said Jim, pointing to it, "and running across the bottom of the page is the famous 'Just Do It' tagline. The subhead reads, 'Go Ahead and Cut.' And I'll read you the body copy," said Jim. " 'Triathletes. Channel swimmers. Hikers of Everest. Compared to the woman facing breast cancer surgery, those clowns don't have a clue about perseverance and courage. Talk to someone who's faced down *this* guy. She knows what hard work is all about. She knows the definition of winning. Survival, baby. Just Do It.' "

There were several more — the "Got Cancer?" ad, the "Absolut Ether" ad, in which a hand with long painted fingernails grips the neck of a half-empty vodka bottle like a claw. Jim handed them all across the bed and she got very close to each one, inspecting and reading them. When she got to the Absolut ad, she offered us a genuine smile.

She continued to smile as she thanked us. We said our goodbyes. We told her to feel better. Out in the hallway, we encountered more nurses and medical equipment. We said we thought she liked them. We asked Joe if he agreed. We said we nailed it, didn't we, Joe? Didn't we nail it? We walked together down the hall. We were a full car heading down the elevator.

"Do you really think she liked those ads, Joe?" asked Marcia. "Or do you think she was smiling because of how atrocious they were?"

"Hey!" cried Jim.

"Sorry, Jim, nothing personal. I just happen to think they're atrocious," she said. "It's not your fault, you did better than any of us. I'm just saying it was an impossible assignment."

We grew introspective and quiet for the remainder of the ride. When we reached the lobby floor, there was a delay before the doors opened, and that's when Genevieve broke the silence.

"Maybe she wasn't smiling because of the ads," she said. "Maybe she was smiling because of us. What we did."

"Because it was a nice gesture," said Marcia.

"Or maybe," said Jim, with uncharacteristic conviction, "you guys just don't know anything about advertising."

WHEN, A FEW WEEKS LATER, they let go of Jim Jackers, we said they lifted him off his seat by the middle belt loop of his jeans and threw him from the building. We said he went flying three stairs at a time until he landed on the curb, where he picked himself up and checked his forehead for blood. After that, we said, he collected his useless shit, which had spilled everywhere during his propeller dive at the sidewalk. Jim was not one to leave without a box.

When next they came for Amber, a few weeks after that, we said she was tossed into the streetlamp outside the building without any concern for her unborn baby. We had just come back from lunch at T.G.I. Friday's when she got the news. It was at that lunch we presented her with things we had bought for the baby — a diaper bag, a stroller — all of which was tossed out with her. She lay trying to recover, head spinning, on the wet cement in a light summer rain. We said people walking past stared down at the spectacle and refused to help, and we imagined the bum with the Dunkin' Donuts cup bending down to the stroller, opening it up, and rolling it away with him.

We said Don Blattner was thrown headfirst into the window of a parked taxi with such force he wheeled around 180 degrees, rolled his eyes a couple of times, and slumped down between the car and the curb. He settled, head hanging down like a heavy melon, and appeared to all passersby like a drunk sleeping off a bender. We said the movie stills that had adorned his office walls were taken down and flung at his drooping head. Most of them just hit the car and shattered, but a few landed, and the cuts began to bleed. More movie memorabilia — action figures, back issues of *Vanity Fair* — was dumped on his prone body. Eventually, we said, Don was carted off by city officials.

It was all fun and games after they were gone. Easier to make cartoons of them than to wonder for any amount of time how Amber was going to find a new job before the baby came, or how unjust they were to let go of her while keeping Larry on. Easier to joke than to feel sorry for Jim, who had been everyone's whipping boy for so long that we had nothing left after his departure but loathsome memories of our bullying and cruel remarks. None of us cared to revisit the fun we'd made of him for fear our laughter might now stick in our throats.

In reality, when we heard Jim was let go we went down to his cubicle, miserable with happiness that he had been chosen over us. Everyone who had spoken ill of him at one time or another was there to offer him condolences. Jim's reaction was magnanimous and pathetic at once. When people extended their hands and told him how sorry they were, he nodded and smiled and said, "Thanks," as if he had just been named Employee of the Month. He almost seemed to be enjoying himself, which was curious but later made sense, because it was probably the only time during his entire tenure that so many people had approached him with a universal consensus of support instead of with ridicule or scorn. He didn't point out the hypocrisy or seek to settle scores. He soaked up the attention with an indulgence he deserved, stretching out his allotted half hour to forty-five minutes until Roland, who was standing against the wall as he had done with Marcia, finally told Jim he really had to be out of the building. So Jim said his final good-byes and shook a few hands and left with his box, never to return.

It was different with Benny. Earnings were down across the board. Stock prices were in free fall. We were just about to awaken from a decade of unadulterated dreaming. Benny had to call his father to come with a car, he had so much useless shit in his office.

"Roland," he said, "have a seat. This may take a while."

"You know I gotta stand, Benny."

"What do they think I'm going to do, Roland? Stab you with a highlighter?"

"They can't take any chances since the incident," Roland tried to explain for the hundredth time. "I'm not even supposed to be conversing."

"I bet I can make you converse."

Soon Benny and Roland were conversing about whether or not Benny could make Roland converse, until Roland, catching himself in Benny's trap, said, "Please, Benny, I'm just trying to do my job."

"Come on, man," said Benny. "I thought you and me were friends?"

"You think this is easy for me?" asked the older man.

When at last Benny's father arrived, it took the three men four trips down the freight elevator. Benny had so much stuff in his office it was like he was moving out of an apartment. If a general sadness overtook us when Marcia and Amber and Jim were let go, a veritable pall cast itself about the hallways during Benny's last hour. Who would regale us with stories now? Into whose office would we go to confide, to gossip, to horse around? And who, what with Paulette Singletary gone, too, could we point to now and agree that there was the one person who stood head and shoulders above the rest? Garrulousness and a natural amiability — that was the nature of heroism in the confines we shared during that more innocent time, and when they took Benny, they took away our hero.

After that we fell into even greater recrimination and bickering. Needless to say, the caffeinated water people went with a different firm, and the running shoe people ended up staying with their original agency. Without any new business things got worse. What little work remained was never any fun. All that summer no one took advantage of the city or the proximity of the lake for an aimless stroll during a lunch hour because we were too rabid with speculation about how dire things had become and who would be the next to go. We could enjoy nothing but our own dull rumoring. Conversation never extended beyond our walls, walls that were closing in on us, and we failed to take stock of anything happening beyond them. One topic — that was all we knew, and it tyrannized every conversation. We fell into it helplessly, the way jilted lovers know only one subject, the way true bores never transcend the sorry limitations of their own lives. It was a shrill, carping, frenzied time, and as poisonous an atmosphere as anyone had ever known — and we wanted nothing more than to stay in it forever.

In the last week of August 2001, and in the first ten days of that September, there were more layoffs than in all the months preceding them. But by the grace of god, the rest of us hung on, hating each other more than we ever thought possible. Then we came to the end of another bright and tranquil summer.

5

FIVE YEARS LATER — WHO'S HANK? — THE DAY OF *THE GODFATHER* — THE MONTAGUES AND THE CAPULETS — JIM GOES TO A MEETING — FOR US IT WAS NEVER A WORRY — HANK'S READING — HANDLEBAR HARRY — TO LYNN, AND LATER, TO TOM — THE REFORMED LAMA — IN THE END

IN THE SUMMER OF 2006, Benny Shassburger received an e-mail from someone he couldn't place. The name was familiar, he knew he should know it, but the longer he stared at it the more it eluded him. He said the name aloud. His cubicle neighbor, a lank, annoying person who never let anything go by without making inquiries, popped his sandy groundhog's head over the cube wall and said, "What'd you say?" Benny hardly had the energy to explain. "I'm just talking to myself," he said. Ian replied that there was a new study claiming that whenever anyone said something out loud and then someone else asked, "What did you say?" and that person responded that he was just talking to himself, that that person wasn't just talking to himself, but in fact was most likely addressing someone specific, even if only subconsciously. Ian kept abreast of all the new studies. Benny felt tired.

Where had we located the energy? Updating our resumes, interviewing again, learning a new commute route. We had spread out across the industry, finding work at other agencies, at design firms and in-house marketing departments, usually the first place that would have us. The less fortunate or talented among us went to direct-mail shops or turned to the temp agencies for uninsured day jobs. The floor plans, the shapes of the desks, the names of the people, and the colors of the corporate logos were all new and different, but the song and dance remained the same. We were delighted to have jobs. We bitched about them constantly. We walked around our new offices with our two minds. All those new faces and names to memorize, the strange coffee pots and unfamiliar toilet seats. We had new W-4s to fill out and never knew if it was zero or one that would give us more money back. HR was there to assist, but they were never as good as our old HR. We spent the first two or three weeks, and some of us more like a month or two, in isolation and anonymity. For an unbearable spell, lunch was a solitary affair. Only slowly did we get folded into the mix, only slowly did the new political realities start to dawn. Who was wrangling and for what, who was crass, arrogant, stupid, powerful, fake, prepossessing, double-crossing, or a good person all around — all this began to shake out. But it didn't happen overnight. It took weeks, it took months, and that we mustered up the oomph to start over again at new agencies was a testament to our tenacity. It was a sign that buried beneath all the bitching, there were parts of the job we loved. It was proof we needed the money.

"You know I'm a friendly guy," Benny said into the phone, peering over the cube wall to be sure Ian hadn't returned. "But I don't know how much more I can take. I'm telling you, this guy Ian? He's destroying my core personality."

Some had adjusted better than others. There was freedom in starting over because nobody knew yet if you were crass, arrogant, stupid, powerful, fake, prepossessing, double-crossing, or a good person all around. You could reinvent yourself. Wasn't that part of the promise of America? A few blissful months passed in which pigeonholing was impossible. Lessons learned from past mistakes held us in good stead. Some of us displayed a rapid growth in political savvy. Others wondered what happened. "I used to be such a mensch," Benny continued. "Remember? People used to come into my office and I would regale them with stories. With the exception of maybe Paulette Singletary, I was the person everybody loved the most. What happened?"

"Why don't you come down to my office and let's talk about it," Jim said to him.

When Benny arrived, there he was. Jim Jackers. Composing an e-mail. If the expression on Jim's face was any indication, thought Benny, the fate of the entire agency depended on that one e-mail. Benny took a seat across from him and waited. He disliked being on *this* side of the desk. He wanted to be on *that* side. Jim's side.

"Okay, listen," said Jim, once he had finished composing the all-important e-mail. "You're next in line for an office, okay? You just have to be patient."

"How do you know I'm next?" asked Benny.

"I'll take care of it, don't worry. But you gotta wait until somebody vacates. We can't just kick somebody out of an office they're already in and send them to a cube."

"I was kicked out of an office and sent to a cube."

"Because you lost your job," said Jim.

"A technicality," Benny replied. He sat back in his chair. "Don't get me wrong, Jim. I'm eternally grateful to you for hiring me. I've been doing freelance too long. But a small agency doesn't suit me the way it suits you. I can't look at the same thirty people over and over again every day. I need multiple floors. I've learned this about myself. I'm a creature whose natural habitat is multiple floors. And I *need* an office. I miss my old office. I miss the people. You know who I miss? I'll tell you who I miss," he said. "I miss Old Brizz."

"How can you miss Old Brizz?" asked Jim. "You never really knew him. If you miss him at all, it's because he was old and he died and nobody here currently occupying an office fits that description."

"Jim, you have turned into a cynical man," Benny said. "I blame the corrupting influence of power. I miss Old Brizz because I got ten bucks a pop from all you Charlton Heston hopefuls when poor Old Brizz kicked off." He got closer to Jim across the desk and lowered his voice. "What I miss, Jim, is Celebrity Death Watch. I can't even get a Super Bowl pool going on around here. What is *wrong* with these people? I'm not clicking and it's driving me crazy. I miss *clicking*. Speaking of which," he said, sitting back. "Who's Hank Neary?"

Jim's attention was seized by the sound of the name. "Hank Neary," he said. "Hank Neary." Furrowing his brow and looking away, he slowly, methodically incanted the name as a word absent of all meaning. "Hank," he said. "Hank. Hank."

"We worked with him, right?"

"Hank Neary," said Jim. "Hank Neary."

"Didn't we work with him, Jimmy? At the old agency?"

"Hold on. Give me a minute," said Jim. "We worked with him."

"Neary," said Benny, slitting his eyes at Jim. "Hank Neary."

"Hank Neary," said Jim. "It's escaping me."

"My memory," said Benny, shaking his head.

"Mine, too. You know what? Call Marcia. She'll know."

Benny shook his head. "Can't call Marcia right now," he replied. "Marcia's mad at me."

"What's she mad at you for?"

"Jim, have I got a story to tell you," he exclaimed. "I've got the best story you've ever heard. Hold on a second while I get more coffee."

"No, Benny —"

"What?"

"I got a meeting in ten minutes."

"Oh."

"Well, don't get defeated," said Jim, seeing Benny's disappointment. "I still got ten minutes."

"All right, I'll do without the coffee. But do me a favor," said Benny. "Let me sit in your chair while I tell it."

"Are you serious?"

Benny got up. Jim got up reluctantly and they switched places. Benny smiled. He was on the right side of the desk again. He could look out into the hall and see all the people passing by and call them in.

"Michael!" he hollered out into the hall. "Michael, get in here and listen to my story. It's a terrific story, you'll love it."

Michael barely paused to stick his head inside Jim's office. "Can't," he said. "I'm on deadline with this newsletter."

He quickly departed, and Benny held up his hands to demonstrate his disbelief. "Do you see that?" he asked. "Do you see now, Jim, what I'm talking about? There's something wrong with these people."

"Benny, he's on deadline."

"Who doesn't have ten minutes to hear a good story?"

"Benny. Tell me the story."

So Benny told Jim the story of why Marcia was mad at him. Since becoming employed full-time again, he had grown aware of a phenomenon that seemed to happen only at work, or at least happened with more frequency at work than other places in life, and the phenomenon was this: one person would say something and the person listening would have positively no idea what he or she meant, but not wanting to appear rude, or worse, stupid, or alternatively, not caring to waste any more time, it was easier just to nod or laugh along than it was to pause and inquire what that person really meant. This was especially true with hallway banter and kitchen talk and other types of inconsequential daily exchanges.

People were indifferent to what was said, or were preoccupied by other things, or had long ago concluded that what passed for speech during the course of a workday was mostly the babble of idiots. "So I thought, Would it make a difference, really? Would it honestly make a difference if instead of replying the way I would normally, I answered everybody with quotes from *The Godfather*?"

Jim was curious. "How would you manage that?" he said.

Benny explained that he gave himself a simple rule: nothing could come from his mouth that had not come first from the mouths of Michael, Sonny, Fredo, Tom Hagen, or the Don himself — or anybody at all in the first two films.

"Why only the first two?" asked Jim.

"Come on, Jim," said Benny. "You know why. Do we have to call Don Blattner?"

"Because the third one sucks?"

"Boy, I miss that old Don Blattner," said Benny.

At the conclusion of a morning meeting, during which he had remained perfectly silent, as everyone was packing up their things, Benny had turned to Heidi Savoca and said, " 'I spent my whole life trying not to be careless. Women and children can be careless, but not men.' " Heidi's expression indicated she didn't know where Benny's comment was coming from, but more pressing than her confusion was her distaste for the remark itself. "That's a very sexist thing to say, Benny," she replied. Later that morning, Seth Keegan stopped by Benny's cube to ask him a question about some revisions for a project the two had been working on over the course of the previous few weeks. "Do you have a minute?" Seth asked Benny. Benny swiveled in his chair. " 'This one time,' " he said. " 'This one time I'll let you ask me about my affairs.' " "Cool," said Seth, who entered the cubicle more fully. "I'm wondering what you think we should do about these drop shadows. What I was thinking we could do is . . ." Benny let him talk, nodding from time to time, and before long, Seth had arrived at a conclusion without needing any input from Benny at all. Just as he was leaving, Benny thought what the hell, and called out to him. "'Hey, it's my sister's wedding,'" he said, angrily. "Oh, yeah?" said Seth. "Your sister's getting married?" "'And when the boss tells me to push a button on a guy,'" Benny continued, "'I push a button.'" Seth stared at him. "Cool," he said. He nodded. Then he walked away.

In the afternoon Carter Shilling came to his cube, and Benny didn't think he could continue if he had to talk with Carter, his scruffy, cross-eyed boss. A rasp or a boom, those were the two ways Carter communicated, and he was currently booming, raving about how stupid the client was to request such stupid changes to their ad. For a long time Benny didn't have to say a word. Finally Carter looked at him and asked him if he agreed that the client was stupid. "'I think if we had a wartime consigliere,'" Benny found himself answering in a small voice, "'we wouldn't be in this mess.'" Carter gazed down at him and asked if that was code for something. "Are you saying we're at fault here?" asked Carter.

"So I swear to god, Jim," said Benny, "I put on my most serious face, man. I mean, I was nothing but business, and I looked him straight in the eye and I said, 'Carter, this sort of thing has to happen every five years or so. Helps to get rid of the bad blood.' And both of us, at the same time, looked back down at the ad, which the client had just ripped to shreds, and he says to me, 'Yeah,' he says, 'I suppose.' As if what I just said made any sense whatsoever. 'Go ahead and make the changes, then,' he says. 'I don't give a damn anymore.' And then he stormed out of my office. It was —"

Just then the two men were interrupted by Carter Shilling himself as he happened by Jim's office on his way to the meeting.

"You're not Jim," he rasped, pointing at Benny. "You're Jim," he said, pointing at Jim. "What's with the switcheroo?"

"Damn, Jim!" cried Benny, snapping his fingers aw-shucks style. "He caught on."

With no visible change in expression, Carter nodded his laughter. He expressed many of his emotions with a simple nod. He turned away from Benny. "You coming to the meeting?" he asked Jim.

"On my way," said Jim.

"Jim, it was priceless," said Benny, once Carter had departed.

"Benny, don't talk to Carter like that."

"I miss Joe Pope," said Benny.

"You still haven't explained why Marcia's mad at you," said Jim.

Benny was only too happy to pick up the story where he was forced to leave off when Carter appeared. He told Jim that as the afternoon wore on, his task got more complicated. His memory of *Godfather* quotes was being heavily taxed, and around three in the afternoon, Marcia started calling him with unusual frequency, almost once every ten minutes. Benny couldn't use the phone because it would be impossible to keep to the rules of the game over the phone, so he let it ring and then checked his voice mail for messages. But Marcia wasn't leaving messages. "I've told you about her brothers, right?" he said to Jim.

"That they eat Jews for dinner."

"Right," said Benny. "Even the youngest is basically just a walking crowbar. The wedding's going to be . . . what are those family names, in *Romeo and Juliet*?"

"The Montagues and the Capulets," said Jim.

"The Montagues and the Capulets," cried Benny. "That's exactly right. How'd you know that?"

"I took a course in Shakespeare last summer," said Jim. "A continuing education thing."

"No shit?" said Benny. "So yeah, the wedding's going to be like the Montagues and the Capulets. Except the Montagues won't have swords, they'll have Saturday-night specials, you know, and us, we'll just have the Torah and whatever shards we can collect from the breaking of the glass. Anyway," he said.

He let his office phone ring the rest of the afternoon, puzzled why Marcia was calling and not leaving messages, and answered his cell phone only after the workday had come to an end and he had departed the building. When he finally picked up, Marcia was in hysterics. Her youngest brother had gotten into a fight — he was still only a sophomore in high school — and had to be taken to a South Side hospital. Marcia's mother was crying, her older brothers were vowing revenge, and her father was sleeping off a night shift. Marcia was trying to get ahold of Benny so he could help her keep things together. Benny rushed over to the hospital and inquired at the nurses' station what room the boy was in.

"When I got there, nobody else was around. Turns out later they were down talking to the doctor. I walked in and took one look at Mikey in his hospital bed — Jim, he was all fucked up. Broken arm, black eyes. Big gash in his chin. But he was awake. The kid was going to be fine. And you know what I said? I just couldn't help myself. I went right up to him and I said, 'My boy! Look what they done to my boy!' "

Marcia found out later why Benny hadn't been picking up the phone, and that's why she was mad at him. She thought it was a thoughtless and juvenile game to play and it explained why he was still in a cube. "Why can't you be more like Jim?" she asked.

Carter Shilling stopped by again. "Jim, you coming?"

"Carter," said Jim, rising at the sound of the man's voice. "Coming."

"Jim, it was priceless," Benny said, once Carter had departed.

"I gotta go do this meeting," said Jim.

He collected some papers off his desk and Benny was left sitting alone in another man's office. He was trying to decide whether or not to get up — he supposed there was some work he could do back at his cube, if Ian didn't interrupt him — when Jim reappeared in the doorway. "So what now?" he asked.

"What do you mean?"

"I mean if you can get by with quotes from *The Godfather*, and nothing you say matters, that's pretty bleak, don't you think? Don't we want what we say to matter?"

Benny swiveled effortlessly in the chair that wasn't his and gave Jim a puzzled, surprised look. He unsteepled his fingers and opened his hands into a shrug. "What is this, Jim, what's wrong with you? I was just having some fun."

"Don't you want people to take you seriously, Benny?"

"But why do you have to phrase it like that? Why does Marcia have to ask me why I can't be more like you, and why can't Michael listen to my story for ten stupid minutes? What's happened to everybody? You're all so serious."

Jim hung in the doorway, ponderous and unresponsive. "Why did you keep Old Brizz's totem pole?" he said at last.

"What?" said Benny. "What are you talking about? I didn't. I gave it away."

"No, you kept it in storage for six months. Why did you do that?"

"Where is this coming from?"

"I've always wanted to know."

"But why are you bringing it up now?" Benny asked.

"Did you think," said Jim, "that he was trying to communicate something to you?"

Benny stopped swiveling and grabbed Jim's armrests. "Like what?"

"I don't know," said Jim. "I'm asking you."

"Maybe he was just playing a practical joke on me. Maybe because he knew I had him at the top of my list in Celebrity Death Watch."

"Maybe," said Jim. "But Brizz wasn't one to play practical jokes."

Benny nodded in agreement. "No, he wasn't."

"And as it turns out, that thing was worth a lot of money," Jim added. "Leaving someone a lot of money isn't a very mean practical joke."

"No, it isn't."

"So why'd you store it? Why'd you keep it for six months?"

"It meant something to me, I guess."

"What?"

"I don't know," said Benny.

"You don't know?"

"I do and I don't," said Benny. "You know what I mean?"

Jim bit the inside of his cheek. He nodded slowly in a sign of respectful resignation.

"Hank Neary," he said finally, shaking his head. He said it again: "Hank Neary." Then he threw up his hands and went off down the hall to his meeting.

— — —

SOME PEOPLE WOULD NEVER FORGET certain people, a few people would remember everyone, and most of us would mostly be forgotten. Sometimes it was for the best. Larry Novotny wanted to be forgotten for his dalliance with Amber Ludwig. Tom Mota wanted to be forgotten for that incident involving the paintballs. But did anybody want to be forgotten about completely? We had dedicated years to that place, we labored under the notion we were making names for ourselves, we had to believe in our hearts that each one of us was memorable. And yet who wanted to be remembered for their poor taste or bad breath? Still, better to be remembered for those things than forgotten for your perfect parboiled blandness.

In other words, amnesty was a gift, but oblivion was terror.

Most of us recalled in a general way this person or that, their features exaggerated by memory, their names lost forever. Of others we could pull up only the murkiest general outline, as if rather than walking past them in the hall a hundred times a day, we'd encountered them in a cloud once, mumbled a polite exchange, and moved on. Once in a great while, every random detail — tone of voice, where the mole was — came screaming out of the clear blue. What a weird sensation that was. And then there were some people some of us could not shake. Janine Gorjanc couldn't shake the memory of her lost child. Benny couldn't shake Frank Brizzolera because Frank had died and bequeathed him a totem pole. Uncle Max would never forget his Edna.

As for us, it was never a worry. We would never be forgotten by anyone.

"You jackass," Marcia said to Benny later that day. "How could you forget Hank Neary?"

Benny hurried down to Jim's doorway. "The black dude!" he cried. "With the corduroy coat!"

"Aw, man! I wanted to tell *you* that!" said Jim. He was reading Hank's e-mail, which had gone to him as well, to an e-mail account he rarely checked. "His face just now came to me," he said. "How could we have forgotten Hank, Benny?"

"I don't know," replied Benny. "I guess it just happens."

EVERYONE HAD RECEIVED the same e-mail as Benny and Jim and we all wondered how Hank had managed to track us down, scattered as we were. Most of us remembered him perfectly and recognized his name right away, because it wasn't every day you worked with a black guy who dressed like a poetry don at Oxford. We used to joke that the only thing missing was a pipe which he could grip with his teeth as he gave ponderous consideration to the iambic pentameter's slow demise. But no, he wasn't a poet, he was a failed novelist, and when we got his e-mail, it was like hearing that one of Don Blattner's screenplays had been picked up by Warner Brothers and George Clooney was starring. It turned out that Hank had published a book, and his reading was taking place at a bookstore on the campus of the University of Chicago. We were intrigued and disbelieving.

We packed the room full. We hardly had time to say hello to everyone when he appeared, book in hand, alongside a stooped, bearded gentleman who took to the podium and introduced him. He had many nice things to say about Hank, whose bashful, averted gaze we took note of as the man spoke. We also noticed that instead of the corduroy coat, Hank now wore a plain white Fruit-of-the-Loom T-shirt that accentuated his dark lanky arms and boyish torso. Without his bulky glasses his face was leaner, more handsome. He wore a pair of jeans and a simple black belt. It was a better look for him all around, and we were pleased to see that he'd moved beyond his weird ersatz professorial phase. We didn't say so at the time, but it never seemed appropriate.

As the introduction continued, we looked around at some of the familiar faces. Amber Ludwig sat at the end of the third row with a kid in her lap, a little girl who played industriously with a dirty, undressed doll. The poor kid had Larry's masculine features but Amber's stout, seal-like body. Larry Novotny himself sat in back, alone, hiding beneath a brand-new Cubs cap. Dan Wisdom was seated next to Don Blattner, and to the right, in the front row, Genevieve Latko-Devine sat beside her husband. He was holding a baby to his chest, which suddenly let out a succession of unhappy cries. In rapid response he shifted the child in his arms and rubbed its back tenderly and it was sleeping again in no time.

Everyone applauded when Hank rose and stood at the podium. We bucked a little at some microphone feedback. He readjusted the mic, gave us a sheepish smile, and began to speak with an endearing quaver in his voice. We could tell he was nervous. All at once, great swells of conflicted emotion flooded over us. One of our own had made good: we were proud, astounded, envious, incredulous, vaguely indifferent, ready to seize on the first hint of mediocrity, and genuinely pleased for him. We were all those things and more. Before sitting down, many of us had taken copies of his book off the display rack, and we thumbed through them now for errata. We read the acknowledgments page to see who he thanked. What was it about, anyway? And who, working our hours, had time to read books? We had to force ourselves to stop and pay attention, as he had finished thanking us for coming and was opening the book to read.

" 'The night before,' " he began. Suddenly he stopped. The room froze with anxiety. He was stiff-arming the podium with a white-knuckled grip and staring down as if trying to recall how to breathe. He cleared his throat. He took a sip of water. The glass quivered in his hand. Then he took a deep breath and resumed.

" 'The night before the operation,' " he started up again, to our great relief, "she has no association dinners to go to, no awards ceremonies, no networking functions. A plan comes to her impromptu in the back of the cab as she steps in and instructs the driver to take the Inner Drive. She envisions her sofa, her two cats, something good ordered in, and a bottle of wine she's been saving. They ask you not to eat anything twelve hours before, but honestly, that's unreasonable, isn't it — your last chance at a normal meal for how long?' "

The room was silent but for a few hushed noises issuing from the faraway registers and Hank's lone, crackling voice, amplified by the microphone, which accentuated the subtle cottony smacks of words formed within his dry mouth. We were so nervous on his behalf that, once he had started up again, it was hard to concentrate on what he was saying. We were just happy to see that he wasn't going to faint.

He shifted his stance from one foot to the other, relaxed his arms a little, and read now with an easier, more pleasing rhythm. " '. . . better to see them *with* someone, though. Alone, there is that awkward ten minutes between the time you arrive and the time they dim the lights for the previews when against all reason you believe everyone in the theater is staring at you because . . .' "

We kept looking around at the familiar faces. Plump Benny Shassburger and freckle-faced Jim Jackers sat together, and between them, Marcia Dwyer with a rather dated haircut. Carl Garbedian was there with Marilynn. He was hardly recognizable. His gut was gone and he was tan as an almond. He was wearing a dark blue linen blazer with an open-collared shirt and he'd done something with his hair. His legs crossed, he was focused on Hank with great curiosity, perfectly still, listening.

" '. . . walking the hallway toward some associate's office. Is she really longing to be a part of *that?* She would replace these bright and open spaces full of the world's best footwear, fashions . . .' "

Karen Woo was there, which we had mixed feelings about. No Chris Yop that we could see. He'd apparently never forgiven us for that long-ago slight. No Tom Mota, either, and we guessed he was probably in the pen somewhere trying to convince the guards to let him grow tomatoes alongside the edges of the basketball court. Janine Gorjanc was changed. She wore a pair of leather chaps over her stonewashed jeans and had a matching leather vest. Dangling silver earrings, which might have been made in Santa Fe, flashed beside her hair, which she had allowed to grow long and turn gray. Before the reading, she introduced us to her boyfriend. He wore a leather vest as well and sported a bushy handlebar mustache. His name was Harry and he had shaken our hands much more timidly than his facial hair indicated he would. They had ridden to the reading on Harry's hog and both carried vintage black helmets like those worn in World War II. It was kind of weird to see that Janine was into motorcycles now. When the reading began, she and Harry settled themselves in one of the back rows.

"'. . . inside now — the place had an airy, echoic atmosphere, rumbling low with hushed voices, and footsteps on marble stairs she could pick out one by one. He took the blindfold off and they spent an hour . . .'"

If Old Brizz had been there, he probably would have cut out for a smoke break, as Hank's reading was taking longer than we had anticipated. We had stopped paying attention altogether. Our long-suffering preoccupations got the better of us — family concerns, projects going on at work, the weekend and what it held in store, something funny said at lunch, the genius of the infield-fly rule, nice jacket there, bad shoes on her, could really use a drink — all that. Hank's soft, steady voice floated over our heads like clouds drifting over the tops of buildings.

"'. . . watching the sky open at her window, it is magnificent, especially after all the work she's put in . . .'"

And we couldn't stop wondering where Joe Pope might be. He had always appeared to like Hank. Odd for him not to come out and support him like the rest of us. And then we thought, wait a minute. Had five years been so unkind to our memories that we could forget where to find Joe Pope at that hour? He was still at the office, of course, working.

Finally Hank closed his book and said, "Thank you." We applauded approvingly.

— — —

AFTER THE READING CONCLUDED, we milled about. We bought copies of Hank's book. We went up to congratulate him. We were all handshakes and hugs and he signed our books with personal good wishes. Someone asked him if this book was the same book as the one he had talked about during our time together, his small, angry book about work. Thanks to being laid off and forced to find new jobs, we had discovered that every agency has its frustrated copywriter whose real life was being a failed novelist working on a small, angry book about work. Work was a fetishistic subject for some of our colleagues, but unlike Don Blattner, who wanted everyone to read his screenplays so long as they signed confidentiality agreements, the book writers played their cards much closer to the vest, and usually ended up folding. Howling screeds went mute inside desk drawers. Lovingly ground axes melted in fireplaces. We felt grateful on behalf of the world.

"No," Hank replied. "This is a different book."

"What happened to the old one?" someone asked. He had such ambition for it.

"That one was put down like an ailing dog," he said. "But how about you?" he asked suddenly, looking around. "What's new with you guys?"

We could tell he was eager to shift the spotlight from his failed novel onto something else, so Benny and Marcia announced that they were getting married in the fall.

"If he doesn't piss me off before then," she said, looking at Benny affectionately.

She wore an achingly modest diamond ring and threaded her arm through Benny's just as Benny shared the equally incredible news that, for all intents and purposes, Jim Jackers was his new boss.

"Can you believe that?" he said. "This guy right here!"

He put his arm around Jim and bent his head down like he was about to give him a noogie. Jim raised his eyebrows in mute and modest capitulation and for a moment the three of them, Marcia and Benny and Jim, were linked physically as if they were a little family.

Carl told us the details of his landscaping company, Garbedian and Son, a modest outfit. "Come on, be honest," Marilynn said. She turned to Hank. "It's a phenomenon, is what it is." "Is that true, Carl?" asked Hank. We all urged Carl to tell us more. Finally he admitted, "We do work in about twenty suburbs." We thought, Holy shit! Twenty suburbs? The guy must be raking it in. "But you're still no doctor, are you?" we expected Jim Jackers to say, but he said no such thing, and it didn't even seem to be on Carl's mind. He was smiling and nodding and he had his arm around Marilynn as if landscaping had changed his life.

Amber introduced us to Becky, who was bashful and hid behind her mother's sturdy leg. We looked around for Larry, but he was gone. We avoided the topic by concentrating on the kid. Eventually we entered back into adult conversation, and that's when Becky came out from behind Amber's leg and approached Benny. She seemed interested in introducing him to her naked and soiled doll. He bent down and made its acquaintance. Everyone congratulated Genevieve on her baby as well, and her husband answered for her when we asked how old it was (ten months), because Genevieve and Amber were lost to stories of motherhood.

The funny thing about work itself, it was so bearable. The dreariest task was perfectly bearable. It presented challenges to overcome, the distraction provided by a sense of urgency, and the satisfaction of a task's completion — on any given day, those things made work utterly, even harmoniously bearable. What we bitched about, what we couldn't let lie, what drove us to distraction and consumed us with blind fury, was this person or that who rankled and bugged and offended angels in heaven, who wore their clothes all wrong and foisted upon us their insufferable features, who deserved from a just god nothing but scorn because they were insipid, unpoetic, mercilessly enduring, and lost to the grand gesture. And maybe so, yes, maybe so. But as we stood there, we had a hard time recalling the specific details, because everyone seemed so agreeable.

At Benny's suggestion we headed out for a drink. There was an Irish pub nearby and we brought tables together and Carl Garbedian bought the first round, which was only right given his twenty suburbs, and we toasted Hank and his accomplishment, and we talked of regrets and of old times and happily recalled that not all had been misery. By the time we had worked down that first round, we had reason to remember that Benny had been a good storyteller, and Jim Jackers a good sport, and Genevieve a pleasure to look upon. And Lynn Mason, we all agreed, had been a better boss than any we'd found since. Next to Handlebar Harry, who defied our drinking expectations by ordering a cup of decaf, Janine sat sipping her familiar frosted glass of cranberry juice, which was somehow comforting. She reached out to tap Hank on the hand. "I've read your book, Hank," she said.

"Oh," said Hank. "Thank you."

"It's about Lynn, isn't it."

"Well," he said. "Some of it is based on Lynn, yes."

We couldn't believe it. His book was about Lynn?

"And is it true?" she asked.

"The book? No, the book is . . . which part?"

"Any of it."

"Well, I visited her several times in the hospital," he said.

Wait a minute, we thought, wait a minute. He had visited her in the hospital?

"In the first book I tried to write," he explained, "the book I put down, I based a character on Lynn, and I made that character into a tyrant. I did it on principle, because anyone who was a boss in that book *had* to be a tyrant. Anyone who believed in the merits of capitalism, and soul-destroying corporations, and work work work — all that — naturally that person wasn't deserving of any sympathy. But when I decided to retire that book, thank god, and write something different, I knew she was sick, so I went to see her. Just on a lark. Because what did I know about her? Nothing, really. I didn't know her — not in any meaningful way. And it turned out she was very open to talking with me, not only about her sickness, but also her personal life, a lot of other things. She was dying at the time —"

Jim Jackers stopped him. "What do you mean?"

"Lynn died in the summer of 2003," Hank replied. "Of ovarian cancer."

"Am I the only one who didn't know that?" Jim asked, looking around.

"And I think she knew she was dying," Hank continued, "and in a way, I also think she hoped that I would write something worth a damn, which I can tell you, I did not. I can assure you I did not. Not with respect to her, anyway."

Janine objected. "I've read it," she said. "You most certainly did."

"Trust me," Hank told her. "I didn't get the half of it."

— — —

GENEVIEVE AND HER HUSBAND LEFT because they had to put the baby to bed, and we lost Amber and Becky, too. Benny didn't want them to go — all his windows were fogged up with nostalgia — but they insisted they had to get home. He demanded that the rest of us stay, and so we stayed. Most of us wanted another drink anyway. Marcia hit the jukebox with about a week's salary and played one saccharine ballad after another and it felt like not a day had passed since we'd parted. Jim Jackers bought the next round, which was only right given his inexplicable rise up the ladder, and the fact that we'd had to suffer him during his weaning years.

We toasted to Lynn Mason's memory and found ourselves telling stories of her, encounters and exchanges we had no trouble recalling the way we had, say, encounters with Old Brizz — she was our boss, after all, and we all had our separate and memorable experiences with her. None of us could forget, for example, the thrill and glory we experienced when she took a particular liking to a concept one of us had come up with, and we recalled with startling accuracy what job it was for, and the concept, and the reasons she gave for her admiration. Nobody's approbation meant more to us than hers, and nothing was easier than recalling her words of approval. We also remembered her expensive and delicate shoes, and the time she showed up at Carl's bedside with a pathetic bouquet of flowers, and how she had put up flyers for Janine alongside the rest of us when Jessica went missing, and Jim told us the story of being in an elevator when she told him that she had once been a hula girl. "She was just joking," he said, "but I took her so seriously." We remembered that despite how formidable she always seemed, a lot of the things she said were funny.

By the end of the second round, Sandy Green from payroll said she had to get home, and so did Donald Sato and Paulette Singletary. Benny begged them all to stay. He wanted to talk about whether or not they were currently happy at their new jobs, what the people were like, and if they had any complaints. "You know," he prodded, "compared to how it used to be." They stayed for a while longer, but when finally they left, Benny looked downcast. "What was that Tom Mota used to say, the send-off he used to give when somebody quit? Anybody remember?"

No one did.

"It was a toast," said Benny, "and it went something like 'So good luck to you.' And then he'd finish off his drink, remember, and sort of burp? And then he'd bring the glass back up and say, 'And fuck you for leaving, you prick.'"

Everyone laughed, though it wasn't strictly speaking very funny — in fact, it was pretty uncomfortable. When the laughter died down, we wondered aloud what had happened to Tom and why he wasn't at the reading.

"You don't know about Tom?" said Carl.

Nobody knew a thing.

"Do you know he joined the army?"

Joined the army? Carl was pulling our leg.

"No, it's true."

"Come on," said Benny.

"Nobody else got Tom's e-mails?"

No one could say they had.

"Strange. He used to write to everybody."

"Come on," said Benny. "They let that nut join the army?"

"Superior marksmanship skills," Carl said simply.

Suddenly a crazy notion almost seemed possible.

"He was looking at jail time," Carl continued, "you know that much. But his wife, Barb, testified on his behalf. And so did Joe Pope. Yeah," he said, to our expressions of disbelief. "And so the DA agreed to reduce the charges down to a misdemeanor. After that, he came to work for me for a time. But not for very long. He kept talking about wanting to join up — after all that had happened, you know. He just couldn't get it out of his head. He was afraid he was too old. And he was afraid they wouldn't take him because of his record. But it kept gnawing at him. He wouldn't go down to talk to a recruiter, though, because he was afraid they'd tell him no — he wanted it so badly. He didn't want somebody telling him no. But one day on a prayer he just went down there, and by sheer luck, he and the recruiting officer hit it off, they just hit it off right away. Tom told him what he wanted to do and how bad he wanted it, and the guy, the recruiting officer, arranged it so Tom could show him what he had to offer. And after they saw him shoot, they said, You want to join up, we're happy to have you. So Tom joined the army."

Carl *had* to be joking.

"No, he's not," said Janine.

We all looked at Janine. Did she get e-mails from Tom, too?

"He wrote me letters," she replied.

"He said it was the best decision he ever made," said Carl.

"And he never regretted it," said Janine. "He was happy to be there. He was happy to be doing what he was doing."

"He believed, you know," said Carl, "in fighting for his country."

"He called it — and I will always remember Tom for many

things," said Janine. "But one thing he wrote I will never forget. I still have the letter. He called this country the best republic that ever began to fade. Those were his exact words. I still have it. He was very proud that they put him in a special marksman's division."

"It comes as no surprise to anybody that Tom had good aim, I guess," said Carl.

The tears that hung in Janine's eyes were familiar, despite all the new leather. "And he was probably a good soldier, too — wouldn't you think, Carl?"

"It was discipline he had needed for thirty-seven years. At least that's how he put it to me," said Carl.

"Which is still very young," said Janine. "Thirty-seven."

"Yes," Carl agreed. "Very young."

"What happened?" asked Benny. "What happened to him?"

Everyone ordered martinis in Tom's honor, and toasted him as a patriot and a scholar, a good soldier, and a lousy corporate citizen. We thanked him for sending outlandish e-mails, for the antics inspired by his consumption of two martinis at lunch, and for all the crazy shit he did that in hindsight had provided us with a lot of entertainment, without which our afternoons would have been longer and our lives more dull. He had been killed by friendly fire in Afghanistan.

"To Tom," we said.

We raised our martini glasses. "To Tom."

"Goodness," said Janine, with a sour face. "How could he have enjoyed such things?"

WITHOUT DON BLATTNER, we might have lost ourselves to the oblivion of drink and dark thoughts, but Hank asked him how his writing was going, and Don let it be known that by some miraculous, persevering nerve of his, he had not given up working on his wretched and unproduceable screenplays. He was in the thick of one even as we spoke, which he believed had real potential. "But I always say that," said Don. Which was true — he always said that. We asked what his new one was about, and he told us that it was the story of a highly revered Tibetan lama who, on a speaking tour of the United States, gets seduced into the lucrative world of endorsement contracts. He finds himself improving the ads in which he appears, much to the awe and excitement of the hapless creative team in charge of the account, whose cynicism and ennui are at an all-time high. The lama ultimately finds his own true happiness in forsaking his fawning followers for the newly rejuvenated advertising agency, becoming the team's executive creative director in charge of the Nike, Microsoft, and BMW accounts. He sleeps with models and dies happily reading *Time* magazine in a whirlpool in Crested Butte, Colorado.

Everyone thought it was going to be a big hit.

"We'll see," said Don.

Carl and Marilynn left us, and we lost Janine and Harry to the exigencies of middle-aged sleep. Some other guy left, and Jim turned to Benny. "Benny, who was that guy who just left? We work with that guy?"

"That was Sanderson," said Benny. "Bill Sanderson."

"Bill Sanderson?"

"You remember Bill," said Benny.

"I have no recollection of that guy."

"Sure you do, Jim. You just don't recognize him without his mustache."

Soon Jim himself was preparing to leave. "It's a school night," he explained.

A school night? When had Jim Jackers become so . . . so . . . *adult?*

"Jimmy, don't *you* leave!" cried Benny.

"Benny, you'll see me tomorrow."

"Oh, I guess that's true, isn't it," said Benny. "Come here, old buddy." Benny was on his last drink, according to Marcia. Jim was forced to bend down and hug him.

"I had better get going myself," said Reiser.

"You can't leave, Reiser!" said Benny. "You haven't said a word about the people you're with now. What are they like? Are you happy?"

Reiser rose as Benny fired off his round of questions, shrugging nonchalantly at each one.

"But do you miss it?" Benny persisted.

"Miss what?" asked Reiser.

"I'll tell you who I miss," Benny said. Suddenly he was pulling out his cell phone. "Let's call Joe Pope!"

We watched Reiser hobble out of the bar, and for some reason it was comforting to see that he still walked with a limp. As soon as he was gone Benny put his phone up to his ear and tried to get an answer.

"I must have dialed the wrong extension," he concluded, hitting end. "That was the desk of someone named Brian Bayer. Anybody recognize that name?"

Nobody did. He must have come after our time. Odd to think they were hiring again. We had a hard time picturing those familiar surroundings peopled by strangers, unfamiliar voices calling out from behind the plasterboard partitions of our old cubicles, unrecognizable men and women sitting in our chairs.

We asked Benny what extension he was dialing. He had it

right — that was Joe's extension. Nobody could forget it, we had dialed it so often. He hit end a second time. "Brian Bayer again," he said. He had the ingenious solution of calling the main switchboard. When prompted, he pressed "P" for Pope. "His name isn't coming up," he said.

Don Blattner came back from the men's room and asked Dan Wisdom if he was ready to go. They had driven together.

"His name didn't come up," said Benny.

"We had better get going, too, Benny," said Marcia. "It's getting late."

Don and Dan threw money down on the table and we said good-bye to them. "Hey, wait!" Benny cried out. But he was too distracted to get off the phone, and eventually they left.

"Where is he?" he said, setting his cell phone down and looking around at the rest of us. "Where's Joe Pope?"

"Come on, Benny," said Marcia, "I'm taking you home."

"He's not in the directory, Marcia. Where is he?"

"Benny, honey, you're drunk."

"It's Joe," he said. "He never leaves his desk."

"Benny," she said.

"Where's Genevieve? Where is she? She'll know where he is."

"Genevieve? Benny, honey, she left hours ago."

She pried him from his chair.

"Hank, you must know what happened. What happened to Joe, Hank?"

But if Hank knew anything, he wasn't saying. We watched Benny stumble drunkenly to his feet. "But it's Joe, Marcia," he said. "Joe doesn't leave."

"Benny," she said. "Sometimes you just lose track."

Soon they were out the door, followed by the last strains of one of Marcia's hair-band ballads.

Most of us followed them out soon after, and, in the end, last call was announced. The lights came up, the jukebox went quiet. We could hear the clink of glasses and the exhausted silence of the waitstaff as they began to clean up, wiping down the shiny surfaces, placing the padded barstools on top of the bar. Their work would soon be done, they could see something waiting for them at home — a bed, a meal, a lover. But we didn't want the night to end. We kept hanging on, waiting for them to send over the big guy who'd force us out with a final command. And we would leave, eventually. Out to the parking lot, a few parting words. "Sure was good to see you again," we'd say. And with that, we'd get in our cars and open the windows and drive off, tapping the horn a final time. But for the moment, it was nice just to sit there together. We were the only two left. Just the two of us, you and me.

Acknowledgments

THE TITLE OF THIS BOOK owes a debt of gratitude to Don DeLillo's *Americana.*

A special thanks to early teachers: Jane Rice, Anna Keesey, and Brooks Landon. A very special thanks to the codirectors of the MFA program at the University of California at Irvine, Michelle Latiolais and Geoffrey Wolff. Jim Shepard made me a better writer, but just as important, a better reader. Thanks also to Mark Richard and Michael Ryan.

Thank you, Julie Barer, agent extraordinaire. Reagan Arthur at Little, Brown and Mary Mount at Viking UK — wonderful editors. A big thanks to the whole team at Little, Brown.

Thanks to Kathy Bucaro-Zobens, Doug Davis, Amanda Gillespie, Robert Howell, Dave and Deb Kennedy, Dan Kraus, Chris and Keeli Mickus, Dave Morse, Barry and Jennifer Neumann, Arielle Read, Grant Rosenberg, Matthew Thomas, E-fly and Tere, and the Kennedys of Naples, Florida.

Thanks to the UCI Humanities Department, and to Glenn Schaeffer, the International Institute of Modern Letters, and the International Center for Writing and Translation at UCI for establishing the Glenn Schaeffer Award, which provided me with crucial funding.

And to my family, from Illinois to Indonesia, without whom, no book.

Kelly Campbell

JOSHUA FERRIS attended the University of Iowa and the University of California, Irvine. His first novel, *Then We Came to the End,* has been published in eighteen countries. It was short-listed for the National Book Award, long-listed for the Guardian First Book Award, and named by the *New York Times Book Review* one of the top ten books of 2007. His short fiction has appeared or is forthcoming in *Granta, Tin House, New Stories from the South, Best New American Voices,* the *Guardian,* the *Iowa Review,* and *Prairie Schooner.* He currently lives in Brooklyn with his wife.

For more information, visit www.ThenWeCametotheEnd.com.

BACK BAY · READERS' PICK

Reading Group Guide

Then We Came to the End

A NOVEL BY

Joshua Ferris

A conversation with Joshua Ferris

Tell us a little about your writing background up to this point.

I lived in Key West as a kid, and there I started writing imitation Alfred Hitchcock stories—not "The Birds" but, given Key West's coastal view, "The Crabs." Many good people, boaters and sunbathers, were eaten alive as Hitchcock turned in his grave. Then in college, at the University of Iowa, I started writing stories again—again imitations but with sights set a little higher, or at least more literary: Nabokov, Barthelme. Shortly after college I got a job in advertising where I wrote ad copy for national brands, which taught me a good many things. And after my time in advertising I enrolled in the MFA program at the University of California, Irvine, where I started *Then We Came to the End.*

So you had experience working in an ad agency. Is that how you arrived at the setting of your novel?

Ad agencies can be a lot of fun. Creative departments are full of toys and games and wacky surprises, and throwing a Nerf football down the hallway to release tension isn't immediate cause for walking papers. I wanted my characters to have the freedom to do certain things that wouldn't fly, say, in a law firm. But I didn't want that freedom to come at the expense of excluding what's universal about office life. Copywriters, lawyers, financial analysts, accountants, waiters, and construction workers all share in an inescapable group dynamic that includes scuttlebutt, in-jokes, disaffection, camaraderie. I hope *Then We Came to the End* taps into some of that.

I did yeoman's work in advertising for about three years, and I was fascinated by the behemoth structure in place—the hierarchies, the coded messages, the power struggles. I thought such an awesome, malignant, necessary, pervasive, inscrutable place deserved a novel's attention.

The characters in *Then We Came to the End* are under the constant threat of layoffs, and that creates a specific group dynamic: the group's unquenchable scrutiny of itself. Who's next on the chopping block? Whom do they value most? What will happen to "us" if the company goes under? Eventually this scrutiny drives the characters in *Then We Came to the End* to distraction, and they do things that even the more carnival environs of advertising can't abide.

Why the narrative "we"?

Companies tend to refer to themselves in the first-person plural—in annual reports, corporate brochures, within meetings and internal memos, and, in particular, in advertising. What used to be the "royal we" might now be thought of as the "corporate we." It's not just a company's way of showing unity and strength; it's also a matter of making everyone feel as if they're a member of the club. This is especially true in advertising, where the work is dedicated to getting more and more people to join the clubs of various clients, who have dreams of greater market share, bigger profit margins, and, ultimately, global dominance.

In *Then We Came to the End,* you see just who this "we" really is—a collection of messy human beings—stripped of their glossy finish and eternal corporate optimism. It returns the "we" to the individuals who embody it, people with anger-management issues and bills to pay, instead of letting the "mystic we" live on unperturbed in the magic land promoted by billboards and boardrooms.

But why not tell the story from one office worker's perspective?

My father took a great risk around the time he turned fifty by starting his own company. It was small at first; he was his only employee. Yet his message machine told callers that "we" weren't in right now, but if you left a message "we" would call you back. Who was this "we"? It was just him! But, of course, he had to be a "we"—few people trust a one-man show. Over time I came to realize that every company refers to itself in the first-person plural. It's not just a way of showing unity and strength; it's also a matter of wanting you to join that club.

So, thematically, the novel's point of view was a no-brainer. Making it work took me up and down a long learning curve.

How does the centerpiece interlude (where the "we" disappears) function in relation to what comes before and after?

The interlude is the book's emotional heart. Without it *Then We Came to the End* would have been only an elaborate, if amusing, game. Lynn is forced to look at the possibility of death when she's diagnosed with breast cancer, and in turn so is the reader. After the interlude it becomes clear that death qualifies everything that came before it and everything that follows.

The novel seems more like borderline farce at the beginning and then borders on tragedy as the reader comes to empathize more with the characters. Was this tonal progression part of the plan all along? Was it a challenge to sustain?

The tonal progression was absolutely part of the plan. I had little interest in writing a book that was only about what's funny at work. There are some pretty effective TV shows that do that. A novel asks more time and attention from its readers than a TV show does of its viewers, and the novel's form has always demanded a scope as all-encompassing of life as its practitioners can deliver. So, at the conceptual level, I knew it had to be, one, more than the complexities of its "we" point of view, and, two, more than the sum of its jokes.

But I had to puzzle out how to make all that work. I initially spent about a year and a half on the book before giving it up. Another year and a half of reflection passed before I returned to it, and I did so only after hearing the voice of the collective in my head and not being able to tune it out. Once restarted, the book was finished in about fourteen weeks. So it took three years and fourteen weeks to gather my wits about me and know how to write a book in the first-person plural that took work as its subject and that included such disparate things as e-mail pranks and the emotional and physical ravages of breast cancer.

Your observations about office life ring so true. Were you working in an office setting when you wrote the book? Or, like your character Hank Neary, did it all come to you after you left office life?

After. Much, much after. Like Hank's fictional book, initial versions of my novel were top-heavy with complaint—the infelicities and pains in the ass that arise day to day when working among other human beings and their foibles. Only after a certain remove—in fact, only after I had settled into the relatively solitary routine of a writer—did I realize that office life has a lot to offer: companionship, the opportunity to clown around, lunch mates. I sort of became, to my surprise, nostalgic for it. Only then did I see that work wasn't all misery. For every part dread, there was one part fun. Hopefully *Then We Came to the End* provides an equal measure.

Almost anyone working in a cubicle world will see her own experiences and thoughts in this book, yet most of us get so caught up in those individual experiences we don't realize how universal typical office life and behavior is. Would you agree?

You get pretty wrapped up. I left a lot of friends behind when I went off to pursue writing, and it would be dishonest to say that our scope of conversation afterwards didn't narrow. We still talked about all the stuff that went on at my old agency, but those things meant less and less to me. Amazing! Stuff I had lived and died for, now mere reportage on the machinations of a far-off land.

But, as you say, it's universal. It's perfectly human to seek out community, especially at work, and with community comes getting caught up in the community's insatiable gaze inward. Especially when that community is under threat, as the group of employees is in *Then We Came to the End.* It's hard to think of anything else when every day there's someone new being twirled unwillingly through the revolving doors.

What tagline do you think Benny, Marcia, Joe, Genevieve, Karen, Yop, Jim, and the rest of the creatives would come up with to sell Then We Came to the End*?*

They wouldn't have a single clue. They would bemoan the assignment while being happy to have a job to bill time to. They would lollygag for a couple of days. Then they'd get down to business and feel woefully inadequate to the task. Jim especially. Eventually something would emerge, but there would be no consensus. *Then We Came to the End* would disappear from bookstores within two weeks and the agency would go bankrupt.

What authors and books are among your favorites?

I mentioned Nabokov and Barthelme. I read and reread Chekhov and Kafka. Same with Philip Roth and Thomas Pynchon, twin engines of a dark machine. I filched the title for *Then We Came to the End* from DeLillo's *Americana,* one of my favorites. I recently read a wonderful book by John Haskell called *American Purgatorio,* which is one of my favorites in recent memory. And it seems to me that the often maligned short story is having a renaissance of sorts, from masters of the craft like Edward P. Jones and George Saunders and Jim Shepard to younger writers like Karen Russell and Miranda July.

Are you working on a second novel? If so, can you share any details with us?

I am. I'm trying out a narrative technique called the "third person." We'll see how it goes.

Questions and topics for discussion

1. Although *Then We Came to the End* is told predominantly in the first person plural, there is a brief departure to describe Lynn Mason's last night before she undergoes surgery. Why do you think the author chose this point in the novel for the shift in perspective?
2. What was the most humorous moment in the novel for you? Does the author's incarnation of the office remind you in any way of your own work environment?
3. *Then We Came to the End* features a large and diverse cast of characters. Which character is your favorite? Which do you find least likable? Does any character closely resemble a person with whom you work?
4. On page 57 the author writes: "Yet for all the depression no one ever quit." Did you find other seemingly contradictory passages in the novel? If so, why do you think the work environment lends itself to such contradictions?
5. The novel contains insights into many aspects of office life, but can you think of any office situations not included that you wish the author had addressed?
6. Near the beginning of the novel Marcia Dwyer accidentally sends an e-mail intended for Genevieve Latko-Devine to the entire office. Have you or anyone you know ever experienced a similarly embarrassing situation in the office? If so, how was it handled?

7. The author presents the office as an environment without secrets, writing of Old Brizz: "He knew it because he was one of us, and we knew everything" (page 4). Do you agree with this statement? If so, why does this dynamic exist in offices?
8. *Then We Came to the End* is a novel that depicts many lighthearted moments and many dire situations as well. Did you find that one, either the whimsical or the grave, outweighed the other?
9. In a conversation between Lynn Mason and her boyfriend, Martin, Lynn thinks that "technology would never advance past primal fear. It would never trump human instinct" (page 213). Aside from Lynn's observation, how does the novel view technology as it relates to social interaction at the office?
10. What do you ultimately think is the overall tone of the novel? Do you think this is the tone the author intended?

Some of Joshua Ferris's favorite books

The Emigrants by W. G. Sebald
Project X by Jim Shepard
All Aunt Hagar's Children by Edward P. Jones
Sixty Stories by Donald Barthelme
Jesus' Son by Denis Johnson
Molloy, Malone Dies, The Unnamable by Samuel Beckett
Sabbath's Theater by Philip Roth
White Noise by Don DeLillo
Gravity's Rainbow by Thomas Pynchon
The Complete Essays and Poems by Ralph Waldo Emerson
Great Tales of Terror and the Supernatural edited by Phyllis Cerf Wagner and Herbert Wise
Pale Fire by Vladimir Nabokov
M31: A Family Romance by Stephen Wright
Slaughterhouse Five by Kurt Vonnegut
The Ambassadors by Henry James
A Sport and a Pastime by James Salter
Ask the Dust by John Fante
Play It As It Lays by Joan Didion
The Complete Works by Nathanael West
The Dog of the South by Charles Portis

The Collected Stories by Amy Hempel

The Great Gatsby by F. Scott Fitzgerald

The Complete Stories by Anton Chekhov

Bleak House by Charles Dickens

One Hundred Years of Solitude by Gabriel García Márquez

Girl with Curious Hair by David Foster Wallace

Airships by Barry Hannah

Travesty by John Hawkes

Catch-22 by Joseph Heller

The Complete Stories by Franz Kafka

Birds of America by Lorrie Moore

The Things They Carried by Tim O'Brien

The Collected Stories by Grace Paley

Gilead by Marilynne Robinson

The Age of Innocence by Edith Wharton

Mrs. Dalloway by Virginia Woolf

The Duke of Deception by Geoffrey Wolff

The Good Soldier by Ford Madox Ford

The Moviegoer by Walker Percy

The Corrections by Jonathan Franzen

The New York Trilogy by Paul Auster

The Complete Works by Michel de Montaigne

The Complete Poems by Emily Dickinson

We Have Always Lived in the Castle by Shirley Jackson

Blood Meridian by Cormac McCarthy